Kay Brellend, the t[...] North London but now li[...] in Suffolk. Under a pseudonym she has [...] historical novels published in England and N[...] America. This is her fourth novel set in the twentieth century and was inspired by her grandmother's reminiscences about her life in Campbell Road, Islington.

Also by Kay Brellend

The Street
The Family
Coronation Day

KAY BRELLEND

The Campbell Road Girls

HARPER

This novel is entirely a work of fiction.
The names, characters and incidents portrayed in it are
the work of the author's imagination. Any resemblance to
actual persons, living or dead, events or localities is
entirely coincidental.

Harper
An imprint of HarperCollins*Publishers*
77–85 Fulham Palace Road,
Hammersmith, London W6 8JB

www.harpercollins.co.uk

A catalogue record for this book
is available from the British Library

ISBN: 978-0-00-746416-6

Set in Meridien by Palimpsest Book Production Ltd, Falkirk, Stirlingshire

Printed and bound in Great Britain by
Clays Ltd, St Ives plc

FSC™ is a non-profit international organisation established to promote
the responsible management of the world's forests. Products carrying the
FSC label are independently certified to assure consumers that they come
from forests that are managed to meet the social, economic and
ecological needs of present and future generations,
and other controlled sources.

Find out more about HarperCollins and the environment at
www.harpercollins.co.uk/green

ACKNOWLEDGEMENTS

Thanks to Juliet Burton, Kate Bradley and the rest of the HarperCollins editorial team. And to Brian McDonald for his fascinating book, *Gangs of London*.

For Susan, Carole, Jackie, Gary – with love.

PROLOGUE

'You can't mean it!' Sophy Lovat stared at her youngest sister in astonishment. 'You're planning on handing in your notice and going back to Campbell Road? You gone nuts, Lucy Keiver?'

'Course not. I won't be there for more'n a few days, not if I can help it,' Lucy replied defensively. 'I'll stop with Mum and Reg just while I'm between things. I can keep Mum company while I'm sorting this out.' She drew from her serge skirt pocket a piece of paper and, having unfolded the crumpled scrap, scanned the advertisement for an assistant lady's maid in a mansion in Bloomsbury. 'Got an interview early next month, and if I get offered the job, I'll be living in straightaway.' Lucy could tell her explanation hadn't impressed her sister. 'Move back to the Bunk for good?' she scoffed in an effort to save face. 'I'm not that daft!'

'After all I did to get you took on here!' Sophy protested indignantly. 'And you've done all right for

1

yourself with my help. Out of the kitchen and upstairs in no time at all, weren't you?'

'It was different before, when the mistress was still alive.' The staff at Lockley Grange still called their employer's late wife 'the mistress'. His current spouse was referred to as 'the madam', and invariably in a disparaging tone.

'You can't throw it all in 'cos you've had a bit of a disagreement with Mrs Lockley.' Sophy was prowling back and forth outside the stable block while reasoning quietly with her sister; she was aware they might be overheard.

'Weren't a *bit* of a disagreement.' Lucy's wry grimace emphasised her point. She was also keeping a weather eye out in case any ears were flapping in the vicinity. 'She called me an insubordinate wretch who should keep to her place. So I told her . . .' She hesitated and guilty colour stole into her cheeks. 'I told her a few home truths, so even if I don't chuck it in, I'll probably get chucked out.' Lucy defiantly tilted her chin. 'She's never liked me and I know I ain't alone in not liking her. Nobody here took to her from the start.' Lucy stepped closer to hiss in her sister's ear, 'We all know she got John Drew sacked from the stables, and Edna couldn't wait to work out her notice before she quit. If you're honest, you know you 'n' Danny don't like her either.'

Sophy struck a finger to her lips and steered her sister roughly against the cover of brickwork.

Lucy had spoken the truth. Sophy and her husband, Danny, had been disappointed, to say the least, on being introduced to the master's new wife. Celia was half his age and only two years older than his own daughter. Monica had wisely decided to decamp to live with her aunt in Yorkshire shortly after her stepmother moved in. Celia's attitude to the staff from the start had been

2

utter disdain, but Sophy and Danny Lovat, older and more mature than their colleagues, had tried to adopt a pragmatic outlook. They had a great deal to lose since they'd been promoted to the top jobs.

After eleven years working at Lockley Grange, and after a year of being man and wife, Danny and Sophy had been summoned to Mr Lockley's study one afternoon. They'd turned up in trepidation, wondering what they'd done wrong, only to learn they'd been doing everything right. Sophy had been promoted to a new position of housekeeper and Danny to that of house steward. With hindsight they'd realised their employers had wanted to free themselves from running the Grange because they'd known their time together was limited. None of the servants had been aware of the mistress's grave illness until near the end.

'How about if I have a quiet word with the master?' Sophy offered unconvincingly.

'Oh, yeah,' Lucy muttered sarcastically, ''cos that's bound to work. We all know she's got him wrapped right around her little finger. And we all know how she keeps him there,' she added sourly. Lucy had previously held Mr Lockley in high estimation but her opinion of him had plummeted when she'd realised what a sucker he was.

Ever since the newlyweds had returned from honeymoon, guttural noises could be heard issuing from the master suite at any hour of the day or night, prompting salacious gossip in the servants' hall. It had not gone unnoticed that the young madam engineered those passionate trysts, and that they invariably coincided with her getting her own way on something.

Sophy felt annoyed at having this bombshell dropped on her by Lucy. It was barely four months since Celia's personal maid had abruptly quit and Sophy had been put in the same awkward spot, having tactfully to find excuses for a colleague who'd had enough. Through threat and bribery, Sophy had managed to persuade Edna Jones to work out two months' notice despite the woman insisting she'd sooner give up her wages and scoot than stay and be bullied and belittled. Now Lucy, who had been Edna's apprentice, was jacking in the same job and Sophy knew the master would question her over why her sister was leaving hot on Edna's heels.

'It's time you learned to take a bit of discipline and curb your tongue, miss,' Sophy snapped.

'I'm not putting up with it!' Lucy exclaimed. 'I don't mind doing me duties and a bit more besides, but I'm beggared if I'll let her look at me like I'm something she's just stepped in in the stables.'

Sophy cast an assessing look on her younger sister. She had an inkling why the madam constantly clashed with Lucy. Little Luce, as her youngest sister was affectionately known by her family, was too pretty by half.

Lucy had started in the kitchens at the Grange at fourteen. She'd recently turned eighteen and had blossomed from a gawky teenager into quite a beauty. Her hair was thick and had the colour and shine of ripe chestnuts; her large eyes were lushly fringed with sooty lashes, and an unusual shade of greenish blue. But Lucy also had their mother's pride and fiery temper to balance her sweet looks. For the past year or so, during her transformation from girl to woman, Sophy had noticed her sister turning a few of their male colleagues' heads. But Lucy could give as good as she got. She was neither shrinking violet nor prude, and always met the boys' lusty impertinence with a few salty quips of her own.

4

'We've all had a bellyful of her, but on the whole it's a good place to live and work.' Sophy gripped Lucy's hands to emphasise what she was about to say. 'Mr Lockley might be a silly old fool but deep down he is a decent man. She's the master's wife so we've all got to accept it and knuckle down—'

'You knuckle down if you want to,' Lucy spiritedly interrupted. 'I'm getting out before there's a right royal dingdong.' She gave Sophy a significant nod. ''S'all right for you'n Danny, you report to the master, but now Edna's scarpered I'm the one at *her* beck and call.'

'Can't believe you're really going.' Sophy sighed. 'You might not get this position you've applied for. With unemployment like it is there could be dozens of women after it. What you going to do then? Move back in with Mum in that poxy hole?'

'Gonna keep applying for jobs in London,' Lucy answered briskly. 'To tell you the truth, it's not just about Mrs Lockley.' She avoided Sophy's eye and stared out at rolling, verdant countryside. 'I'm bored stiff here.' She gestured with a hand at the quiet scenery. 'What is there to do on me day off 'cept go and stare at cows or the sea, or window-shop old-fashioned frocks I couldn't afford even if I wanted one.' She shrugged in frustration. 'I want to go in some of the big London stores and wander around just looking at all the lovely clothes . . . and Yardley compacts and lipsticks and perfumes . . .' She broke off and giggled. 'Then I'd go down the market with Alice and Beth and buy a dress that looks the same but costs a few bob instead of a few pounds.'

'We've got a market here!' Sophy stated huffily.

'Yeah,'Lucy agreed wryly. 'When I want fresh fruit 'n' veg I'll know where to come. But a cheap costume or a fancy silk blouse that don't take me for ever to save for is gonna be hanging up down Chapel Street or Petticoat Lane.'

Lucy knew her sister was confused and alarmed by what she'd said. Sophy and Danny had been sweethearts since school age. The only ambitions Sophy had ever had were marrying Danny and securing regular work. Lucy knew it was all very sensible and admirable but she wasn't yet ready to settle for just that.

'I'm too young to get stuck in a rut out in the sticks. I want a job in town.' She gazed earnestly at Sophy. 'I never knew what it was to work in London. This was me first job, and I'm grateful to you for getting it for me, but perhaps I'm a city girl at heart. I'm going back there, Sophe, to find out . . . and that's that.'

After a short silence, Sophy put out a hand. 'Let's have a look then.'

'Won't be leaving fer a while yet, anyhow, so can work out me notice and a bit more if you want. Interviews are being held next month 'cos the girl who's leaving is going off to get married, so no rush as such.' She handed over the paper for Sophy to read.

'You *can* work out yer notice 'n' all,' Sophy said grumpily, frowning at the letter.

'Probably be stuck on a pallet in an attic with a few others,' Lucy admitted with a wry chuckle. But even if her quarters were just a shared top-floor dormitory, Lucy would jump at the chance of it. Without a glance at the place, she knew it would knock living in a dirty room in a tenement house in Campbell Road into a cocked hat. But at least she'd be closer to her poor, ailing mum and would be able to visit her on her days off.

'Put your notice in then, if you want to,' Sophy said,

thrusting the paper back at her sister. 'Go and see if smog suits you better'n fresh air. But mark my words: I reckon you might just find you've jumped out of the frying pan straight into the fire.'

The crunch of feet on gravel brought the two young women to atttention. Tim Lovat, Danny's brother, who worked as the master's valet, suddenly appeared around the side of the house and waved to them as he sprinted closer. 'Mistress is after you, Lucy. Stomping round with her chops on her boots.' He grinned. 'Rather you than me.'

CHAPTER ONE

September 1930

'If . . . if . . . if! I'm fooking sick of hearing about if!'

Reg Donovan shoved over two battered chairs as he strode towards the door. He'd hoped to escape further hostility between himself and the irate redheaded woman confronting him, arms akimbo. But Matilda Keiver was having none of that. Today she was prepared for him trying to take the coward's way out. In a trice she was between him and the exit, though the exertion left her wincing and gasping. He'd listen to some more of what she'd got to say if it killed her. And it was what had nearly killed her that caused them constantly to scrap.

'You might be fucking sick of hearing about it, Reg Donovan, but I ain't,' she wheezed. 'Ain't you in pain every minute of the day, is it? Ain't you stuck indoors most o' the time 'cos it's an ordeal just getting down the stairs to nip to the shop. I'm suffering something chronic, and though it ain't *all* your fault I blame you fer a good part of what happened.'

'I can't be having this argument over and over again wid yer, Tilly.' Reg's defeated plea for a truce had thickened his Irish brogue.

'If you'd been where yer should've been that night, I wouldn't be in the state I'm in, would I? Deny it, can you?'

'I can't! I know it . . . you know it!' Reg's voice again thundered at the ceiling. 'But what can I do about it now?' His hands balled into fists close to his contorted features. 'Give over about it, woman. I can't stand having it thrown in me fooking face a hundred times a day.'

'You can't stand it 'cos it makes you feel guilty.' Tilly was using the wall as support, whilst teetering on her toes in an attempt to keep her weight forward and away from the ache in her back.

Two years ago she'd come out of hospital after a stay of five and a half months following a dreadful fall that had almost killed her. It had finished off the man who'd deliberately sent them both hurtling out of a first-floor window in Campbell Road to certain death, impaled on railings below. Jimmy Wild had expired almost instantly, but then he'd already been mortally wounded when he'd turned up, intending to take Matilda to hell with him. Despite several broken bones and an iron spike piercing her waist, Tilly had miraculously lived to tell the tale . . . over and over again, according to Reg. And Reg had had a bellyful of hearing it.

Despite her extraordinary luck in having survived, eating away at Tilly like a cancer was the knowledge that if Reg, the man she'd hoped to marry shortly after that stormy summer evening, had done what he'd set out to do and fetched them home a couple of brown ales, she'd have completely escaped Jimmy Wild's lethal

10

malice. Jimmy had always been a coward when it came to a fair fight with a man; he would have crawled away to die alone had Reg been the one to open the door to him that night. But instead of joining her in a drink at home the selfish git had forgotten about her brown ales and gone to the Duke with a pal for a few whiskies.

'You got to admit now, you let Jimmy in that night, Tilly. No point kidding yourself over it.' Reg had edged closer to the door and casually manoeuvred a hand in readiness to yank it open. He felt sorry for Tilly, but not a lot more, and he knew pity wasn't enough to keep him with her. At forty-nine she was a decade older than he was. Once the age gap had been unnoticeable – in fact at times he'd had trouble keeping up with her – but now she looked her age. The stiffness in her bones following the accident sometimes had her hobbling like a pensioner instead of sashaying about as she had a few years previously. She'd taken a few tumbles since she'd been out of hospital, which had set back her recovery, but she was too proud and stubborn to heed anybody's warning to take things easy or accept help with her chores.

The good times had gone; the only passion the engaged couple now shared was during fights and arguments. She wasn't even a drinking partner for him any more. She'd been a patient for a long time in a Spartan hospital, and enforced abstinence had curbed Tilly's addiction to heavy drinking. To dull her aches and pains she'd down a few tots at home so she didn't have to smarten up and drag herself out. But Reg considered himself still a young man. He needed a bit of a social life and a breath of fresh air outside of the stinking room on the first floor of the tenement house in Campbell Road that they called home. Reg knew he needed to get away from her, not only so he could calm down, but to decide whether he ever wanted to come back. If it took a bit of honest cruelty to cut himself free he was prepared to use it.

'You brought a lot of this on yourself, Tilly. You'd known for years that Jimmy Wild was no good. You told me yourself he was an evil fooker. Yet you invited him in.' Reg pointed accusingly at her. 'You're a stupid woman and you've got nobody to blame for the state you're in but yourself. It's time to face up to it.'

It was the first time Tilly had heard that from him and shock dropped her jaw. Usually Reg pinned the blame for her attempted murder squarely on Jimmy and recounted what he'd like to do to the bastard to pay him back, if only he could.

She whacked away his blunt finger quivering close to her nose. 'I reckon *you're* at fault and *you'd* better fucking face up to it!' she suddenly roared, her blue eyes almost popping from her head in fury. 'And if yer don't like hearing the truth of it you know where the bleedin' door is.'

'Well, if you'll move aside I'll be out and leave you in peace.'

Matilda felt her guts tighten; he meant it this time. He wanted to go, not just to cool down, but for good. She flung back her auburn head, exposing silver wings close to her temples where her fiery locks were fading. For a moment she was close to capitulation and apology but her pride tilted up her chin an inch higher and she shifted aside. 'Go on then, get out and good riddance.' She limped back towards the wooden table, picked up her cold cup of tea and gulped at it. She didn't even turn her head when she heard the door bang shut.

* * *

'He'll be back, Mum, when he's had time to calm down.'

'He won't be back.' Tilly's dull eyes settled on the groceries her daughter Alice had tipped onto the table but she didn't elaborate on how she knew she'd been abandoned.

She'd heard Reg creep in a few nights ago and gather together his meagre bits and pieces. She'd pretended to be asleep although an inner voice had been urging her to rear up haughtily onto an elbow and bawl at him to sling his hook. She'd lain there undecided before wearily concluding she'd no more stomach than he had for another slanging match. So she'd listened to his soft footfalls, and doors and drawers opening and closing, until the key had again grated in the lock and he'd taken himself off for good. As the tears had trickled to dampen her pillow she'd impatiently dashed them away, and with them the suspicions that, if she didn't know deep down that he'd had a point when he'd put the blame on her, she'd have struggled up and flayed him with her tongue.

If only she'd locked the door and turned a deaf ear to Jimmy's weasel pleading that night, two and a half years ago, she'd still be the Tilly of old: confident and bold, with the will and energy to turn her hand to anything to earn a few bob. Prior to that calamity she'd had a personal taste of Jimmy Wild's brutality, yet she'd opened up to him and once more suffered the devastating consequences.

'Did you remember to get the bread from Travis's bakery? You know I only like his loaves.' Matilda banished miserable memories to prod at a crusty Coburg, testing its freshness.

'Yeah,' Alice sighed. 'Got it from Travis.' She sat down

13

at the table adjacent to her mother and plonked an elbow down, supporting her chin in a cupped palm. 'D'you want to go for a walk today to get a bit of exercise? I haven't got to be back till four o'clock. Josh is doing a late shift at Houndsditch warehouse and is indoors with the kids.'

About to snap she couldn't be bothered Tilly gazed quietly at the cup between her palms. She knew she should get out instead of mouldering away inside, feeling sorry for herself, day after day. She gave her daughter a quirk of a smile and a jerky nod, accepting the invitation for an outing. Tilly knew she was fortunate to have daughters who put themselves out for her. But displaying her gratitude didn't come easily, as Reg would have readily testified.

Having made a laborious descent of the rickety stairs, Alice assisting her mother every step of the way, the two women emerged on to Campbell Road into autumn sunlight. As though several neighbours had foreseen Matilda's rare appearance they immediately converged on her. Beattie Evans abandoned her conversation with a friend and came straight over. Margaret Lovat diverted from her march to Smithie's shop and headed her way too. Then Connie Whitton caught sight of Matilda, ceased trying to sweet-talk her rent collector into being lenient till next week, and trotted towards the group.

'Look a mile better'n when I last saw you,' Beattie announced with a beam.

The trio of neighbours stood eyeing Matilda up and down.

'Don't feel it,' Matilda grumbled.

'No, you do, honest, Mrs K,' Connie piped up. 'Nice day 'n' all for a bit of a walk about. Where you off to, then?'

'Might take a stroll around the park,' Alice answered brightly.

'Ain't goin' that far.' Matilda was immediately contrary.

'Yes, you are,' Alice countered firmly, rolling her eyes in exasperation. 'You're out now and going to stay out for a while. Being cooped up in there all day is enough to send anyone bonkers. Anyhow, you know what the doctor's told you: you got to keep moving about or the stiffness won't ease off.'

'Need anything up the shop?' Margaret Lovat offered. 'Bring it down for you later if you do, Til.'

Matilda shook her head; she didn't like relying on her neighbours although she knew their offers of help were genuine. But it was her daughters' duty to make sure she was all right. 'Alice just got me some stuff, thanks anyhow.' It was an abrupt answer.

'I'd come for a stroll 'n' all, to keep you company, but I'm gonna have that fat git Podge on me ear'ole in a minute 'cos of the rent.' Connie scowled over a shoulder.

'Bleedin' hell,' Matilda muttered. 'That don't sound too nice, Con . . .'

All the women guffawed, even Connie. Beattie gave Tilly's shoulder an appreciative pat and wiped her eyes. It was good to know that Tilly Keiver still had her sense of humour, despite what she'd been through.

It was well known locally that Connie, currently working as a waitress, was not averse to going on the game when she needed cash. It was also known that she'd let Podge Peters into her room for payment in kind when she was really desperate. And she wasn't alone in that. Even married women classed as respectable were not beyond opening up to Podge behind their husbands' backs when things were really grim and they were

15

determined to keep a roof over their kids' heads. With two million people unemployed there was no realistic chance of earning the money any other way.

The women proceeded up the road together at a slow pace so Tilly wouldn't feel under pressure to keep up. Beattie drifted away with a wave after a few yards, having seen that her neighbour was impatiently pacing in the hope of resuming where they'd left off gossiping.

'Oh . . . 'ere 'e is again,' Connie muttered as a fat, florid man emerged from a doorway and stared determinedly at her. She sighed. 'Better go 'n' see him or he'll be round hammering on me door later.'

'Good luck with that,' Tilly said drolly as the petite blonde walked off.

'You heard from your Lucy?' Margaret Lovat blurted out as the three women ambled on.

'Not for a week or two,' Matilda answered. Her eldest daughter, Sophy, was married to Margaret's eldest son. They'd started at Lockley Grange during the Great War and had been there ever since. Four years ago, when Lucy, Matilda's youngest, turned fourteen, Sophy had got her a job in service there too. Then Danny had done the same for his brother, Timothy, so the Lovats and the Keivers were closely connected as well as being neighbours. When news came from 'the kids' in Essex, whether it came to Margaret or to Tilly, it was usually shared around.

'You heard anything from them?' Alice asked, glancing at Margaret.

'Come on, out with it,' Matilda duly prompted her neighbour, having noticed the woman looking uncomfortable. Nothing escaped Matilda Keiver; she might be a bit battered about the body but her mind was as sharp as ever. 'If you've got a bit of gossip, let's hear it, good or bad.'

'Just . . . Tim wrote and said he reckons your Lucy's getting itchy feet. Said he's gonna miss her if she goes. Reckon my Tim's always been a bit sweet on your Lucy.' Margaret frowned at Tilly. 'Don't you say I told you none of this. 'S'pect Lucy's gonna speak up in her own time if she's planning on a move elsewhere.' Margaret halted as they drew level with a gloomy tenement, similar to the one in which Matilda had rooms. The Lovat family were at least housed closer to what was known as the 'better' end of Campbell Road.

'My Luce is too cute to give up a job as good as that,' Tilly stated. 'She got early promotion to lady's maid a short while ago when her senior left.'

'Yeah, course,' Margaret replied, and quickly changed the subject. 'Seen anything of Reg, Til?'

'No, and don't want to neither,' Tilly growled and, grabbing Alice by the arm, she urged her on.

It was only by leaning heavily on Alice that Tilly made it back up the stairs after their constitutional. By the time they were on the landing and unlocking her door Tilly was breathing heavily and frowning in pain.

'You've got to come and live with me for a while, Mum,' Alice gently insisted as she helped Tilly to sit down at the table. 'While Reg is away you'll never manage on your own. You've got to come and live with me and Josh in Wood Green—'

'Ain't going nowhere, so you can shut that up,' Tilly tersely interrupted. 'Told you lots o' times, ain't I, the Bunk's fer me, cradle to grave?'

'Well, you'll be in your grave sooner than you think

if you take another tumble down those stairs. And it's on the cards, 'cos I can't be here every minute of the day fetching you in stuff.' Alice inspected the cups in the bowl to see if they'd been washed up and were ready to use. 'Sooner or later you're going to want something and try and go out and get it yourself. You know how impatient you can be.'

'Got Beattie 'n' Margaret if I'm desperate,' Tilly returned harshly.

'Yeah,' Alice said drily, 'But you never take up their offers of help, do you?'

'Haven't needed to. And I can yell out o' the winder at people, if needs be. Don't think I'm relyin' on you 'n' Beth to that extent.' Matilda looked a bit sheepish because she knew that last statement was completely untrue. Bethany lived closer than Alice but had just had her second child, Joey, so wasn't able to help out as often as Alice. 'Can get about on me own if it comes to it . . . just slowly,' Matilda mumbled.

'You've got to come to mine for a while,' Alice insisted, setting the cups on the table in readiness for tea. 'If you really want to come back to this fleapit when you're better . . .' She shrugged as she glanced about with distaste at the room in which her mother chose to live. She and her sisters had been brought up in a couple of equally squalid rooms. That tenement house had been near the junction with Seven Sisters Road, at the rougher end of the street. Tilly had moved in the right direction and her home was now situated close to Paddington Street, which sliced Campbell Road into two distinct halves. As far as all the Keiver girls were concerned, Campbell Road, top or bottom, was a slum. Sophy, Alice, Beth and Lucy had promised themselves from an early

18

age to escape the Bunk, as the road was nicknamed due to its proliferation of dosshouses. And they'd all made good on their vows.

'Ain't going nowhere,' Tilly enunciated, planting her palms on the tabletop and leaning towards her daughter. 'And no time fer tea. You'd best be off home right now if you don't want Josh to be late getting hisself to work.'

Alice buttoned her coat with a sigh at her mother's curt dismissal. It was better to leave her to stew in her own juice than end up bickering with her.

'D'you reckon Lucy might be getting itchy feet?' During their stroll Alice had avoided discussing the subject. She'd listened to Matilda puffing and panting with the effort of walking along so hadn't wanted to put any additional pressure on her. Alice had mulled things over in her mind as she'd kicked through autumn leaves in Finsbury Park. And she knew that, quiet as her mother had been beside her, she was also brooding on what Margaret Lovat had told them about Lucy.

'She'd best not have got herself sacked,' Matilda replied grumpily. 'Or she'll have me to answer to.'

'Lucy wouldn't get herself sacked, Mum,' Alice said with a rueful smile. She liked to think she knew her little sister better than anyone. If Lucy was moving on, Alice reckoned it was because she'd chosen to do so. At present Sophy and Lucy visited only about twice a year and, whereas Alice accepted that Sophy and Danny were now settled elsewhere, she'd harboured a hope that Little Luce, still single and fancy-free, might one day return to London to work so they could see more of one another.

But her youngest sister wouldn't want to come back to Campbell Road to live. That was certain.

CHAPTER TWO

'That ain't what we agreed.'

'What you talking about . . . what we agreed?'

The woman listening outside the door recognised her husband's mean, scoffing voice.

'We didn't agree nuthin', as I recall.'

'Reckon you must have a right problem with yer memory then. I told you a monkey, and a monkey it is, or no deal.'

Winifred Finch shrank aside as, through a sliver of space, she saw her husband whip a glance her way. In her eagerness to concentrate on what was going on she'd gripped tightly at the door knob, making it squeak in protest. She crept backwards, still craning her neck in the hope of hearing more.

The two men had frozen at the suspicious sound with their fists planted on the table and their torsos almost touching across its square cloth-covered top. A single lamp was burning to one side of them and it put sallow colour on their snarling profiles, and jagged shadows on the opposite wall.

The younger of the men suddenly sprang half out of his chair and swept the gold on the table towards him with the edges of his palms. Broad, bristle-backed fingers then crouched protectively over the jewellery as he slunk down into his seat. 'You don't want this fair and square,' William Black spat, 'don't fucking have it. I got other places to go. This ain't high street crap, y'know, Finchie. This is stuff most likely come out of Tiffany's and Mappin & Webb and the like. I'll have people rip me arm off to get hold of it, so fuck you.'

'Now . . . now . . . now . . .' the older man soothed. His slitted eyes darted back to the glitter visible beneath his associate's hand. He was sure his wife was spying but he'd deal with the nosy cow later. He relaxed back in his chair and spread his arms, gesturing for a truce. 'Didn't say I don't want it, did I, Bill? Just said we ain't agreed a price yet. Certainly ain't agreed the sum you come out with.' He snorted a laugh, hoping he was conveying how farcical he thought Bill's figure. His mockery sounded false and nervous, and did nothing to alleviate the tension in the gloomy room.

Eddie Finch had known Bill Black for many years. He did business with him on a regular basis despite Bill living Lambeth way and Eddie being an Islington resident. Bill might turn up, unannounced, any evening, and unload from his car several cases stuffed with stolen goodies. Eddie knew Bill made the journey to see him north of the water because he liked the way he did business. If Bill had any better associates over Lambeth way paying good prices Eddie knew he wouldn't have seen so much of him. He'd no intention of being railroaded into paying over the odds. He slew a crafty glance at the jewellery.

This little stash was entirely different from what he usually got offered. As a rule Bill brought him a few boxes filled with luxury items of leather and linen, knocked off from some top West End store. But this wasn't fifty quids worth of nice stuff from Derry and Toms or Selfridges, which he'd get a handsome profit on by channelling it through market stalls and clothes dealers. This was serious money. But Eddie wasn't about to let Bill know how keen he was; neither did he relish getting into a scrap with the nutter.

For one thing, he had his wife and kids about the place, and he didn't want a tear-up occurring in his own home. For another, Bill was almost half his age and about a stone heavier. He'd seen the damage Bill could inflict when in a paddy. Last week, when in a south London pub for a business meeting with another of his partners in crime, Eddie had seen a fellow who looked a right state courtesy of Bill's vicious temper. Apparently, he'd spoken less than respectfully to one of Bill's lady friends. Bill was known to have plenty of women always on the go. In all probability it had been a slag he had no real feelings for that had been insulted yet it had resulted in a bloke nearly getting kicked to death. Eddie could see that Bill hardly had a mark on him so the fellow must have either been too pissed to put up a proper fight or had a lousy punch on him.

Eddie's excitement at the prospect of getting his hands on some lovely stuff had given him a racing heartbeat and guts that gurgled, but he'd no intention of letting Bill know he was seriously rattled. For a long, long time he'd wanted a plump sum to add to his little nest egg and Eddie reckoned he'd found one. He wasn't going to let it slip away.

'Winifred!' Eddie summoned his wife in a bellow. 'Take a drink, won't yer, Bill?'

A diminutive woman with frizzy brown hair and a sullen expression immediately shuffled into the parlour from the adjoining kitchenette. A small boy peered about the edge of the door with huge dark eyes, but when Bill noticed him and gave him an exaggerated wink the child shrank back out of sight.

'Get us a couple of whiskies while we sort out some business.'

'Ain't gonna make no difference to the price.' Bill Black gave a sour smile. 'I'll take a drink with you, Eddie, but I still want a monkey or nothing doing.' As Winifred beetled back to the kitchenette Bill noticed Eddie's eyes dart again to his humped hand so he temptingly wriggled his fingers, exposing the shimmer beneath. Weak lamplight caused the diamonds to spark fire and the dark stones appeared huge and profound.

'Fuckin' hell, that *is* nice,' Eddie whispered, lunging to pick up a ring by its platinum shank. The huge sapphire at its centre appeared black until he angled it towards the light and it burst into colour.

'Get most o' yer monkey back on that piece alone, won't yer?' Bill softly drawled, watching Eddie with foxy eyes. 'Tell you the truth, I reckon I must be nuts lettin' it go.' He inclined closer to whisper, 'Betty took a fancy to that sapphire and I nearly had to break her finger to get it back off her, the greedy mare.' He continued watching Eddie's expression as he turned the ring this way and that, letting the lamp work its magic.

Eddie fumbled under the edge of the tablecloth to pull open a drawer and find an eyeglass. Having screwed it in, he went to business.

'Don't let yer missus get a gander at that one. Go missing, it will, 'fore you've had a chance to shift it.'

Eddie snickered and continued twisting the ring to and fro.

Words were unnecessary. Bill knew the weasel sitting opposite would throttle his missus or his kids if any of them so much as touched anything of his without his say so.

Eddie put down the sapphire and began examining a square-cut diamond ring set in yellow gold. He carried on until every single item had been thoroughly studied. He didn't have much of a clue what to look for; the gems looked big and clean under inspection and that seemed enough. But he'd once had a job as a goldsmith's apprentice in Hatton Garden and liked to think he knew a bit about the trade despite the fact he'd been sacked for stealing a bracelet before he'd been employed six months.

'Well?' Bill prompted, having impatiently observed his companion staring transfixed at the collection of gems neatly arranged in the centre of the table.

'Give yer four.'

'Get stuffed.'

Winifred shuffled in and nervously put down two tumblers half-filled with Scotch. She audibly swallowed and gawped, dumbstruck at the jewellery adorning her dirty tablecloth.

'On yer way,' her husband gruffly ordered, jerking a thumb in the direction of the kitchenette. Immediately she did as she'd been told, pulling the door to after her.

'Shut it!' Eddie barked. He waited until he heard a click, then said, 'Bleedin' nosy cow's probably got her eye stuck to the keyhole instead.'

'Can't blame her. All women love jewellery, Eddie.

You'll probably get the shag of yer life if you just let her wear a couple of bits. Betty likes to slip on a few baubles when we're at it . . . says it excites her . . .'

'Give yer four fifty,' Eddie wheezed out. 'Can't say fairer'n that.'

'Can, Eddie,' Bill sighed. 'Can say five hundred and you're still getting a steal.' He chuckled at his little joke. He knew he'd got him. Eddie desperately wanted the stuff and he couldn't blame him. It was the bargain of the century. If Bill had had more time to shift it he'd have gone elsewhere. He knew he could have got closer to a grand if he'd sold the stuff individually. But he wanted shot of it quickly because it was hot and he might at any time get a visit from the boys in blue.

He also needed some money pronto to pay off what he owed on other deals. His spare bedroom at home was stuffed floor to ceiling with fur coats, and the bad girls who'd hoisted the stuff for him were giving him earache about getting their share of the loot. He needed to keep Betty and her crew sweet because they earned him a fortune, and a few of the girls didn't mind joining him in bed when Betty's back was turned. Bill glanced at Eddie; he knew he had a wad about the place somewhere. Much as Eddie Finch liked to plead poverty, the miser always had ready cash.

Bill glanced about the parlour with distaste. Considering the dump Eddie lived in it wasn't surprising he had a stash; he certainly didn't spend any of his money on his home or his family.

Eddie swiped a hand over his bristly chin. 'There ain't gonna be no comeback on this, is there?'

'Nah! The girl I got working for me, she's young but real cute. No flies on her. We've covered her tracks.'

'Nothing going to be in the papers, then, to identify it? No list of items up Scotland Yard getting looked at?'

'Got hoisted off some posh bloke's tart.' Bill shrugged. 'When I say tart, course I mean a right high-class brass. Set up in style, she is, in Mayfair. The old boy, who I can tell you is an MP, 'n' all – but no more clues,' he joked playfully – 'well, he ain't gonna want it splashed all over the papers that his mistress's jewellery got robbed when it's probably a damn sight better than anything he's ever bought fer his missus, is he?'

'Who is this girl you use? Is it Betty?' Eddie was playing for time while he thought things through. He doubted that Bill would have used Betty Pickering to steal this lot. For one thing, she was the woman in his harem he fancied the most and he wouldn't risk getting her banged up on a long stretch for something serious. Betty already had a police record for shoplifting and had done short sentences. Her face was well known; she wouldn't easily get a job in service, even with false references.

'My business, that is, Eddie.' Bill tapped his nose. 'Can't expect me to go telling you me trade secrets. Don't you worry, she's a pro all right. Weren't there working as a maid for this tart more'n a week.' He made a diving motion with a hand. 'Straight in, she were, had a mosey around, found where the jewellery box were hid and Bob's yer uncle.' He abruptly drew the gems into his fingers, his expression grim. 'Time's up. Ready or not?'

'What you doin' downstairs, Jenny?' Eddie had scrambled to his feet at the sight of one of his teenage daughters stationed in the doorway. 'I told you to stay in yer room, you disobedient little . . . Winnie!' he roared, summoning his wife.

Winifred shot out and gawped at Jennifer. 'You know

26

yer dad don't like you downstairs when he's got company,' she wailed. Her bony hands began flapping in front of her pinafore to shoo the girl away.

'Only after a drink of water,' Jennifer breathed in a high nervous voice, but she couldn't stop her gleaming eyes from sliding towards Bill Black.

'Leave her be; ain't doin' no harm.' Bill sent the girl a subtle smile. He knew Eddie and Winnie had twin daughters who were about fourteen. This was the little minx who gave him come-on looks; the prettier one, called Katherine, seemed a right stuck-up cow. Considering who she was and where she lived she'd no right to such airs and graces, in Bill's opinion. He'd seen Jennifer before, watching him out of an upstairs window when he'd been unloading stuff from the boot of his car. He knew her sort – had a throb in her fanny before her tits were big enough to be of interest. Bill was wise enough to decline gaol bait but he wasn't averse to stringing her along and letting her know he'd be ready when she was . . .

'Fetch her a bleedin' cup of water and get rid of her,' Eddie growled through set teeth at his wife. He'd seen Jennifer stare at the pile of gems before her eyes skittered away. Once Bill was gone the little slut would feel the back of his hand.

A moment later, Winnie thrust a chipped cup at her daughter, slopping some water down the front of Jennifer's nightdress in her haste to get rid of her.

Once Winnie had taken herself off back into the kitchenette and the stairs creaked quietly, Bill said, amused, 'Now . . . where was we, Finchie? You want this stuff or not, 'cos I'm on a promise and I don't want Betty to go off the boil, if yer know wot I mean . . .'

'All right,' Eddie muttered in defeat. 'Give yer half

now and half on Friday.' He pulled out of his pocket a thick roll of notes and, having slowly counted out, slapped most of it down on the tablecloth. 'Look . . . just left meself a tenner to get by.'

Bill laughed at his sulky expression as he picked up the cash. 'You know that ain't how it works, mate.'

'Fucking hell,' Eddie snapped, slamming himself back in the chair. 'Yer reckon I've got five hundred notes about the place?'

'Tell you what.' Bill tilted his head, eyeing him shrewdly. 'I'll take yer two 'n' 'alf and leave you them.' He pushed some rings towards Eddie. 'Then Friday I'll come by with the sapphire and you can settle up.' He waved the ring beneath Eddie's nose before pocketing it.

Eddie jerked immediately to his feet. He reckoned come Friday Bill would have sold it elsewhere. 'You don't trust me to pay up?' He was all huffy indignation.

'Course I don't, mate.' Bill also got to his feet. 'What kind o' mug d'you take me for?' He picked up the whisky and downed it in one swallow. 'Say thanks to the missus fer the drink, won't you now, just in case she can't hear me.' A sardonic glance was sent towards the kitchenette.

'No . . . hang on . . .' Eddie stopped him by the door that led into the gloomy passage. He swiped a hand over his jaw. 'I'll see what I can rake up.' He went into the kitchen and closed the door quickly behind him. Raised voices could be heard, then a shove from her husband sent Winifred, holding her son by the hand, hurtling out of the small room. The momentum was too much for the boy's balance and he fell to his knees, but Winnie immediately hoisted him up by an arm before flouncing out of the parlour. A moment later the stairs started creaking again.

28

Bill chuckled to himself as he heard Eddie turn the key in the lock. Wherever it was Eddie had hidden his money in the kitchen he wasn't about to let him, or his wife, know about it. 'Wise move, mate,' Bill called drily. 'Can't be too careful. Winnie finds yer stash you won't see her nor it no more.'

Garbled muttering was heard coming from behind the door, then a few moments later Eddie was back with a roll of notes. 'There, take the fuckin' lot. You've cleaned me out.' He threw the money on the table.

'Know what I reckon, Eddie?' Bill grinned as he collected fivers and tenners. 'I reckon I should've asked fer more because you could pull a grand out of this place if necessary, couldn't yer?' He shook his head. 'Crafty old git.' He retrieved the ring from his pocket. 'There, have that, and a good leg-over later, if you let Winifred slip it on. She'll be staring at that instead of the ceiling for a change, and fantasising you're Ramon Navarro and she's Tallulah Bankhead.' Ignoring Eddie's scowl he went out guffawing, one hand curved about the cash in his pocket.

Even before he'd heard the front door click shut behind Bill, Eddie was drawing his belt from his trousers. He was seething to have been forced to pay so much for the jewellery. He wasn't happy either that he'd been forced to scrape together his nest egg in front of his wife; he now needed to find a new hidy-hole. Winifred would have the kitchen upside down looking for it as soon as his back was turned. But there was nothing left to find. Bill had cleaned him out, and Eddie never liked to be without a little bit tucked away. He sent a vicious look ceiling-ward, his lips flat against his teeth as he started towards the door.

CHAPTER THREE

'Why didn't you let me know you was coming?'

'Wanted it to be a nice surprise for you.' Lucy managed to shield her shocked expression against Matilda's shoulder whilst giving her a fierce hug. Once she'd composed herself she looked up.

Lucy had last seen her mother many months ago during the Easter holiday and had thought then she looked rough. In the meantime, as the hot summer months had passed by, she'd prayed the fine weather would help Matilda recuperate in body and mind, rather than the heatwave exhaust her, for she'd seemed worryingly depressed even before Reg took off. But moments ago, Lucy's optimism had dwindled. While waiting on the landing to be let in, she'd realised her mother was finding the simple task of opening the door an irritating effort.

Having lugged her trunk and a bag of shopping up the rickety flight of stairs to the first floor, Lucy's light, teasing ratatat had drawn slow shuffling footsteps and muttered cursing from inside the room. Her first glimpse of haggard features, grey with strain, had been viewed through a narrow aperture and had made Lucy's spirits plummet. Having identified her visitor Matilda had then found the energy to shove the door wide open and hoarsely whoop in delight. But despite her mother's enthusiastic welcome Lucy was dismayed by her relapse.

Alice had sent a letter to Essex over a month ago to let her and Sophy know that Reg had done a runner. A long time had passed with no news of him, she'd added, so it seemed unlikely he'd soon be back. Alice had also informed them that their mother was still struggling to get about on her own and was stubbornly refusing to accept neighbours' help, or to move to Wood Green so Alice could properly care for her.

'How long you got off work?' Tilly asked, gripping tightly at Lucy's hands and pushing her back so she could study her lovely face. 'Be a treat if you could stay till the weekend.' Matilda's customary gruff tone bubbled joyfully at the prospect of having her youngest daughter's company.

'I can stay, Mum,' Lucy confirmed, a smile in her voice. 'In fact I'll be able to stay for a while 'cos I've got something to tell you.'

'Good or bad?' Tilly immediately elbowed free of her daughter's renewed embrace and took a suspicious peer at her flat belly.

'Well, I think you'll reckon it's good. I've come back to London to stay.'

'To stay?' Matilda parroted. 'It's true then what Margaret said.' She frowned at Lucy. 'You after a change of scenery or you got sacked?' It was barked out indignantly rather than angrily. Of all her daughters, Lucy tended to be proud and impetuous. As a child she'd got into numerous scraps with other kids because of it. Not that Matilda had chided her for that. When you lived in the Bunk you brought up your kids to give as good as they got or they'd have the life bullied out of them. But her youngest could be a bit naïve at times as well as hot-headed. Matilda felt annoyed with herself for not pursuing the matter of Lucy's employment when Margaret Lovat had first hinted at it, weeks ago.

'Not got sacked, Mum!' Lucy chuckled. 'Got an interview for a job in Bloomsbury.' She struck a hoity-toity little pose.

Tilly's lined face softened in relief. 'In town, eh?' She nodded to show she was impressed. 'More money, then?' she asked, ever prosaic.

'Hope so; 'cos of my age and lack of experience and so on it'll all be discussed at the interview. It says so in the letter they've sent me. But if it's a few shillings less I'm not bothered. I'll be closer to you, anyhow. So even though I'll be living in I can come 'n' see you on all of me free afternoons,' Lucy rattled off. 'And I'll be able to meet up with Alice and Beth. I'll take you out places and we can have some fine times again. It'll be like before I went away when it was just us two.'

After her other sisters had left to set up their own homes, Tilly's maternal instinct, no longer diluted by being channelled four ways, had condensed and targeted Lucy. They had grown very close, and her sisters still referred to Lucy as their mother's blue-eyed girl. The bond had survived Tilly's volatile nature and heavy drinking, and Lucy leaving home to work in service.

'And what if you don't get offered this job, my gel? Bound to be lots of women applyin' fer a position like that.'

Lucy shrugged insouciantly. 'I'll find another agency and go after another job. But I want to have a taste of London life, and I ain't going back to the sticks and that's final.' She gave a crisp nod, setting her thick chestnut hair waving. 'Not that I could go back anyhow 'cos I told that snooty bitch that married Mr Lockley just what I thought of her before I carried me case out of the back door.'

Matilda grinned despite herself. She liked to know that her daughters didn't stand for any nonsense, and she recalled that Sophy had described the new mistress as 'bleedin' hard work'. 'Well, you'll have to get this job then, and once you've got it, you keep hold of it.' Despite being overjoyed to hear her Little Luce was going to be close by, Tilly wagged a cautioning finger at her. 'Good work's hard to come by these days. You was lucky getting a job straight from school. And you got yer sister Sophy to thank fer that. You've never had it hard, so take it from me, being skint ain't fun.'

'Not renting the back room now you're on yer own?' Lucy had opened the connecting door and peered in to a dismal space that held nothing but an iron bed with a stained mattress on it, and a wonky tallboy that had a gaping hole right in the centre where the largest drawer should have been. She gazed enquiringly at her mother. Most people who lived in the Bunk and had a bit of spare space would rent it out. Lucy could recall that even when their rooms had been filled to overflowing with family members, Tilly would sometimes take in a temporary lodger for a bit of extra cash. Being the youngest, she'd usually share a bed with her mother and free up just enough space in the back room for another young woman to kip down with Bethany and

Alice in the back. It was so unlike her mother to overlook such an opportunity that Lucy repeated her question.

Matilda shook her head. 'Could do with the rent money all right but can't be doing with the company.'

'You *can* do with the company,' Lucy disagreed, closing the back room door and approaching her mother. 'Alice reckons you could do with a hand most days. If you had a lodger . . . perhaps a widow or a spinster about your own age who could help out with other things . . .'

'Don't want no strangers nursemaiding me,' Tilly brusquely asserted. 'So don't think you lot are landing one on me. What else yer sisters been telling you about me behind me back?'

'It's not like that, Mum,' Lucy said briskly. 'We're all worried about you, you know. Why won't you go and live with Alice for a while till you're feeling better?'

'Has Alice told you to get on at me about it? If she has I'll have her hide fer pokin' her nose in where it's not wanted.'

'Alice hasn't said more'n she's worried you'll take another bad fall and end up looking a worse state than you do now.'

'Look a mess, do I?' Tilly challenged with grim amusement.

'I've seen you look better. In fact you looked better at Easter,' Lucy immediately came back with an honest reply. 'I expected you to be well on the mend by now.'

Matilda ignored that, instead demanding, 'And I suppose you've all been having a chinwag about Reg 'n' all. What've you all been saying about him?'

'He's done a runner and left you on yer own.' It was a concise reply.

'That's about the size of it,' Matilda agreed. 'Ain't talking about him neither. He's gone and forgotten, and that's that.' A moment later she'd rescinded that vow. 'You don't seem surprised about him going.'

Lucy shrugged. 'Last time I was here I could tell things weren't right between you. You were both snapping and snarling more than usual.'

'He's gone back to Ireland.'

'Back to Ireland?' Lucy echoed, her eyes widening in surprise. None of her sisters had heard that bit of news as far as she was aware. 'What, for good?'

'Dunno,' Matilda replied. 'Yesterday I went up to Smithie's shop.' She sent her daughter a sour smile. 'See, I can do the trip on me own, if I have to. Anyhow, I bumped into Reg's friend Vince. He looked a bit embarrassed; don't know why 'cos I never had a habit of questioning him about Reg. So, he just come out with it and said Reg had caught the boat back a few weeks previous.'

Lucy had met Vince a few times and thought him a weasely sort of fellow. 'Perhaps he was just saying that, Mum, 'cos he felt awkward and wanted to nip off.'

'Just said I never pestered him over Reg. Don't matter anyway; let him stay in Ireland, for all I care. Seen him in his true colours now, ain't I?' Matilda pursed her lips. 'Bleedin' good job, weren't it, we never did the "in sickness and in health" bit,' she added bitterly.

Despite Matilda's bravado Lucy could tell her mother was getting upset talking about the man who'd abandoned her. She and her sisters, along with most of Campbell Road's inhabitants, were aware that Reg ought to have been at home with their mother on the night their evil uncle had turned up with murderous intentions. Nobody really blamed Reg for allowing himself to be waylaid by a pal for a drink in a pub; but then nobody blamed Tilly either for being unrelentingly resentful that he had.

That horrible night had been a catalogue of calamity for their family. On the very same night, their cousin, Robert Wild, Jimmy's son, had been beaten up so badly by thugs that he'd nearly died. The disasters had been like toppling dominoes: one setting the other in motion. A shiver rippled through Lucy at the memory of the dreadful months that had followed when they'd feared Matilda and Robert might both die of their injuries.

Determinedly, Lucy cheered herself up and, to impress on her mum that she was definitely not returning to Essex, she briskly dragged her case in from the landing. She left the trunk against the wall but plonked the shopping bag down on the table. 'Here,brought us in a nice couple of currant buns so let's get that kettle on.'

'Those from Travis's?' Tilly grumpily interrogated. 'You know I only like stuff from the Travis bakery.'

'Yeah, Mum,' Lucy mocked in a dreary tone that transformed in to a chuckle. Like her sisters, she was used to Tilly's deliberately contrary ways. 'They are from old man Travis. The dirty old git don't change, do he? Still stares straight at me chest when he serves me.'

Tilly opened the paper bag and her eyes lit up as a spicy scent wafted to her nostrils. It was a treat for her to have something fresh and tasty. To save herself the ordeal of a trip out, or the need to ask a neighbour for a favour, she ate little and made what she had last.

Lucy picked up the kettle and gave it a shake to see if there was enough water in it for a pot of tea. She pulled out a chair for her mother to sink into, for she'd noticed Tilly had been holding on to the table edge to ease the weight off her legs. 'Sit yourself down again, Mum, and I'll make a brew. Have you got any jam to put in these buns?'

Ten minutes later the tea was made and the buns split and spread with marge as Tilly hadn't got any jam.

'So when's your interview?' Tilly took a large bite out of the warm, aromatic bun. Any currants that escaped were picked from her plate and popped in her mouth.

'Ten o'clock on Friday, Bloomsbury.' Lucy brushed crumbs from her lips with her fingertips. 'A Mrs Venner is the housekeeper and a Mrs Boyd is me senior. I'll be seeing them both in Mrs Venner's office. It's a posh establishment, by the sound of things; belongs to a Lord and Lady Mortimer in Bedford Square.' She raised her eyebrows, displaying pride at the prospect of working for the aristocracy. 'Don't suppose I'll get to see much of them. The housekeeper and the lady's maid'll be me guvnors.'

Tilly nodded sagely. 'You turn up all nice and tidy with manners to match then, my gel, and the job'll be yours.'

Lucy grinned and delved into a pocket. She pulled out an envelope. 'Should be mine, no trouble; if not, I'll have Mrs Lovat's hide.' She playfully waved the envelope under her mother's nose. 'The housekeeper at me last job's done me a lovely reference, don't you know . . .'

Winnie Finch thrust her son's coat at him. 'Get that on and get yourself off or you'll be late for school, Tom.'

The boy grimaced as he gingerly stuck an arm in a sleeve. 'Can I stay home today, Mum?'

'No, you can't. I've got me job to do, you know that.' Winifred avoided Tom's pleading eyes.

'Can I stop home with Jenny?'

'No, you can't; she's off out to find herself work.' Winnie knew her son was still suffering from getting a belt off his father earlier in the week. Not that Eddie had intended to discipline Tom when he pounded up the stairs that night, face contorted in rage. Tom was his favourite and he rarely laid a finger on him.

Jennifer, the brazen little cow, had been his target because she'd defied him and poked her nose in while Eddie had been doing a deal with Bill Black. Winnie knew her husband hated any of them to see or hear what was going on when his associates called round. If Eddie could, he'd arrange it so Bill always turned up at an appointed time, rather than whenever he felt like dropping by with a box of stuff or, as he had this time, a pocketful of gemstone rings.

Winnie was aware too that the fact one of his daughters was turning into a little tart before she'd been out of school six months was less worrying to Eddie than knowing Jennifer had seen the jewellery. Jenny's jaw had sagged open in the way Winnie imagined her own had done when she'd spotted those sparklers on the table. What she desperately wanted to know – and had tried hard to discover – was whether the lovely stuff was still in the house. Since that evening, Winnie had been through the kitchen with a fine-tooth comb and turned up nothing at all. She'd even accidentally dislodged a cupboard from the wall in her search and had made a very inexpert job of screwing it back in place. If the gems were in the house, and Winnie could find them, or Eddie's stash of banknotes, she'd take herself and Tom off as fast as she could. The twins were old enough now to sort themselves out, in Winnie's opinion.

Katherine was a good, hardworking girl – she'd been doing her little job serving in the kiosk at the local flicks the evening Bill Black turned up – and Winnie would feel a twinge at leaving her behind. But Katherine had a good brain on her and Winnie was confident she would eventually get a nice full-time position in a factory. Katherine talked constantly of training to be a nurse and Winnie reckoned she had the right attitude to see it through. As for Jenny, Winnie feared if she didn't change her ways, she'd be hanging around on street corners touting for business from the likes of Bill Black. But, brazen as she'd been that night, Jenny hadn't deserved the beating Eddie had given her. Her daughter's legs were still black and blue, despite the fact that the blankets she'd dived under had given her some protection from her father's fury. If Katherine had been home she'd also have got a taste of Eddie's brutality because she always stood up to him if he set about her sister.

Jennifer's howls had brought her brother running in from his bedroom and, though just six years old, Tom had jumped on his father's back to try to protect her, and got a bash for his trouble.

Winnie helped Tom on with his coat, uncomfortably aware her impatience to get him out of the house was making him wince. It had been her job to stop Eddie's rampage that night, not her son's. Jennifer had deserved chastisement. Besides, whenever her husband was in one of those moods, Winnie always paid later . . . in bed, and on that particular evening she hadn't seen why she should have to put up with the bastard setting about her twice.

'There's an advertisement for an assistant in the Dobson's shop window,' Winnie barked at Jennifer, who was descending the stairs, hunched into her dressing gown for warmth against the draught coming through the open front door.

'I'm going down the labour exchange with me friend later this morning . . .'

'Yer friend can go on her own. You go along to the sweet shop straight away and apply for the job.'

'I don't want to work in a poxy sweet shop. I'm gonna get a job in Oxford Street, in Selfridges . . . or somewhere like that.'

'You won't be getting no jobs in the West End, miss,' Winnie hissed at Jennifer. 'You can give over with your fancy ideas and act a bit more like yer sister. Katherine's had a job since the day after she finished her schooling. Time you got off yer backside. Now get yourself dressed and get along to Dobson's and don't come back without a job or it'll be the worse for you.'

CHAPTER FOUR

'Like it here, do you?'

'Like having me here, do you?' Lucy returned, equally sarcastic. She knew who'd spoken without taking a look so she finished leisurely positioning Lady Mortimer's combs on the dressing table before turning to confront the woman behind her.

Lucy had just about had her fill of Audrey Stubbs spying on her. Since she'd started work at Mortimer House at the beginning of the week, whether she'd been brushing clothes or refilling scent bottles and cosmetic pots, the housemaid had seemed to materialise at the corner of her eye. Audrey could have been hovering on the threshold of her ladyship's bedroom for some time before Lucy realised she was again being stalked.

'Don't make a blind bit of difference to me if you're here or there,' Audrey answered airily, lazily polishing the brass door knob with her pinafore.

'Could've sworn it did,' Lucy retorted. ''Cos ever since I started on Monday you've been on me back about something.' She glanced past Audrey to check nobody was nearby to overhear. 'What's got your goat?' Lucy demanded sharply. 'I taken a job you was after?' She'd stabbed a guess at the reason for Audrey's animosity and seemed to have turned up trumps. The maid's lips tightened and the malice in her eyes was concealed behind her eyelashes.

'Let's face it, if you'd been up to the work you'd've got it 'cos you was here first,' Lucy pointed out with vague amusement. 'Must be a reason why you was overlooked.' She went back to the dressing table and picked up a delicate comb. She leisurely turned it this way and that. 'P'raps Mrs Boyd ain't any keener on you than I am.'

'Think yer clever, don't you? Coming here 'n' swanking around, 'cos you managed to land a plum job. I've seen you eyeing up the men, don't think I ain't.' Audrey had approached stealthily to jab twice at Lucy's arm to gain her attention.

'What?' Lucy glanced over a shoulder, her features crumpled in incomprehension. She'd been used to getting attention from male colleagues when she'd worked at Lockley Grange. But there, or here, she'd never yet met one who'd interested her enough to make her stare back. Since she was a little girl she'd been told she was pretty. But all the Keiver women were lookers in their own way so she had never felt the need to boast about it.

'If Mrs Boyd gets a sniff of how you've been carryin' on with Rory Jackson, you'll be out on yer ear, and serve you right.'

Lucy itched to slap the smirk off Audrey's face but was puzzled by what the housemaid had just implied. 'Carrying on with Rory?' she echoed, frowning.

Rory was one of two chauffeurs who ferried about

Lord and Lady Mortimer and their children. Apart from a bit of bantering at breakfast time earlier in the week, when they'd sat next to each other in the servants' dining hall, she'd had little to do with Rory. They'd passed on the back stairs earlier that day, he descending and she travelling speedily in the opposite direction as she'd been told to fetch her ladyship's favourite kid boots to be soled and heeled. The lad appointed to run to the cobblers had been impatiently waiting by the kitchen door for her return so she hadn't dawdled, and had exchanged with Rory just a good morning. The most she could bring to mind about him was that he'd got fair hair, a pleasing face, and looked smart in his chauffeur's uniform. Suddenly the penny dropped and she realised Audrey probably had a crush on him. Lucy raised her eyes heavenward in an effort to persuade her colleague there was no reason for her to be jealous on that score.

'If you've got yer sights set on Rory Jackson, you can have him with my compliments.'

'Not good enough for you, is that it? Proper full of yourself, ain't you, Miss Keiver?'

Lucy huffed in disbelief. 'What's up with you? Look, I'm telling you you're welcome to him. From what I've seen so far there ain't one fellow here I'd walk out with, let alone pine over.' Her tone was all mock sympathy. 'Now, why don't you sling yer 'ook so I can get on 'n' do what I'm supposed to be doing 'stead of listening to your stupid prattle.'

'I've met your type before.' Audrey grabbed Lucy's arm and jerked her around. 'Butter wouldn't melt one minute, then the next you're round the back o' the washhouse with yer drawers round yer ankles.'

'Let go of me arm.'

'Why, what you gonna do . . . make me?'

As Audrey's spittle flecked her face Lucy instinctively shoved a hand hard against her shoulder. Audrey tottered backwards with a grunt of surprise and ended on her posterior on the polished floor just as her ladyship's maid walked in.

'What the *devil* is going on here?' Mrs Boyd barked, her round, bespectacled face a study of shock and disgust.

'Lucy Keiver just pushed me over, Mrs Boyd.' Audrey had immediately turned on the waterworks and was dabbing at her face with the pinafore she'd whipped up. She scrambled on to her knees and continued whimpering, presenting a picture of hurt innocence.

Determined to keep the disturbance, which had vexingly occurred on her patch, undetected until she'd had some facts, Mrs Boyd immediately hurried to shut all connecting doors. 'Explain yourself, Lucy Keiver,' she hissed.

'I didn't want this to happen,' Lucy began. 'I was just setting out her ladyship's brushes and combs like you asked me to when Audrey come up behind and started accusing me of stupid stuff.' She moistened her lips. She didn't want to tell tales; at the Grange the servants had had an unspoken pact that, barring gross misconduct, they never grassed one another up. But Audrey hadn't hesitated in immediately putting the blame on her. Lucy had not even finished one full week in her new job. She'd been growing to like it here too, despite having been put in the same dormitory as Audrey Stubbs. All she'd done was try to get the stupid cow to back off and leave her alone. It was her own fault she'd ended up on her backside, snivelling.

'Accusing you of what?' Mrs Boyd snapped, inclining stiffly forward. 'Come on, out with it.'

'She thinks I'm flirting with the men. She thinks I'm after Rory Jackson and I only met him Monday and haven't said more'n half a dozen words to him.'

'I reckon you've done more'n that with him,' Audrey sniped, and narrowed her gaze on Mrs Boyd to gauge the woman's reaction.

'Enough!' Clare Boyd had heard about Audrey being involved in a scuffle over a different male employee. Allegedly, she'd been found outside, smoking and flirting with one of the gardeners and a tussle had ensued in the kitchen with another girl. It had been Mrs Venner's responsibility to sort that one out but apparently she'd let it pass because there'd been no witnesses to the fight and neither girl had made a complaint.

Mrs Boyd felt relieved that she'd had no hand in taking on Audrey. The housekeeper had been solely responsible for her recruitment. But Clare had been present when Mrs Venner interviewed Lucy Keiver and she had sanctioned her employment. Lucy had seemed to have an honest forthright manner – and an excellent reference from her previous employer – and Clare had believed she'd make a good addition to the household. She sighed to herself. In the old days, before the war, you could get decent staff, but these youngsters coming through were no good at all. They had no interest in anything but dancing, smoking and flirting with the opposite sex.

'Don't think it's gone unnoticed by me that you have no business being here in Lady Mortimer's chamber,' Mrs Boyd snapped at Audrey. 'The upstairs cleaning was all finished hours ago. And I believe it's not two weeks since you were reprimanded for shirking outside instead of working.' She looked from one downcast face to the other. 'I'll speak to Mrs Venner later and you can each explain to her your disgraceful conduct. Now get about your duties.'

As Lucy proceeded along the corridor she was aware of many pairs of eyes following her and a hush descending where moments before had been heard lively chatter. She pursed her lips and inched up her chin. Of course, the other servants had been gossiping over the brouhaha upstairs concerning her and Audrey Stubbs, and the likely punishments they would receive.

At the Grange, if Lucy had been given a ticking-off for some misdemeanour – and she'd certainly had some from her sister and brother-in-law – she'd have got sympathetic smiles from her colleagues. Not here. Cold glances and turned shoulders met her lonely progress towards the kitchens. Once she'd passed by she heard a few sniggers and her fingers curled at her sides.

She'd just had her dressing-down from Mrs Venner and had been told her punishment was the loss of her afternoon off next week. It had come as a bitter blow because she'd planned on persuading her mother to take a trip round to her sister Beth's house. But she hadn't felt it prudent to argue or even offer to have her pay docked instead. She'd simply bitten her lip and waited to be dismissed by the housekeeper.

She was the newest member of staff and had not yet made any friends amongst her colleagues. Prue Bates, who was the other girl sharing the dormitory in which she and Audrey slept, had been standoffish from the start and had marked her territory very clearly in the cramped attic room. Lucy considered most of them quite snooty for hired help. But it didn't worry her; she liked her work, learning to care for her ladyship and her daughters' swish clothes and accessories. She'd also fetched bits and pieces from the haberdashers and milliners. Lucy didn't mind at all being an errand girl for it got her out of the house for a while. After the sedate pace of life at Lockley Grange the crowds and the bustle in London fascinated her. She'd walk along looking about and jumping out of her skin when hooting vehicles chugged past. Mostly the fellows were just impatient to get going in traffic but she'd noticed a delivery driver had done it to get her attention and give her a saucy signal.

So far she'd had little contact with the mistress or her two young daughters. Mrs Boyd kept her in the background as much as possible and took all the praise for jobs well done. But Lucy knew there was time enough to make her mark; she was being trained to be the Mortimer girls' personal maid when they were older.

On the whole she'd found Mrs Boyd a fair boss and wasn't resentful about being disciplined. But Lucy felt dejected that camaraderie, so much in evidence at the Grange when the mistress had been alive, seemed to be lacking here. Rory Jackson seemed friendly but his harmless attention to her had got her into trouble. Reflecting on him seemed to have conjured him up. Her sideways glance through the open door of the servants' hall landed on his lean figure. He saw her too and strolled up to her.

'You didn't hang about in getting yourself into trouble, did you?'

Lucy kept on walking without replying to his amused

47

statement. He followed her as she carried on towards the kitchens.

'What started it off?'

'As if you didn't know,' Lucy muttered.

'What you on about? Why would I know anything?'

Lucy halted and planted her hands on her hips. 'Don't tell me it ain't gone round like wildfire. No doubt Audrey's got her side in first. As I'm the new girl I'm the culprit, right?'

'Touchy, ain't you? Carry on like that and everybody *will* think you're at fault.'

'They can think what they bloody well like!' Lucy gritted out through set teeth. '*I* know what went on, and that's enough for me.'

'It's enough for me too. You say it's her fault, I believe you.'

'Why's that, then?' Lucy started off again at a slower pace, slanting him a look.

'Ain't the first time Audrey's got caught out. Don't suppose it'll be the last. Only next time she'll get the boot. Everybody's allowed a few warnings here at Mortimer House, and she's had hers.'

Lucy recalled that Mrs Boyd had snapped at Audrey because she'd recently been in trouble.

'What started it off?' he again asked.

As it concerned him, and was a bit embarrassing, Lucy considered telling Rory to mind his own business, but instead she blurted out the truth. 'Audrey thinks I've got me eye on you and she don't like it. If you and her have a thing, you've got my sympathy, 'cos she's a right nasty cow, as far as I can see.' She eyed him frostily. 'On the other hand, if you've been winding her up on purpose, saying I'm after you, when I ain't, then the two of you deserve each other, 'cos you're no better than she is.' Lucy made to walk quickly on but Rory grabbed her elbow and tugged her back.

'I don't know her much better'n I know you. As I said, she's only been here a short while. Neither of you takes my fancy . . . no offence.'

'None taken . . . and likewise,' Lucy rattled off. But she felt miffed by his clipped words and amused air, and ripped her elbow free of his grip.

Rory followed a few paces behind her marching figure. 'Is that all you were fighting about? Audrey thinking we'd been flirting?' he asked lightly.

'We didn't *fight* over you so don't go getting conceited ideas. If anything, I reckon she's more narked she didn't get my job.'

'She did want it. Everybody knew that. That's why you shouldn't be surprised that a lot of people aren't jumping to any conclusions over what happened today.'

Lucy turned and gazed up at his lean profile.

'Where was you when she started on you?'

'In the mistress's bedroom.' Lucy took the last few steps to the kitchen and stopped outside the door. She was going to ask for a sandwich and eat it in her room rather than sit with her colleagues glaring at her at teatime.

'Ain't the first time she's been caught dawdling in a place she shouldn't be. She's workshy, that one.' Rory plunged his hands into his pockets.

'She had a set-to with anybody else?'

He nodded. 'Couple of times since she's been here. Millie . . .' He saw Lucy's frown and explained, 'Housemaid who comes in twice a week, you've probably not yet met her . . . she gave Audrey a smack when

49

she found out she'd been canoodling with her sweetheart. Jack helps out in the garden and, officially, him and Audrey were just sharing a crafty smoke, nothing more to it.'

'And unofficially?' Lucy suggested drily.

'Jack couldn't help boasting to a few of us men that he'd been on the verge of getting a roll in the hay.' He chuckled softly. 'Right puffed up, he were, the little tyke, 'cos he reckoned Audrey wouldn't take no for an answer.'

Lucy blushed, feeling indignant that the brazen trollop had had the cheek to accuse *her* of being the sort to drop her drawers out in the open! 'Who else has she been in trouble with?' Lucy's question tumbled out.

'Susan Reeves; your predecessor came across Audrey in her ladyship's room just after she'd laid out some of her clothes for a fancy evening do. By all accounts she gave Audrey a right piece of her mind.' Rory propped an elbow against the wall, casually supporting a cheek on an open palm. 'Audrey had only been here a few days and got away with saying she was confused and didn't know it was the personal maids' job to bring up the mistress's clean linen.'

Lucy gave a little nod to let him know she'd appreciate knowing more.

'Susan reckoned that Audrey was overawed seeing all her ladyship's finery,' Rory resumed. 'When she disturbed Audrey she'd got one of Lady Mortimer's frocks held up against her and was staring at herself in the glass.' He shrugged. 'Susan just packed her off with a flea in her ear. She never told Mrs Venner or Mrs Boyd about it. No harm had been done and as Susan had already put in her notice and was leaving at the end of the week to get wed it wasn't worth making a fuss.'

'Susan confided all this in you, did she?' Lucy asked waspishly.

Rory grinned. 'Nah . . . her fiancé, Gus Miller, did. He's a friend of mine. Don't suppose I'll see much of old Dusty now he's leg-shackled and gone off to Essex.'

'That's where I've just come from,' Lucy offered up automatically. 'Big manor house with a farm and acres and acres of land, close to the coast.'

'Yeah? Whereabouts?'

'Southend way.'

'Know Southend.' Rory nodded in emphasis. 'No good for you there?'

Lucy shrugged. 'It were a lot better a while back before Mr Lockley's first wife died and he got remarried to a right dragon.' Lucy snapped her lips together. She barely knew Rory and regretted being indiscreet. You never could tell who might know who. 'Found it a bit dull there so I've come back to London to be closer to me mum,' she added briskly. 'She's not been at all well.' Lucy changed the subject as she sensed Rory to be on the point of questioning her about her family. 'So, Audrey Stubbs is gonna be one for me to watch, by all accounts.'

Rory twisted about to lean back against the corridor wall so they were face to face and he could study her properly.

'She'll hold a grudge against me.' Lucy grimaced. 'Not bothered, though. If I find her fiddling about with her ladyship's belongings I'll wring her neck.'

'I reckon you would too.'

He was smiling and Lucy noticed he had nice even white teeth and grey eyes with long lashes. 'Perhaps you should tell her and put her out of her misery,' Lucy said abruptly.

'Tell her?' he echoed, mystified.

'You said you don't fancy her . . . perhaps you should tell her and no doubt she'll turn her attention back to Jack in the garden.'

'Pity him if she does,' Rory said, his eyes warm and humorous.

'Pity *her* if she does, 'cos from what you've said, Millie won't take kindly to it and might lay her out next time.'

Rory chuckled appreciatively, his gaze becoming intimate, making Lucy's cheeks sting with heat. 'Just getting something for me tea,' she blurted. 'Ain't sitting in there with 'em all staring at me, thinking I've done wrong when I've not. I'll end up telling somebody their fortune then I'll lose another of me afternoons off . . . or it might even be me job next time.'

'Lost yer afternoon off?'

'Made arrangements to take me mum out, too.'

'Where does your mum live? Far is it?'

Lucy stabbed a look at him and nibbled her lower lip. From the age of about eight years old, when she'd first done a bit of doorstep scrubbing for coppers at weekends, she'd had it drummed into her by her mum and older sisters that you never disclosed to an employer – or for that matter any stranger – that you were out of the Bunk. Campbell Road had a notorious reputation as being the worst street in north London and those who lived there were discriminated against as being the dregs of society. She certainly didn't know Rory Jackson well enough to confide in him anything as important as where she'd been reared, and where, despite it all, she still considered her real home to be.

'She lives in north London; not that far.' It was a

brusque reply and Lucy made to open the kitchen door to go to find her tea.

'Big place, north London. Hampstead way, is she?' Rory stabbed a guess.

Lucy snorted a laugh. 'Bit too rich for us.' She could see he was keen to know so she said airily, 'Finsbury Park way, if you must know.' Before he could probe further she'd pushed open the door.

'You don't want to hide yourself away.' Rory put a hand out to bar her way into the kitchen. 'If you chicken out teatime there'll be some who'll think you're feeling guilty. Turn up, sit down and eat your grub.' He grinned down at her. 'Don't worry, I'll talk to you if nobody else will.'

'Yeah, thanks a lot.' It was drily said but Lucy couldn't prevent a small smile curving her mouth. 'That's how I got in trouble in the first place, Rory Jackson, you talking to me, and making Audrey jealous.'

'Told you, I ain't taken no notice of her, and I've given her no reason to think I ever will.' He tilted his face to watch Lucy's evasive expression. 'I don't tell lies.'

'That right? Why you being so nice to me then? Anybody'd think you fancied me. Yet you've just said you don't.'

A look of mock thoughtfulness put a furrow in his brow but he appeared unabashed by her accusation. 'All right, I'll own up. Once in a while I tell a little fib.' He sauntered off towards the butler's office. 'Got to see Mr Collins about some pay I'm due. See you in the dining hall later. Keep your chin up.'

CHAPTER FIVE

'I've had enough, I tell you! I won't never have a chance to get near her ladyship's jewels now this new girl's got taken on. Fucking Lucy Keiver is watching me like an 'awk.' Ada Stone flung herself back against brickwork and took a long drag on a cigarette while staring sulkily into the night. 'Shame Susan quit. She were a pushover, that one. But it ain't easy now slipping in and out of the bedrooms.'

Ada was stationed in an alleyway beneath the weak flicker of a gas lamp. A few feet away a tall, muscular man was silhouetted against the same wall. A fashionable homburg was pushed back on his head and he was dressed in a loose-fitting check suit. The dusk hid the fact that the cloth was garish, if of fine quality. Next to him, Ada appeared like a small dark drab in her voluminous servant's cape.

It was close to one o'clock in the morning and Ada had slipped out of Mortimer House just over an hour ago to meet Bill Black on the sly. It wasn't the first time she'd done it. She knew that there were only so many

54

times she could use a pretence of having raging bellyache and desperately needing the outside privy, rather than settling for the little po under the bed, before her bunk mates started getting suspicious. She wouldn't put it past Keiver to follow her, the inquisitive bitch.

But Ada Stone – or Audrey Stubbs, as her colleagues and employers at Mortimer House knew her – no longer cared about getting sacked. In fact she'd been tempted to be purposely insolent just so the prissy housekeeper might finally lose patience with her. The only reason she hadn't was because she feared the full force of this man's wrath if she got booted out of Mortimer House before she'd got him what he wanted. She longed to be away from the drudgery of working in service and back to excitement and easy pickings: hoisting expensive clothes around the West End with her light-fingered friends.

Ada was twenty and had been sent to work in service in Kent at the age of fourteen. But she'd got bored and left after a year, travelling here and there taking on jobs in shops or laundries. On returning to south London, she had been introduced to Bill by her brother, who ran a market stall. She'd jumped at the chance of working for him, and had been recruited to his gang despite her age. That suited Bill Black. He could always find a use for a fresh face unknown to store detectives and the local coppers and magistrates. And Ada had proved her worth from the off.

Bill was prepared to turn his hand to any form of criminal activity. He came from the same area of Elephant and Castle as Ada Stone and her family and was five years older than she was. Her brother Derek was a seasoned member of his team and was presently doing six months' hard labour following a heist that had gone sour. The driver of the lorry he and his accomplices had hijacked had done a very silly thing. Instead of playing dead after a crack on the head he'd fought back and got stabbed for his pains. Derek hadn't wielded the blade but it was more than his life was worth to say who had, so he'd been resigned to doing time along with the culprit while the unlucky hero recovered in hospital.

'I'm handing in me notice, Bill, so don't go trying to persuade me otherwise.' Ada flicked ash with jittery fingers, avoiding his inscrutable gaze. 'It's been a bleedin' waste of time 'n' I told you it would be from the start. But you wouldn't listen to me, would yer?'

A tense minute passed in silence and Ada realised Bill had no intention of answering her. 'Nearly a soddin' month I been stuck in that house and what we got? Nuthin'.' Again she turned to him for a response but he kept staring ahead and smoking. She knew he was ignoring her on purpose, as a punishment, because he didn't like what he was hearing.

'Tell you what, I'll lift a few bits of silver to make it worthwhile, eh, Bill?' Ada hissed a reconciliatory offer into the dark. 'Old Collins, the butler, ain't doing the inventory till the end of the month. He won't even notice it's missing till then and I could be long gone . . .' She tailed off, squinting through the gloom at Bill's immobile profile.

Finally, she sighed, realising he was not going to be swayed by any of her suggestions. 'Should never have gone in the poxy place,' she said peevishly. 'Could've made a good few quid fer meself by now round the West End instead of being stuck workin' me fingers to the bone as a bleedin' skivvy.'

His withdrawal was beginning to unnerve her. She dragged desperately on her cigarette while pacing to and fro. Tears of frustration started prickling her eyes; she'd be going back; he'd make her. He wouldn't let her give up until he'd got what he wanted. She might be there till Christmas before the safe was opened and out came the jewellery box for her to rummage in. Ada reckoned she could handle Mrs Boyd, no trouble. It wouldn't occur to that stuffy old cow that a little nobody would dare rob her precious employers.

Ada had overheard Venner and Boyd talking about her just that afternoon. They'd called her flighty, and thought she might encourage too many followers – as they named the housemaids' boyfriends. Ada had stuffed a fist to her mouth to stifle her raucous guffaw on hearing that. She'd not wanted to give the game away that she was eavesdropping on them. Ada liked the boys right enough, a lot more than those two dried-up old biddies could ever imagine, but that wasn't the half of it. If they only knew what she was *really* about they'd both have a blue fit!

Keiver was a different kettle of fish. Ada had immediately got her measure, just as Lucy Keiver had recognised her sort straight away. Ever since their tussle they'd been circling each other, waiting for the inevitable to happen. And it would; and despite Ada believing she was a bit of a rough handful, she wasn't completely confident she'd come off best in a bust-up with the under-lady's maid.

'Listen, Bill, I'm gonna get sacked soon anyhow if I don't jack it in.' Ada sounded coarse and angry. 'I'm just about riled up enough to give someone a thump.' She dropped her cigarette butt to the ground, stamped on it, and immediately put out a hand for another.

Bill fished a packet of Weights out of his pocket and having lit one he took it from his lips and gave it to her.

'Come on now . . .' He finally broke his silence and soothed her with a touch of his manicured fingers on her mousy hair. 'Don't go gettin' all het up. You did just dandy in that other place, didn't you?' His hand continued stroking. 'Got the stuff out sweet as a nut and nobody knew who you was and no comebacks, 'cos you acted like a real pro, didn't you, *Annie Smith*.' Playfully he chucked her under the chin as he used Ada's previous alias. 'This time, *Miss Audrey Stubbs*, you're gonna be even better at doing me a good job—'

'That other time were different,' Ada interrupted. But she preened beneath his praise and his touch. 'That silly tart was always out of her mind on drugs 'n' booze. Could've walked out of that gaff with a fuckin' crystal chandelier under me arm and she wouldn't have noticed.'

Bill chuckled. 'P'raps you should try a different angle.' He cocked his head and looked down at her. 'How about you pretend you want to be this new gel's pal? Instead of goin' at it hammer 'n' tongs, Ada, you could be a bit subtle. Then this Lucy might think you're hangin' around her ladyship's bedroom to be friends with her instead of clocking when the jewellery box gets an airing.'

'She ain't that stupid! She knows I hate her and she don't like me neither. She's too cute by half.'

'Well, you're gonna have to be that bit cuter then, ain't you, Ada?' Bill returned with sinister softness.

Ada darted a narrowed glance at him. She knew he could switch from friend to enemy in seconds. She'd been caressed and clumped by him in her time, and from bitter experience knew that sometimes just seconds separated the two.

Although they'd only been talking for fifteen minutes or so Ada knew he was already impatient to be gone back to the gin palace on the corner. She, on the other hand, would stay with him all night, given half a chance. She needed to get out of that house, not just because she was bored rigid, missing her shoplifting jaunts and the luxuries they brought in, but because she was a woman with basic needs. And neither of those needs was being met in Mortimer House. Every night she was desperate for a stiff drink, and a horny man.

'Got a flask with you, Bill?' she asked.

Bill produced a pewter bottle from a pocket and courteously unscrewed the top for her. After she'd taken a long swig he helped himself before the flask disappeared whence it came.

'Let's have another,' Ada complained immediately, having noticed the whisky disappear.

'Don't want to go back stinkin' of booze, do you, gel? Give the game away, that will. I reckon it's time you was on yer way. It's getting late.' He made a show of checking his wristwatch beneath the milky lamplight.

Ada huffed sulkily, eyeing his crotch from beneath lowered lashes. 'Got anything else for me before I go?' she whispered crudely. She felt no humiliation in having to ask for what she wanted.

She knew that if Betty Pickering, one of her girl gang comrades, hadn't last week been taken into custody on a charge of shoplifting sables from Selfridges, Bill would doubtless have been with her tonight. Ada was resigned to being second best while Betty was available. But at present Ada had Bill more or less to herself. If Betty got a stretch inside – and Ada privately hoped she would – then Bill might start treating her as his number-one girl. Of course, Ada knew he had different little scrubbers he saw on and off but they didn't bother her; neither had they seemed to bother Betty too much. Bill was a big attractive hunk of a man who always seemed to have plenty of cash to flash around because he was a successful criminal with a crafty streak. So far, he'd avoided imprisonment, unlike many of the Elephant and Castle boys, by managing to implicate others and fabricate watertight alibis.

'Come on, get goin', Ada.' Bill sounded harsh and impatient, apparently deaf to her suggestiveness. 'Ain't took all the trouble to get yer set up with false references to come out wi' nuthin' 'cos you've blown yer cover.'

'Don't have ter come out with nuthin'. I can get us some silver, like I said, and—'

'I've told you that silver ain't what I'm after,' Bill snarled. 'I'm after first prize, not consolation prize.' He made an effort to calm down and smiled at her. 'I can get any of Betty's crew to lift me some nice shiny silver out of Gamages. But none o' the others has got the class to fetch me out a special bit of jewellery. That's your speciality, sweet'eart.'

He prowled away a few steps, his dark head down so she had no glimpse of his expression and had no idea what he was thinking. A moment later he'd whipped back in front of her. 'It's emeralds me client's after, see. He's a rich gent, upper crust, and his little ladybird's got a yen for a big green stone, and she's seen the one she wants round her ladyship's neck. Giving him gyp, she is, over having it. Now I'm getting gyp off him 'cos I've said I've got a sure way of nabbing it for him. Boasted to him I've got the best hoister in the whole of London on to it. Now you don't want to make me look like I'm a chancer, Ada, do you? Can't have that, can I?' Bill tilted his face close to hers.

'What if her ladyship ain't got that big green stone in her box in the safe? If it's good as that it might be held in the bank vault. I heard Mrs Boyd saying some of her heirlooms are kept there.'

'According to my source she had it on recently so I reckon it's still at the house. Any case, we ain't gonna know, are we, 'less you get to work and take a gander.'

'I dunno . . .' Ada whined.

'Never mind dunno,' Bill growled. 'You just get the bleedin' necklace and we'll be in the money.' He stuffed his hands impatiently in his pockets. He regretted having said so much. Ada was his workhorse, not his partner or confidante. This was a delicate situation and involved people in high places. He would have thought twice before disclosing to Betty what was going on. He put his lips against Ada's cheek, taking her pointed chin in a stinging grip that made her squirm. 'You goin' against me?'

Ada carefully shook her head.

'Good gel. Course you ain't. I know you *could* bring a fuckin' crystal chandelier out that house with you if you really put yer mind to it, Ada.' Suddenly he laughed and swooped his lips to hers. He kissed her hard on the mouth, grabbing a breast through the cloth of her heavy cloak.

Immediately Ada dropped her newly lit cigarette to the ground and wound her arms about his shoulders, plunging her tongue greedily into his open mouth. Her pelvis ground against his groin, and a hand began frantically stroking his erection beneath wool.

Bill laughed, mingling their alcoholic breath before

lifting his head. 'You're a right dirty gel, know that, Ada?' His words were coarse, with no hint of affection. But Bill didn't really believe Ada expected any wooing, neither did he care if she did. She might once have had an ambition to be a proper girlfriend to him, but he reckoned by now she'd got the message that Betty was his favourite.

But Ada was passably attractive and had a reasonable figure on her so no red-blooded fellow was going to turn down what she willingly offered, even if he knew it might have been given elsewhere ten minutes previously. It was no secret in their neighbourhood that Ada Stone behaved like a regular nymphomaniac.

'Begging fer a seeing-to right here, are you, Ada?' Bill goaded her, squeezing harder at her nipple. He waited for her to nod, as she always did, before barking contemptuously, 'Get yer drawers off then, dirty gel.'

Ada nipped Bill's lower lip with teasing teeth as a little thank you. "S'another reason I got to get out o' that bleedin' house, Bill,' she moaned breathlessly, whilst kicking away her underwear and drawing up her night-dress beneath her cloak. She fell back against brickwork, getting into position for him to hoist her up against the wall as he had on other occasions when they'd met on her afternoon off and he'd needed to coax her to obedience. 'Need yer, don't I, Bill? Want this all the time. Been ages since we done it . . .'

'Been a week,' he grunted, lifting her and shoving her back then up and down till he'd managed brutally to impale her.

The rough treatment didn't worry Ada; she had a constant itch between her legs and any man's attention to it was encouraged and gratefully received.

Bill Black heard her sigh of utter relief, felt her impatient bucking, and he chuckled. 'Don't tell me there's not a bloke in a house as big that can't keep you going till yer day off.'

'I reckon they're all bleedin' eunuchs in that place,' she gasped, bouncing against him, clawing at his back. 'All too scared of their shadows to act like real men. Nobody there like you, Bill . . . wish there was,' she moaned. 'Might stay for ever then . . .' Her panted words tailed away into a guttural mewing sound.

'How about one o' them starched-up women then, if yer real desperate?' Bill whispered, then realised he liked the idea of that and the fantasy prompted him to drive into her with such force that she started to shriek and gyrate.

Bill clapped his hand over her mouth and took a startled look about. 'Fuckin' shut up, will yer?' he growled. 'You'll bring a crowd down on us.'

Ada felt exhausted and hungry on returning to the house; Bill hadn't even offered to walk back with her so she'd flitted through the dark, deserted streets as fast as she could, her cloak wrapped tight about her. Being a criminal herself she knew a lone woman out at night was easy pickings and she hadn't fancied a crack on the head from a mugger.

Having gratefully reached her destination she slipped in through the side door and tiptoed along the corridor towards the kitchens, hoping there might be a few easily found titbits lying around. Though she doubted anybody would be about at two o'clock in the morning, nevertheless she took pains to proceed quietly. As she was passing Mrs Venner's office she heard a sound and started to attention. She frowned in disbelief; she'd believed even that conscientious old biddy would have taken to her bed by now. Ada froze against the wall her heart thumping loudly in her ears. She knew if somebody senior caught her up and about at this hour, with a reek of alcohol and tobacco about her, awkward questions would be asked. It was obvious from the way she was dressed that she'd been out, and she'd just faithfully promised Bill that she'd get the necklace, not the sack . . .

Having strained to listen, and caught low whispering coming from behind the door, Ada's curiosity overcame her caution and she noiselessly turned the handle. It was locked, but on glancing down she saw a faint light leaking from beneath it. A whimpering little sigh was heard next and it increased her suspicions. She crouched to put her eye to the keyhole. A few moments later she'd stuffed a muffling fist to her mouth and had tumbled backwards onto her posterior in scandalised shock. Her jaw sagged towards her chest, then she silently scrambled up, her features now set in a soundless laugh. She scratched against the door with a fingernail then flattened herself against the wall. She was aware of the quiet within, then a moment later she heard the key turn in the lock and knew one of them would come out to investigate. Before the door was properly open Ada had burst in to confront the two women.

Felicity Venner recovered composure first. 'What on earth do you think you're doing, Stubbs? How dare you burst in like this? Why aren't you in your dormitory? What have you been doing?' she breathlessly demanded.

'Not quite what you've been doing with Mrs Boyd, that's fer sure,' Ada whispered, her face alight with lewd amusement. She backed against the door until it clicked quietly shut while putting a warning finger to her mouth. 'My preference is for boys. But I'll admit I've been enjoying meself tonight, like you two. My "follower" I reckon you'd call Bill. Big lusty chap, he is, but course you wouldn't be interested in knowing about any o' that . . .'

By the light of the small oil lamp it could be seen that Clare Boyd's face was crimson, and where she'd hastily done up her bodice most of the little pearl buttons were in the wrong hooks. At forty-two, she was only three years younger than her lover but she could have passed for her junior by a decade. Her skin was smoother and her character less robust at times of need. She darted a glance at Felicity Venner, moistening her lips, pleading with the older woman to keep up the bluster and find a plausible way to extricate them both from this awful mess.

'Don't bother denying what you've been up to,' Ada muttered, intercepting Clare's frantic look. 'I seen you at it through the keyhole, and if I give a yell and bring 'em all running you're gonna have some explaining to do, ain't you?' She nodded at Clare's flushed face. 'Now what would *she* be doing here at this time o' night, and with her blouse all skewwhiff?' She glanced at Felicity, then at the floor. 'Them your drawers or hers?' she asked, having spotted the discarded linen. Before the housekeeper could retrieve her undergarments Ada stamped a foot on them, and drew them out of reach. 'Never mind . . . ain't the end of the world, you know, getting caught out like this, 'cos I've had an idea . . .'

Still in a half-doze, Lucy heard Audrey return from her jaunt but didn't bother rolling over to confront her roommate about her absence. She'd guessed what Audrey had been getting up to when she went off at night, and sleepily wondered if Jack from the garden had after all succumbed to having a roll in the hay. When a moment later Audrey's mattress creaked and Lucy heard a ribald giggle being smothered by bedcovers she knew that whoever Audrey had been with, he'd shown her a good time.

CHAPTER SIX

'I'm being *sacked*?'

'No, not sacked, Miss Keiver,' Mrs Boyd hastily interrupted. 'There will be a vacancy for you here, as a housemaid, should you wish to accept it.'

'But why . . . but . . .?'

'Enough! A decision has been made and it is not up for discussion.' Clare Boyd shot a glance at the housekeeper. But it seemed on this occasion no assistance was to be forthcoming from that quarter. Mrs Venner was tight-lipped, staring straight ahead, taking no part in Lucy Keiver's dismissal. Clare knew that she *was* effectively dismissing her junior despite having made an offer of alternative work. Lucy was a proud and intelligent young woman who knew she'd given them no reason to treat her shabbily, and rather than be demoted she would pack her bags.

The trio of women were closeted in the housekeeper's office. The two senior members of staff were ranged behind a large oak desk; Lucy was seated opposite on a hard-backed chair, her face a study of furious bewilderment.

'What've I done wrong?' Lucy abruptly stood up with a savage shrug. 'I've not moaned or been insubordinate. I've done everything you've asked and made a good job of it too. I know I have.'

'You were told that you would be on a trial period when you started work here,' Mrs Venner finally said.

'I know, and I've made sure to do me best, so there'd be no complaints about me. *Has* anybody complained?' she demanded, frowning.

'They have not,' Mrs Venner replied stiltedly. 'But her ladyship knows that Mrs Boyd and I both feel you are not suited to the particular work. Lady Mortimer is in agreement that a position elsewhere should now be offered to you—'

'I don't want a position elsewhere!' Lucy interrupted indignantly.

'In that case, Miss Keiver, we accept your resignation, and in the circumstances, as you feel so strongly, you will not be obliged to work out your notice period. You may go today.' Felicity Venner had been a little unnerved by the forceful arguments issuing from Lucy Keiver. She had imagined the girl might cause a scene by bursting into tears, or pleading for a second chance. But Lucy looked more likely to leap into battle than collapse, snivelling. A significant glance at her partner in crime enquired if Clare had anything further to add before they might speedily end the interview.

Mrs Boyd cleared her throat, shuffling some paperwork together on the desk in front of her. 'It seems there's nothing more to say on the subject. I'm sorry—'

'So you bloomin' well should be sorry!' Lucy gritted through her teeth and stormed towards the door.

'A reference will be prepared for you . . . and your wages . . .'

'I'll take me pay but you know what you can do with your reference, and if you don't, I'll tell you quick enough—' Lucy suddenly swallowed the rest of her impulsive insolence.

Her shock and anger had made her oblivious to some of what had been said, but important bits were drifting back into her mind. 'A vacancy for a housemaid's come up, has it?' It was a vital question. 'So who is it took me job so you can give me theirs?' She stepped back into the room swinging a narrowed glance between the two stiff-backed, middle-aged women. As the lady's maid blinked rapidly behind her glasses Lucy grunted a laugh. 'Well . . . well . . . I wonder how Audrey Stubbs managed to swing that one,' she drawled acidly. 'You know as well as I do that the ding-dong me and Audrey had a while ago, upstairs in her ladyship's bedroom, was her fault not mine.' She watched with sour satisfaction as Clare Boyd shifted uncomfortably on her seat. 'But you've gone ahead and got rid of me so you can give her me job. Something fishy's going on, and I don't reckon Lord and Lady Mortimer knows the first thing about it.' She gave a crisp nod. 'Audrey Stubbs is a wrong'un, and take it from me, you've made a bad mistake giving in to her. You're gonna regret what you've done.'

When the sound of the slamming door had died away Clare continued to avoid Felicity's eyes but muttered bitterly, 'How right she is about that.'

She knew she'd been a fool to allow herself to be seduced by the housekeeper because, once started, and conducted unnoticed, it was an affair that, for her, survived indifference and was easier to carry on than bring to an end.

When Clare had arrived in London five years ago she'd felt lonely and in need of comfort, having recently been widowed. She'd nursed Bernard at home until he'd died of his war injuries and had found the task mentally and physically gruelling. Before the conflict they had both been in domestic service and had married when barely nineteen. But those few youthful years with an active virile man seemed to Clare just a hazy memory. She would have liked to find another fellow to love, but she'd never been a sought-after beauty, even in her prime. A shortage of men following the carnage of the Great War had left widows and spinsters alike yearning in vain for husbands.

When Mrs Venner had seemed to single her out as a companion Clare had gratefully lapped up her support and friendship, thinking it was just in the woman's nature to be kind. Now she knew her better and understood that it hadn't merely been a friend the housekeeper had been after. Although Felicity Venner styled herself 'Mrs', Clare had since learned she had never been married. And the reason for that was obvious to Clare, even if her noble employers deemed it a ruse for respectability rather than a smokescreen.

Following four years spent as colleagues and lovers, a scheming minx had discovered the shameful truth about them and was using it as a tool for blackmail. Clare knew that Lucy Keiver wasn't going to be the only person to suffer for Audrey Stubbs's wickedness.

'Once Miss Keiver has left and Stubbs has taken up her position as my apprentice, I shall find an excuse to tender my notice.' Clare abruptly got to her feet.

'There is no need to do anything so drastic . . .' Felicity gasped, shooting upright.

'Of course there is!' Clare struggled to keep her voice low. 'Stubbs will never stop mocking us, and we will never be rid of the rotten girl now she knows she has us pinned beneath her thumb. Do you really think I will have her working alongside me, tormenting me with every sly look and word?'

Felicity came over to Clare, attempting to put a comforting arm about her but was immediately shrugged off.

'I'm bitterly ashamed, and worried, and you should be too,' Clare said bleakly before quitting the room.

'What's given you such a sour puss?' Aren't you pleased to see me on yer afternoon off?' Tilly beamed at her youngest daughter.

Lucy had wordlessly sunk down into a battered chair by the table when she'd arrived seconds ago. Instead of the happy chatter Matilda usually received in greeting the moment her daughter turned up on a visit, Lucy had planted her elbows on the table and shielded her dejection with her hands. Realising the door had been left ajar, Matilda limped over, muttering, to shut it and kick the sausage of rags into place at its base. It was unusual for Lucy to be careless on a blustery November day. Keeping everything closed against the cold was standard practice for people used to living in the Bunk. But as she put a hand on the door knob Matilda stood stock-still, having noticed the packing case on the landing, leaning against the wall.

'What's gone on?' Matilda gasped, swinging about to confront Lucy.

'Chucked it in,' Lucy admitted through muffling fingers.

'You done *what*?' Matilda roared. 'Christmas nearly here and you've chucked in a good job?' She hobbled over to Lucy as fast as her aches and pains would allow, and ripped her daughter's hands away from her cheeks so she could read her expression. 'What you been up to? You pulled a stroke and got found out?'

'I ain't done anything . . . apart from shoot off me mouth when I should've kept quiet. But somebody's pulled a stroke all right, and I've suffered for it,' Lucy added bitterly.

Matilda could hear the tears in her youngest daughter's voice and some of her anger withered. Having dislodged a chair from under the table she collapsed into it. 'Had the dirty done on yer?' she asked, astonished. 'How? Who done it?'

'I've lost me job, Mum,' Lucy mumbled. 'I liked it too. And I was good at it.' She gazed at her mother through misty vision. 'I've not done anything wrong, swear, but the housekeeper and me senior told me me job's gone to somebody else. They said I could have a housemaid's job instead but . . .' She threw back her head in despair and blinked at the cobweb-covered ceiling.

'But you told 'em to poke it,' Matilda guessed, her lined face still displaying her shock.

Lucy abruptly stood up. 'I wasn't thinking straight, I was in such a paddy. But I know now I should've bit me tongue and played it clever. If I'd stuck around till after Christmas we'd have had more money to help us over the holiday, and I might've found out what's been going on in that place. I know fer definite that something has. A nasty cow's got given me job and I want to know why.'

Matilda gawped at her daughter. She knew this blow couldn't have come at a worse time of the year, and jobs were getting harder than ever to find. The papers were always full of the woes of unemployment and the length of the labour exchange queues. Although she didn't get out and about very much, Matilda was keen to listen to her neighbours' news about the locals who were unsuccessfully looking for jobs. But she understood why Lucy had reacted in the way she had. All the Keiver clan – men and women – had hot tempers and fast tongues, and were likely to explode if they believed they'd fallen foul of underhand trickery.

'Didn't clump anyone, did you?' Matilda sounded rueful.

Lucy gave a gruff laugh on realising her mother was slowly calming down, having digested her bad news. 'I felt like it, Mum. That's why I got meself out of there quick as I could. Just packed me bags, got me pay, and got out.' The mention of her wages prompted her to pull from her pocket the little envelope that held a small amount of cash.

'Gave you a reference, though, didn't they?'

Lucy slid guilty eyes to her mother's face, inwardly wincing as she saw Matilda's optimistic expression crumble.

'You never told 'em to poke that too!' Matilda burst out. 'Heavens above, Luce!' She thumped a fist on the cracked wooden table top. 'How you gonna get another job in service without a character?'

Lucy shot to her mother and enclosed her in an apologetic hug that was so fierce it made Matilda totter on

73

her feet. 'I'll find something, swear I will,' Lucy promised. 'I'll be employed again before Christmas, you'll see.'

'Got another afternoon off, Lucy? You're doing all right!' Connie Whitton had called out on noticing Matilda's daughter emerging from Smithie's shop with a small bag of groceries in her hand. She was surprised to see her because Lucy had been about in the street earlier in the week and Connie thought she'd not be back yet.

Lucy gave a welcoming smile as she noticed Connie crossing the road to speak to her. Despite the fact the woman was more than a decade older than she was, Lucy had always liked her. She knew Connie was a bit of 'a goer', as her mother would call the tarts she had time for. Those Matilda didn't like were called something else entirely. But Connie had an appealingly mischievous way about her that didn't put up the backs of other women in the way some brash local prostitutes did.

In her time Connie had had some proper swanky sugar daddies looking after her. She was a good-looking blonde in her early thirties, who'd got engaged twice but never married. At present, she was fancy-free, working shifts as a waitress in a West End supper club. But it was well known she'd supplement her earnings by going on the game when tips were scarce, and she didn't care who knew about it. Despite some of her neighbours being hostile to her because of her part-time profession she could be indiscriminately kind-hearted. If a family were in deep trouble, she'd give those particular kids coins for sweets in the full knowledge that they'd run home and hand them over to their mums. Some of those women would have shoved the money back at Connie if she'd given it to them directly. But so long as it filled empty bellies in a roundabout way, it was acceptable.

When Connie had been in her prime Lucy had been about six or seven and she could remember being struck by how beautifully glamorous the young woman looked wearing her fur coats and red lipstick. Lucy had been one of the street urchins treated to pennies and thrupenny bits when Connie was feeling flush. But only seconds after receiving her treasure her mother would materialise at her side and remove it from her fingers before she could hide it away.

'Not at work today?' Connie had stopped by her side, folding her arms in readiness for a chat.

'Been out searching for work this morning,' Lucy told her, pulling a long face. 'I've just come back to have a bite to eat with Mum. Then I'll be off out again hoping to spot a job posted in a shop window. It's too busy up the labour exchange to hang around waiting. Couldn't even get in the door it was so crowded. I'd sooner pound pavements and save time. Know of any vacancies going, Con?'

'Thought you was settled in a good job.'

'Long story . . .' Lucy replied in a tone of voice that deterred further questions.

'Ever done any waitressing?' Connie resisted the temptation to be nosy.

Lucy nodded. 'Course. Used to help out serving at table when I worked with me sister Sophy in Essex. We all used to pitch in together doing different jobs when we needed to.' She smiled. 'Actually, I've just been and asked for a job in Ken's caff, and the Lyons Corner House, but nothing doing.'

'Fancy a job working in the supper club with me?'

Connie asked brightly. 'A girl's leaving at the end of the week. She's got a better offer . . . off one of the gents who's a regular client.' She chuckled as she saw Lucy's dubious frown. 'Oh, you don't have to get involved in any of that if you don't want to. Most of the girls are above board and just serve and smile and take their tips home.' Connie had comically mimed waitress duties as she was speaking, making Lucy laugh, especially when she acted out shoving cash into her brassiere.

'The Cuckoo Club is in Piccadilly. There's a bit of gambling now and again, and late drinking, and a jazz band playing most nights. Mainly we get gentlemen come in on their own, but some bring their lady friends,' Connie explained. 'If you get pestered by randy fellows, I'll see 'em off for you, Luce.'

'Oh, come on, Con,' Lucy drawled with a smile. 'D'you want me mum to wring me neck before I'm much older?'

'Don't have to tell her you're working with me. Just say you've got a job as a waitress in a restaurant. Ain't a lie. Honest, there's plenty of us gels prepared to do a bit extra, if he looks nice and the price is right, so you won't need to worry.'

'Ain't interested, Con. Seriously . . . have you seen any jobs posted about?'

'Dobson's sweet shop in Blackstock Road had a card in the window. Don't know if it's still there, though, 'cos I saw it last week.'

'I'll go straight away and find out,' Lucy said quickly. 'Do us a favour, Con, would you, and drop this bit of shopping into Mum? Tell her where I'm off to and that I shouldn't be long.' Lucy thrust the shopping bag in Connie's direction and hurried off.

'What's happened then?' Connie skipped after Lucy,

to catch her up. Her curiosity had got the better of her. She wanted to know why Lucy was unemployed when earlier in the week Matilda had been boasting just how well Lucy was doing working for the aristocracy. 'Did you chuck in your job? Matilda said you liked it.'

'Tell you later,' Lucy called, jogging away.

It was the best bit of news she'd had all morning. She'd traipsed for miles and had spotted only two cards advertising for assistants. Neither the tobacconist nor the cobbler had thought her suitable for their vacancies and had told her so. Inwardly she cursed that she'd not gone directly to Blackstock Road earlier but had headed off in the opposite direction. The most interesting notice she'd seen all day was a newsstand placard declaring, LORD MAYOR'S SHOW: OVER 30 INJURED AS ELEPHANTS STAMPEDE.

'Thanks, Connie,' Lucy threw over a shoulder, followed by a breathless, 'Wish me luck.'

When Lucy rushed up, puffing, to scan the sweet shop window her heart plummeted. There was nothing advertised behind the glass but the shop's wares. She took a glance past bottles and jars filled with colourful candies and saw Mrs Dobson. She appeared to be alone inside so Lucy decided it might be worth asking, just in case the card had fallen on the floor, and lain there unnoticed.

The bell on the door announced her and she received a sour look from the shopkeeper. Lucy had always thought Mr and Mrs Dobson a pair of miserable gits. When young and saucy and still at school she'd once told him to suck what he sold 'cos it might sweeten him up a bit.

'Good afternoon to you, Mrs Dobson. Heard you wanted an assistant,' Lucy started politely. 'I'd like to apply for the job.'

'It's taken,' Mrs Dobson returned flatly, then glanced up again and levelled an interested look at Lucy.

She'd hired Jennifer Finch last week but was beginning to regret it even though she was paying her a low rate because of her age. The girl had showed no aptitude for the work. She stood daydreaming at quiet times rather than stirring herself to tidy up or refill bottles and jars. Jennifer had gone off on her dinner break yesterday and returned ten minutes late. Mrs Dobson glanced at the clock on the wall. She was late again today; it was twenty-five minutes to two and she had been due back at half-past one.

'I'm giving somebody a short trial to see if they suit. You can come back tomorrow, if you like, and I'll let you know if I'm satisfied with her.' Mrs Dobson knew when Jennifer eventually returned she'd tell her she could keep her coat on and go back home.

Mrs Dobson was aware that Lucy Keiver came from a rough family in the Bunk, but some of that clan had done all right for themselves and were known to be hard workers. Besides, she looked to be at least eighteen, whereas Jennifer was virtually a school leaver and acted as though she needed to return to the classroom and pay attention this time.

But Mrs Dobson knew her husband would disapprove of Lucy Keiver; he had always been prejudiced against people from the Bunk, lumping them all together as liars and thieves. Mrs Dobson, however, was prepared to speak as she found and so far she'd nothing against Lucy. Besides, as her husband left it to her to earn them both a living running the shop during the week, while he swanned off to council meetings and sat on his backside drinking tea and eating biscuits, she reckoned it was up to her who she employed as help, and if he didn't like it, he knew what he could do.

Lucy turned to go, smiling her thanks, but felt none the less dejected. She was sure that whoever had got the job would make sure they kept hold of it with Christmas looming and work being so hard to come by.

Having closed the shop door she turned the corner and bumped straight into Jennifer Finch. Lucy didn't know the girl well as Jennifer was about four years younger than she was, and their mothers tended to be prickly with one another. Nevertheless, having gone to the same school, they usually said hello and perhaps stopped for a brief chat. Lucy was aware that in the past Jennifer had seemed to admire her from afar because she'd been popular and had had a lot of friends at Pooles Park School. Out of the two girls, Lucy preferred Jennifer's twin, Katherine. She'd always seemed more interesting and less sulky. Since Lucy had been back living in London she'd seen Katherine out and about a few times and they'd waved at one another.

'Where you off to in such a hurry?' Lucy asked with a smile.

'Late back fer work after me dinner break,' Jennifer replied, coming to a halt. 'Hope the old bag sacks me, actually. Never wanted to work in that poxy sweet shop anyhow. It was me mum's idea; I only took it to shut her up moaning.'

'You've got the job at Dobson's?'

Jennifer nodded glumly. 'Worst luck. I'm after getting a position in one of the big department stores. I'm applying to Selfridges after Christmas. I've just turned fifteen.'

Lucy affected to look encouraging despite knowing

Jennifer would have to wait till she was older, and had an impressive reference, to get a sales position in Oxford Street. But Lucy believed everybody was entitled to dream and have ambition.

'Well, if you don't want it, I'll take it. I'm after a job.'

Jennifer looked surprised. 'Thought you was working in service.'

'I was, but I'm back home now so I can look after me mum.'

'She's still limping badly, ain't she?' Jennifer said sympathetically, leaning back against the wall as though she'd forgotten about getting back to work and was settling down for a long chat. 'I saw her out walking with one of your sisters and she was struggling to keep up.'

'Hadn't you best get back to work if you're late?' Lucy cocked her head towards the sweet shop.

As Jennifer trudged on with a grimace, Lucy turned to watch her. Suddenly she realised she might not be wasting her time going back to see Mrs Dobson tomorrow . . .

CHAPTER SEVEN

Ada Stone knew she was being watched.

She strolled away from the rack of elegant day dresses and approached a display of winter coats. With practised nonchalance she checked the size of a garment and smoothed her fingers over the tweed, inspecting its quality. A legitimate customer with twelve guineas to spare would have felt entitled to inspect an intended purchase. But Ada wasn't about to buy anything from this shop, although she had previously selected several nice blouses. At present those were secreted about her person in cavernous pockets within her clothes, roomy enough to hide more choice items, and before she left the store, Ada was determined to fill them.

The thin-faced fellow in a pinstriped suit moved to follow Ada, stopping at a display counter adjacent to the coats. He positioned himself so he could still covertly observe her from beneath the brim of his hat.

Ada could have laughed. If he thought he was a professional he was mistaken. She'd spotted him a mile off, not long after she'd entered Debenham and Freebody.

In her opinion he resembled a pensioned off flat-foot who'd got himself a store walker's job to keep out of his wife's way.

Her amusement withered away. Luckily, he'd only been on her tail since she'd settled by the dresses. She'd managed to get one off the hanger and had been ready to stuff it out of sight when she'd noticed he was on to her. With great composure she'd strolled to the nearest mirror, held the gown up against her and deliberated on her reflection. Then she'd carefully returned the garment to the rail. He hadn't caught her out and she wasn't about to confirm his suspicions that she was up to no good. If he tried to arrest her, she was confident she could outrun him to the exit but she was hoping it wouldn't come to that. She'd got her eye on several other nice pieces to nab; Bill would praise her to the skies if she managed to return to Lambeth up to the gills in classy merchandise.

And if her useless associate would play her part properly Ada knew it was possible she *would* saunter out onto Oxford Street in a few minutes' time looking as though she'd doubled in size.

Today, Ada Stone would have been unrecognisable to her erstwhile colleagues at Mortimer House. She had a polished veneer as befitted a patron of an expensive store. A smart velvet cloche hat was perched at a jaunty angle on her sleek bobbed hair; her coat was of dark blue cashmere and her new court shoes and matching gloves were of soft kid. Yet beneath her breath she began swearing like a navvy.

Mavis Pooley was supposed to be causing a distraction while Ada got on with the delicate business of thieving. Her co-conspirator, was just seventeen and on her first shoplifting jaunt. Mavis was equally well attired: she was not supposed to arouse suspicion before the appointed time. But her cues were going unheeded. Several times, Ada had given her a discreet nod yet still the young blonde remained dithering by a display of hats, looking nervous. Ada hadn't wanted Mavis tagging along with her today; she'd guessed the younger woman would end up as more of a hindrance than a help.

But Bill had insisted Ada be the one to teach the new recruit the ropes. She was convinced that if the little trollop hadn't been dropping her drawers for Bill for weeks, he wouldn't have let Mavis wangle a place in their gang at all.

Ada squinted fiercely at Mavis, in the hope she'd snap out of her jitters, remember she was supposed to go to the door with an expensive item, and pretend to examine it in the light.

It was a trick Ada had learned from Betty Pickering. They'd made an excellent team and had used it successfully many times in the past. A store detective would always be drawn to a person who gave the impression they were about to leave with unpaid goods. The chief hoister was then left free to pilfer at will for some minutes. If lucky, they could disappear, unchallenged, into the crowd of West End shoppers.

Fifteen minutes ago Mavis had managed to keep a sales assistant occupied while Ada slipped the silk blouses out of sight. But they'd moved now to the more expensive stuff and Ada was keen to get done and escape.

It seemed Mavis had finally plucked up the courage to make her move. The young blonde grabbed a feathered hat and barged swiftly towards the exit, bumping into several people in her blind haste. Ada chuckled beneath her breath as the flat-foot started to attention, then raced after her. Ada realised that if the new girl got herself arrested on her first day it wouldn't bother her one bit. She'd have Bill all to herself . . .

Mavis's panic made it seem she would run out onto Oxford Street with the hat but she remembered to halt sharply by the door to inspect it. Giggling softly, Ada turned her attention back to the rails and it took less than thirty seconds for three dresses to join the blouses she'd already tucked away. She liked the look of the tweed coat but knew it was too bulky to go into an inside pocket, despite the fact the clothes she wore were specially tailored to conceal large quantities of booty. Instead, she whipped it off its hanger and swung it casually about her shoulders like a cape.

Feeling unbearably hot and heavy, Ada made her way swiftly towards the exit, endeavouring to remain inconspicuous by keeping close to groups of people. As soon as she noticed Mavis blushing and batting her lashes at the security guard, who now looked soppy, Ada went out of another door, and melted away into the West End throng.

Despite icy gusts cooling her face Ada was sweating by the time she reached the alley where her receiver was waiting to relieve her of the clothes. Gratefully she shrugged off the heavy tweed, then began to pull the dresses and blouses from their hiding places.

Charlie North packed the merchandise into a suitcase. Within three minutes of their efficient meeting, they were both going their separate ways, due to reconvene later to repeat the exercise.

Once more 'clean', Ada sauntered back into view and began mingling again with early Christmas shoppers with the intention of raiding a different store. First, she needed to catch up with Mavis and she hoped the pest hadn't forgotten where their rendevouz point was.

Ada had hardly gone a hundred yards towards Marble Arch when through the crowd she spotted the weasel-faced store detective with a policeman at his side. She realised immediately the fellow had found the empty hangers and had rumbled that she'd been in cahoots with a decoy. Now he was out searching for her, perhaps both of them. Mavis had been instructed to make herself scarce immediately after she'd fulfilled her role and head to their meeting place. Ada just hoped that her accomplice *had* got clean away because she wouldn't put it past the snivelling wretch to grass them all up under police interrogation.

With a bitter curse Ada ducked down her head, pulled up her collar and weaved a path to safety. She knew she'd be going home to Lambeth early and that annoyed her because she'd seen some smashing shoes recently in Selfridges.

'I've been hanging about waiting for her by Marble Arch!' Ada was so enraged that the finger she had pointing at Mavis was violently trembling. 'I'd've been better off doin' the job on me own. The cowardly bitch nearly got the both of us arrested in Debenhams.'

Ada continued stamping to and fro in the back room of the Windsor pub, sucking on a cigarette. 'And I ain't taking her with me again, so don't go asking me, Bill. See if one of the others will have the useless article on their backs.' She glowered, waiting for Bill to side with her and bawl the new girl out.

If anything, Bill was sliding his latest young fancy encouraging glances.

'Time she was sent packin', Ada stormed, unpinning her hat and throwing it down on the table.

'Cut her some slack, will yer, Ada?' Bill drawled soothingly. 'Be different next time. Virgin at it today, weren't she?' He twitched his head, giving Mavis a sly, sideways wink.

'Only way she could be a bleedin' virgin 'n' all, ain't it?' Ada snarled sarcastically, staring hatefully at her rival for Bill's affections.

A few minutes ago her resentment for Mavis had escalated when, hot and bothered, she'd entered the Windsor public house on Garnies Street and found the young blonde hadn't bothered going to their rendezvous spot so had beaten her back from Oxford Street. Not only that, Mavis had been looking like the cat with the cream, cosying up to Bill's side, sipping gin and tonic.

Having completed her initiation into the gang without mishap Mavis had begun to feel relaxed . . . until Ada burst in, vinegar-faced and spouting her mouth off. As she listened to Ada's criticism of her debut performance Mavis's pretty features turned sulky. She knew there was truth in it but she wasn't about to admit that to anybody, least of all Bill, even though she reckoned it was his fault she'd put on a poor show.

She'd spent last night with him and if she'd been acting dozy in the shop it was because she'd been tired: Bill hadn't let her get any sleep till the early hours of the morning. Besides, she might be a novice thief but her parents weren't, so in Mavis's opinion Ada could get stuffed. The Pooleys' criminal pedigree was superior to the Stones' and that, Mavis calculated, gave her the right to be part of Bill's set-up.

As soon as Mavis left school, she'd have happily gone

into the family business. But her father had been against any of his kids taking up his and his wife's seedy career. Mr Pooley had since died and Mrs Pooley had been less against seeing Mavis follow in her shoes as a shoplifter. Times were hard, and in Gill Pooley's opinion, a girl did what she had to these days to get by. She'd encouraged Mavis's relationship with Bill because she knew he'd look after her daughter while she learned the ropes. But she'd warned Mavis not to let the other girls push her around or to rely on Bill for too long. Mavis was heeding her mum's advice. Bill Black might want her for now but as soon as Betty Pickering came out of gaol, she knew he'd drop her like a hot potato . . . just as he would Ada.

'Ain't my fault you let the store detective get onto yer,' Mavis sighed. She got up and sauntered towards Ada, swinging her hips and her gin to and fro. 'If it hadn't been fer me timing it just right you'd've had yer collar felt.' She gave a contemptuous smirk. 'I weren't being a coward, see, I was being clever. I hung back playing me part on purpose. You're lucky I helped you out best I could even though you was to blame for getting clocked. Then I scarpered straight away 'cos I knew the fellow would check the rails and call the police when he found stuff gone. You ought to be more subtle, Ada.'

'That subtle enough for yer?'

Ada, her face boiling with rage, suddenly jerked Mavis's arm up, flinging her drink into her face. She followed that up by punching the side of the young blonde's head, sending her staggering into a chair, which crashed over.

By the time Bill sprang to separate them, Mavis was

screaming abuse at the top of her voice and twisting a fistful of Ada's mousy hair. A moment later Mavis howled as Ada bit her hand. As they wrestled back and forth, bashing into tables, one wobbled, sending several glasses smashing on the floor.

The landlord suddenly barged into the back room pulling the door to behind him. 'Chrissake . . . what's going on, Bill?' he ground out in an undertone. 'Can hear the commotion in the saloon bar.'

Bill managed to elbow Ada forcefully away from Mavis, and the older woman went tottering back and landed on her backside on the floor. Mavis was shoved more gently in the opposite direction.

''S'all right, Jim,' Bill breathlessly told the landlord. 'Just a bit of a disagreement between the ladies, that's all.'

'Fuckin' hell!' Jim muttered. 'I'll be bleedin' glad when Betty's out.' Jim Trent knew that most of the bust-ups between the women in Bill's crew were caused by jealousy over him, not the value of the stuff they stole. Bill couldn't say no to any of the little scrubbers. At least when Betty was about he managed to keep his fly buttoned a bit more often.

'Get going.' Bill jerked his head at the door, but gave Mavis a little smile to soften her dismissal.

Mavis straightened her clothes in a couple of tugs. Having patted her blonde waves into place she collected her handbag and sashayed out. The landlord followed her, then stopped at the door, wordlessly pointing at the broken glass and overturned furniture.

'I'll see to damages, Jim,' Bill said, all affable. 'You know I always do, mate.'

Jim couldn't argue with that. On a previous occasion

when Bill had caused mayhem and nearly killed a bloke in his pub, a pile of banknotes had been slapped down onto the splintered bar counter before the victor and his cronies sauntered on their way. Jim gave a nod of acceptance and disappeared.

Bill turned back to Ada to find she was still sitting on the floor examining a stained hand. Suddenly she scrambled up and started pulling hysterically at her clothes to view the back of her skirt. She held out crimson fingers towards him, shaking them angrily. 'Look! I've only sat on glass and cut me bleedin' arse! That fuckin' bitch! She's made me cut me bleedin' arse! I'm gonna have her right now!'

Bill scraped together shards with a foot while grabbing at Ada's arm to prevent her charging after Mavis and starting another scrap. He began rubbing and patting Ada's back in an attempt to calm her down. 'Let's take a look,' he said soothingly. 'Probably ain't more than a scratch.'

Ada tried to tug free of his grip but when he lifted her skirt and petticoat she quietened and sent him a sideways look. Turning her around so her back was to him he pulled aside her bloodstained drawers then bent to take a look at the gash. It was long and deep, and he knew it needed stitches. Bill drew out a handkerchief from his pocket and folded it into a wad to press against the wound and staunch the flow of blood. He could sense Ada was still bubbling with rage and knew of only one sure way to distract her from going after Mavis and creating merry hell. His free hand began sensually kneading the spare flesh of her undamaged buttock.

'We'll get a stitch or two put in that for you by the doc and you'll be good as new come supper time.' He leaned closer and nipped at her ear with his teeth. 'Then later on, Ada, I'll kiss it all better for yer. Like that won't yer, gel?'

Ada shoved her spine against his chest, squirming her bottom against his fondling hand and deliberately parted her thighs in wordless demand.

As Ada's head fell back Bill impassively watched her grimace and groan as he thrust his fingers to and fro. Of the two women, he preferred Mavis. She was better looking and, even at her tender age, had a bit more finesse about her, in and out of bed.

But Ada was the one to keep sweet because she was an instinctive, versatile thief with rare skills that were earning him a fortune. Only Betty was her superior, and she was languishing in Holloway and no use to him at all.

Bill had guessed that Mavis might not be up to much when she was under pressure. He'd also known that if anybody could teach her tricks, Ada could.

Ada had done a fine job at Mortimer House, lifting fabulous jewellery. She'd got him more than he'd wanted by bringing the suite of emeralds out with her and getting clean away. It had been days ago and he was now confident there'd be no comebacks. After the tale Ada had told him about those perverted women he'd expected it might get hushed up. It still made him chuckle and feel horny just thinking about Ada catching those two old girls at it . . .

As Ada writhed and bucked Bill jerked free his fingers and wiped them clean with his handkerchief. He then pressed the linen back against her bleeding bottom. 'Hold that on there, Ada,' he ordered and started counting out some cash pulled from his pocket to give to the landlord on the way out. 'Now, come on, gel, get a move on,' he barked impatiently as Ada wallowed in a sensual haze, propped against a table. 'It's time to go and get your backside sorted out.'

As Ada gave him a torrid low-lashed look, Bill inwardly sighed. He knew he'd be glad when Betty had done her time and saw the fucking lot of them off for him . . .

'You can shut that noise up right now before I really give you something to cry about!'

This time Jennifer ducked her head aside and the back of Winnie's hand cracked against her shoulder, spinning her around.

'Get yourself upstairs and don't bother coming down tea time. You'll be getting nuthin' to eat in this house, miss, till you've found another job. So if you don't want to starve get yerself down the labour exchange first thing in the morning.'

Having darted past her irate mother Jenny hared up the stairs to the room she shared with her sister and flung herself prostrate on the bed. Grabbing a pillow she pulled it over her head to muffle her sobs.

In Jenny's opinion, everybody was always against her. It wasn't her fault that she'd got back from her dinner break twenty minutes late. If it hadn't been for Lucy Keiver holding her up she'd only have been ten minutes overdue. Only an old misery would moan about that. But Jenny realised she probably shouldn't have said so to Mrs Dobson when she was ticking her off.

She scrubbed her eyes on the pillowcase to dry them and a watery chuckle grazed her throat as she recalled the old cow's expression on hearing her insolence, as she'd called it.

A few minutes later Jenny was feeling more cheerful. She'd hated the job anyhow. She sat upright, slouching on the coverlet picking her nails.

Kathy wouldn't be back for hours. Jenny knew she'd get little sympathy from that quarter in any case. They might be twins but they'd never been close friends, even as children. In Jenny's opinion, Katherine always got away with misbehaving because she was prettier and cleverer. Her sister had always done better at school lessons and been more popular with classmates.

But when the headmaster had tried to persuade Winnie that Kathy should continue studying rather than leave at the end of term following their fourteenth birthdays, their mother wouldn't hear of it. There had been no favouritism then. The twins were out to work, she'd bluntly told him, and that was that. Their father had also taken a rare interest in his daughters' futures by backing Winnie to the hilt over the necessity of two extra wage packets. Jenny couldn't recall her father bothering much with his son's upbringing either, other than an occasional mutter about Tom moping about indoors when he should be out kicking a football. No doubt when it was Tom's turn to leave school, Eddie would have more to say, Jenny thought acidly. But at least Tom was lucky in that he got odd presents bought for him by their father. He'd brought in the football for him only a few weeks ago. Her and Kathy got next to nothing; last Christmas they'd received a hairbrush to share.

The front door slammed and Jennifer got up, peeking from behind the net curtain at the street below. She saw her mother, holding Tom by the hand, striding off up the street, shopping bag swinging at her side. Jenny knew whatever it was her mother was off to buy in the way of groceries she'd get none of it later. It wasn't the first time she'd been sent to bed hungry for annoying her parents.

Jenny brightened, realising there was an opportunity to nip downstairs and root about in the pantry for something to eat before her mother returned. She doubted she'd find much, but a few stale biscuits would be better than nothing. With a sniff she started along the landing.

The street door banged shut and Jenny grimaced, guessing her mother had forgotten her purse and had returned for it. She peered over the banisters and saw her father go in the parlour. A moment later she heard him chuckling softly to himself and, curious as to what was amusing him, she crept down a few stairs and angled her head to see through the open parlour door.

Eddie had just passed his wife in the street, on her way to the shops, so he knew he was alone and could have a Scotch without hearing her miserable muttering behind his back. He got the whisky from the sideboard and poured a tot, smacking his lips and savouring it. A moment later he drew from his pocket an envelope and tipped out of it a stream of banknotes. He'd just been to Finchley and done a sweet deal with a goldsmith and he was very happy.

He hadn't expected the old Shylock to be in such a generous mood. On previous occasions when they'd done business, Eddie had thought it'd be easier squeezing blood from a stone. He'd almost doubled his money on the rings he'd had off Bill Black and was now feeling pleased as punch. He scrunched a handful of tenners then let them flutter back to the table. 'Luvly stuff . . .' he purred. 'Think you deserve another one o' these,

Eddie boy . . .' He topped up his tumbler with whisky, immediately tossing some back. A moment later he was neatening the pile of cash and squashing it back into the envelope.

Jenny watched her father darting thoughtful glances here and there before approaching the small radiogram. He bent down and started fiddling with the speaker grille at the front until it came loose in his hand. The envelope was placed in the cavity behind it before being fixed back in place.

Eddie sauntered back to the table to finish his drink. He wasn't worried about anybody in the family wondering why the speaker wouldn't work. All of them, even Winnie, knew to ask permission before turning on his radio. And in future he wouldn't be letting them use it.

CHAPTER EIGHT

'Your Lucy in, is she?'

Matilda could tell from the way Winnie Finch had barked at her that she'd come to have a ruck. Jutting her chin, she slowly looked the younger woman up and down. 'What's it to you if she's in or out?'

Having just made slow progress across the road following a chat with a neighbour, Matilda had been taking a breather, leaning on the railings outside her house, while summoning the energy to climb the stairs to her rooms. On Lucy's orders, Matilda tried to get herself out and about for a short stroll every day, whatever the weather. Today she hadn't hung about chinwagging with Beattie Evans as it was a cold Saturday morning.

The moment Matilda had spotted Winnie marching in her direction, pulling along her young son by the hand, she'd guessed why the woman looked riled up. Yesterday, Lucy had come home jubilant with the news the job in the sweet shop was hers as Mrs Dobson wasn't satisfied with the person she'd taken on. Lucy had told

Matilda she'd bumped into Jennifer Finch the day before and had recounted the gist of their conversation. Jennifer had made it clear she didn't want the work so Lucy had declared she didn't feel at all guilty taking over from Winnie's daughter.

'Your Lucy's taken my Jennifer's job round at Dobson's and I want to know what she thinks she's playing at.' Winnie had jabbed Matilda twice on the shoulder to emphasise what she was saying and received harder prods in return. 'I heard Lucy Keiver reckoned herself above shop work, what with her mixing with posh people in big houses. Seems she ain't; and she ain't above doin' the dirty on kids who've managed to find themselves their first proper job.'

A few years ago, when Matilda was in her prime, Winnie would never have dared to confront her in such a way because she knew she'd have got a hefty clump. But since her terrible accident, the woman was frail and Winnie guessed it might not take more than a shove to put Matilda on the ground despite she'd once been a notorious local bruiser.

'Reckon you ought to go back home and ask your Jennifer why she got the boot,' Matilda snarled. 'And don't yer come back here trying to throw your weight about, Winnie Finch, or you'll not find me in such a good mood next time.'

Winnie shrank back a bit and Tom, white-faced and wide-eyed, crept behind her. Matilda might not be in top form, or as young as she was, but the savagery shaping her features told Winnie her opponent was ready to go down fighting.

'She in?' Winnie jerked her head at the first-floor window. ''Cos if she is I'll have it out with the bleedin' cow right now.' She pushed back her coat sleeves, gathering the courage to barge past.

'Ain't nuthin' to sort out. My daughter's got the job and that's that.' Matilda limped quite nimbly to block Winnie's path into the house. 'And you're wasting yer time here anyhow 'cos she ain't in. My Lucy's at work.' Matilda added an intentionally infuriating smirk to the information.

Winnie looked as though she might explode with rage on hearing that. Jennifer hadn't been offered Saturday morning although Winnie had nagged her daughter to ask for it as overtime. Mr Dobson worked at the weekend and Jennifer had been told she wasn't needed. Yet Lucy Keiver had managed to wangle herself extra hours straight away.

With a deep breath that puffed out her bony chest Winnie turned and marched back up the street, pulling Tom along behind her.

'Want a word with you.' Winnie burst into the sweet shop, sending the bell clattering madly. She let go of Tom's hand and stamped up to the counter, grim-faced, while her son stuck a thumb in his mouth and watched nervously.

The customers inside swivelled about, mouths agape. A moment later it was obvious the two young women, with kids in tow, were loitering expectantly in the hope of watching this drama unfold.

Winnie's pointing finger was levelled at Mrs Dobson, rather than at Lucy, who was in the process of tipping gobstoppers onto the scales. Mr Dobson suddenly came out of the back room carrying a jar of barley sugar.

'What's the noise all about?' he huffed tetchily, and shot his wife a stern frown.

'You gave my Jennifer the job. What's *she* doing here in her place?' A curt nod indicated Lucy. 'You didn't even let me daughter see two weeks out. You've got a bloomin' cheek . . .'

Mrs Dobson closed her dropped jaw with a clack. Having conquered some of her shock, her eyes narrowed on Winnie. '*You've got a blooming cheek,*' she mimicked sarcastically. 'Don't expect *me* to teach the girl manners and diligence because you've made such a bad job of it. Your daughter's timekeeping was appalling and her attitude to serving customers no better. You're lucky I gave her a chance to prove herself for a few days.' She raised her eyebrows at a dangerously whitening Winnie.

Winifred had harboured a suspicion that perhaps Jennifer hadn't been as upset as she'd made out at getting the sack. Her daughter had insisted she'd been unfairly dismissed and complained that Mrs Dobson shouldn't have changed her mind about taking her on just because of her young age. It wasn't her fault, Jennifer had cried, following a cuff round the ear, that Lucy Keiver had nipped in and stolen her job. Winnie turned her attention to Lucy, who had her lips pressed together and a spark of amusement in her eyes. Winnie was determined to wipe the look off the smug so-and-so's face.

'Least my Jenny ain't been raised in a slum,' she spat with a sneer. 'She's from a decent home and she wouldn't come back here now if you was to beg her. If you like having scum out of the Bunk working for you, that's yer own business. You can stick your job, and none of us'll be in here again buying yer sweets neither.'

Lucy was around the counter in a flash, yanking at Winnie's elbow and spinning her around as she made to flounce out of the shop. 'Who you calling scum?'

Winifred shook her arm but Lucy tightened her grip. 'Jennifer didn't want the job, she told me so, so I reckon you owe me an apology, and Mrs Dobson too.'

Winnie shoved at Lucy, who held ground and shoved back, sending the older woman tottering against the door, making the bell swing wildly. The two customers exchanged a pop-eyed look. One of them clapped a hand over her gaping mouth.

Mr Dobson finally overcame his embarrassment to spring into action. Dumping down the jar of sweets, he dragged Lucy back just as Winnie made a lunge for her, grabbing a handful of her long dark hair.

'Enough!' he bellowed. 'How dare you come here and cause such a commotion!' He smacked at Winnie's hand to loosen her grip on his employee's scalp while trying to prevent Lucy from swinging a fist in retaliation.

'Don't you worry, I won't be coming here ever again,' Winnie bellowed breathlessly, dusting herself down and trying to dislodge her son from where he'd sprung to cling to her hip. 'Nor will none of me friends and neighbours when I tell 'em wot's gone on.' With a sniff, and yanking Tom behind her, she went out, slamming the door.

When the bell's reverberation had died away Mr Dobson turned an enraged stare on his wife. 'I told you it was a mistake taking on someone from Campbell Road,' he snapped. 'Only trouble ever comes out of it. Now we'll be gossiped about by the likes of *that* woman.' He jerked his head at the door where the bell was still silently swaying following the Finches' departure. 'Why do you never listen to a word I say?' Without a glance Lucy's way he ordered, 'Please wait in the back room, Miss Keiver. Once I've served these customers I'll be out to speak to you.'

Lucy knew she was about to be sacked and a surge of indignation rose in her chest. She felt inclined to follow Winnie's lead and tell the Dobsons they could poke their job and their gobstoppers too. She'd worked hard since she started in the shop and had stayed late yesterday as a favour to clean shelves and show willing. But she knew there was no point in causing further commotion.

She noticed the youngest child in the shop, who looked to be about the same age as Tom Finch, had tears glistening in his eyes and was gazing solemnly at his mother for reassurance. Moments ago, she'd seen similar distress crumpling Winnie's son's face. Lucy could cope with fights and name calling, and always gave as good as she got, but she'd no stomach for frightening little children. Suddenly she felt guilty and thoroughly ashamed of her behaviour. With nimble fingers she took off her overall and threw it on the counter before going into the back room.

A week later, Lucy was walking swiftly towards home, hunched into her coat for warmth, when she heard someone shout out to her.

'Wait up, Lucy.'

Lucy pivoted about and squinted into twilight. Jennifer's sister, Katherine, was trotting down the road towards her, her fair hair glinting as she passed beneath the gas lamps. The girl came to a halt puffing out steamy breath into icy air.

'I've been keeping a lookout for you,' Katherine rattled off. 'I would have come round to your house to see you but didn't know how Mrs Keiver would take getting a visit from any of us Finches after what went on.' She pulled a face.

'So you've heard all about it then,' Lucy said.

'Oh, yeah . . . know it off by heart . . .' Katherine rolled her eyes in mock agony. 'I knew Jenny would never knuckle down to working at Dobson's. She reckoned from the start it wasn't good enough for her. She's got pie-in-the-sky ideas, you see, about fancy jobs in posh London stores. So, I just wanted to say I'm sorry it all turned nasty and that you got the sack as well.' She sighed. 'I know what Mum can be like when she's het up. Really, she was angrier with Jenny than you, 'cos she knows she's bone idle. It's just . . . you'll see a cow jump over the moon before she'll admit one of her own kids is useless to someone outside the family.'

Lucy smiled wryly. Her own mother had exactly the same attitude to protecting her family's reputation.

'Over and done with now, Kathy.' Lucy shrugged magnanimously.

'Should've heard the row coming out of ours later that day,' Kathy resumed. 'I was glad to get out and do me afternoon shift at work and leave them all to it. Dad was sticking his oar in, 'n' all . . .'

Katherine stuffed her hands deeper into her pockets, feeling ashamed, as she often did, of her parents. They might think themselves better than people living in the Bunk, but they weren't. She knew first-hand that Eddie Finch was a brutal man because she'd had tastes of his fists, usually at times when she was trying to protect Jennifer from his temper. After Kathy had found out her father had whacked her little brother Tom, her disgust for him had deepened until she wasn't sure whether she hated him.

She knew that as well as being cruel he was a crook who dealt in stolen goods. She'd witnessed over the years her father's 'friends', as her mother described the men who visited, carrying boxes of stuff into the house. Jennifer had told her she'd sneaked downstairs and glimpsed a mass of fabulous jewellery on the parlour table on the last occasion that Bill Black came over. Katherine knew her twin fantasised about Bill so she wasn't really sure whether to believe that one. But Katherine had seen the bruises on her sister and brother, following Bill's last visit, and realised something more serious than Jennifer trying to get Bill's attention by parading about in her nightie had set her father off on a rampage that night.

'Where are you working?' Lucy had noticed that Kathy didn't seem in a hurry to be on her way. Neither was Lucy in a rush to return to the cold, depressing rooms she shared with her mother. Besides, it was a good opportunity to quiz Kathy over her employment and discover whether any vacancies were going.

When Kathy had stopped her, Lucy had been on her way home from the Chapel Street market, where she'd managed to pick up a temporary job on a second-hand clothes stall. Lucy had bumped into one of her old school friends last week when she'd been to the market at the end of the day in the hope of picking up some bruised fruit and veg, and Nora Brightman had told her she was going away for a bit so she could have her job till she returned. Lucy had noticed the small bump straining her friend's coat buttons and had guessed that once the bun was removed from the oven Nora would be quickly taking back her wages. Late this afternoon, after just four day's of sorting smelly old clothes to sell, dawn to dusk, she'd been proved right on that score. Nora's mother, who ran the stall, had handed over seven and six as her pay and told her that she was no longer required as her daughter would be showing up tomorrow.

'I've got a job doing shifts at Barratts sweet factory in Wood Green,' Kathy told Lucy. 'I don't mind it 'cos the people there are nice and the wages aren't bad either, especially if you manage to wangle a bit of overtime. But they don't let us "kids", as they call us, do nights. Anyway, it'll do for now. As soon as I'm old enough I'm going to train to be a nurse.'

'You want to go into nursing?' Lucy looked impressed.

Kathy nodded. 'It'll take a long time 'cos I'll need to work during the day to earn me keep, then study in me own time for qualifications. But I'm determined to do it.'

'Good for you,' Lucy said spiritedly before her thoughts returned to her own prospects. 'Any vacancies going at Barratts?'

'Don't know of any,' Kathy replied. 'Mum's already told me to keep me eyes and ears open for a job for Jenny. I said I would but, between you 'n' me, I won't 'cos I know I'll be wasting my time. She'll get herself booted out, like she did at Dobson's, and probably lose me my job into the bargain. But I'll put in a word for you, Lucy; just keep that to yourself, though, or me mum'll be round to sort you out again.' She grinned.

'I think I can handle your mum,' Lucy said drily. 'But I'd be grateful to know if anything comes up. Getting a bit desperate now it's so close to Christmas.'

'Something might come up in the New Year.' Kathy gave her a sympathetic look.

'Yeah . . . thanks anyway . . .' Lucy said, trying to sound bright. She needed cash now, not in the New Year.

'Better be off.' Kathy turned to go.

Lucy trudged on down the road towards home, her face low so she could muffle her freezing cheeks with her coat collar. She knew her mother would be very disappointed that Mrs Brightman had put her off after so short a time working on her stall.

'How's it going? Found anything?' Connie was emerging from her house, buttoning up her coat, when she saw Lucy approaching and enquired about her hunt for a job.

Lucy shook her head. 'Found a few days' work down the market but just got put off by Mrs Brightman 'cos Nora's took her wages back.'

'There's still a job going at the supper club. We're pretty short now, and old Boris is getting agitated. Another one of the gels handed in her notice 'cos she's getting set up in an apartment by a customer, lucky thing.' Connie started to move on, anticipating Lucy's rejection. 'Gotta go or I'll be late fer me shift. Bleedin' freezin', ain't it, Luce?'

'Hold on a moment, Connie . . . would this Boris mind if I took a job just till after Christmas?' Lucy asked on impulse.

Connie halted, surprised. She'd not really believed that Matilda's daughter would be tempted to agree. 'If you're serious about it don't tell Boris about your plans, 'cos once he sees how pretty you are I'm guessing he won't like losing you too soon. You'll pull in the punters all right.' Connie cocked her head; she could tell Lucy was still dubious about the work and she didn't want to push her into it. 'You thought of asking your cousin Rob for a job?' Connie asked gently. 'He's got his own business, ain't he?'

'Mum says don't ask him 'cos once he knows we're struggling, he'll feel obliged to help out. Rob's good like that.' Lucy paused. 'But since he got badly injured and his warehouse went up in flames his business has suffered badly. Last thing he needs right now is us on his ear.'

'Rob Wild might have got badly beaten up but he's still a good looker, ain't he?' Connie winked. 'I know I would if he asked . . .'

'Shut up!' Lucy scolded, but with a grin. 'He's married to Faye and she'll have yer eyes out and serve you right.' Lucy grew serious. She desperately needed a job; it wasn't fair to expect her mother to support her on her tiny widow's pension. She knew her mum was missing Reg, not just as a companion but because he had contributed to the household. Now it was her turn to do that. 'It's work, I suppose,' Lucy sighed. 'What's the pay like?'

Connie grimaced disgust. 'But you get to keep yer own tips and there's a good dinner thrown in.' She started to walk away. 'I'm gonna be late if I don't get a move on.'

'All right,' Lucy called after her on impulse. She knew if she didn't make a snap decision the vacancy might be taken by the time Connie returned from work. 'I'm interested. Will you find out when I can start?'

Lucy carried on towards home, thinking again what a fool she'd been to turn down the housemaid's job at Mortimer House. But it would have been purgatory trying to act as though nothing had happened while Audrey Stubbs lorded it over her in a job that was rightfully hers. She wondered if the nasty cow had yet managed to get her hooks into Rory Jackson. The way Audrey had gone on about him Lucy knew the woman fancied him. As she had herself. There was no point in denying the truth: she'd found him attractive and missed seeing him. Their friendship had been blossoming and she'd have liked it if eventually they'd grown close enough to become sweethearts.

CHAPTER NINE

'I think I've managed to get myself a job in a restaurant, Mum.' The news was casually given as Lucy sat down at the table opposite her mother. 'What's for tea?' she asked brightly in an effort to deflect questions.

'You ain't working with Connie, and that's final!'

Matilda carried on reading the newspaper. She'd been studying the situations vacant section for some time while her youngest daughter had been working at the market. Earlier in the day Matilda had spied Nora Brightman close to the junction with Seven Sister's Road, looking dispiritingly trim and healthy. In anticipation of Lucy again returning home unemployed, she'd bought a gazette before trudging back to the Bunk.

'See . . . good position there for a lady's maid in Hampstead, but says references required and followed up.' Matilda jabbed a finger on newsprint, huffing in exasperation. 'Can't you go back to Mortimer House and get one off the housekeeper?'

'How d'you guess I'm waitressing in Connie's supper club?' Lucy asked, baffled.

On several occasions, Matilda had spied her daughter and Connie Whitton chatting together in the street. She'd guessed where that friendship might lead if Lucy continued struggling to find a regular job. 'Nuthin' gets past this.' Matilda gave her daughter an old-fashioned look, tapping the side of her nose. 'Ain't got nuthin' against Connie, but she's a working gel, and it'll be the finish of me if you follow in her footsteps.'

Lucy had intended to keep details of her new job offer to herself because she'd feared this reaction from her mother. She didn't want to upset her, and she didn't relish doing the work, but things were desperate. Earlier in the week, Matilda had bawled out of the window at Podge Peters that he'd better come back another time to collect the rent. Lucy knew they were in arrears. Her mother always lived hand to mouth and Lucy had very little left of her meagre wages from Mortimer House to eke out. If this continued she and her mum would be in the queue for the soup kitchen, never mind the labour exchange.

'If I get offered the job I'm giving it a go,' Lucy said firmly. 'Con said it's a proper dining room and you don't have to get involved with anything you don't want to. I'm gonna take the job till after Christmas, then see . . .'

'I said you ain't working with Connie!' Matilda roared, and repeatedly thumped a fist down on the paper. 'That's how she started out on the game. Waitressing my eye! Before you know it some flash sod's gonna offer you more than you can refuse. Then it's a slippery slope to the gutter.'

'Well, thanks very much, Mum!' Lucy jumped to her feet. 'Says a lot about what you think of me. I ain't Connie Whitton and I ain't sleeping with any man; don't care how rich he is.'

108

Matilda roughly gestured apology then dropped her forehead into a hand. 'Know you wouldn't,' she said gruffly. 'But can't blame a mother fer being anxious at times like this. If only I could get meself out charring I could bring in a bit. Wouldn't all be left up to you then. Not as if I'm *that* old! Bleedin' hell, Beattie can give me a few years and she's working in a laundry three days a week.'

Lucy heard her mother's deep sigh and enclosed her in a hug; she'd noticed how careworn was her expression. 'You're not well enough to be out working. That's for me to do. I've got a job offer . . .'

Matilda shrugged off her daughter's comfort. 'Look at how Con's turned out, doin' that work,' she mumbled. 'Lots of men passed through her life but she's never got herself married or had any kids, has she?' Matilda slanted a bleak look up at Lucy. 'Men don't marry spoiled goods and I want to see you get yerself a nice fellow like yer sisters've done. Want to see you happy and settled, Luce.'

'I'm only eighteen, Mum,' Lucy replied gently. 'Time enough yet . . . and I won't be spoiled goods, but I *will* be happy, I promise.'

'How about if we get in touch with Sophy again and tell her she's *got* to do you another character?' Matilda raised enquiring eyes to her daughter.

Lucy had written weeks ago to ask Sophy if she'd urgently supply another glowing recommendation. But 'the madam' at Lockley Grange had found out that her housekeeper had taken it upon herself to give her sister a character reference and it had put her nose out of joint. Mrs Lockley had told Sophy that any further enquiries about Lucy Keiver were to be directed to her so she might reply to them personally.

Given that Lucy had told the madam that she was stuck up and impossible to work for, true though it was, she had to accept there'd be no good word forthcoming from that quarter. Neither could she rely on Sophy's endorsement. The last thing Lucy wanted was for her sister, perhaps her brother-in-law too, to risk upsetting the Lockleys and losing their livelihoods because of her. She'd allowed temper to get the better of common sense when she'd stormed out of Mortimer House with just her pay in her pocket. So Lucy believed she alone should suffer the consequences of her hot-headedness.

Sophy had told her to button her lip and knuckle down. Now Lucy understood the wisdom in her sister's advice and her warning that she might jump out of the frying pan straight into the fire. In the past Lucy had been pampered and protected by her doting mum and older sisters; now it was time to face up to disappointment and danger all by herself. She was about to experience just how tough life could be and she felt a peculiar thrill of pride and excitement at the prospect.

'I'll only stay working at the Cuckoo Club a short while and I'll keep looking for something else, promise.'

'You gonna tell yer sisters what you're up to?' Matilda asked after a long silence. 'They're gonna be disgusted with you, especially Sophy, after all she did to get you promoted to lady's maid.'

'I won't say if you don't want me to.' Lucy knew her mother was becoming resigned to the idea of her working with Connie, but she was still bitterly ashamed at the thought and wanted Lucy to know it.

'Don't matter what I want, do it?' Matilda snapped testily. 'You've made that pretty clear. If I was fit enough to stop you, you'd not get past me and out of that door to go to such a dive. You'd get a clip round the ear, my gel, just for mentioning it.' Matilda looked sulkily at the ceiling. 'Anyhow, soon as Beattie finds out – and she will 'cos Connie'll let on – the whole bleedin' world'll make up its mind about what *you* do fer a living.' Matilda abruptly stood up and ambled to her bed to lie down. 'Good job yer father ain't alive to see the day,' she muttered over a turned shoulder and the sound of creaking springs. 'Break his heart, you would . . .'

Connie removed two hairgrips from her mouth and slid them into place close to her temples. She primped her blonde curls, inspecting her appearance in the large mirror hanging on the wall before turning to the new recruit.

'Remember what I told you, Lucy?'

Lucy was hovering nervously behind Connie, tugging at the hem of her skirt in a vain attempt to lengthen it. When Connie had eyed her up for size, then taken from a cupboard a uniform for her to put on, Lucy had at first noticed nothing unusual. It had seemed to be a basic outfit of black dress and stockings and white pinafore and cap. It was only as Lucy pulled on the dress that she realised the skirt stopped at mid-thigh.

'Don't let Molly Warner barge you aside and take the best tippers,' Connie instructed. 'The greedy selfish cow'll do it if she can. All the gels are fed up of her. I'll give you the wink when I spot a regular coming in who likes a good feed and nuthin' much else to go with it.' Connie reapplied her lipstick, then dabbed a hanky at the corners of her mouth. 'The older blokes might be willing in mind but the old sods can't do much about it. A pat on the backside's all you'll get off them.'

'You didn't tell me we was expected to wear uniforms like this,' Lucy wailed.

Connie sent her an amused sideways look. In her time as a hostess she'd sashayed about in far more revealing costumes than the one the girls wore at the Cuckoo Club. 'You didn't reckon you'd be serving randy blokes their dinner in yer overcoat, did you, Luce?' She picked up Lucy's tiara-shaped cap and plonked it on her head. 'There . . . suits you . . .' Having straightened the frill on Lucy's starched pinafore she brushed her down with the backs of her hands, then stepped back to assess her new colleague's appearance. 'Reckon you're ready to go . . . and don't you look good. There'll be green eyes about the place when the other gels see you.'

Connie planted first one then the other of her stylishly shod feet on a stool to more easily adjust her suspenders. Lucy could tell from the inexpert stitching about the hem of the older woman's dress that Connie had deliberately shortened her uniform so that a glimpse of pale flesh was visible between skirt and stocking top.

Connie chuckled on noticing Lucy's frown. 'More you show, more o' this you'll be taking home.' She rubbed together a thumb and four fingers under Lucy's nose. A moment later she was unhooking the top buttons on her bodice to reveal some cleavage.

'Well, for heaven's sake don't tell me mum what you've got me wearing,' Lucy said on a wry sigh. 'She'll have a heart attack.'

'I won't say nuthin'. I already promised not to blab that you're working with me in the West End, if you don't want me to.'

'Me mum's guessed already but she's worried Beattie

might find out and start spreading it around. You know what a gossip she is.'

'Girls . . . come . . . I don't pay you to chat . . . chat; customers outside waiting . . .'

Boris Papadopolous had poked his oily black curls around the door of the vast store cupboard that also served as a restroom. Spare waitress uniforms were kept inside in a makeshift wardrobe, and a small table and chairs was shoved against one wall for the girls to use to have their dinners on their breaks. At one end a jug and bowl for freshening up stood on a marble-topped chest. A bare electric light bulb dangled over the old mirror.

Boris spotted Lucy and his swarthy features split into a grin of pleasure. He came into the room and circled her, hardly recognising her. 'You done me well bring this pretty lady,' he praised Connie in his thick Greek accent, patting her arm.

When Boris had interviewed Lucy he'd thought her a beautiful fresh-faced kid but a bit too prim-looking, dressed as she was in a thick woollen coat and low heeled lace-up boots. But he'd given her the job straight away, knowing that in the right get-up she'd attract customers. The younger and prettier the girls, the better most gentlemen liked it. Women in their early thirties, like Connie Whitton, were coming to the end of their usefulness in a place like the Cuckoo Club. But Boris was loath to get rid of Connie because she had a jaunty personality that some of the older clientele found appealing. She also had an on-and-off romance with one of the constables who did the beat round Piccadilly Circus. That liaison was very valuable to Boris. He resented paying protection money to bent coppers but he'd rather pay a little bit to Ralph Franks than shell out a lot to thugs sent round by rival club owners who were keen to put him out of business.

Now Boris had found another reason to keep Connie on: she might find more pretty friends like young Lucy to introduce to him.

He cocked his head, professionally inspecting the allure of his latest employee. The nipped-in waist of the black dress accentuated Lucy's curvy figure and the pinafore ruffles sat very nicely over her pert bosom. He was pleased to see that beneath her black stockings were slender shapely legs, and that this evening she had on her dainty feet more attractive shoes. He nodded while pondering if Lucy would be willing to do more than serve drinks and dinners. He knew if she could be persuaded to do some extras for gentlemen she could make herself . . . and him . . . rich.

'You have some lipstick for your friend to put on?' Boris addressed Connie while sliding one of Lucy's silky chestnut tresses over his palm. 'This colouring needs red . . . very red lips, like you got.' He whipped a finger to and fro in front of his mouth before pointing at Connie.

Lucy gave Connie a glance, then determinedly removed her hair from her boss's olive fingers and edged away from him.

'Yeah, got some in me bag,' Connie replied, and fished out a gilt tube. 'Boris is right, y'know, Luce. Just a bit of brightening up and you'll knock their socks off out there. I've got some rouge in here somewhere 'n' all.' Connie rummaged again in her bag.

'Good girl . . . you find me more like this Luce, I give you bonus.' Boris beamed at them. Before disappearing, he hissed, 'Hurry now.'

'If he thinks he's getting boss's perks after I've done me shift this evening, he can think again!'

Connie hooted a laugh on noticing Lucy's indignant expression. 'Oh, you don't need to worry about Boris. He's excited 'cos he knows the customers'll take to you like a shot and that's money in the bank to him. He ain't interested in any of us like that.' Connie struck a pose, with one hand on a jutting hip and the other limp at the wrist. 'I know he don't look it being as he's all big 'n' hairy, but he's got a boyfriend . . . or two . . .' Connie thrust the tube of lipstick at Lucy. 'Put a bit of that on . . . Come on, hurry up,' she heckled as Lucy hesitated. 'He'll be back after us otherwise.'

Lucy, in common with all the women in her family, had never worn lipstick, or any makeup at all, as such things were associated with a certain class of woman. Lucy inwardly sighed. Lipstick or no lipstick, she'd be considered disreputable by most people who found out she worked at the Cuckoo Club.

She stepped to the speckled mirror and frowned at her reflection, pushing the gilt base till a slim scarlet column appeared. A pleasing perfume came with it. She slid the lipstick on her mouth but ducked aside and shook her head as Connie attempted to dab rouge on her cheeks. 'You'll make me look like a bloomin' clown,' she protested.

Connie dropped the rouge pot back in her bag. 'Quick, come on, rub yer lips together, but don't get none on yer teeth, 'cos that don't look good,' Connie instructed as she watched Lucy inexpertly applying the lipstick.

From a very young age Lucy had got used to being amongst men and women drinking heavily and having fun. She could still remember being about three years old, sitting up in a pram that had been left in a cold corridor, with her older sisters minding her. Her parents would regularly disappear behind closed doors that led off that draughty passageway. Through the frosted glass panels she'd stare at blurred images and listen to raucous noise. Even at that tender age she'd understood she was being denied some enjoyment, so she'd cry until one of her sisters pulled on a big iron handle and called through an aperture to the adults. If they came to see to her their cooing – especially her mother's – was impatient and they were soon gone again, the door swinging shut on a secret smoky atmosphere.

As Lucy took another step towards a room of muted light and conversation, there was a strengthening redolence of those bygone times in the Duke of Edinburgh public house. But her parents had drunk in the saloon bar with friends who stank, as they did, of grime and sweat. In the Cuckoo Club's supper room were sweeter notes of floral perfume and roasting meats mingling with the alcohol and tobacco.

A *frisson* stole over Lucy as she hovered on the threshold of the dining area, watching men in expensive suits arrive at the top of the stairs, some escorting ladies in sumptuous furs. Intuitively, she suspected that of the two environments, this might be far the more sordid and dangerous.

A nudge in the ribs from Connie brought Lucy to attention.

'Fellow in the old-fashioned suit, about seventy, he's a sweet old stick, and got a bob or two. Get yerself over there and take his coat from him. If he takes to you he'll let you serve him all night. He's quite generous with tips when he's in the mood. Greg Randall is his

116

name.' Connie noticed Lucy's hesitation. 'Come on, I'll introduce you to him before Molly sticks her oar in,' she said kindly.

Lucy licked her red lips and took a nervous couple of steps. Mr Randall did look harmless enough with his iron-grey hair and small white moustache; nevertheless she slowed down.

'Come on!' Connie hissed, gripping Lucy's elbow and urging her forward.

They arrived at Mr Randall's side at the same time as another hostess.

'Sling yer 'ook, Molly,' Connie hissed undercover of a delicate cough. She discreetly bumped a hip against the almond-eyed redhead, sending her away a pace.

'Come to introduce you to our new member of staff, Mr Randall,' Connie lilted sweetly. 'Lucy's her name and I've told her what a nice gentleman you are. What'll you have? Scotch and soda, as usual?' Connie was deftly helping the portly fellow off with his coat. She was pleased to see that the old duffer had his smiling eyes on Lucy as he murmured agreement to having a drink. 'I'll just show you to your seat, sir. Saved you a nice one close to the window 'cos I remembered that's where you like to be . . . not too close to the band when they start up later. Noisy bunch, they are!' she clucked her tongue, chuckling. 'Lucy'll fetch your drink for you, then she'll take your dinner order.' Connie discreetly jerked her head at Lucy, urging her to fetch the Scotch and soda from the bar, which ran the length of one side of the dining room. Once she'd seated Mr Randall she quickly intercepted Lucy, who was on her way back, balancing a tumbler on a small silver tray.

'Ask him what he wants for dinner . . . recommend

the lobster or beef . . . keep him topped up with drinks . . . more he spends, better Boris'll like it. More he drinks, better you'll like it 'cos his tips'll get bigger as he gets tipsier.' Connie pulled out a little pad and pencil from her pinafore and slipped them into Lucy's pocket. She gave a chuckle. 'Knew you was going to put some noses out of joint; Molly's got a face like a bag o' spanners.' She glanced across to where the sulky redhead was watching them.

Lucy knew that Connie had forfeited bagging Mr Randall and his tips for herself so she could have an easy ride on her first night in the job. 'Thanks, Connie,' she murmured.

The older woman smiled and shrugged. 'This is as good as it gets, Luce. You'll be on yer own on nights when I ain't on shift with you, so toughen up smartish.'

Lucy nodded, took a deep breath, and pinning a smile to her face carried on towards Mr Randall.

CHAPTER TEN

A couple of urchins about seven or eight years old, inadequately clothed against the biting cold, were playing hopscotch on the pavement ahead and they turned and grinned at Lucy, daring her to interrupt their game. She obligingly stepped into the road.

'Get yerself indoors, Davy Wright, it's past yer bedtime,' she told the cheeky-faced boy, attempting to sound severe. He stuck out his tongue at her while his pal made grotesque faces, twisting his ears back and forth. 'If the wind changes,' she called over a shoulder, 'you know what'll happen to you, don't yer?'

'Me brother fancies you, Lucy Keiver,' Davy called after her, swiping a finger under his chapped nose. His boots looked too big for him and his trousers too small. But cold and ragged as he was, he continued grinning happily.

Lucy walked on, shaking her head in amusement. She knew that Samuel Wright liked her because he always blushed when they passed in the street. The Wrights were one of the poorest families living in the Bunk. The father had up and left years ago when Davy was a toddler. Ever since then Mrs Wright had struggled to bring up five boys on her own by hawking bits and pieces off a barrow that she pulled around the local streets. Lucy knew her mother tried to help the woman out by buying small amounts of her soda and matches and soap. Most people in the Bunk would try to give such support and, in turn, hoped to have a favour returned when it was needed because nobody liked charity or interference from the authorities.

It wasn't the Wright family's extreme poverty that put Lucy off Samuel, or the fact that he was younger than she was. Not many men had made much of an impression on her in that way. When working in Essex, Tim Lovat and a few of her other male colleagues had tried to win her over. She'd preferred Tim's company on her days off, and had gone out walking with him, or to the flicks on a number of occasions. But she'd made it clear from the start she considered him just part of her extended family as he was Sophy's brother-in-law. Tim had accepted that with no hard feelings.

At present Lucy was too busy with important things, like finding herself a respectable job, to bother pining for love. But as she sank further into her introspection she realised she was still missing a fellow she hadn't seen in a while. At quiet times she often found herself thinking about Rory Jackson and how much she regretted that their flourishing relationship had been abruptly nipped in the bud. The afternoon she'd left Mortimer House in high dudgeon, Rory had that morning taken his lordship to Newmarket races so there'd been no opportunity for farewells between them . . .

Suddenly, from a corner of her eye, Lucy glimpsed a

vehicle she thought she recognised. It was such an incongruous sight that she snapped up her head and gawped as it slowly approached. Her heart started pounding and she almost stumbled in alarm: thinking about someone couldn't conjure them up . . . could it?

Several other people stopped and stared too. Beattie Evans and Margaret Lovat had been having a gossip while ambling away from Smithie's shop. Beattie sank to her knees, scrabbling on the pavement because she'd dropped her shopping bag in amazement at the sight of a cream-coloured Rolls-Royce sailing up the Bunk. Open-mouthed, she and Margaret watched the luxurious tourer come to a halt by Lucy Keiver. A moment later a tall fair gentleman in uniform jumped out, looking very angry.

'Why the hell did you go off without saying a word? Was it too much trouble to leave me a message? D'you know how long it's taken me to find you?' Rory Jackson strode up to Lucy whilst grinding out his questions in a suffocated voice. He seemed about to reach out and jerk her against him, but instead thrust his hands into his pockets and frowned down at her, his lips tightly compressed.

Despite being stunned by his appearance Lucy sensed her hackles rising at his curt interrogation. 'Who do you think you are, Rory Jackson, that I'm obliged to keep you informed of me movements? I didn't ask you to come looking for me.'

He stared silently at her before replying stiffly, 'I thought we were good friends, getting to like one another. And I thought you might be interested to know what's gone on at Mortimer House since you quit. Perhaps I've made a mistake about all of it and have been wasting me time driving around in circles searching for you since you left. I've kept on believing Audrey was the only one to blame for what happened. But . . . can't deny it's entered me head that you might've been in it with her. It could have been a clever ruse, pretending to be at loggerheads when you was really best pals. Was that your plan?'

'What on *earth* are you talking about?' Lucy hissed, trying to concentrate, but being distracted by more people congregating to watch them. The sight of a smart young chauffeur and a flash vehicle at the kerb was making numerous pairs of eyes pop with excitement. She knew she'd be cross-examined at length about this incident by neighbours, and by her mother when she came to hear about it.

Her pleasure at seeing Rory was strengthening despite the prickliness between them. Nevertheless she was deeply embarrassed that he had tracked her down to the Bunk. She had never wanted anybody at Mortimer House to know she'd been reared on the worst street in north London and had now returned there to live with her mother.

'All right over there, Lucy?' Margaret Lovat called. A moment later, Beattie waved to attract her attention.

'I've got to go,' Lucy muttered, waggling some fingers at the two women to reassure them. 'You're making people stare. Bit of an unusual sight around these parts, a chauffeur-driven Rolls-Royce.'

'I know it's best not to talk here.' Rory took a glance about, top lip curled in distaste. 'Reckon if I don't watch it, I'll lose the hubcaps.' His tone was only faintly jocular. 'Come for a drive and I'll tell you what's gone on. I reckon you'll want to know, even though it's dreadful news.'

'Why should I be interested in any of 'em?' Lucy burst out in an under-breath. 'I got the dirty done on me by those two old cows at Mortimer House, and Audrey Stubbs was a thorn in me side from the start. You must be nuts to think we're secretly pals; we hated one another. Don't matter anyway, 'cos I'm over all of it now,' she added. 'Audrey's welcome to me job and I'm glad I'm out of there.' Despite the truth in it Lucy knew she'd give her eyeteeth to have the security of such a good job again.

'Audrey wanted your position all right,' Rory said quietly. 'But not for a reason anybody could've guessed at. And she's long gone now.'

'Weren't up to it, eh?' Lucy scoffed. 'What a surprise! I told Boyd and Venner she were no use. And if you think you can get me to go back and apply for me old job that got took off me, you can think again,' she rattled off heatedly. 'I wouldn't set foot in the place after the way I got treated.'

'No, it's not that . . .' Rory said. He broke off and rubbed a hand across the back of his neck. 'Come for a drive so we can have a talk.'

'I can't! It'll really start them all chinwagging if I go off in a fancy motor with a stranger,' Lucy interrupted.

'They'll gossip anyhow,' Rory returned logically. 'Besides, I'm not a stranger to you, and I haven't got an ulterior motive. Don't worry, I'm not about to kidnap you and carry you off so I can have my wicked way with you on the back seat of his lordship's limousine.' He smiled as Lucy blushed, clucked her tongue and discreetly punched his arm. A moment later his expression was again grave. 'It's not a time for larking about, actually. Not with what I've got to say. And I reckon you ought to be told what's gone on as you were sort of caught up in it. It's not good news,' he repeated with a sorrowful shake of his head.

Uneasiness rippled through Lucy. Rory had always seemed to her a straight-talking, positive sort of fellow, not one to wallow in a melodrama. 'I'll come for a drive.' She stepped towards the car parked at the kerb. 'If you carry on towards Seven Sisters and look for somewhere out of the way to park up, we could have a quick natter.' She sent him a cautionary frown. 'Can't stop out long 'cos me mum's expecting me back and she'll start to fret if I'm late.'

'Guess what, Til.'

'What?' Matilda carried on dunking a biscuit in her tea, seemingly unperturbed by a flustered-looking Beattie having burst in uninvited.

'Just seen your Lucy get in a Rolls-Royce with a bloke who looks like he's a film star. All done out in fancy togs and handsome as yer like, he is.'

Matilda gave her neighbour an old-fashioned look. 'Bit early, ain't it, fer you to be on the turps, Beattie?'

'Ain't been drinking, Til. I'm telling you straight, your Lucy's gone off with a bloke in a posh car.'

'Come over here, Beattie.'

Beattie stepped closer, her expression still displaying her gleeful wonderment.

Matilda planted her fists on the tabletop and pushed upright. She sniffed close to Beattie's face. 'Don't smell of booze, do you, so perhaps you've lost yer marbles, eh, gel?'

'I saw 'em going off together with me own eyes, I tell you.' Beattie slapped her hip, then pointed at Matilda's

124

sash window. 'So did other people out there in the street. Margaret's still hanging about hoping to get a gander when he brings her back.'

Matilda's frown became thoughtful. If what Beattie had said was true – and she hoped it was – it must mean a person from Mortimer House had come over to see Lucy. There could be no other reason for that visit than to offer Lucy her old job back. Matilda prayed that was the case. She was still deeply concerned and anxious about her youngest daughter working at the Cuckoo Club although Lucy had so far returned safely – and sober – in the early hours of the morning with her pockets chinking with the tips she'd received.

But Matilda was fearful that one evening that might not be the case, and she'd lie awake every night that Lucy was on shift, never rolling over with a contented sigh until she heard her daughter's key in the lock.

'I could do with a smoke,' Rory said, turning off the Rolls-Royce's purring engine.

'I don't mind if you have a cigarette,' Lucy said with a smile.

'Yeah, I know you wouldn't mind, but I reckon his lordship might if he gets a sniff of it,' Rory replied wryly. 'I dropped the family off in Chelsea to have tea with friends this afternoon.' He turned to Lucy, settling himself back in the leather seat. 'I've got to pick them up in an hour's time and take them home for a late supper.' He checked his watch with a grimace. 'I wasted too much time searching around the other side of the park before coming here. I remembered you said your mum lived Finsbury Park way so I've been driving around the area whenever I had a bit of time off. I knew it was a long shot, hoping to sort of just bump into you,' he glanced at her rather bashfully, 'but it paid off in the end.'

'Tea then supper; how the other half live,' Lucy muttered wryly. She'd forgotten just how well fed she'd been when working in service: regular meals and plenty on the plate. Nowadays she only got a good tasty meal when doing a shift at the Cuckoo Club. Even then she would put practically all of it in a basin to bring home to share with her mother. 'You've not got much time to hang about if you're due back in Chelsea in an hour.' She'd noticed Rory staring fixedly towards the junction with Campbell Road. She knew why he'd concentrated on looking for her on the other side of the park: the properties were better and he'd not imagined she'd be found in a rundown street.

She wanted to distract him from pursuing the subject of where he'd chanced upon her. Although he'd heard Beattie Evans address her by name he couldn't be sure she lived in the Bunk, and Lucy knew she wasn't about to volunteer the information. But it seemed Rory's thoughts were elsewhere.

'Her ladyship's been laid up indoors for months. So it's good to see her out and about again.' Rory shoved the peaked cap back on his head. 'Course, the daughters don't know a thing about the scandal. It's all been hushed up . . .'

Lucy swivelled on her seat to frown at him. 'Scandal?' she whispered, feeling a pang of uneasiness.

'I know I can trust you to keep what I'm gonna say to yourself. All of us staff at the house are loyal and respect Lord and Lady Mortimer. We agreed we wouldn't want to hurt them any more than they have been already so we've sort of taken a vow of secrecy on it all. But I reckon it's all right telling you because you still would be staff but for Audrey Stubbs' scheme to get you out of the way.'

'So you believe I'm not her pal now, do you?' Lucy asked waspishly.

'Yeah. Sorry . . . it's just, I've been desperate to find you and just seeing you like that, strolling along all carefree, it made me see red. I've been worried about you.'

'Why?'

'Why d'you think?' He turned away, shielding his expression. 'Found yourself work, have you?'

Lucy nibbled her lower lip. She'd no inclination to disclose where she worked or where she lived. She was ashamed of both facts. But especially, she realised, that she was still employed as a hostess in a place where she was expected to wear a uniform that barely covered her behind.

She'd been working at the Cuckoo Club for over a month. Christmas had come and gone; it had been a frugal yet cosy affair for her and her mother, spent with her sister Beth. Previous Christmases had been more lavishly celebrated at her sister Alice's house, where a roistering good time was always on the cards. But this year Alice had gone to stay with her in-laws. Many people in the Keiver clan were feeling the pinch financially, in common with families up and down the country.

Beth and her husband George lived close by in Islington, and Lucy had enjoyed eating a Christmas meal of roast pork and apple sauce, with a helping of plum duff covered in lashing of custard to follow. After dinner she'd played with her little niece, Sally, for a while and had delighted in the fact Sally was very taken with the rag doll Lucy and Matilda had clubbed together to buy her. It reminded her of the one her father had bought for her when he was a soldier serving in France. She still had it tucked away in a drawer.

But the New Year had brought with it no improved job prospects, in fact the beginning of January had seen the local labour exchange crammed full of desperate people searching for work.

Lucy became aware that Rory was awaiting her reply. 'Got a job as a waitress . . . not much good, looking for something better. So what's this scandal all about then? Something to do with Audrey, is it?' Lucy rattled off to distract Rory from questioning her further.

'Knocked her ladyship for six, what that bitch done. I'll start at the beginning but I'll warn you it gets worse as it goes on.' He paused. 'Audrey wasn't in your job for long when it happened. Master and mistress were going to a ball in Berkeley Square. Her ladyship's emerald jewellery came out of the safe so she could wear it. Audrey managed to get her hands on it and she scarpered with the lot: necklace, bracelet and earrings. The suite was an heirloom handed down through Lord Mortimer's family.'

Following a sharp intake of breath Lucy squeaked, 'Audrey Stubbs was a *thief*?'

'A bleedin' good one at that,' Rory confirmed with a bitter smile. 'The crafty cow knew exactly what she wanted 'cos nothing else went missing in all the time she worked at the house. Old Mr Collins was straight away counting out the silver and all of us staff were checking our belongings in case anything had gone walkies. But it was all present and correct.' He gave Lucy a bleak look. 'No wonder she was so keen on having your job and getting close to her ladyship's valuables.'

Momentarily, Lucy's expression froze in shock and dismay, then she angrily pursed her lips. 'Now I know why she was always hanging about, watching. She never stopped spying on me.'

'All becomes clear, don't it?' Rory gave a mirthless grunt.

'Have the police caught up with her and arrested her?' Lucy demanded. 'I don't remember seeing anything about a theft like that reported in the paper.'

'Weren't in the papers. And, as far as we know, the police were never called. All hushed up,' Rory said. An expectant quiet followed before he added on a sigh, ''Cos of the terrible scandal that would have followed an investigation.'

'That *isn't* the scandal?'

'It's only part of it.' Rory slanted Lucy a glance. 'You not been wondering why Mrs Venner and Mrs Boyd might give Stubbs your job in the first place?'

Lucy's jaw sagged. 'No! They weren't in on it too?' She raised a hand to cover her gasp of disbelief.

'They were being blackmailed.' Rory's voice was emotionless but a muscle leaped close to his mouth and he cleared his throat. 'That's why they caved in and let Audrey take over your job. They both swore they had no idea what she was up to and just thought she was after promotion. We all did, 'cos we knew she'd got ambitions to be under-lady's maid when Susan left.'

'So what happened next?'

Rory's closed expression and prolonged quiet made Lucy prompt him for more information. 'You said she was blackmailing Mrs Boyd and Mrs Venner? How?'

'Audrey caught them . . . canoodling one night . . . in Mrs Venner's office.' Again Rory concealed his embarrassment beneath an impassive tone.

'*Canoodling?*' Lucy selected the perplexing word and frowned. Slowly her features displayed her enlightenment. 'Oh my God! You're joking!'

"Fraid not . . .' Rory rubbed a hand about his lower face. 'Course, it were exactly what Stubbs was after. She had the two of 'em pinned right beneath her thumb finding out something like that.' He glanced solemnly at Lucy. 'They swore they didn't know any more than we did about what the wicked cow was planning, and we all believe it. I reckon you do too.'

Lucy simply nodded agreement, feeling too stunned to speak. 'What's happened to the two of them? Were they dismissed by Lord Mortimer?' she asked eventually.

'Mrs Venner left as soon as she could; quick and quiet, middle of the night she was out of the back door.'

'And Mrs Boyd?' Before her anger at being ousted from her job had coloured her judgement, Lucy had liked the woman and thought her a fair boss.

'That's the worst of it,' Rory said huskily, rubbing at the bridge of his nose. 'Mrs Boyd couldn't live with what she'd done. She blamed herself for the jewellery going missing, and for her ladyship having a real bad turn over it. She kept saying she should have been more vigilant. But that evil bitch would have found a way to get rid of Mrs Boyd. She only needed a few seconds alone to steal the stuff. She was a pro, that one.'

'What's happened to Mrs Boyd?' Lucy whispered, a queasy sense of uneasiness stealing over her.

'She was found dead in her room a couple of days after Mrs Venner left. Arsenic poisoning . . .' Rory cradled one of Lucy's hands on hearing her little groan of anguish. 'She left a folded note and one of the maids found it. That's how it all got out, 'cos I don't reckon the master and mistress would ever have told us the whole story, being as it was so embarrassing. Once they knew the letter had been seen by a member of staff . . . well!' He gestured hopelessness. 'Suppose they thought they'd better trust us all with keeping a secret than let a load of half-cocked stories start circulating. I reckon we were all more outraged by what Audrey did than finding out about Mrs Venner and Mrs Boyd liking one another a bit too much.' He broke off, staring moodily into the night. 'Her ladyship was very fond of Mrs Boyd. We all reckon that it was her suicide rather than the loss of the jewels that sent her into such a state they was talking of putting her in a sanatorium for a while. She was laid up in bed with the doctor coming over twice a day for nearly two months.' He sighed. 'Needed a bit more'n smelling salts to sort that one out. Today's the first day she's been out for any length of time.'

'The police will run Audrey to ground eventually,' Lucy blurted, before recalling that Rory had said the Mortimers wanted it kept hushed up. And no wonder!

'Got to go.' Rory looked at his watch. 'Don't want to. Could sit here talking to you for hours. But got to pick the family up in Chelsea.'

'Course, you get off or you'll be late.' Lucy made to open the door but he held her in her seat with a gentle grip on an arm.

'Chauffeur's job, madam, to assist you to alight.' In a trice he was out of the car and opening her door, a hand held out to her.

They stood for a moment on the pavement, their gazes merging before breaking apart.

'Can't believe what I've heard,' Lucy said huskily. 'I'm very sorry that Lady Mortimer's had such a rough time of it. As for Mrs Boyd . . . well, I don't know what to say. Did she have any family? I know she was a war widow, but she never mentioned any kids.'

'I think she had a son, and her mother was still alive, living with her spinster sister. Probably best if they don't ever find out all of what went on. We're all keeping quiet on it out of respect for everyone.'

'I won't repeat what you've told me, I swear.'

'Know you won't,' Rory said. 'Can I see you again? We could go out somewhere.'

'You'd better get going. You'll be late.'

'Don't you want to see me again?'

'I'd like to. But I'm trying to find meself a good job,' Lucy truthfully said. She didn't want Rory coming back to the Bunk or enquiring again about her employment. But she'd like to resume their friendship to see where it might lead . . .

Rory caught one of her hands in his.

'If I manage to get took on in service I don't know where I'll end up. Might be the other side of London. But I know where you are so I can write a letter to you with me address when I get settled.' Gently she withdrew her fingers from his clasp.

'Promise?'

'Promise.'

CHAPTER ELEVEN

'Ain't interested, Bill. You'd better clear off. Winnie'll be back soon.' Eddie Finch was edging away to open the door, hoping his visitor would quickly depart. But his bulging eyes were still fixed on an elegant, if battered, tortoiseshell box standing open on the table.

'Course yer interested,' Bill lilted persuasively. 'You're always interested in a sweet deal, Finchie, y'know you are. And they don't come no sweeter'n this one.' Bill Black lounged against the stick-backed chair in Eddie Finch's parlour. 'You've had a lovely bit of stuff off me, can't say you ain't. Remember them rings? Sold them on at a tidy profit now, didn't yer? Don't go tellin' lies; I know you did,' he remonstrated playfully as Eddie started to deny it. 'This time I've brought you *real* top-class gear. Aw . . . woss wrong, Ed?' Bill asked affably as Eddie started violently shaking his head.

'Woss wrong?' Eddie spluttered. 'You think I'm nuts?' He barked a hoarse laugh. 'I heard that someone got his fingers burned nicking heirlooms off a toff. I heard too that the prat's been trying to off-load 'em all over the

place with no luck,' he continued, pointing a quivering finger at the suite of emeralds while slinking further away as though it was poisonous. 'You only come to me 'cos nobody's taking and you're desperate to be shot of it. But I ain't a mug! I've heard whispers 'n' know what'll happen to me if I get caught up in it.' Eddie licked his dry lips. 'Don't mind risking a stretch inside, but I ain't ready to push up daisies. So get going and take the jewellery with you before Winnie gets in and clocks it.'

Bill defiantly cocked his head, picked up his glass of Scotch, and sipped leisurely. When he'd turned up fifteen minutes ago Eddie had been nice as pie, pouring him a drink before he'd sat down. Then Finchie understood the purpose of his call and his attitude had changed. But Bill wasn't ready to give up trying to persuade Eddie to take the emeralds off his hands. He was banking on the sly old git's greed eventually getting the better of him. Finchie's eyes were constantly being drawn like magnets to the glitter on the table. Bill was hoping Eddie would cave in and shell out simply for the privilege of getting hold of such exquisite gems.

Bill started tapping his feet, quashing his irritation as he sipped the whisky. Eddie had guessed right: he was his last port of call before he dumped the stuff, and the idea of it ending up in the Thames was making his guts writhe.

Not that Bill was expecting to get anything like the emeralds' true black-market rate; he'd come to the appalling realisation that the suite was truly priceless. It had no value because none of his contacts would touch the jewellery with a bargepole. Even those who'd usually jump at the chance of prising fabulous stones from their settings then refashioning them into new pieces had shied away. He just wished *he'd* steered clear in the first place.

Bill never liked losing face, or money, especially not on a transaction that should have made him a fortune to brag about, but instead had turned sour as a barrel of vinegar.

When Ada had first brought the box to him Bill had been elated. To his fury, he had since discovered he'd landed himself with a white elephant. The chinless wonder who'd commissioned him to pinch the necklace as a gift for his mistress had gone yellow and weaselled out of the deal as soon as he'd heard in his gentlemen's club what game Lord Mortimer was playing.

His lordship wasn't going through the usual channels of the police and insurance company to recover his property. Eddie realised he'd been an idiot not to have guessed how it all might end. Ada had told him the tale about the two lesbians at Mortimer House, and her plan to blackmail them so she could get close to the valuables. They'd both had a good laugh about it. But they weren't laughing now.

Mortimer knew he and his family would be made a laughing stock throughout London once the scandal hit the papers. So he'd kept quiet for some time and not involved any authorities. But it transpired that neither was the old boy taking the loss of his heirlooms lying down. A rumour had started spreading through the underworld that an aristocrat was out for blood following a theft of a centuries old parure of emeralds. And he was expecting to get his revenge due to a huge reward he'd put up. Bill had heard that it was many thousands of pounds; he knew even people he classed as pals would be tempted to turn him in for a few hundred quid.

Eddie Finch would. But Eddie knew that if he

squealed, Bill would find out and eventually retaliate. He was praying his other associates would also keep mum for fear of reprisal. Bill was known to have a long memory when it came to bearing grudges.

But the reward wasn't open to all comers: his lordship had apparently chosen his bloodhound but nobody could find out who it was. For that sort of money Bill knew it might be a small army coming after him.

Lord Mortimer was obviously shrewd and had guessed the housemaid who'd pinched the gems was just a pawn in a bigger game. Bill knew he was his lordship's target and even if he tried to return the jewellery – no questions asked – he might still taste Mortimer's revenge. He'd sooner the box of emeralds was found floating in the Thames than he was.

'Come on, finish yer drink and get off, will yer?' Eddie had been shifting nervously from foot to foot waiting for Bill to empty his glass.

'Tell yer what, we've been pals a good while now, Eddie, ain't we? Forget the grand. I'll cut me own throat and let you have the whole bleedin' lot for seven hundred notes.' Bill stuck out a hand for his mate to shake. 'And if you're running scared of it being a bit hot, put it by. If you sit on them emeralds for a few years till it all dies down you'll end up a millionaire. Y'know that ain't a lie . . .' He nodded at his extended hand, urging Eddie to take it and seal the deal. 'If you don't do it you'll be kicking yourself.'

Eddie averted his eyes and started shaking his head again. He heard Bill's deeply disappointed sigh, then his extended hand thumping back on the table. It curved around the tumbler and Bill sipped his whisky, refusing to budge.

When the glass next hit the table, Eddie whipped it up in a panic and tossed back the remainder himself. 'Missus is due back right now.' Eddie snapped shut the box, as though afraid Winnie might creep up on them and get a glimpse of the gigantic emeralds. 'Can't help yer on this one, Bill.'

Bill collected the box and got up. He gave Eddie a menacing stare. 'Ain't gonna forget this, Eddie. You're gonna want me before I want you, mate. You remember that when you're after a nice bit of gear to shift.'

Bill was driving slowly, scowling at the tortoiseshell box on the seat beside him as he turned the corner into Holloway Road. On looking up he recognised Jennifer Finch walking towards him. She'd spotted him too and he noticed her move closer to the kerb so he couldn't miss her as he passed by. She was fiddling with her hair, a coy little smile on her mouth, her wide eyes fixed on him.

About to ignore her pleading look and drive on, Bill's expression suddenly turned calculating and he stopped sharply. He leaned across and opened the passenger door.

'How are you doing? Jennifer's yer name, ain't it?'

Jenny ducked down to speak to him. 'Yeah, I'm Jenny,' she answered breathlessly. 'Just on me way home from work. You been round ours to see me dad?'

'Yeah, just seen him . . . So where you working, then?'

'Factory. Can I get in?' Jenny blurted out. She'd no intention of telling this sophisticated man she was packing custard powder in a factory at King's Cross, earning a pittance because her mother had made her take the first poxy job that came along after the Dobsons sacked her. She didn't want to seem boring or useless to Bill Black. She imagined he had glamorous girlfriends who worked in top places and wore furs, and jewellery like the fabulous rings she'd seen months ago on their table at home.

Jennifer wanted to be such a woman. She wanted a boyfriend like Bill, who would treat her to nice things and take her to swish places in his smart blue car. It was what she deserved and, with a thrill, she realised her ambitions might not be impossible if she could keep Bill Black interested.

'Course you can get in sweet'eart. Be my guest,' Bill drawled, moving the tortoiseshell box off the seat and onto the floor. 'Want to go for a little drive?' he suggested casually. 'If you ain't gonna get in trouble with yer mum 'n' dad, that is.'

'They won't mind,' Jenny lied. She knew she'd get the belting of her life – off both her parents – if they found out.

Bill put the car in gear and set off.

'How old are you now?' His low-lidded eyes dropped to her small bosom.

'Turned fifteen long time ago.'

'Growing up, aren't yer . . . quite the little lady . . .?'

Jenny gave him a swooning smile, smoothing her fingers over the soft leather of the seat. This vehicle was wonderful compared to the small smelly van her father owned. Eddie never used it for family outings, only to ferry his business goods back and forth. The Finch family were expected to walk or get public transport if they needed to go anywhere, including the doctor's surgery.

Jennifer had been yearning for a private meeting with Bill so she could get his full attention and let him know she liked him. She was sure he fancied her; she'd caught his subtle smiles and winks when her parents' backs were turned and she remembered fizzing with pleasure and excitement after those secret glances, much as she was doing now.

She was aware Bill was a bit of a crooked character; but then so was her father, and as far as she knew he'd avoided getting in bad trouble. At least Bill looked rich and important; in comparison Eddie just seemed a drab nobody. Jennifer reckoned Bill was different in other ways too, like being good fun, and generous with his cash. Her father was a tight-fisted bully who'd shout at Winnie if she dared to buy herself a new pinafore.

One thing Jenny vowed she'd never do was follow in her mother's footsteps and get tied to a man like her father. Bill was the sort of fellow Jenny longed to catch. She realised she needed to prove to him she wasn't a know-nothing kid just because she was a lot younger than he was. She was ready to grow up fast and do whatever he said, so long as he promised to marry her.

'Like yer job, do you?' Bill asked.

'No, hate it . . . So you've been to see me dad?' Jenny rattled off.

'Yeah . . . that's where I've been, Jennifer, to see your dad. But we didn't agree on nuthin' today, more's the pity 'cos I had some top stuff on offer.'

Jenny darted a look at Bill's dark profile. She thought he was handsome in a heavy, foreign sort of way. His hair was thick and black and quite long. He was nothing like her dad, who had wispy fair hair, receding at the front, and a spare build. Bill glanced at her, making her blush for staring.

'I saw those smashing rings you brought Dad last time

you came over,' Jennifer blurted in a whisper. 'Thought they was beautiful, I did.'

'Did yer now?' Bill purred. 'Like jewellery, do you, Jenny?'

'Course I do. I'm gonna have lots of fancy stuff like that one day when I'm rich. But I won't be selling 'em on, like my dad does. I'll be keeping 'em to wear meself, like a film star.'

Bill steered into a quiet backstreet and pulled up. He turned to Jenny. She was hardly a beauty, like her blonde sister, but she wasn't plain either. She had nice clear skin and, although her hair was more the colour of Winnie's – a nondescript light brown – it was thick and wavy. Her figure was blossoming and he could see curves forming in the right places.

'Knew you was a girl after me own heart soon as I saw you.' His voice sounded throaty with affection and he raised a finger, slowly tracing Jenny's cheek, making her eyelids flutter.

'Maybe your dad didn't sell them rings on, or if he did perhaps he lost out on the deal 'cos he seemed a bit narky when I was speaking to him earlier.' Bill paused, waiting for a comment. None came so he tried again. 'I used to get Eddie quality stuff out of West End stores but I reckon we're finished now and I won't be back this way again. Shame, 'cos I'll miss seeing you, sweet'eart.'

'You won't be back? Why not?' Jenny burst out.

'Well . . . I'm a businessman, and doing all right fer meself; but I reckon your dad might not be doing as good as me. I got the impression he's embarrassed to admit he's struggling fer cash and can't afford to have stuff off me no more.'

'He's got money!' Jenny snorted. 'I've seen it. He's mean and selfish.' She bit her lip, alarmed at her outburst.

''S'all right; you can trust me,' Bill soothed. 'I ain't ever gonna tell him what you tell me. It's private . . . just between us.' He moved closer and his stroking finger slid to tickle behind one of her small ears.

Jennifer angled her head, revelling in his caress, but when she remained quietly entranced Bill removed his hand.

'Me dad just pretends he ain't got money, and hides it so he can keep me mum short,' Jenny said, sensing Bill was waiting for such information. 'Then she goes on at me 'n' Kathy to put more in the kitty.'

Bill put a hand on Jenny's knee, squeezing gently. 'Pretty gels like you want to spend their wages on nice frocks, don't they?'

'Yeah . . .' Jenny murmured, instinctively clamping together her knees as his fingers slid upwards.

'Got a sweetheart, have you, Jenny?'

Jenny blushed and shook her head. One of the boys who did sweeping up at the factory had been whistling at her but he was younger than she was, and besides, she wasn't interested in factory hands. She wanted a man like Bill, who knew how to treat a lady.

'Reckon the boys are after you, though, ain't they? But you're a clever gel who knows there's more to life than what yer mum's got.'

'Never ending up like her,' Jenny vowed, top lip writhing. 'Feel sorry for her putting up with him.'

'So you don't reckon yer dad's struggling money-wise? Perhaps it's just me he don't like. Perhaps he knows I've had me eye on you for a while.'

Jenny's complexion turned pink again and she dimpled in pleasure, feeling more confident. 'Oh, he's got money,' she said. 'What's in that?' She nodded at the tortoiseshell box by her feet.

'Take a look, if you like,' Bill invited.

Jenny swooped on the box and with an excited smile slowly lifted the lid.

'Is this what me dad didn't want off you today?' she croaked, having spent a full minute staring in wonderment at the sumptuous emeralds and diamonds nestling on velvet.

'Yeah, that's it,' Bill returned insouciantly. 'Only wanted seven hundred for 'em 'n' all. They're worth a lot more but I thought I'd give Eddie first refusal, being as we've done good business in the past.' He took the box from Jenny's clinging grip and closed it. 'Never mind . . . I know somebody else who'll rip me arm off to have 'em. Make a fortune out of them, the lucky bleeder will.'

'Wish I could have 'em,' Jenny murmured wistfully. 'Never seen anything so lovely, 'cept in portraits hanging on the wall in big old houses. Me mum took me 'n' Kathy once to a mansion when we was on holiday. Going all up the stairs was pictures of ladies without eyelashes wearing weird old dresses. They had on necklaces as big as that.'

'Can see you know yer onions, Jenny,' Bill praised her. 'Reckon you'd be a natural at business 'cos you've got an eye for quality. When you get a bit older perhaps you should think about taking over from yer old man. I can promise you there's good money to be had.' He leaned closer and gave her a little peck on the cheek. 'Better'n working in a factory, eh?' he whispered before angling her face towards him and kissing her full on the lips. He felt her eager little pant and gave her a quick taste of his tongue before sitting back in his seat.

'Now . . . better get you home or you're gonna be in trouble, and we can't have that, can we?' He slanted her a smile. 'Told you things today perhaps I shouldn't have. But I reckon me and you are friends, ain't we, Jenny?'

Jennifer nodded, beaming.

'I don't tell everyone me trade secrets, y'know, so I reckon you must be special.'

'You're special to me. And you can trust me . . . swear,' Jenny whispered, eyes aglow. She inclined closer, hoping he might be tempted to kiss her again.

Bill leaned in and touched his lips to hers, watching her face take on a rapturous expression as her eyes closed.

'You've got to come back again,' Jenny whimpered, clinging to his hand to try to prolong their conversation. But he continued jamming the car into gear. 'When will I see you otherwise?'

'Well . . . when you're more grown up . . .' Bill let off the handbrake.

'I ain't a kid, and I'm sick of working in that poxy factory.'

'Can see you ain't a kid, sweet'eart,' Bill said, chucking her under the chin and giving her body a long appreciative look. 'You save a bit of money out of yer wages and who knows, in a few years' time you might be ready to do a bit of business with me. Course, it's the classy stuff like them big emeralds where the real money is. But never mind, yer dad didn't want 'em.' He shook his head. 'He's gonna regret not buying them, y'know. Double his money easy as anything, he could.'

Bill drove back towards Holloway Road.

'Better not take me right home,' Jenny blurted as soon as she saw landmarks she recognised. If anybody reported to her parents that she'd been seen getting out of a man's car she'd be flayed alive.

'Got yer,' Bill said with a grin. 'Don't want either of us getting into trouble, do we?'

He pulled over to the kerb. 'Tell you what. I reckon I might have a deal to do on Friday over this way. Could meet you just round the corner here, if you like, and we can have another little chat about things. Say five o'clock. If I ain't here, you'll know there weren't a deal to be done; and if you ain't here, I'll know you've got better things to do.'

'*I'll* be here,' Jenny vowed solemnly. 'I reckon me dad's mad not to have that jewellery.' She was furious with her father for cutting his ties with this man because she had a feeling that Bill would be too busy with important people to meet her later that week.

'He'll regret it,' Bill confirmed sadly. 'But I ain't one to crow over somebody making big mistakes. Just make sure you don't make big mistakes, eh, Jenny?' He nodded at the car door. 'Off yer toddle then, sweet'eart. Might see y'around . . .'

Jenny seemed reluctant to go. '*I'd* buy them emeralds off you if I could.'

Bill's features slowly transformed into a foxy smile as he glanced at the box on the floor. He wanted rid of it. She was putty in his hands. Perhaps he'd found a safe haven for the emeralds for a while. It was certainly a better option than chucking the box off Tower Bridge. With any luck, if he gave her the jewellery she might feel obliged to plunder Eddie's savings to pay him for it.

144

Bill suspected Jennifer knew where the money was stashed. She was a little minx itching to break free, and to do that she'd need more cash than she'd get from a factory job. He reckoned she'd already made it her business to locate her escape fund.

'Tell you what, Jenny,' he said, all magnanimous. 'I'm gonna let you have the jewellery on trust 'cos I reckon you're fair and'll find a way to divvy up eventually. You know same as I do when your dad comes to his senses he's gonna be grateful he's got a clever gel like you fer a daughter.' Bill collected the box and put it on her lap.

Jennifer audibly swallowed as she stared at him open-mouthed. 'You'll let me have it fer nuthin'?'

Bill squeezed her knee. 'Not fer nuthin', is it, sweet'eart? I know you'll come across with what's owing soon as you can. Now you ain't gonna wear any of it or anything silly like that, are you?' He tapped the side of his nose.

She shook her head in mute amazement. 'Wouldn't ever do that. It's our secret, ain't it?'

'That's right. And don't ferget, sometimes all it takes is a nudge to put daft sods right. Not mentioning no names, o' course . . .' Again Bill tapped his nose. He knew Jennifer would never let on to Eddie – or Winnie, for that matter – about their meeting today.

'I don't know if I should . . .' Jennifer was beginning to comprehend Bill's hints. He wanted her to steal her dad's nest egg to pay for the box of jewellery. She was sure he was correct in thinking her dad had missed out on a bargain. She felt compelled to take another look at the fabulous jewels. She lifted the lid of the box and gawped at the treasures within. Her indecision melted away. 'I'll see what I can do, promise I will,' she croaked.

145

'Thank you.' She raised huge eyes to Bill's face. 'I won't ever let you down 'cos I know you trust me.'

Jennifer sucked in a breath that took her higher in her seat and lit her face with pride. She felt grown up – important – and knew this was a monumental moment for her. Her life was about to change for ever, for the better.

CHAPTER TWELVE

'You're getting a big girl, Sally, and too heavy for your poor old auntie's arms.' Lucy put her three-year-old niece down on the rug but the child immediately held out her hands for another cuddle.

'She's a bruiser, all right,' Beth said, fondly eyeing her chubby little girl. 'George has got to stop feeding her biscuits. He will spoil her.'

'Easy to understand why he does,' Lucy said, tickling Sally under the chin. 'She's a beauty. Gonna break some hearts, this one.'

'Sit down and drink your tea or it'll go cold.' Beth pointed at the table, urging her sister towards a chair. With her other hand she continued rocking a pram holding Joey, her eight-month-old son.

'Leave Auntie alone,' Beth chided as her daughter tried to climb on Lucy's lap the moment she settled down. 'Play with your dollies.'

Sally obediently toddled off to pull a few toys from the settee, then kneeled on the rug to line them up in front of a spitting fire protected by a high mesh guard.

It was March and the weather still sharp enough to necessitate burning logs.

Beth and her husband, George, rented the ground floor of a Victorian house a few streets away from Campbell Road. In comparison to the decrepit rows of properties in the Bunk this unremarkable terrace seemed in splendid condition.

Beth's home was spotlessly clean, and of an adequate size for a couple with two young children. It comprised a bay-windowed front sitting room, two back rooms used as bedrooms, and a kitchenette behind which sat an outside privy with a tin bath hanging on a hook. There was a small rear garden with a patch of lawn for Sally to play on, and behind the coal bunker, hidden from view from the back windows, was a narrow border where George's spring vegetables were already making a show.

Confident that her son had nodded off to sleep, Beth tiptoed away from the pram to take the chair opposite Lucy at a compact oak table. 'You look browned off,' she said bluntly, having noticed her younger sister frowning at her tea rather than drinking it. 'Penny for 'em.'

Lucy gave a wry smile. 'Nothing really . . . just wish I could turn up a decent job 'cos Mum's always chewing me ears off about the one I've got.'

Lucy had told both Beth and Alice that she was working in a disreputable club. At the same time their youngest sister had warned them that Matilda was up in arms about it.

Lucy had written to Sophy to let her know she'd found work in London as a waitress. But she hadn't elaborated. Lucy knew Sophy would not gossip;

148

nevertheless she didn't want any of her old colleagues at Lockley Grange to overhear her sister and brother-in-law discussing how sour things had turned for her. Lucy had quit Southend in high spirits and was feeling daft now for having easily dismissed Sophy's warning that she might not find a good job as quickly as she'd imagined.

As Joey made a mewling sound, Beth got up with a sigh and started wheeling the pram to and fro. 'Think he's got colic,' she muttered while sending a concerned glance at her glum-faced sister.

Beth couldn't deny having been shocked at first to think of Little Luce working in the Cuckoo Club alongside the likes of Connie Whitton. But having ruminated on it for a while Beth had taken the philosophical view that Lucy was nobody's fool and wouldn't allow herself to be pushed into doing anything against her will. It was a job. And those were increasingly hard to find. Beth knew that if she were in Lucy's place she too would have scraped the barrel for a wage packet to ease the burden on their mother's small pension. Sophy and Alice would have acted the same. Of course, none of them would go as far as Connie Whitton was prepared to in order to pay the rent . . .

None of the Keiver girls was a sponger. From the age of about eight each of them had done chores for coppers. They'd spend Saturdays cleaning doorsteps or rubbing brasses for families that lived in respectable neighbouring streets and could afford such help.

Having left school as soon as was possible, Sophy, Alice, Beth and Lucy had all gone straight into full-time employment. But the luxury of picking a suitable job was not easily come by nowadays. Even well-to-do people were cutting down on domestic help now the Depression was a fact of everyone's life. Pride and preference had to be put aside when there weren't enough jobs to go round.

'Have some of the men at the club tried to take liberties with you?' Beth demanded, anger stirring inside at the very idea of her youngest sister being touched up by a lecher.

Lucy shook her head. 'Some have a go at pushing their luck, but if you tell 'em no, they'll just try it on with one of the other girls. A few of them are quite nice fellows, it's just . . . I feel uncomfortable being there at all, wearing that silly outfit. It ain't me, doing that sort of work, Beth.'

'Something'll turn up for you,' Beth said kindly. 'How about if you contact this Rory you used to work with and ask him to put in a good word for you to get your old job back? Then you might not need a new reference 'cos they already know you.'

'Couldn't go back there . . . not after what went on . . .'

Lucy hadn't related the whole tale of woe that had occurred at Mortimer House. She'd promised Rory she wouldn't repeat what he'd told her so couldn't break her word, even to trusted family members.

But she had told Beth – and her mother, of course, who'd been agog with curiosity to find out the identity of the handsome fellow who'd given her a ride in a posh car – that she'd bumped into an old colleague from Mortimer House. Lucy had explained that Rory Jackson had tracked her down to let her know that the nasty cow who'd taken her job had since left. And the Mortimers and the staff all thought it was good riddance to bad rubbish.

On hearing about it, Matilda's immediate response had been that her daughter now had the upper hand. The others were bound to be feeling awkward, she'd gleefully said, so Lucy should take advantage and apply for her old job.

Canny as her mother's advice was, Lucy knew she couldn't follow it. The Mortimers and her old colleagues certainly might be feeling a bit guilty that she'd been ousted from her job but they wouldn't thank her for showing her face again. Unfortunately, she'd been entangled in a tragedy when she'd been demoted so Audrey could take over as Mrs Boyd's assistant. If Lucy returned to work at the house her presence would be a constant bitter reminder to one and all of the dreadful goings-on.

'Mum's been writing letters to Reg, y'know.' Lucy decided it was time for a change of subject; she also wanted to let Beth know that Matilda hadn't got over the man she'd lived with for years.

Beth peered in the pram at her son to make sure he'd dozed off, then came and quickly sat down at the table. 'Are you sure about that?' She frowned in disbelief. 'Mum told me she didn't have his address in Ireland.' She paused. 'Besides, I don't think she's ever written a letter before in her life. Even when Dad was fighting in France she got Alice or me to do that for her.'

The Keiver girls knew that neither of their parents had had proper schooling. Jack Keiver had been keen for his children to do their lessons so they wouldn't be as disadvantaged as he and his wife. Matilda's attitude to her daughters' education had veered towards considering it an obstacle to the girls getting full-time jobs quickly enough. Filling the kitty to keep a roof over a family's head was a priority for most Bunk wives. It was the reason Alice had lied about her age and started work in a factory before she'd turned fourteen.

'I'm not sure if Mum's actually *sent* any letters yet. I've not seen an envelope addressed to Reg. All I've come across are screwed-up notes. I wouldn't have flattened them out and looked at them if I'd realised they were so personal,' Lucy explained sheepishly. 'Mum had left them on top of the stove, probably 'cos she was going to burn them when she got it alight.' Lucy chuckled. 'Her spelling hasn't improved, bless her, but I understood what she was trying to say. If she'd sent them I expect Reg would've got the gist of it too.' She sighed. 'She's missing him badly, and for all her bluster wants him back.'

'He's been gone months so I don't reckon there's much chance of that, do you?' Beth frowned. 'Perhaps she's missing his contribution to the rent more than him.'

'Can't blame her for that.' Lucy paused. 'I was going to offer to write to him for her, but then she'd know I'd read her letters.'

'Best keep shtoom on it and see what happens.' Beth swung her rosy-cheeked daughter back from where she'd been roasting in front of the flaming fire and plonked her on the settee to cool down.

'Another cuppa?' she asked Lucy. At that moment little Joey let out a howl.

'Best be off and leave you to get on,' Lucy answered wryly.

Having given her niece a kiss on the forehead and blown another towards the pram for her nephew, Lucy let herself out into a blustery March afternoon and headed home. A sigh escaped her on remembering she was on shift at the club that evening; not that the prospect of spending evenings cooped up with her mother in their rotten rooms was any more appealing.

Yet . . . much as Lucy found depressing the thought of travelling to Piccadilly and not returning till the early hours of the morning, she couldn't deny that on occasions the club's atmosphere could be thrilling.

Only last week a whisper had gone around that a famous actor had entered the club. Even when pointed out to her he hadn't been recognisable to Lucy, yet she became as infected with excitement as the other girls. He'd seemed smaller than she'd expected him to be, but it had been wonderful to know a film star seen on screen at the flicks was a real person.

On other evenings, when she was rushed off her feet and every customer seemed to moan about something, Lucy vowed to take the first job she got offered at the labour exchange.

Lucy and Connie were strolling out of the Hornsey Road baths, having spent a leisurely time soaking in tubs and carrying on a conversation across the echoing sound of running water and high-pitched female voices. After an hour they'd emerged from the steamy atmosphere hot and pink cheeked.

It was a warm Saturday in early April and they were contemplating whether to take a look at the stalls on Chapel Street market. Connie suddenly stopped and walked backwards to peer into a side road they'd just passed. On realising she'd been talking to thin air Lucy turned around then went to find out what had caught her friend's attention.

'I *thought* I recognised that bloke down there. And blow me, ain't that Jennifer Finch with him?' Connie sounded shocked. 'Bleedin' hell! I bet her mum don't know she's hanging about with *him*!'

'Who is he?' Lucy frowned at a couple in the distance standing at the side of a dark saloon car, apparently deep in conversation. It was indeed Jennifer Finch and the swarthy-looking fellow with her appeared to be quite a lot older than she was.

'Bill Black's his name. Well, that's what he told me, but bloke's like that don't always tell a gel the truth. He used to come in the Cuckoo Club quite a bit but I've not seen him there for some time. He's bad news, that one.'

Lucy gave Connie a glance.

'Only once or twice,' Connie confessed with a mischievous smile. 'Paid up all right, he did, but I heard off some of the other gels that he's a wrong'un, and violent with it if he gets crossed. So I made me excuses from then on 'cos I was seeing quite a lot of Ralph at the time.' She chuckled, nodding in Bill Black's direction. 'I made sure *he* never knew I was involved with a copper in case he thought I was a grass. Didn't fancy getting me face bashed in. Bill weren't bothered anyhow when I started avoiding him in the Cuckoo Club. He just turned his attention to somebody else, like they all do.'

Lucy knew that Connie had had a casual relationship with a policeman for many years. She knew too that Ralph Franks had once worked the beat around the Bunk area of Islington. But that had been when she was a little girl. Constable Franks was long gone now, having transferred to a different neighbourhood. Currently he was stationed in central London and Lucy knew that Connie sometimes met up with him after finishing her shift at the club.

154

'Don't know what Bill thinks he's playing at. Wouldn't've thought even he would stoop so low as to go after a kid Jennifer's age.' Connie shook her head in disgust. 'He must be twenty-five at least, and bet yer life Jennifer ain't yet turned sixteen.'

'Might be innocent enough,' Lucy pointed out. 'According to me mum her father ducks 'n' dives with dodgy characters. Perhaps he's a pal of Eddie's and she just stopped to say hello.'

They glanced back at the couple in time to find Lucy's theory proven false. Jennifer was on tiptoes, her arms about Bill's neck, kissing him on the lips.

The passionate display drew a whistle of foreboding from Connie. 'It's gonna end in tears,' she said beneath her breath.

Lucy could only murmur agreement. Winifred Finch had a high opinion of herself and her family. If the woman discovered what her daughter was up to Lucy reckoned Jenny would get her marching orders, and a toe up the backside to hurry her on her way. What Mr Finch might make of it all was anybody's guess.

Lucy knew nothing about Eddie Finch other than what she'd heard her mother say about him. Matilda certainly hadn't been complimentary. In fact Lucy had got the impression her mother thought him a nasty so-and-so and she felt sorry for Winnie being married to him. Considering the antagonism between the two women, Lucy had concluded that Mr Finch must be a horrible man if her mother preferred Mrs Finch.

'Wouldn't want to see that poor little cow come a bad cropper listening to his lies,' Connie said. 'I know Bill had a regular girlfriend 'cos a few times he brought her to the club with him.'

Connie wasn't the sort of woman to relish others' misfortunes. And, much as Winnie Finch looked down on her, treating her as though she was something she'd stepped in if they passed in the street, Connie wouldn't like to see the Finch family suffer if a quiet word could avert it. 'Perhaps I should set Jennifer straight on Bill; might not be too late,' she said with a frown.

'Well, now's your chance,' Lucy murmured. 'She's heading this way.' Lucy had watched Bill Black get in his car and set off in the opposite direction. Jennifer was now strolling towards them, and as she came closer, Lucy realised she was looking like the cat that had got the cream.

'Oh, hello, Lucy,' Jennifer blurted, having caught sight of the two women hovering at the junction with Hornsey Road. It was the first time they'd chanced upon one another since the stupid bust-up over the sweet shop job. But her sister, Kathy, had told her that she'd made a point of speaking to Lucy Keiver and she hadn't seemed too bothered about being sacked by Mrs Dobson.

It was the sight of Connie Whitton that was causing Jenny to blush and feel uneasy. She knew her mother might froth at the mouth if she found out she'd spoken to 'that brassy old bag', as she called Connie.

Jenny had always thought Connie quite a friendly, well-dressed woman. Today she was wearing a fashionable frock that Jenny had seen in a shop window, and she longed to own such a garment herself. In Jenny's opinion her mother was probably envious of Connie because she was lively and pretty, whereas Winnie looked like a dog-tired drudge from morning till night. Besides, Winnie never had a good word to say about anybody, especially those who lived in the Bunk.

'Saw you a moment ago with Bill Black,' Connie said airily. 'One of yer dad's pals, is he?'

Jennifer turned scarlet. She hadn't realised they'd been observed together. When Bill had pulled up she'd worried that it was a bit too close to home. The fear of one of her parents spotting them together was always at the back of her mind. But he'd said they were in a quiet backstreet and out of sight of prying eyes.

'Me dad does know him,' Jenny mumbled, averting her face.

'Not as well as you do though, eh?' Connie said, nudging Jennifer's arm.

Jenny understood Connie's hint and whipped up her head, about to deny everything. But the older woman's sly smile was infectious and involuntarily Jenny mirrored it. 'He's me boyfriend,' she whispered proudly. Although Jenny desperately wanted to keep from her parents the news, she was dying for other people – especially other women – to know she'd caught herself a sophisticated handsome man.

'Told you that, has he? That he's yer boyfriend?' Connie asked gently.

'Course . . .' Jenny said, feeling deflated. Something in Connie's attitude was troubling her. 'How do you know him?' she demanded suspiciously.

'Bill gets about a bit,' Connie said, her expression kindly. 'And you want to remember that, Jennifer. He's best avoided. I expect if yer mum and dad knew you was kissing him in broad daylight . . . well, the least they'd do is tell you the same.' Connie knew Winnie would explode even if the fellow Jennifer was knocking about with were decent and a similar age to her daughter.

'Don't care what they say.' Jenny cocked her head

157

defiantly. She looked the two women up and down. The glimmer of pity in their eyes made her bristle. They were both just jealous of her because she'd hooked a man like Bill. 'Don't care what you think neither . . .' A moment later she realised that wasn't quite true. 'You ain't thinking of telling me mum you've seen us?' she gabbled out.

'Telling you fer yer own good, love,' Connie said shortly. 'Don't say you wasn't warned when he drops you in big trouble then clears off.'

Jenny licked her lips then whipped on by, head high, a smile skewing her lips.

But her smirk needed a boost before she'd got a few yards. She knew Bill was getting impatient with her. He wanted her to pay for the box of jewellery and was hinting that she should use Eddie's money to buy it. But Jenny knew if she did steal from her father her bridges were burned and there'd be no way back home. Presently, she liked the way things were: it was exciting having Bill as her secret boyfriend, and knowing she had hidden away beautiful jewellery she could wear when she was on her own at home. She knew Bill wanted more from her. He'd said he could find her work in lots of top stores so she could pay him for the jewellery that way. He'd told her he knew girls who were making a good living, but he never quite told her what they did when she asked. Neither had he offered to let her live with him if she left home. All he said was that he'd see her all right on that score . . .

Something was holding her back from cutting ties with her family although she'd had enough of the lot of them – even her sister, Kathy, who was always preaching to her about knuckling down to a job so she could put by for the future. But she'd miss Tom. She'd grown very fond of her little brother since he'd tried to protect her from being beaten by her father.

Bill drove back towards south London scowling. He'd been banking on Jennifer finally bringing him Finchie's savings this afternoon. He'd been sure he'd got her wrapped right around his little finger but his insinuations were falling on deaf ears. She was playing dumb. And he didn't think she was, so he was starting to worry that she might be playing a game of her own.

Once a week for over a month he'd been meeting the silly little cow in backstreets and giving her a kiss and cuddle in the hope she'd pay up. He'd even hinted he'd take five hundred at first, then the rest later if she could manage that, but she simply clung to him, like a limpet. He was determined not to lose on the deal. He'd have Jennifer working with Ada and the other girls if necessary so she could clear her debt to him in stolen goods.

Bill nodded to himself, feeling a bit more chipper; there was always a way round things.

CHAPTER THIRTEEN

'Blow me down, don't see nuthin' of Bill Black for ages, now it looks like I'm in danger of tripping over him.'

Connie nudged Lucy, nodding at the doorway as a well-built man stepped over the threshold of the Cuckoo Club with a pretty young blonde on his arm.

Lucy deftly picked up a loaded silver salver as the barman shoved it towards her across polished mahogany. She turned round carefully to see Molly Warner leading a couple towards a table close to the dance floor. It did indeed look to be the same fellow she'd seen with Jennifer Finch last week.

'Is that his girlfriend?' Lucy asked, balancing the tray and straightening the linen cloth draped over her arm.

Connie shrugged. 'Ain't the woman I used to see him with. Her name was Betty, but she's probably had enough of Bill's roving eye. She was more his age and had dark hair. That one over there don't look much older than Jennifer.'

Lucy had to agree that Bill's companion could have

been a lot younger than he. Nevertheless, she was glamorously turned out and wearing plenty of makeup.

'Not seen *him* in here before.' Again Connie's vigilant eyes had darted to a new arrival. 'Cor! Hope he's gonna be a regular, 'cos I wouldn't say no if *he* asked.'

Connie's dirty chuckle encouraged Lucy to take a look and immediately she understood her colleague's enthusiasm. Boris was greeting, with theatrical sweeping gestures, a tall dark-haired gentleman. The stranger appeared distinguished and attractive, but Lucy knew that good looks were no indication of good character. They could veil very black hearts.

Her late uncle, Jimmy Wild, might have been a looker but he was also a devil, so Lucy and her sisters had regularly heard their mother declare when they were growing up. And Matilda had been entitled to judge. When the fiend had committed suicide he'd tried to murder Matilda by dragging her with him as he plunged from a first-floor window. Even though Jimmy had been dead a while just the thought of him could stir profound anger and hatred in Lucy's guts.

The dreadful day that she and Sophy had got word their mother had been involved in an accident and wasn't expected to survive would remain branded on her memory. They'd left Lockley Grange that same afternoon and travelled home, sobbing on the train, expecting to prepare for their mother's funeral.

But Matilda had pulled through. She'd said afterwards that she'd go to her maker in her own time, not when it suited a scumbag like Jimmy Wild.

While reflecting on wickedly handsome men Lucy had been staring at the stranger. She snapped her eyes away, realising he appeared amused to have caught her at it.

'Damn!' Connie chuckled beneath her breath. 'Wish I'd been a bit closer to him. I'd've made sure to elbow that lot aside.' A trio of hostesses had simultaneously bolted towards the newcomer in the hope they'd be picked to serve him. Vera Markham appeared victorious in the race.

'Girls! Serve those drinks before fizz gone.' Boris Papadopolous had come over, huffing his disapproval at seeing them standing idly together with trays of cocktails. 'Too much chat . . . you and Luce always chatting.'

'That's 'cos we're the only two who work here who ain't at each other's throats,' Connie cheekily returned. But she sashayed away from the bar towards a cloth-covered table, laid with glittering crystal and silverware, around which sat a party of middle-aged gentlemen. A moment later Lucy was heading towards Mr Randall, stationed as usual by the windows, to serve him his Scotch and soda.

Boris gave a philosophical shrug as he watched them go to work. He couldn't deny that what Connie had said was true. Although he'd never admit as much he appreciated that Connie Whitton and Lucy Keiver were friends and worked well together as a team. At times he fretted that the rivalry between the hostesses over men and tips might be affecting his profits. Gentlemen didn't want to see sulky faces, although a few of the vulgar fellows enjoyed watching catfights when girls rolled on the floor displaying knickers and stocking tops. Boris thanked the Lord that scraps in the dining room were few and far between.

Punch-ups in the restroom were another matter. He had forced his bulk between battling employees to separate them on numerous occasions. When off shift the girls were less inclined to keep their lips buttoned and their tempers in check.

Lucy spent a few minutes passing the time of day with Mr Randall, her attention flashing intermittently through the dark window to a neon-lit street scene below. He was a pleasant gentleman who reminded her of her old boss Mr Lockley in manner and looks. Having sipped his drink, smacked his lips and wiped his white moustache carefully with his napkin, he dug in a pocket and produced a silver sixpence, which Lucy graciously accepted as a tip. A moment later she began weaving between tables to fetch his roast beef dinner.

Her eyes were drawn to the stranger as she passed his table and she hesitated when he raised a finger beckoning her. Feeling oddly apprehensive she approached him with a smile pinned to her lips.

'What do you recommend?' he asked.

Lucy glanced at the menu he'd turned towards her. She was aware that Vera Markham had seated him and considered him hers for the evening. 'I'll find your waitress, sir, and get her to tell you about tonight's specials.'

'I'm asking you.'

Lucy recognised a hint of authority and an accent that reminded her of Reg. But whereas her mother's fiancé had a coarse voice, this man's Irish brogue was smooth and cultured.

From a corner of an eye Lucy saw Vera rushing over. She knew there were unofficial rules about poaching other girls' clients and she'd no intention of causing ructions. She was happy to bow out and leave them to it.

'Just fetching your whiskey, sir,' Vera said with a glimmering glance at Lucy. 'Have you decided what to order?'

Lucy stepped away, then swiftly turned and went over to the bar. Connie was filling her tray with fresh drinks and chuckling quietly to herself.

'Nice work,' she praised. 'He's still got his eye on you.'

'Well, he can take it off 'cos he'll get the same answer as all the rest.' Despite sounding casual, Lucy felt breathless as though she'd run instead of walked away from him.

Bill wasn't a possessive man and usually he wouldn't have minded any of his girls eyeing up somebody else while out with him. Apart from Betty. He'd have slapped her down for doing it.

He was always on the lookout for business and he knew there was good money to be made from a horny gentleman with a fancy for a young woman. Unfortunately, Mavis was on heat but the Irish fellow a few tables away – who Bill had heard the waitress call Mr Napier – looked cold as ice. Bill was taking Napier's lack of interest in Mavis as a personal insult and in turn he was feeling irritated with his dinner companion.

He was starting to wish he'd chosen to bring Ada out this evening with him. She was always more appreciative of his attention. She'd sulk if she found out she'd been overlooked but Bill had known Ada would expect more than dinner from him. She'd expect him to service her all night. At least Mavis would roll over and go to sleep when he was finished and too pissed to perform again. And tonight he fancied a good drink.

'Flash yer fanny at him, like the waitresses,' Bill snapped petulantly. 'You might have better luck attracting his attention. He seems more taken with every one of them than you, gel.'

Mavis reddened and snatched up her drink. 'What you on about?'

'You been staring at that paddy since he sat down, and getting ignored for yer trouble.'

'Ain't staring at nobody. Where's me dinner? We ordered a while ago . . .'

'How you doing? Connie, ain't it?' Bill had transferred his attention to the waitress walking by, with every intention of riling Mavis. He'd teach her not to flirt unless he said she could. 'Not seen you in some while, luv. Yet you don't look no older, do you?'

'Not been in for some while, have you?' Connie returned. Despite knowing his compliment was simply old flannel she was flattered. 'If you had been in, Mr Black, you'd have seen me. I've been right here all the time.'

'Remember me name, do you?' Bill sat back, puffed up with conceit. He placed a rewarding hand on the back of her knee then stroked upwards. His fingers found warm silky skin under a suspender.

Mavis's eyes flicked at Bill's fondling hand and her mouth tightened into a crimson bud. But she knew not to question him on anything he did. 'Any chance of getting me dinner, is there? I'm starving.'

'I'll hurry it along for you,' Connie answered agreeably. She gave Bill a subtle smile on moving away. She remembered he'd been a run-of-the-mill punter. Quick and rough, as most were; they'd no need to be anything else. But he'd paid up, no arguments. And she was short this week because Podge Peters had insisted on having all Mr Keane's back rent. Apologetically, Podge had told her that the landlord was going to check over his books before meeting his accountant.

'Thought you were seeing Ralph later,' Lucy said as she crossed paths with Connie in the clanging corridor outside the kitchens. She'd just emerged, pink cheeked, from the steamy atmosphere with two lobster dinners. For about an hour they'd been nipping to and fro without a word or glance passing between them. But Lucy had witnessed the incident between Bill and Connie and she'd worked with her friend for long enough. Such sly behaviour usually ended up with Connie disappearing with the fellow at the end of her shift.

'Don't reckon it'll come to nuthin'.' Connie pulled a face. 'His girlfriend's got a gob on her and I don't reckon she'll be easy to shake off. Course, not all of 'em want to shake the girlfriend off; the more the merrier, if you know what I mean . . .' She laughed as an expression of disgust flitted over Lucy's youthful features.

'Lucy . . . Lucy . . .' Connie sighed mockingly. 'You've got a lot to learn, my gel.'

'Yeah, and how to get meself a decent job's top of me list right now.' Lucy's smile was sour as she brushed past, balancing a dinner plate in each hand.

Connie followed her and whispered in her ear, 'His name's Sean Napier. Just thought you might like to know that.'

Lucy hesitated; she'd no need to ask Connie who she meant. She'd sensed the Irishman watching her on several occasions. 'Why would I want to know that?'

'Perhaps 'cos he asked Vera what your name was,' Connie grinned. 'Put her nose right out of joint, you have. Couldn't have made it plainer who he's keen on, could he?'

Lucy carried on out into the dining room. Immediately she cast a glance in the direction of Sean Napier's table and saw it vacant. She was uneasily aware of feeling disappointed rather than relieved. He'd been in for a dinner and nothing more. He hadn't even been interested in the entertainment.

By the time the jazz band started playing at eleven o'clock, most of the customers' meals had been served. The waitresses were then able to look at the rota to see when they could take their fifteen-minute dinner breaks.

Lucy blew a wispy damp curl off her brow as she read the notice pinned to the wall outside the kitchen door. She saw that in half an hour's time she was timetabled to have her break with Molly.

Having placed their hot plates of roast beef and vegetables on the table, Lucy and Molly pulled out hard-backed chairs and sat down. Simultaneously they eased off their shoes then leaned back, eyes closed, to rest quietly. After ten minutes, when her food had cooled down, Molly sat forward with a sigh, opened a napkin and started putting the beef and potatoes into it.

Lucy watched her from beneath lowered lids that felt too heavy to open fully. She'd noticed before that Molly ate very little and wrapped up most of her meal to take home with her . . . as she did herself.

'Do you share yours?' Lucy asked.

'What's it to you?' Molly snapped. They'd never become friendly, despite having worked together at the club for some months.

Lucy shrugged, sitting forward. 'Just making conversation, that's all.' She reached for her bag and withdrew a small china basin into which she put the contents of her own plate. Then she put a clean hanky on the top and carefully placed it back in her bag.

'You share yours as well, do you?' Molly asked brusquely.

'Yeah, with me mum. Live at home with her, see.' She glanced at Molly. She looked to be her senior by some years but not as old as Connie.

'This is for me little boy,' Molly blurted. 'Me mum minds him for me. He'll have this tomorrow.' She gave a faint smile. 'He always looks forward to Thursday morning after I've done me shift. Knows it's beef, see, Thursday. His favourite's beef.'

Lucy smiled. 'How old is he?'

'Seven.'

'Your husband on night shift as well?'

'No husband.' Molly got up, went to the jug and bowl and began sluicing her hands of gravy stains.

'Sorry . . .' Lucy said, feeling awkward. 'Wasn't prying.'

''S'All right; ain't bothered no more who knows I'm on me own.' Molly dried her hands on a scrap of towel. 'Prefer it that way. Men are a pain in the arse at the best of times.' With that she combed her titian hair, reapplied her lipstick, picked up her empty plate, and went out.

After a moment, Lucy followed the same ritual of washing, tidying and clearing up used crockery and cutlery, feeling relieved that she had just an hour to go before she could head home.

'Oh, there he is.' Connie had spotted Ralph Franks across the road.

Lucy had clattered down the stairs from the club behind her friend and peered around Connie to see a policeman standing under a gas lamp on the opposite

168

pavement. He looked to be very officially checking his watch for the time, then he began scribbling in a notebook. He moved on immediately, walking around the corner as though continuing on his beat.

'He's clocked me; he always pretends he ain't.' Connie gave a chirpy laugh.

Ralph and Connie never met out in the open; both knew it wouldn't do their respective reputations any good to be seen together. The Cuckoo Club attracted the sort of clientele that might just have come out of prison or was soon due a spell inside. The last thing Connie wanted was for her tips to dry up because she'd been seen cosying up to a copper.

Connie gave Lucy's arm a squeeze. 'G'night, then, Lucy. Get going or you'll miss yer bus home.' With that she set off at a leisurely stroll in the direction Ralph had taken.

Lucy never liked walking alone at night despite the fact that the area – even at past one o'clock in the morning – was crowded and brightly lit. A lot of the people out and about at such a time were drunk, and the men seemed to assume all lone women were tarts keen to have their attention.

Connie often went home in her short waitress uniform when she couldn't be bothered to change. Lucy never did. She left hers behind in the cupboard. The staff were expected to take care of their own outfits but rather than launder hers at home – and risk her mother getting a scandalised look at it – Lucy used the kitchen sink at the club to wash it. There was an old flat iron kept in the storeroom cupboard and she'd arrive for her shift early and press the dress and pinafore. Her mother would have a fit if she saw her wearing lipstick so that too was removed before she returned to Campbell Road.

As she turned quickly in the direction of the bus stop, Lucy pulled a hankie from a pocket and scrubbed her mouth clean with it while walking.

The flare of a match in shadows made her start in alarm.

'Want a cigarette?'

Lucy's tongue flicked to moisten her dry mouth as Sean Napier stepped out a few yards in front of her, cigarette smouldering in a hand.

'Don't smoke . . . thanks . . .' She intended to hurry on by but he seemed to be blocking the whole width of pavement.

'Don't want anything else from you either.' Lucy avoided looking at him. When she'd spoken to him briefly in the club earlier she'd tried to escape his penetrating blue-eyed gaze. 'I've had me wages and that's enough for me. Speak to Boris . . . or one of the other girls.'

'Yeah, I will speak to Boris . . . he needs to sack that chef.' His drawl was husky and amused, and he smiled before sticking the cigarette in his mouth.

Lucy relaxed slightly, huffing a laugh. They'd had several complaints that evening about the overcooked beef. 'He's a relief cook,' she explained. 'The regular one'll be back at the weekend. Pierre had to go off to a funeral out in the sticks somewhere.'

'I'll come back then . . . give the other feller a try.'

Finally, Lucy glanced directly at a lean profile and a curve of thin lips shaded by the brim of his hat. 'Right . . . well . . .' She cleared her throat. She was unused to dealing with sophisticated men other than in the confines of the club. In there it seemed so much easier to be flip and witty when turning them down.

'Do you want a lift home?' He angled his head, indicating a large vehicle parked at the kerb.

'No!' Lucy remembered her manners. He was being polite, after all. 'Thanks all the same,' she added.

It was the first time she had been accosted outside. Customers seated at dining tables had frequently propositioned her. But Connie had told the truth: if you rebuffed them most of them were happy to turn their attention to girls who were willing.

'Why do you work there?'

'It's a job.'

'But you're not suited to it, are you?'

'I'll take that as a compliment,' Lucy snapped under her breath, stepping into the road to get past him.

'It was meant as a compliment.' He stepped off the kerb too.

'Look, I've told you no.' Lucy sensed her voice sounded high and panicky, and she was annoyed with herself. She didn't want him to think he could frighten her. From the age of about fourteen she'd slapped boys' faces if they tried it on with her. But Sean Napier wasn't a boy, and for some reason she wasn't angry enough yet to hit him.

'Does your friend know the policeman well?'

Lucy darted an alarmed look at his darkly handsome face. He'd guessed Connie and Ralph were going to meet up round the corner. With an amount of pique Lucy realised that Mr Napier might not be as interested in her as her conceit had led her to believe. He could be a shady character trying to find out about any detective work involving the club. Or he could be investigating police corruption. She knew Boris handed over protection money to Ralph; Connie had let that slip. Lucy's mind raced to and fro as she considered which side of the law Sean Napier might be on. She bit her lip. It didn't matter to her either way; he'd get nothing out of her but a clump if he didn't let her pass this time.

'Sorry, don't know what you mean. Now, if you'll excuse me . . .' Her fists tightened into little balls. But he let her go, watching her until she'd turned the corner. He dropped the cigarette butt and ground it beneath a shoe.

Bill Black had emerged from the Cuckoo Club with Mavis just after Connie and Lucy finished their shift. He'd opened the car door for Mavis, then fiddled with lighting a cigarette while watching interestedly from beneath the brim of his hat the tryst taking place across the road.

He understood why the Irishman had taken a fancy to her: he'd noticed her himself and thought her a pretty little thing. A corner of his mouth lifted in a smirk. It seemed the girl wasn't as smitten as Mavis had been by the paddy. She'd gone on her way having given Napier the brush-off, by the looks of things. Bill glanced at Mavis, who was inspecting her reflection in a vanity mirror while she waited for him to get in the car. If he thought the fellow might be interested in a substitute he'd go across and have a word.

At that moment Napier turned and saw him watching. Although his face was in shadow something in the fellow's stance made Bill make a show of putting away his cigarettes and matches before getting in the car. As he drove off he knew for some reason he wouldn't forget Sean Napier in a hurry.

CHAPTER FOURTEEN

'What are *you* doing here?'

Kathy Finch had returned from work to find her twin reclining on the double bed they shared, flicking over the pages of a magazine. It was just after three o'clock in the afternoon and Jennifer should still have been working at the factory. Kathy knew if her sister were again shirking – or worse, had been sacked – there would be pandemonium when their mother found out. Jennifer's stubborn laziness was causing a constant bad atmosphere at home and Kathy was thoroughly fed up of it.

'What's the matter?' Kathy realised her unexpected appearance had startled Jennifer, but she frowned on seeing Jennifer's hands spring to cover her throat.

'Got the bellyache,' Jennifer muttered. She quickly struggled to sit up, looking flustered, her hands still clasping her neck. 'Told the supervisor I was going off sick.'

'Why are you strangling yourself?' Kathy looked Jennifer over. Her sister seemed fit enough and she knew

Jenny's heightened colour was more likely to be caused by guilt than fever.

Kathy wasn't sure why her sister was acting coy. She'd seen marks on Jenny's neck before. While they were still at school Jennifer had got herself a reputation for messing about with boys. Their mother had taken up the cudgels with a neighbour who'd delighted in telling her so. When their parents were around Jenny made sure to keep hidden under her collar lovebites lads gave her; but she proudly displayed them when they were alone in their bedroom.

Kathy had known for a while that her sister was slipping off to meet a secret boyfriend. She'd seen Jenny cramming her bag with a comb, powder compact, and a scent bottle before telling her mother she was meeting a friend from the factory. Kathy had guessed her twin was intending to stop off somewhere and get ready away from their mother's eagle eyes. Impatiently Kathy prised Jennifer's fingers away from her throat to see if she was attempting to hide a bad bruise.

But what met Kathy's astonished gaze was far more beautiful than an enormous lovebite. She fell back a step in shock, gawping at the huge green stones strung about Jennifer's throat.

'What . . .? Where on earth did you get it?' she gasped, craning to get a better look. 'What's that?' She touched an emerald with an unsteady finger. 'Is it a real jewel?'

With a defeated sigh Jenny slouched back onto the bed. She was desperately wishing she'd heard Kathy come in, but she'd been singing to herself and hadn't heard the key in the lock or the footsteps on the stairs to warn her of her sister's arrival.

The tortoiseshell box was customarily kept out of sight

beneath their heavy chest of drawers, but Jennifer had thought it safe to admire her prized possession this afternoon while she had the house to herself.

Noticing the direction of her sister's gaze, Jenny pounced to close the lid of the box lying on the coverlet. But it was too late. Kathy had seen more sparkling pieces.

Kathy slapped away Jennifer's hands as her twin tried to quickly shove the box under the pillow. She ripped open the lid, eyes popping at what was inside. 'Did you find it downstairs?' she whispered. 'You'd better put it back quickly. If he gets back and finds it missing God knows what he'll do to you.'

'It's not Dad's, and you'd better not tell what you've seen.' Jenny quickly snatched back the box, hugging it to her chest. 'Dad didn't want it, more fool him. So I've got it instead, but don't you say nuthin'.'

'What d'you mean, Dad didn't want it?' Kathy sensed foreboding creeping over her. 'How did you get it?'

Jenny bit her lip. She knew Bill would be furious if he found out she'd risked betraying him. She'd promised him faithfully he could trust her but she'd let him down.

'Could ask *you* why you're home early, if it comes to it.' Jenny sniped. Her sister's shift at Barratts sweet factory ended at six o'clock. Sometimes it was close to seven before she got back. Jenny was feeling so agitated she was tempted to jump up and slap Kathy for spoiling everything by turning up early.

'Machines broke down on our section. We all got sent off home.' Kathy's eyes darted to the box. 'Where d'you get that? Who gave it to you? Have you stolen it?' she demanded.

Jenny hid the box under the pillow. She had no

intention of letting her sister know where she usually concealed it. She picked up the magazine, pretending to read.

'You'd better tell me what's gone on or I'll tell Dad about that.' Kathy pointed a finger at the pillow.

'You do and you might just get more'n you bargained for off somebody I know.' Jenny's stare was bold and challenging. 'If he didn't like me a lot he wouldn't have give me this, would he?' She couldn't prevent boastfulness getting the better of her.

Enlightenment dropped Kathy's jaw. 'You got it off Bill Black, didn't you?' she uttered in amazement. Kathy had imagined her sister was meeting a boy from the factory. She knew Jennifer had had a crush on Bill for a long time, but never in her wildest dreams would she have thought a man like Bill would go after her fifteen-year-old twin.

'You've not slept with him, have you, you stupid cow?' she asked, aghast. 'He won't marry you, y'know, if he gets you in trouble. He's too old for you.'

'He's not. He's me boyfriend.' Jenny tilted her chin. 'We haven't gone all the way 'cos he's respectful and waiting till we get engaged. He's getting me a good job in the West End and I'll be moving out soon. So no need to worry about any of this.' She patted the pillow.

They both jerked to attention as the front door slammed. Jennifer's brashness disappeared and she jumped up in alarm, fumbling at the clasp on the necklace to remove it.

'Promise you won't say nuthin!' she hissed at Kathy. 'Promise!' she demanded tearfully.

Kathy raised her eyes heavenwards in despair. But she nodded. Her sister was acting idiotically and taking great risks, but in a way she understood Jennifer's desperation to get away from their miserable home life.

Kathy also wanted to escape. But she was prepared to work hard and save to do it. Their parents despised one another and for Kathy it was a relief to go to work to avoid their constant bitterness. She couldn't comprehend why Jennifer preferred idling at home to earning and saving for a decent future. But one thing Kathy understood very well: her sister was going to regret getting involved with Bill Black. Kathy had never had a proper boyfriend, but even at fifteen years old she intuitively knew that men like Bill were trouble.

'I'll go down and help Mum get tea ready,' Kathy sighed. 'You'd better come down and give a hand as well, then when she asks why you're home early she might take it better.'

Jenny nodded, wiping her wet eyes and straightening her hair. 'I'll say . . . dunno what I'll say 'cos I'll get a belt if I say I was sick. She never cares about that. You can be ill as yer like and she expects you to work.' Jenny shrugged. 'Don't want no tea anyhow. I'd rather go out and walk about than stay in here with you lot.'

'You gonna tell me what you done with the jewellery? Ain't seen that box fer quite a while.'

Ada was sitting opposite Bill in the George pub close to the Elephant and Castle. Bill did most of his business in the Windsor, closer to Peckham. He liked to keep a moderate distance between the 'office' he had in Jim Trent's back room where he rendezvoused with his girl gang, and the neighbourhood where he lived. Besides, of all the watering holes he frequented, the Windsor seemed to have the most trustworthy landlord. Jim Trent wasn't above doing under-the-counter deals and was more inclined to take philosophically a tear-up in his establishment. For pleasure Bill usually drank closer to home, or motored into central London.

Ada took a swallow of her beer and wiped her mouth with the back of a hand, growing impatient for Bill's answer. But he was ignoring her as he always did when she threw at him questions he didn't like. Ada gulped again at her ale, although she was already feeling tipsy; if she hadn't been drinking steadily for a couple of hours she wouldn't have found the courage to confront him over the emeralds at all.

'You said last week you'd give me my whack out of the Mortimer House hoist,' she hissed. 'All this time gone by and still you ain't weighed me out *that*, have you?' She clicked her fingers close to his nose. When he continued ignoring her, she prodded his arm. She'd seen him eyeing a buxom brunette sitting in the corner with a spiv-like fellow. The woman looked a bit like Betty Pickering, and the fact that Bill was favouring a dark-haired woman was something else riling her.

Ada knew Bill was more attracted to Mavis Pooley than to her so she'd bleached her hair in an attempt to resemble her rival. He'd laughed when he'd seen her new platinum style, accusing her of trying to look like a film star, so she'd said she'd done it to change her looks after the Mortimer House hoist. It was a good enough reason. She certainly didn't want to be recognised as the maid who'd run off with those heirlooms. Bill had kept her informed about Lord Mortimer being up in arms about losing his jewellery and that a reward was on offer for their return. She'd also heard that dangerous people were out to get them back and claim the reward. Ada had considered pinching them back off Bill and returning them herself as she'd been the one to lift them, but she knew all she'd get for her pains was her collar felt and a long stretch inside. Then Bill would be waiting for her when she got out . . .

She didn't blame his lordship for wanting revenge. But she did blame Bill for sending her in there in the first place. It had all been a waste of time and she'd told him it would be from the start. Ada reckoned she deserved to be paid for her trouble whether Bill made a loss or not.

Ada thumped down her empty tankard, puffing impatiently. She rarely drank spirits but could sink pints of bitter quicker than most men, and keep on going after they'd slid under the table.

'Want another?' Bill asked affably, head still turned towards the brunette in the corner.

Ada's constant whining was grating on his nerves, as was her vulgar, mannish behaviour. If he didn't know how much she liked the opposite sex he'd have taken her for a bloke the way she carried on.

Bill knocked about with women who were hard as nails but on the whole they had curves and a bit of pleasing femininity about them. Ada was straight up and down and crude as they came. He heard, then smelled her belch beer fumes beside him and grimaced distaste; but she was still too useful to offload. If she'd just shut up about the money he owed her he'd feel more inclined to tolerate her presence.

Bill hadn't given up on Jennifer coming up trumps and handing over Finchie's money. To gee her along he'd hinted he might ask her to get engaged when she turned sixteen and she'd leaped on him, covering him with wet kisses like a little puppy. He smiled privately at the memory of it.

He was irritated that Jennifer hadn't already brought him her father's cash, yet he found her soppy ways oddly endearing. The women in the gang used him for money or sex much as he did them. Except for Betty. They were made for one another, like soul mates. Despite his attachment to Betty he sometimes found to his surprise he was looking forward to seeing Jennifer Finch. Her innocence made a refreshing change after he'd been with mercenary cows all day long.

'Waited long enough. Want me money.' Ada banged a fist on the table, making Bill spear her an aggravated look as beer slopped from his glass onto his hand.

'Shut up,' he spat, aware she was drawing attention. He raised a hand to an old school pal drinking at the bar as he looked their way. The last thing he wanted was a row out in the open about the Mortimer jewels. He was very aware you never knew who might be listening. He wanted to find out more about the crew searching for the emeralds but information had dried up.

Ada sent him a glimmering look from under her brows. She was certain Bill was preoccupied thinking of Mavis and she was sick of being overlooked by him because of that maggot. But for Mavis and some of the other girls being on a shoplifting jaunt out of town, Bill would probably have chosen to be with her tonight and she'd have been left at home.

Ada had refused to go with them to Brighton. She'd been working hard in the West End and bringing Bill the best merchandise. But things had got a bit hot for them all lately in the top stores. The floor walkers were getting wise to them, so they'd been forced to try their luck further afield where their faces weren't known. Bill was always on the lookout for fresh talent and Ada reckoned he'd already got somebody new lined up. She knew he wasn't always seeing Mavis when he did a disappearing act.

'Leave off!' Bill snarled, snapping his head towards Ada as she pinched his arm to draw his attention. He could see she was drunk and brewing for a fight before the night was out. He didn't want any commotion likely to bring the boys in blue running, asking awkward questions. The state Ada was in she was likely to let her mouth run away with her. With an effort he dredged up a boyish smile, hoping to pacify her.

'Got some good news about the box,' he whispered, giving her a wink. 'Was saving it fer later when we got home so we could celebrate.' He nuzzled her neck. But tonight, Ada was too inebriated to be swayed by soft-soaping, and she flounced her head aside. 'Acquaintance of mine reckons they've found a buyer for the set. Few more days and should know for sure if it's a sweet deal.' He shoved back his chair. 'Time we got you home, ain't it, Ada?' He tickled her under her chin. 'Don't want you falling asleep on me too soon, gel. Night's young . . .'

Again, Ada snapped her face away from his touch. She was starting to convince herself Bill needed her more than she needed him. She did the donkey-work and brought in the good stuff. He often let the other girls get away with nabbing table linen or underwear and cosmetics. She got bawled out if the coats she lifted weren't furs. In her woozy state Ada reckoned she'd easily get other buyers for her merchandise, then she'd tell Bill he was a parasite and he could sling his hook . . .

'Ain't going home yet; get us another drink.' Defiantly, she shoved her empty tankard towards him across the beer-soaked tabletop.

Bill abruptly stood up but instead of going towards the bar he weaved a path through a merry throng, heading for the exit.

Outside on the gloomy pavement he loitered impatiently till he saw Ada stumble out of the pub. As the door swung shut cutting off muted light only her silhouette swaying in the darkness was visible. He'd known she'd follow him rather than stubbornly carry on drinking alone.

It was mid-May, but a cool cloudy evening, and he hoped the night air might sober her up. But she ambled along swinging her white head to and fro, searching for him in the darkness. She was mumbling drunken curses Bill knew were directed at him. As she came level with the wall he was lounging against he stepped into her path, making her shriek. Grabbing her arm, he gave her a short sharp jab to the jaw. She crumpled immediately and much as he was tempted to step over the mouthy cow, and leave her where she'd fallen, he didn't. He hauled her against his side and half dragged her to where his car was parked at the kerb. It was a bit of a walk and he grimaced jokily at a couple strolling towards him. 'Had a few too many, she has, daft mare,' he explained, making them chuckle.

He watched the couple enter the George, then bundled Ada onto the back seat and headed off home.

CHAPTER FIFTEEN

Lucy was walking past Pooles Park School, on her way to visit her sister Beth, when she saw little Tom Finch being roughly pushed up against the wall in the playground. He appeared to have been cornered by a few older boys and looked white-faced and scared. She recognised one of the bullies as Davy Wright.

Lucy and her sisters had been brought up by their parents to give as good as they got if picked on. No classmate had ever managed to bully Lucy. On one occasion their mother had come to hear about a scrap she'd had with a neighbour's daughter. Matilda had immediately set off up Campbell Road, dragging Lucy by the hand behind her, to have it out with the aggressor. And her mother too, if need be.

Matilda had never shied away from an argument, whether with men or women. Often, minor disputes between children who lived in Campbell Road – who if left alone usually settled their differences – resulted in feuds lasting for years between their warring parents.

'Leave him alone, Davy Wright, or you'll feel my boot

up your backside.' Lucy had stopped by the school railings to yell that out.

Davy turned towards her, looking startled. 'He's got a football 'n' he won't let us play with it.' It was a whining excuse for tormenting Tom.

Lucy hurried through the gate as she saw one of the other lads punch Winnie's son in the side of the head. The offender looked belligerent but sidled away as she stormed closer. The Keiver family's reputation preceded them in these parts.

'Push off, all of you, or I'll get the headmaster out and he'll cane the lot of you when I tell him what you've done.'

'Sissy . . . sissy . . .' the boy who'd punched Tom catcalled as he sauntered away with his friends.

Lucy bent to examine Tom's face. He had a graze on a cheek but was manfully trying to blink away his tears. Lucy recalled how upset he'd looked months ago when witnessing the fight between her and his mother over the sweet shop job. At the time she'd thought he seemed a little lad in need of toughening up if he were to live in the neighbourhood. But he was a polite, nice-natured boy, and quietly murmured his thanks to her while cuffing tears from his eyes.

'Can't let 'em push you around, y'know,' she said, dabbing blood from his face with her hanky. 'Let 'em do that and they'll never leave off.' She gave him a gentle smile. 'Best ask yer dad to show you a few punches . . .' Lucy did a bit of shadow boxing in front of him in an effort to cheer him up.

Tom gazed at her as though she'd spoken double Dutch.

'Will your dad do that for you, d'you think? Show you how to look after yourself?'

Tom shook his head. 'He won't let me share me football with 'em either, 'cos they live in the Bunk,' he declared solemnly. 'That's why they hit me all the time.'

'I see . . .' Lucy said, although she didn't. Why any parent would be so mean was beyond her.

''Ere! What do you think you're doing?'

Winifred Finch had bawled that from across the road on seeing Lucy crouching to talk to her son in the playground. In her hand she had Tom's PE kit, which he'd left behind that morning. She knew he'd be in trouble so had decided to bring it along and tear a strip off him later for his forgetfulness.

Winnie burst through the gate and stomped up. Having seen the mark on her son's face her lips disappeared into a thin line as she confronted Lucy. 'Have you hit him?' she barked, pointing a finger at Tom's cheek. 'Has she hit you?' She jabbed her son roughly on the shoulder to hurry his reply.

Tom shook his head, embarrassed by his mother's behaviour, as he often was. 'She helped me. Got set about by some boys, but she made them clear off.'

The bell was rung loudly and the children began filing inside the school. Tom edged away but his mother gripped his elbow, yanking him back.

'Take that . . . forgot it, didn't you,' Winnie snapped, thrusting at her son the cloth drawstring bag that held cotton shirt and shorts and plimsolls. 'I'll speak to you later,' she threatened, clipping his ear. 'I'll speak to *you* now.' She turned to Lucy, arms akimbo.

'Go ahead,' Lucy invited calmly. 'But if you're thinking of thanking me for stopping those kids belting Tom, you don't need to,' she added sarcastically. 'I'd've done it for any of 'em. Can't stand bullies.' She gave Winnie a significant look that brought bright red colour flowing up to the woman's frizzy hairline.

'*Thank somebody like you?*' Winnie sneered, index finger quivering close to Lucy's small nose. 'I wouldn't do no such thing fer the likes of *you*. Think I don't know what *you're* doing to earn a living since you got the sack from Dobson's?' She huffed disgust into Lucy's face. 'Everybody round here knows you're working with that tart Connie Whitton. And we all know how *she* gets her money. Doin' a double act, the two of yers, I wouldn't be surprised.' She twisted her features into a mask of contempt. 'Don't know how you or yer mother, or yer sisters fer that matter, have got the brass neck to show faces since you went on the game.' She looked Lucy up and down as though she was diseased. 'So you stay away from all of us, especially me little boy. Don't want a trollop anywhere near him.'

'That right?' Lucy asked calmly, although her face had whitened in fury at Winnie's malice. 'You'd better keep your Jennifer away from her brother, in that case. Why don't you go home and ask her what she's been getting up to?'

Normally, Lucy would never grass up anybody. But Winnie had riled her so much she'd spontaneously retaliated and she knew for two pins she'd hit the woman if she didn't stop bathing her face with bad breath. Lucy turned on her heel and started towards the school gate.

Winnie had grabbed hold of her arm before she could get through it. Lucy shoved her away, using the heel of a hand on Winnie's skinny breastbone.

'What d'you mean by that?' Winnie had recovered from her stumble. 'You tell me what you mean by that, you wicked bitch. Don't you dare run me own daughter down to me face.'

Lucy continued walking away. She had no intention of saying more. She already felt a twinge of guilt for dropping Jennifer in it.

Winnie wasn't going to let the matter end there. Previously Winnie's main bugbear with Jennifer had been her shirking at home at every opportunity because short wages affected the family kitty. At the back of Winnie's mind had lurked a suspicion Jennifer might be involved with a boy. Her daughter had been acting secretive, coming in and running straight upstairs to her room so no questions would be asked, and that made Winnie suspect she'd been with someone who was trouble. She'd smelled cigarettes on Jennifer's clothes but had not made a fuss before: people at the factory smoked on their breaks.

A maternal instinct was telling her that if Jennifer *was* smoking it would be the least of her worries. That particular daughter would be eager to please even a thug from the Bunk to keep him hooked. The idea that Lucy Keiver knew more than she did about it all was making Winnie feel ready to explode.

'Don't you walk away from me, when I'm talking to you,' she roared. Again she grabbed at Lucy's arm, digging her nails in when Lucy tried to shake her off.

Lucy dislodged the woman's grip by giving her fingers a backhanded slap. When Winnie grabbed a fistful of her hair instead, Lucy had had enough. 'Let go of me,' she enunciated through set teeth. 'Only telling you once.'

'You evil bitch.' Winnie started jerking Lucy's head to and fro. 'You don't know nuthin', do you? You're just a spiteful cow tellin' lies about me daughter.'

Winnie's voice was shaking with such emotion that Lucy actually started to feel quite sorry for her despite

187

the pain the woman was inflicting. But she wasn't about to let Winnie scalp her so she punched her on the chin. Winnie tottered back a few steps before collapsing on her backside. Lucy brushed a clump of her hair off her shoulder and glowered at Winnie. Still she felt a bit of sympathy for her because it was obvious from the woman's defeated expression that Jennifer's misbehaviour had come as no real surprise.

Without another word, Lucy carried on towards Beth's house.

Usually it was only on a Friday – their paydays – that Winifred eagerly awaited her daughters' return from work. When she heard a key scrape in the lock she darted into the hallway, but it was Kathy who entered the house.

'Thought you was Jennifer,' Winifred muttered. 'She's usually back first. Why're you early?'

'Machine's gone down again,' Kathy explained, looking curiously at her mother. Winnie seemed deflated on seeing her, yet also agitated. Then Kathy noticed the small graze on her mother's face. She knew it wouldn't be the first time Winnie had felt Eddie's fists, but until she knew more about it she was willing to give her father the benefit of the doubt. 'Have you bumped your chin?' Kathy followed her mother into the parlour, slipping out of her cardigan.

'Yeah, bumped meself,' Winnie mumbled, absently scrubbing her jaw as though to remove the blemish. In her preoccupied state she'd forgotten that Lucy Keiver had clumped her and might have left a mark.

Kathy wasn't convinced by that answer. 'Has Dad hit you?' she asked quietly, angling her head to read her mother's averted features.

'Said I bumped meself, didn't I?' Winnie snapped, pacing to and fro.

'What's the matter?' Kathy put an arm about her mother's tense shoulders but Winnie elbowed her away.

'One time I need to catch hold of yer sister she's nowhere to be seen.' Winnie continued prowling the room. 'Usually can't get the pest out from under me feet, she's so keen on skiving at home.'

A reason for her mother's urgent need to speak to Jennifer darted into Kathy's head. It was quickly followed by an explanation for Winnie's bruise.

If her parents had somehow found out about Jennifer seeing Bill Black there would have been an almighty row between them. Eddie would have blamed Winnie for not keeping their daughter's behaviour in check. Her father's attitude was that business was his concern; everything to do with home and family was her mother's duty.

'Is Tom upstairs in his room?' Kathy asked. She was anxious that her little brother might have witnessed a fight between their parents.

Winnie shook her head. 'He'll be home late. He's doing heats for running races after school for the sports day.'

Kathy felt momentarily relieved before realising Tom's arrival might coincide with Jennifer's. Kathy felt the sooner her mother and her sister had a bust-up the better it would be, because Tom might still be at school and miss it.

'I'll go and see if I can find Jenny, as it's urgent,' she gabbled, then wished she'd kept quiet. Her mother had turned suspicious eyes on her face.

'You know what she's been getting up to, don't you?' Winnie jerked on Kathy's arm to hurry an answer. 'Who's she been knocking about with? Come on, out with it!'

189

Winnie knew her daughters had never been close. They were like chalk and cheese and had always preferred spending time with their own friends rather than with each other. She wouldn't have guessed Jennifer would confide in her twin; but she'd glimpsed a spark of guilt in Kathy's evasive eyes.

'It's one of those louts from the Bunk, ain't it?' Winnie barked. 'Might've known she'd show us right up! When her father gets in, she'll get the hiding of her life . . .'

Winnie spun about on hearing the front door slam. A moment later she was flying into the passage and slapping Jennifer across the face.

Kathy rushed out of the parlour to find her sister leaning against the wall clutching an inflamed cheek.

'Why d'you tell her?' Jenny had leaped to the conclusion that Kathy had betrayed her. 'You mean cow . . . you promised you wouldn't say anything!' she cried.

'Weren't her told me, so you can shut that up,' Winnie bellowed, drowning out Kathy's protestation of innocence. 'Saw Lucy Keiver today and she give me this!' Winnie stuck a rigid finger on her bruised chin. 'Got it fer telling the bitch she was making up lies about me daughter, only she weren't, were she?' Winnie bounded at Jennifer again, whacking her on the shoulder. 'Had to hear it from the likes of a Campbell Road girl, didn't I? Wait'll yer father gets in and I tell him what you've been up to, you deceitful little tart . . .'

Jennifer pushed her mother away as Winnie again raised a hand.

'Bill'll give *him* a good hiding if he sets about me. We're getting engaged. Bill said so. So you'd better all leave me alone, or it'll be the worse for the lot of you.' Jennifer's fingers were still pressed to her stinging cheek but her eyes were glaring with defiance. 'Dad's just jealous of Bill 'cos he's important and doing well and got more money.'

In the long silence that followed, Winnie blinked in astonishment at Jennifer. '*Bill?*' she finally croaked, looking mystified.

Kathy's forehead dropped to be cradled by her palms, then she turned about and trudged into the parlour.

'*Bill?*' Winnie whispered at Jenny. 'Who d'you mean? Who's got more money? Bill Black?'

'You said Lucy Keiver told you about him.' Jennifer licked her parched lips nervously. 'I thought you knew about us . . .'

Winnie flinched as though she'd been punched in the guts. Slowly she sank to her haunches, then collapsed on the floor, sitting with her legs sticking straight out in front of her.

Jennifer yanked on one of her mother's arms to get her to her feet. But Winnie refused to budge and sat gawping trancelike at the opposite wall.

Having yelled for her sister to come and help lift Winnie, Jennifer and Kathy got either side of her, attempting to hoist their mother by gripping her under the armpits.

And that's how Eddie Finch found them when he came in a few moments later.

Jennifer let go of her mother and tried to scoot out of the front door, but her father blocked her path. Eddie had digested enough of the scene to understand a calamity had occurred and as Jennifer was keen to escape he knew she'd caused it.

'What you done now?' he growled at her.

The sight of her husband seemed to galvanise Winnie.

She struggled up with Kathy's help. 'I'll tell you what she's done! The little tart's been dropping her drawers for Bill Black. Still is, for all I know.'

Eddie gawped from one to the other of the three women. His chin dropped further as he guffawed in disbelief.

'Tell him!' Winnie shrieked, incensed by his reaction. She leaped at Jennifer and started jabbing her arm. 'Tell yer father what you've been up to.'

Jennifer bolted in the opposite direction this time, heading for the stairs.

Still Eddie stood, mouth agape, half-smiling. His jaw clacked shut suddenly and he turned a savage expression on his wife. 'You've let her open her legs at her age?' he roared. 'Why aren't yer watching her?'

'I can't keep me eyes on her every minute of the day,' Winnie screamed back. 'You was the one brought a dirty bastard here who interferes with little gels . . .'

'Ain't Bill's fault!' Eddie thundered, raising a fist as though he might strike Winnie, but he shoved it against her shoulder to move her so he could stamp up the stairs, unbuckling his belt. 'I've seen her parading herself in front of him.'

Her father's last comment was spoken in a deadly calm voice and it frightened Kathy more than his fury had.

She ran up after him but was too late to prevent her father's first blow. He'd dragged Jennifer out from the coverlet she'd rolled herself in as a form of protection and thumped her across the backside with an open palm. He shoved Jennifer back on the bed and used his belt this time, his lips pressed together in concentration as he aimed whips at her legs.

Kathy grabbed at his arm but he elbowed her off so she ran out onto the landing and yelled for their mother. She could see Winnie hovering at the bottom of the stairs but she didn't even look up and continued pacing to and fro with her hands cupped either side of her head.

Kathy shot back into the bedroom as she heard Jennifer's piercing scream. She made a more courageous attack on her father this time and was knocked aside more viciously. But finally he let the belt fall limp in a hand.

Winnie appeared in the doorway and winced beneath the look Kathy gave her. 'You're almost as bad!' Winnie pointed a finger at her, shaking it to gain her husband's attention. 'She knew all about it. Been covering up for Jennifer, ain't she? Deceitful little cows, the two of 'em.'

Eddie turned, took a step towards Kathy and dealt a blow to the back of her thighs that crumpled her at the knees.

'Do you want a cup of tea, or anything? They've both gone out.'

Kathy had poked her head around the bedroom door and whispered that to her sister, sitting on the edge of the mattress. She knew that Jennifer had barely eaten or drunk anything in the two days since her relationship with Bill had been revealed.

The uproar that had taken place that afternoon had seemed to shake their house to the rafters and hadn't ended when their father went downstairs. Having laid into Jennifer, their parents had spent the next hour or so spitting bitter abuse at each other. Of Bill Black's part in it all there'd been no further mention. Kathy knew

193

that neither of her parents had the guts to confront him over it.

Tom's appearance had briefly quietened them. Sensing the boiling atmosphere, Tom had picked up his football and sloped off to play in the street on his own. And the commotion had started again.

Kathy rubbed a hand across the backs of her thighs, where her father's belt had left a weal. If Eddie had found out she knew Jennifer was hiding expensive jewellery upstairs she'd have got double the punishment. But she'd kept her sister's secret safe.

Kathy had gone off to work as usual the following day. And for the first time Jennifer had been keen to get to her job too. But she hadn't been allowed out of the house.

Winnie had gone to the custard factory to excuse her daughter's absence as a bout of colic. The bruising to Jennifer's legs and arms would give rise to awkward questions. Apart from that, her constant crying had made her face red and puffy.

'Do you want a cup of tea?' Kathy asked again, coming into the room to perch on the edge of the bed beside Jenny.

Jennifer shook her head. She knew her parents were out because she'd been downstairs moments ago and, finding the house empty, had headed straight for her father's radiogram. 'D'you know where they've gone?'

'Mum's probably gone up the shop. 'S'pect Dad's at work.'

'Your machine's still broken?'

'It's mended. I came home early to see you.'

Jenny looked surprised but smiled. She was glad to see Kathy, perhaps for the last time.

194

'I'm worried about you, y'know,' Kathy declared on a sigh. She'd noticed the carpetbag that was usually kept at the top of the wardrobe was on the pitch-black floorboards beside it. 'You're not going to do anything daft, are you?'

'No . . . I'm going to do something sensible.' Jenny sounded calm and quiet as she stood up. She went to the chest of drawers and drew out from under it the tortoiseshell box. 'Thanks for not telling them about this.'

'I would never have said about Bill either,' Kathy said solemnly. 'I don't break promises.'

'I know. That cow Lucy Keiver did it.'

'How did she know?'

'Her and Connie Whitton saw me and Bill together. Bad luck, eh?'

Kathy bit her lip. She felt tempted to tell her sister it was her own stupid fault for carrying on where she was likely to be seen. Nevertheless, she was surprised that Lucy had told tales to their mother. The Keivers didn't seem the sort to grass people up.

Methodically, Jennifer began opening drawers and got together some things: underwear and other clothing; brush and comb and toiletries, then crammed them into the bag.

'You really leaving?' Kathy whispered.

Jenny nodded. 'Should've done it ages ago. Hate it here with them.'

'Do you know where he lives? Will he let you stay?' Kathy knew without asking that her sister was intending to go to Bill Black.

Jenny shrugged. 'I'll find him. Lambeth can't be that big a place. He did say about us getting engaged; I'm

195

not making it up. So I reckon he'll look after me. If not
. . .' Again Jenny gestured hopelessness. Kathy clasped
her arms but Jennifer pulled out of her sister's restraint
and picked up the bag containing her few possessions.
'Don't tell me not to go. I'm off and I ain't coming back.'

'They won't ever let you back, you know that, don't
you, Jen?' Kathy said quietly. 'If he turns you out, what
you gonna do?'

'I'm on me own, I know that.' Jennifer's voice wobbled
but she started towards the door with her bag.

Kathy followed her sister down the stairs, trying to
talk some sense into her. But she seemed deaf to all
warnings.

In the hallway, Jenny turned about with a bright
smile. She dropped the bag to the floor and abruptly
gave Kathy a hug before picking it up. 'Wish me luck?'

Kathy could only nod, tears glistening in her eyes.

Before Jennifer could open the street door her mother
had beaten her to it, stooping with the weight of her
shopping bags as she entered. Winnie stared at Jennifer
with expressionless eyes. A moment later she turned her
back to the wall in the narrow passageway, allowing her
daughter to walk past unhindered. Before Jennifer had
got to the end of the front path Winnie had shut the door.

Jennifer tilted her chin as she set off in the direction
of the tube. Normally she'd have struggled to find the
fare for the journey. Not today. At the bottom of the
carpetbag was an envelope containing eight hundred and
fifty pounds of her father's savings. She also had a box
of valuable gems to sell, if need be. After the beating she'd
taken she'd decided not to leave those for her father.

When she found Bill, she reckoned he'd be very
pleased to see her.

CHAPTER SIXTEEN

'There's a good-looking fellow over there and I think he's waving at us. Crikey Moses! That car must've cost a bob or two.' Connie had been about to take a drag on her cigarette but instead nudged Lucy in the ribs.

The tooting had reached Lucy's ears but she'd dismissed the sound as it wasn't the first time a man had used a car horn to draw their attention.

She and Connie were standing on the pavement outside the Cuckoo Club. Inside was a full house and the atmosphere was unbearably humid, even with all the windows wide open and the ceiling fans whirring. So they'd nipped outside to get a breath of fresh air instead of being cooped up in the small staff room on their dinner break.

Having glanced over a shoulder, Lucy felt her heart leap to her throat. It was close to eleven o'clock yet the dusk hadn't properly descended over a light starry sky. Through the throng in Piccadilly Circus she glimpsed Rory Jackson weaving Lord Mortimer's Rolls-Royce between vehicles, obviously with the intention of pulling over to talk to her.

'It's an old colleague from the place I used to work,' Lucy explained breathlessly. The sight of Rory's quirky smile beneath his peaked chauffeur's cap was more worrying than pleasing to her.

Lucy had been thinking a lot about Rory and how she'd like to see him again, perhaps go out with him. But she knew that there were things about her life that might disgust him. So she hadn't yet written that letter to him at Mortimer House arranging for them to meet up because she couldn't bring herself to be blasé about his opinion of her when he got to know her better. She was proud – too proud, her mother said – and she'd bite back at any insult, imagined or otherwise.

'Gonna stop and have a chat with him, are you?' Connie asked, grinning. 'I will if you won't,' she added saucily, cigarette wagging in her lips.

'I'd like to but . . .'

'But you don't want him to know where you work.' Connie tilted her head, blowing smoke arrow-straight into the air. 'Won't take a genius to work it out, will it?' She glanced up at the open windows from which was issuing an aroma of cigars and gravy, and the sultry sounds of a saxophone.

'Don't want him to know where I live either,' Lucy said a little self-consciously.

'Thought he already knew that.' Connie frowned. 'Beattie told me half the street was having a gander when a bloke in a big car stopped in Campbell Road to talk to you. Took you for a ride, didn't he? It's him, ain't it?' Connie jerked her head at Rory. He'd parked at the kerb and was in the process of disembarking.

'Didn't tell him I lived there. I could've just been visiting the neighbourhood. Don't you tell him,' Lucy hissed.

'Can see now, Luce, why you liked working in service.' Connie was admiring Rory's tall athletic physique as he came around the Rolls. 'Are all the men like him?'

''Fraid not,' Lucy muttered, keen to get rid of Connie so she could talk privately to Rory. Lucy liked Connie but she could be embarrassingly lewd, even with men she'd never met before.

'I'll let you have him to yourself.' Sensing her presence was unwanted, Connie dropped her dog-end, stepped over a threshold set in the wall behind them, then sashayed up the stairs that led to the Cuckoo Club. Before the door swung shut she turned and gave Lucy a mischievous smile over a shoulder.

'Blimey! Didn't expect to see you. What are you doing out at this time of night? How have you been keeping?' Rory fired off his questions while approaching, and was now leaning a hand on the brickwork to one side of Lucy's head.

'I'm fine, thanks . . . and you?' Lucy asked, edging back into the shadows so Rory wouldn't notice how short her skirt was. She'd barely had time to get to know him but sensed he might be a traditional man who'd disapprove of a 'decent' woman displaying her thighs.

So far, Winnie Finch was the only person who'd openly sneered at her because of her job. On a few occasions she'd noticed that neighbours stopped gossiping as she approached but they continued to greet her in a friendly manner. Her mother would put a flea in the ear of anybody who was disrespectful to any member of her family. Matilda now seemed to tolerate her dubious work because her wages and tips, and the good meaty dinners they shared, were very welcome. But Lucy knew her mother would still prefer to see her settled in another job.

Rory glanced at the brightly lit name over the club entrance. 'Not working in there, are you?'

'Why not? Job, ain't it?' Lucy sounded curt and defensive because she'd caught the surprise and distaste in his voice.

'Thought you was gonna apply for another post in service.' There had been a long pause before Rory replied.

'No chance of getting taken on without a reference, have I?' Lucy tilted her chin. 'Mrs Venner offered me one but I stormed out over the way I got treated. Regret it now but . . . too late.'

'Never too late; you could apply for something back with us.' A pessimistic expression turned down the corners of Rory's mouth. 'Course, there's a lot of new people got took on already: new housekeeper and lady's maid, and a new junior in your old job. Mr Collins has quit too. Think it badly affected his health . . . y'know, what went on.' He paused. 'We've got a new butler from up North. Quite a whippersnapper, he is, compared to his predecessor. Not sure yet what I think of him.' Rory grimaced in consideration.

Lucy often found herself contemplating what had gone on at Mortimer House. It was dreadful for everyone concerned but especially for Clare Boyd's relatives. A suicide in any family was a tragedy, but Clare's people would also have to deal with inquisitive questions about the scandal that had led up to it.

One of Connie Whitton's sisters was a lesbian and Lucy knew that Connie and her younger sister, Sarah, had taken pains to keep the news from their neurotic mother. Ginny Whitton had gone to her grave thinking her eldest daughter, Louisa, was living with a man called Sonny, not a woman called Sonia.

'Have things settled down at Mortimer House?' Lucy asked, genuinely hoping they had.

'Yeah, but it ain't the same there. Never will be again, I don't reckon. Bad atmosphere when the chinwagging starts up.'

Rory's eyes travelled Lucy's sweet features, settled on the vivid red bow of her lips before continuing down her curvy figure. Deliberately he angled his head to get a better view of her lissom legs sheathed in black silk. 'That certainly ain't the sort of outfit you was wearing in Mortimer House.'

Again Lucy heard the light condemnation in his voice.

'Just on me break. Got to go back in now,' she said. 'Have you dropped his lordship off in town?'

'Mayfair casino.' Rory checked his wristwatch. 'He'll be gambling for hours so I'm at a loose end.'

'Pity her ladyship . . .'

'Why? She's well on the mend now.'

'Perhaps she is, but you'd think he'd keep himself home with her and give her and the girls some attention.'

'Ain't how those sort of people behave.' An indolent shrug undulated Rory's broad shoulders.

'Yeah . . . suppose not.' Lucy turned to go in but he caught at her arm, staying her.

'Any chance you can get off early? We could stop off and have a drink somewhere, then I'll give you a lift home if you like.'

'Sorry . . . can't . . .' Lucy smiled an apology.

'Come out with me on me day off, Thursday, then?'

Lucy hesitated. She knew she was attracted to Rory: whenever he was close to her like this she felt a little fluttering in her stomach. But there was something unsettling in his attitude to her tonight. She'd rather not go out with him if he were going to spend the evening sniping about her working in the Cuckoo Club.

'Come out with me, Lucy. I've waited long enough,' he coaxed with a winning smile. 'I'm not about to give up, you know, not now I've found you again.'

Lucy dipped her head and chuckled, avoiding his warm humorous eyes. 'Do you know Lyons at the old Angel Islington?'

'Yeah, I know it.'

'Meet you on the corner there at seven o'clock Thursday if you like.'

'I do like,' he murmured with throaty satisfaction. He glanced at the glaring bulbs winking out the name of the club. 'Not working here Thursday?'

'Not my shift.' Lucy flashed him a farewell smile and went through the door. She closed it immediately behind her so he wouldn't get a view of her stocking tops and suspenders as she ran up the stairs.

Bill was sauntering out of a tobacconist's on Lambeth Road when he spotted Jennifer. He stopped dead in his tracks. The match he'd scratched alight burned down to scorch his cupped palm and with a curse he dropped it, snatched the cigarette from his mouth and stuffed it in a pocket. Instinctively he whipped behind the news-vendor's stand by the kerb, concealing himself. As his surprise was brought under control he fished in his pocket for the Woodbine, struck a match, then took a long drag on it. From under the brim of his hat he stared broodingly at the young woman across the road.

Jennifer was in the process of closing the gate of a building that had a bed-and-breakfast sign pinned on its front wall. Bill swiftly deduced she was this side of the water because she was after him, and she had money to pay for bed and board because she'd finally turned up trumps. She'd got Eddie's cash with her and was ready to hand it over for the jewellery.

But something was niggling at Bill, preventing him from yet bowling over to greet her and relieve her of her father's savings. Jennifer appeared to have stayed away from home overnight, so her parents were either sick with worry, or had kicked her out. It was this latter option that was annoying Bill. Teenage girls got the boot when their parents found out they'd been misbehaving with the opposite sex. He was hoping he wasn't in the frame for that; he'd only kissed her and he'd like a bit of breathing space before Eddie came looking for him for his money.

As Jennifer had got this far, it was likely Eddie didn't yet realise he'd been robbed blind; Bill reckoned the old miser probably only took the notes out of their hidy-hole once in a blue moon to count them. He imagined Jennifer had been a crafty little sod. Like father, like daughter, Bill smirked. But when Finchie eventually discovered his cash had been swapped for a box of hot emeralds he'd soon put two and two together and come up with Jennifer as the culprit, with him pulling her strings.

Bill sucked strongly on his Woodbine, his expression turning belligerent. If Jennifer's old man wanted to come after him to do something about it, let him. He'd encouraged Jennifer's infatuation but he hadn't slept with her. And she could have given back the emeralds at any time.

Bill didn't think Eddie would find the guts to confront him, even to defend his daughter's honour. Finchie knew that he had a reputation for putting in hospital people who double-crossed him.

Business was business and morals didn't come into it.

Eddie's daughter had taken jewellery off him and he was about to accept payment for it. If Eddie had a beef with anyone it was with Jennifer. As far as Bill was concerned it was a deal sewn up and all fair and square.

Jennifer set off along the road towards the bus stop, her carpetbag bumping against her leg, unaware she was being watched from behind a newsstand that announced, GOVERNMENT SAYS UNEMPLOYMENT BENEFITS WILL NOT BE CUT. She'd been in south London for two days and was rather enjoying the freedom she now had. She'd asked the proprietor of the guesthouse she'd stayed at whether he'd heard of Bill Black. But he'd not, and he'd stared so suspiciously at her that she'd feared he might ask her outright if she'd run away from home. So she'd paid her tab and left early, immediately after breakfast, in case he called the police.

Jennifer glanced sideways, catching sight of her reflection in a shop window. She slowed down, tilting her head to and fro to inspect her face from different angles. She knew she looked young and innocent and so was off to buy some lipstick and smart clothes to make her look grown up. If anybody asked her outright if she'd run away she could truthfully say that she hadn't. Her mother could have stopped her leaving that day. But Winnie had made it perfectly clear she was glad to see the back of her. The only reason her father would set out after her would be to get back his cash. When Eddie found it gone he'd know she'd taken it.

Reflecting on her father's revenge made a cold shiver ripple through Jennifer, despite the warm morning sun heating the top of her head. Her fading bruises from that last beating would be nothing to what her father would do to her if he caught up with her and Bill wasn't around to protect her. She realised she desperately needed to find Bill before Eddie tracked her down . . .

A low whistle made Jennifer glance over a shoulder, then pivot about. A moment later she was racing back the way she'd come, sheer joy and relief animating her youthful features.

As Jennifer dropped her bag and launched herself at him, Bill caught her and spun them both around, infected by her gaiety. He put her back on her feet and she gazed up adoringly, breathlessly at him.

'Pleased to see me, are you?' he asked, his eyes darting to the bag on the ground.

'Yeah, been looking for you.' Jennifer immediately clung to his arm, hugging him as though she'd never let go. 'Got here two days ago and been staying over there.' She pointed to the guesthouse. 'Landlord hadn't heard of you so I was going to ask in a few pubs instead 'cos I thought afterwards you'd probably be well known in pubs 'stead of hotels . . .'

Bill placed a finger on her lips to quieten her burbling. 'Well, no need to ask anyone about me. You found me now, ain't yer. What you got in there?' Bill cut to the chase. The sooner he could get down to business then drop her off back in Islington, the better he'd like it.

'Guess!' Jennifer teased, grabbing up the bag and holding it behind her back.

'Well, I reckon whatever it is, Jenny, we'd better take a look somewhere a bit more private, don't you?' He relieved her of the bag in a way that looked courteous. 'Car's parked round the corner there. Come on.' He jerked his head to the left and allowed her to hang heavily on his arm as they walked.

* * *

205

'Me dad had more than that put by but I thought I ought to leave something behind.'

Jennifer and Bill were sitting in his car. A few minutes ago she'd delved into her bag then handed over to him the envelope containing the cash. Bill had deftly counted it out in seconds, eased it back in the envelope, then slipped it out of sight in an inside pocket of his jacket. Jenny had been disappointed to see it all disappear. She'd hoped to have a few notes returned for her new clothes and cosmetics. But she'd ask for that later. For now she simply wanted to appreciate Bill's company and his protection.

Eddie's savings had amounted to nine hundred pounds, and Jennifer had left just fifty behind in the cavity in the radiogram. She was feeling very apprehensive about the consequences of what she'd done. She knew she should feel guilty too; but she didn't.

The whoosh of leather cutting through air and the grunting noise her father had made in his throat as he'd wielded his belt against the backs of her buttocks remained fresh in her mind. She could taste the coppery salt of blood flowing as she'd bitten her tongue against the searing pain while wriggling to escape his ferocious thrashing.

Jennifer's regrets were for her sister and brother. She knew Kathy and Tom were likely to suffer for what she'd done. To stop herself thinking about it she leaned across to clasp Bill about the neck.

'You're a good gel.' He tickled her cheek, shifting her back onto her own seat. 'Where d'you leave the box of emeralds for Eddie? In the hidy-hole where you found the money?'

Jenny moistened her lips. 'Didn't leave him nuthin','

she muttered, diving into the bag again to pull out the tortoiseshell box. She pulled up her skirt tilting on the seat to display the huge bruise on her thigh. 'See what he's done to me? He don't deserve the emeralds.'

Bill had seen prize-fighters looking better, but that wasn't important to him right now. 'If Eddie knows you've taken his money, how did you get away?' he barked.

Jenny felt miffed that Bill wasn't more affected by the sight of her suffering. 'I took it when they was all out. Course, if he's checked in the radiogram, he'll know it's gone by now.'

'Why's he walloped you, then?'

'Found out about us,' Jenny said, sliding a look at him from under her lashes. 'Somebody saw us together and told me mum. Went berserk, they did. Mum clumped me too. I hate 'em. Ain't never going back.'

'Think you are, Jenny,' Bill said quietly. 'I don't welch on deals. Your old man's paid fer them emeralds, so he gets 'em.' He slung himself back in the seat and turned the ignition. 'I'll take you back to Islington and you can hand 'em over.'

Jennifer gawped at him, blinking back tears. 'I can't go back. Dad'll kill me. I've come to stay with you.' She placed the box of emeralds on his lap.

'You stupid little cow.' Bill grabbed her shoulders and shook her. 'I don't want the fuckin' emeralds. If I had, I wouldn't have given them to you in the first place.' He made an effort to control himself. 'Now listen, I've got a reputation to keep, see. Don't want it getting round I don't hold up my end of a bargain. So them emeralds belong to yer dad, got it?'

Jenny nodded.

'Good. I'll take you back to Islington and you make sure you give 'em to him.'

'Ain't going back.' Jennifer sobbed and clung to him. 'Gonna stay with you. You said you had a job for me. Don't mind what I do. Just don't make me go back there.'

Bill patted her back while ideas rotated in his mind. Jennifer was an all-round amateur but an eager kid. Ada needed a fresh face alongside when out shoplifting. All the girls were getting too well known to be of use in the West End. They were dispensable but Ada wasn't; but she needed a new assistant . . .

'How about you hand them over to yer mum in a few days then, if you don't want to risk meeting yer dad?' Bill cooed, stroking Jenny's hair. 'Can catch her when she's out, can't you, if you don't want to go back home to see her?'

After a quiet moment, Jennifer sniffed and brightened enough to give him a watery smile. Unbeknown to either of them, they were both mulling over the same notion: Winnie Finch would snatch at the box of emeralds because it would provide the means to leave Eddie once and for all.

CHAPTER SEVENTEEN

On noticing the china basin on the table, Matilda glee-fully rubbed together her palms. She looked forward to the mornings after Lucy's shifts at the club. 'What've we got today?' she murmured to herself, sniffing the air for telltale aroma.

Having lifted the cloth covering the top of the basin she saw inside was a good portion of sliced roast pork and three large roast potatoes. The gravy had congealed but the sight of a large brown globule didn't put Matilda off. Her stomach growled and her mouth watered in anticipation. She knew once the food went on the hob to heat through a rich brown sauce would drip over the meat and potatoes and a wonderful savoury smell would waft through her dank rooms.

Matilda didn't expect Lucy to rise for a few hours yet because it had been close to two in the morning – barely six hours ago – when her daughter had arrived home from work. Matilda still waited for the sound of her return before she'd allow herself to sink into a deep sleep.

When mother and daughter sat down to eat at one

o'clock, Lucy was feeling unrefreshed. She found it difficult to sleep in during the summer because the flimsy
threadbare curtain that covered the window in her back
bedroom did little to keep out the bright June sunshine.

'If it weren't so fatty this wouldn't be a bad bit of
meat,' Matilda declared, cutting into her dinner with
relish. The pork and potatoes had been shared equally
between them right down to the third potato being sliced
in half down its centre.

Lucy's lips quirked at the damning praise; it was the
closest her mother came to thanking her for providing
her with a very lean roast pork dinner. She was glad to
see that Matilda's health and vigour was improving with
a better diet. Recently she'd seemed more able to get
out and about on her own.

'Are you coming with me for a walk round to Beth's
today?' Lucy asked.

'Might just do that,' Matilda agreed, wiping up every
smear of gravy from her plate with a thick crust of bread.
She sat back patting her stomach. 'Reckon I could see
that off again.'

'You'll have to wait till next week if you're after a
fatty roast,' Lucy mocked. 'Probably get steak and kidney
pie later in the week.'

To round off their meal Matilda went to the hob to
put the kettle on for tea. She halted, kettle poised in
midair as a knock on the door startled her.

'Ain't expecting anybody.' She frowned at Lucy.

Lucy knew her mother was waiting for her to answer
the door so she pushed away her empty plate and got
to her feet.

For a long moment, Lucy stared in silence at Reg
Donovan before shifting aside and sending an

apprehensive glance in her mother's direction. Matilda was busy stretching up for the biscuit box on the shelf and hadn't noticed her prodigal fiancé's hesitant step over the threshold. When she eventually turned about she dropped the tin with a clatter onto the table in shock.

'What the fucking hell d'you want?' she growled.

'Come to see you, Tilly,' Reg replied gruffly.

'Well, you've seen me; now you can clear off again.'

In the tense quiet that followed Lucy flicked a glance between Matilda and Reg. Their eyes were locked; Matilda's hard and challenging, Reg's meek and appealing.

'I'll just get off round to Beth's. Wonder where I've got to, she will . . .' Lucy attempted to inject levity into her tone.

'You ain't going nowhere. He is.' Matilda followed her blunt declaration by turning her attention to the teapot.

'You look well, Tilly.'

'Yeah . . . feel well. A whole lot better'n I did when you was here making me life miserable. Got me daughter back looking after me and doing a better job than you ever managed. So sling yer 'ook.' She jutted her chin at him over a shoulder. 'Go on, piss off . . .'

Lucy remembered the unposted letters Matilda had written to Reg wishing him back with her and she knew her mother's rudeness sprung from her need to wound rather than to speak truthfully. She decided it would be best if she made a diplomatic retreat so the couple could be private. Besides, she knew her sister would be keen to have this news, as would the rest of the family.

'Don't want tea, Mum. I'm off to see Beth.' Lucy determinedly avoided her mother's eyes and, unpegging her jacket from the hook on the back of the door, she slipped out.

Halfway round to see Beth, Lucy caught sight of Kathy Finch coming towards her on the opposite side of the road. Lucy felt a twinge of guilt on remembering the set-to she'd had with Winnie after the woman called her a trollop. As they drew closer Lucy sensed Kathy's awkwardness and knew the girl was unsure whether to wave or walk on. It was all the proof Lucy needed that repercussions had followed her fight with Winnie that day.

On impulse she crossed the road to speak to Kathy. She liked the young woman and would rather they didn't fall out.

'I suppose you've heard about that bust-up I had with your mum round at Tom's school.'

Kathy nodded while shuffling her feet. 'Mum jumped to the conclusion Jenny was knocking about with a boy from the Bunk and that sent her into a right paddy. When she found out it was someone even worse – Bill Black – well . . .' Kathy's voice faded away but her rolled eyes spoke volumes.

'I didn't intend dropping your sister in it, swear I didn't. I'd stopped to speak to Tom because some kids in the playground were giving him a hard time. Winnie turned up and told me to stay away from Tom 'cos I was a trollop.' Lucy grimaced regret. 'I shouldn't have let her rile me. Then it wouldn't have slipped out about Jennifer.'

'Thanks for helping Tom,' Kathy said. 'I didn't know about him getting bullied.'

'Have things quietened down indoors?' Lucy asked.

'Jenny's gone . . . packed her bags a few days ago. She left home after Dad gave her a hiding for chasing after Bill.' Kathy sighed. 'It's all her own stupid fault. She's got herself into a right mess.'

For a moment, Lucy was too taken aback to reply. 'Sorry to hear that,' she eventually murmured. And she was. It was hard for a grown woman with a skill and experience to make her own way with the dole queues growing ever longer. Jennifer Finch probably hadn't even turned sixteen and had only scant experience in dead-end jobs. She would struggle to earn enough to keep a roof over her head. 'Perhaps it'll blow over and your sister'll turn up again—' Lucy started optimistically.

'No point in her coming back now and Jenny knows it,' Kathy interrupted dolefully. 'They'll kick her out if she so much as shows her face. You recognised Bill Black with Jenny . . . so you know him, do you?' Kathy cocked her head waiting for a reply.

'It was Connie recognised him, not me. But I've seen him since that afternoon. Never spoken to the man, though,' she quickly added. And she hadn't. Although Bill had visited the club again, on his own, Lucy had avoided serving him. In her opinion he was too flashy and loud.

And very unlike Sean Napier, who had also been back on the same evening as Bill. He too had been alone but Sean hadn't tried to touch up all the waitresses as they passed by, as Bill had, despite a few of them – Connie included – loitering about his table to tempt him to do so.

Both men had left alone.

'Bill's been round ours lots of times to do business with me dad. Don't know what Jenny sees in him,' Kathy said. 'He always seemed a smarmy sort to me.'

'Where's Jennifer gone to?'

'South London, to try and find him.' Kathy answered. 'I've not heard a word from her.' She blinked back tears.

'Mum doesn't care. The day Jenny left, she just shut the door on her and carried on as usual. Dad seems to have forgotten her too.' Kathy bit her lip, wondering whether to say any more about her parents' shocking callousness. 'I reckon they're more worried the neighbours are gossiping that she's been chucked out 'cos she's in the family way.'

'Is she?' Lucy whispered, eyes widening.

'Don't know. She doesn't look it. She said Bill was "waiting" until they got engaged.' She shook her head.

Lucy mirrored Kathy's scepticism by snorting a laugh. 'She surely didn't believe *that*?'

'He's lying, I know.' Kathy glanced at Lucy for confirmation of that statement.

'I have seen him out with a woman . . .' Lucy's expression was sympathetic.

'Mum 'n' Dad won't give her a farthing if she gets in trouble . . .' Kathy bit her lip as her voice cracked. She feared her sister might already be on the road to ruin.

'Daughters turning up on the doorstep with a baby worries the life out of parents. My mum was always checking up on all of us in case we'd been misbehaving with boys.'

The two young women stood quietly for a moment, lost in contemplation of Jennifer's bleak future.

'Where you off to?' Kathy asked.

'See me sister Beth. Got some news for her.' Lucy smiled faintly. 'Mum's fiancé has come back from Ireland.'

'Thought they'd broken up ages ago,' Kathy said, mildly interested.

'So did all of us, Mum included.' Lucy's face was a study in ruefulness. 'Could go home later and find 'em all cosied up drinking tea; on the other hand, could go home and find the place upside down. Never know with Mum how she'll take things.'

'Good luck then,' Kathy said, and forced a smile before walking on.

'So what did Beth say?'

Lucy had the question fired at her before she'd got properly inside the door.

Matilda was standing, hands on hips, with her head cocked to one side and her thick eyebrows winging over her piercing blue eyes. But Lucy was relieved to see that behind her mother the furniture looked no more battered than it had when she'd gone out a couple of hours ago. Matilda's mood appeared more or less the same too.

'What did Beth say about what?' Lucy was aware that her mother was challenging her to admit to gossiping with Beth about Reg Donovan's reappearance.

But he was nowhere to be seen. Lucy felt disappointed because she'd hoped her mother and Reg might patch things up. They'd been together a good many years and had seemed content to rub along together before her vile uncle Jimmy Wild had caused such terrible ructions in their family.

'You telling me you didn't say nuthin' to yer sister about Reg turning up here today?'

'Course I told her,' Lucy admitted. 'Beth hopes, same as I do, that you'll be friends with him again. We both liked him. Alice and Sophy thought he was all right as well.'

'You lot didn't have to live with him,' Matilda grumbled, but her lips twitched suddenly in a smile she was unable to subdue.

215

It was then Lucy's turn to cast a shrewd eye. 'You've made up with him, haven't you?'

'No I ain't! Not completely,' Matilda insisted less sharply. 'Ain't letting him off the hook that easily. That's why he's not here. Sent him away, didn't I?' She glanced at her reflection in the mirror, unconsciously smoothing some fiery coarse hair into her bun. 'No man gets his boots back under me bed that easily, and I told him so.'

'That's right . . . you tell him, Mum,' Lucy praised softly.

Matilda turned an old-fashioned stare on her amused daughter. 'Apologised . . . lots of times, he did, fer going off like that. So he should, 'n' all,' she muttered. 'Said he's been missing me fer ages but only just plucked up courage to come back to England and tell me so.'

'You've been missing him too, I know you have,' Lucy said gently. 'I bet if you'd had his address in Ireland you'd've written and told him so, wouldn't you?'

'Didn't miss him that much.' Matilda made a dismissive gesture, avoiding her daughter's eye. 'Got used to having him around the place, that's all it was. Course, since you come back home it's been different 'cos we've had each other . . .'

'But I might not be around for much longer. You know I'm after another job in service, don't you, Mum?'

'Yeah, that's what I thought,' Matilda agreed. 'Or if you ain't working and living in somewhere you might be getting married. I hope you do take up with a nice fellow and settle down,' she added, matter of fact.

On hearing that, Lucy's thoughts were drawn to Rory Jackson and their meeting the following evening.

'I know you won't be around for ever, Luce. And I know I ain't up to living on me own. Need a bit of

216

company, and a bit of help paying me way, don't I? So . . . I did say I'd meet Reg later round in the Duke for a couple of little drinks so we can talk about things. He can tell me what he's been up to all these months, for a start.' She pursed her lips in determination.

'Not too many drinks, though, Mum, eh?' Lucy smiled. 'You don't want to fall back into bad habits.'

Matilda knew all her daughters had been glad to see her drinking less following her accident. But in typical style she found it hard to admit that she was also relieved a long stay in hospital had helped her conquer her addiction to Irish whiskey.

'Never had no bad habits in me life,' she muttered, but the corners of her mouth jiggled at the fib.

CHAPTER EIGHTEEN

'Wasn't sure if you'd still want to go out with me as you're not getting a ride in a Rolls-Royce this evening.'

'Well, I don't mind admitting it crossed me mind to stand you up, Rory Jackson,' Lucy teased in return, strolling closer.

She'd seen him as soon as she'd approached their meeting place and had been aware when he noticed her too. He'd thrust his hands in his pockets and cocked his head to one side as though assessing her appearance and liking what he saw.

Lucy had taken pains to make sure she looked attractive . . . and ladylike. She'd put on her best summer dress – which covered her knees – and was wearing a new lemon-coloured cardigan that reflected a summery light onto her cheeks and was a perfect foil for her chestnut hair. That afternoon she'd gone to the hairdresser and had her shoulder-length locks trimmed into a sleek fashionable bob. Before heading off out into Campbell Road, she'd taken a last look in her mother's freckled mirror hooked over the mantel and had been satisfied with her reflection.

Rory seemed to have taken a pleasing amount of trouble with his appearance too. He was out of uniform, as was expected, but looked equally handsome and imposing in a brown suit and smart tie as he did in grey flannel and peaked cap. Lucy could see his shoes were highly polished and the angular planes of his jaw looked freshly shaven. As she came closer to him she could smell the citrus cologne he'd used.

'Don't you look a sight fer sore eyes.' Rory smiled down at her, grey eyes twinkling. 'Where d'you fancy going? Have a drink, shall we? Or would you prefer to see what's on at the flicks?'

'How about a stroll first, while we decide?' Lucy suggested. It was a glorious June evening and it seemed a shame to be cooped up too soon in a hot picture palace or a smoky pub. 'We could go along Upper Street till we reach Highbury Fields, if you like?'

Rory offered her his arm, wordlessly agreeing to her suggestion, and they set off in that direction.

'How's your mum doing now? Is she better?' Rory asked conversationally.

A swift enquiring glance from Lucy met that remark.

'You told me ages ago, when you first started work at Mortimer House, that your mum was poorly,' Rory reminded her.

'You've got a good memory,' Lucy responded lightly.

'I have where you're concerned, Lucy Keiver.' Rory gave a gruff chuckle. 'I remember you said you was going to write to me, but if I hadn't caught sight of you outside the Cuckoo Club earlier in the week I don't reckon I'd've heard from you again. Why's that?' he asked bluntly.

Lucy turned away and shrugged. 'Said I'd get in touch when I was settled; don't feel I am yet . . . not properly.'

'Glad to hear it, 'cos the Cuckoo Club ain't exactly the sort of place any fellow would want his girl working in.'

Lucy flicked him a glance. His remark had nettled her but she returned lightly, 'Don't remember agreeing to be your girl, Rory Jackson, just to taking a walk out with you.'

'Don't remember asking you to be my girl,' he countered. 'Just making a general remark about women that work in those sorts of places.'

'Talk about something else then, shall we?' Lucy turned her head towards a shop window display. The pleasure she'd felt moments ago at the prospect of a summer evening stroll with a handsome man was already fading.

Rory's attitude annoyed and disappointed her. What did he know of the hardships that sent women to work in seedy clubs? He had no idea that Molly Warner had a little boy to rear yet no man around to act as husband and father; or that the woman often went hungry to feed her son. Neither did he know that Connie and her sisters had fended for themselves as children because their father had walked out on their alcoholic mother. Her own mother's health had greatly improved due to good nourishment from the dinners she received courtesy of the Cuckoo Club. Lucy might not be proud of her job but it had vital benefits and she wasn't about to justify her actions to anybody, least of all a man who took for granted regular pay and three square meals a day.

'Fancy a cup of tea?' Rory jerked his head, indicating the Lyons Corner House, to which their walk had returned them. Through the windows could be seen the white hats of Nippies darting between tables.

Lucy murmured agreement, hoping the atmosphere between them might ease. Rory again seemed affable and she wondered if she was being too sensitive. Nevertheless she couldn't prevent her mind flitting to find an excuse to return home early.

They settled at a window table.

'Like what you've done with your hair,' Rory touched a finger to her shiny fringe. 'Suits you shorter like that.'

A Nippy came over, pad and pencil in hand, and he gave an order for a pot of tea and two buttered currant buns without asking Lucy what she'd like.

Lucy bit back a retort that an iced bun would have been her choice and looked about the interior of the busy teashop.

She was beginning to relax, determined to enjoy her refreshment when the bell on the door clattered, drawing her attention. She put down her cup and instinctively averted her face her heartbeat increasing tempo. Although Sean Napier's expression remained impassive, Lucy knew he had seen her and recognised her too. Lucy also knew the man accompanying him. She'd never spoken to Ralph Franks but remembered Connie had discreetly pointed him out when Ralph had been loitering outside the Cuckoo Club to meet her when her shift finished. The two men made their way to a table on the opposite side of the room.

Lucy was confident that Ralph didn't know her: on the evening she'd seen him outside the club he had walked away, disappearing from sight seconds after he glimpsed Connie emerging from the doorway. Yet Lucy felt a sense of foreboding creeping over her without understanding what was causing it. She knew she had done nothing wrong but recalled that Sean Napier had questioned her over Connie's friendship with Ralph. She was relieved she'd told him nothing because the two men looked to be friends . . . or colleagues. She'd wondered at the time if Sean Napier might be an undercover copper making enquiries about goings-on at the club. The last thing she wanted was to lose her job or be drawn into any police investigation.

Feeling very apprehensive, Lucy blurted, 'Perhaps we could go to the flicks if something decent's showing.'

'Know them, do you?' Rory asked, a sideways flick of his head indicating the new arrivals.

'Just . . . someone from the club.' Lucy had discerned disapproval in his tone and she was annoyed to have answered him sounding apologetic. She'd done nothing to be ashamed of, she reminded herself.

'Ah . . . clients, are they?' Rory muttered, and swallowed what remained of his tea. 'Finished?' He jerked a nod at Lucy's half-empty cup.

'No, not quite,' Lucy said. 'But I am ready to go,' she added tightly, standing up. She walked swiftly to the exit, leaving him to settle the bill.

Outside the café, Rory caught up with Lucy and grabbed her arm, spinning her around. 'Hold on, I thought you wanted to go to the flicks?'

'I've changed my mind. I'm off home. Meeting up was a mistake. I think you know that as well as I do.'

'Something wrong?'

He sounded genuinely surprised and Lucy stared at him, then huffed a disbelieving laugh. 'I know we didn't work long together at Mortimer House, but either I've changed or you have. You're not the man I remember at all. Has anybody told you that you can be rude and domineering?'

'You're not the girl I remember either,' he came back immediately, ignoring her criticism of his character. 'You're the one who's changed, not me, Lucy Keiver. Never reckoned for one moment you'd lower yourself to do what you do.'

'And what do I do?' Lucy snapped, her lips pursing while she awaited his reply. She could tell he hadn't been expecting such a direct question.

Colour began seeping into Rory's cheeks but Lucy knew he was feeling more embarrassed than guilty. She'd challenged him to call her a name but he didn't have the guts to do more than snipe and hint she was on the game. Lucy tried again to wriggle her forearm free of his fingers.

'I'll tell you what I do,' Lucy spat through her teeth, squarely meeting his hard grey eyes. 'I serve drinks and dinners to customers . . . mostly men but some women too. And that's *all* I do at the Cuckoo Club. Not that it's any of your business.' Finally she flung him off.

Rory shoved a hand across the back of his neck, looking sheepish. 'Sorry . . .' he muttered with bad grace. 'Didn't mean . . . just I don't like the idea of you working there.' He plunged his hands in his pockets and stared sideways into the distance.

After a quiet moment Lucy said, 'It's all right; perhaps we just didn't know one another as well as we thought we did.' She'd sooner they didn't part as bad friends so she gave him a wry smile. 'No harm done. Thanks for tea. I'm gonna get off home.' She'd barely moved a yard before Rory again had hold of her arm.

'We're going to the flicks, aren't we?'

Lucy shook her head. 'I'm getting off home.'

'I'll walk you back, then,' Rory muttered through tight lips following a small strained silence.

223

'No need for that . . . but thanks for the offer.'

'I said I'll walk you back.' He roughly threaded her arm through his and set off at a brisk pace. 'It's getting dark . . .' He glanced up at clouds gathering on the horizon, buffering the low evening sun. The atmosphere had turned cool and a breeze was whipping strands of Lucy's glossy hair across her eyes.

Impatiently she cleared her vision, then yanked her arm free of Rory's grip. She wasn't about to be ordered around. She'd told him no nicely . . .

'You embarrassed about living in that dump?' Rory's voice held a slight sneer as he watched her backing away from him. 'Is that why you don't want me walking you home? 'Cos you don't want me to think you live there?'

Lucy bristled. The Bunk *was* a dump – she knew that better than anybody – but she didn't like it brought to her attention in such an arrogant and intentionally unpleasant way.

'Campbell Road, ain't it?' Rory grimaced disgust. 'I was going to come back and search for you again when you didn't get in touch. But I decided against it when I found out it's got a bad reputation. Never know what you might pick up loitering in such a place. Can see why your mother's ailing, dossing in that slum.'

'She's doing much better, actually,' Lucy informed him icily. She'd feared Rory might be disgusted when he discovered more about her and so had wanted to hide from him the truth about her home and work. Now she felt guilty for having been ashamed of herself. But she felt a burden on her easing because she no longer gave a damn what Rory Jackson thought . . .

'If I'd known from the start where you'd come from, I'd never have let you get your hooks into me.'

'What're you on about?' Lucy demanded. 'I've never even tried to get me hooks into you.'

'Little tease, that's what you are . . . or there's a better name fer girls like you. But then you'd know all about that, wouldn't you?' Rory backed her swiftly against the wall of a building and forced his body's length against hers. He took her chin in a brutal grip, then swooped to kiss her with punishing force.

Lucy swiftly kicked him in the shin and tried to wrench her face away from his grinding mouth. But his fingers simply increased pressure on her jaw until she cried out in pain.

'All right there?'

Neither of them heard the softly drawled question. But Lucy was aware of being greatly relieved when Rory was jerked backwards by a large hand that appeared on his shoulder.

Sean Napier cocked his head, looking from one of them to the other. His narrowed blue gaze settled on Lucy. 'Let me know if I'm not wanted, won't you, now?'

Mortified, Lucy knew why he had addressed her. He was enquiring if she wanted to be left alone with her rough punter.

Months ago she'd rebuffed his overtures when he'd waited outside the club for her; nevertheless, he still imagined she might be a part-time tart. What he'd just witnessed between her and Rory had no doubt reinforced his suspicion. No decent woman would be seen in daylight shoved up against a wall, tussling with a man in the street.

'You're not wanted,' Lucy clipped out. She turned her attention to Rory. 'And neither are you.' She retreated two steps, swung a proud defiant look between them,

225

then spun round and headed off towards home, angry humiliated tears burning the backs of her eyes the moment she was sure neither man could see them.

Rory and Sean clashed gazes. The Irishman's mouth was aslant as though he was amused. But Rory wasn't fooled by his casual stance. Sean had his weight lightly balanced on the balls of his feet and his hands seemed carelessly plunged into his pockets. Rory suspected they might spring free in an instant and deliver a blow. The fellow didn't appear to be taller and his breadth of shoulder was roughly the same as his own, yet for some reason Rory instinctively felt intimidated. With a poisonous look he strode off across the road in the opposite direction to the one Lucy had taken.

CHAPTER NINETEEN

'Will you stop and talk for a moment?'

'No.' Lucy dodged past and kept on walking. She'd felt her heart vault to her mouth when Sean Napier's car had pulled up at the kerb in front of her and he'd got out and blocked her path.

'You used to work with him at Mortimer House, didn't you?'

Lucy's pace faltered. 'How d'you know that?' she demanded hoarsely, pivoting about.

'Well, now, if you stop a while I'll tell you,' he drawled with a half-smile.

Lucy stubbornly moved on, a frown furrowing her brow and blood pounding in her ears. But she'd barely covered a few yards when she halted and swung round again. Sean was resting back against the flank wall of a house, hat tipped forward on his head, waiting for her. The fact that he'd anticipated curiosity would get the better of her and she'd retrace her steps put an indignant flush on her face.

'How d'you know my business?' Slowly she approached him.

'Because it's my business to know about the staff at Mortimer House.'

'Why's that?' Lucy demanded, although she already had a niggling suspicion that the theft and dreadful tragedy at the house would be his reason.

'You quit just before a box of valuable jewellery went missing, did you know that, now?' Sean asked neutrally. 'Has Rory Jackson told you what went on at all?'

Lucy's cheeks prickled as alarming possibilities assaulted her mind. The worst of them was that Sean Napier *was* a detective who imagined she'd information about the crime. Rory had virtually accused her of being in cahoots with Audrey Stubbs, the two of them simply feigning hostility. Lucy had been incensed to hear it; now she felt numb with shock at the idea a policeman might believe she was a thief's accomplice.

On the evening of their brief conversation outside the Cuckoo Club, she'd imagined Sean Napier's professional interest would be in Boris or his customers and his interest in her was personal. Inwardly she squirmed in embarrassment at her conceit.

If Lord Mortimer had changed his mind about keeping quiet to quash the scandal, and had decided to get in the authorities to recover his stuff . . . Lucy felt her mouth go dry as she realised Mr Napier might be able to arrest her if she didn't co-operate in answering his questions.

'Did Jackson tell you about the theft?' Sean again asked.

Lucy moistened her lips. 'Yes . . .' she murmured. His quietly authoritative manner withered her ready denial.

'But I wasn't working there when it all happened so can't be of any use to you, can I?'

His answering smile seemed brimful of mockery and disbelief.

'Who are you to be asking questions, in any case?' Lucy's natural sparkiness came to her rescue and she stepped closer. 'You know a bit about me but I don't know you from Adam.' She was about to demand if he was one of Ralph Franks' colleagues but swallowed the words. Better to leave the police out of it for now, she reckoned, and act dumb on that score.

Sean held out a hand. 'Ah, apologies, Miss Keiver, although I know you and you know me, we haven't been formally introduced, have we? Sean Napier, at your service.'

Lucy glanced at his long outstretched fingers, suddenly grabbed them, gave them a single pump, then snatched back her hand. 'Apart from that, who are you to be asking me questions?'

'I'm not a policeman.'

Lucy's eyes flitted to his face. Again he seemed amused at her expense. 'In that case you've no right to be harassing me.'

'Sorry, I hadn't realised you saw it that way.' He raised his hat to her and strolled towards his car.

'Just you hold on a minute!' Lucy spontaneously yelled, sprinting after him. Now she knew he was not on official business she felt relieved enough to want an explanation from him. 'If you've been making enquiries about me I want to know why.'

Sean halted by his vehicle with a hand resting idly on the dusty black roof. 'Lord Mortimer was very upset about losing his jewellery and wants it back.'

'Can't blame him for that,' Lucy said succinctly. 'And how do you fit into it all?'

Sean smiled at his drumming fingers. 'I'm after getting it back for him.'

A fat raindrop, then another, fell on the car's roof and he smeared them away with a thumb. 'Want a lift home?'

Lucy shook her head. A gust of wind got beneath her floral frock taking the skirt up high about her thighs.

He gave her slim summery figure a slow look. 'Do you like getting wet?'

'Not far to go,' Lucy said hoarsely, spontaneously heating beneath his low-lidded gaze.

'Campbell Road's far enough in a downpour. Get in.'

Lucy blinked rain from her lashes and instinctively ducked as a sudden crash of thunder broke overhead.

Sean took off his hat and plopped it on her new hairstyle to give her some protection. He opened the car door. 'Get in.' The note of authority was again in his voice. But it was a need within that prompted Lucy to obey and slide onto the seat.

'How d'you know where I live?' Lucy rubbed together her moist palms to warm them.

'I followed you home.'

Lucy speared him a look through damp lashes. She knew she should feel alarmed or outraged to know that, but she didn't. Neither did she feel awkward because he knew she lived in a slum. 'Why did you do that?'

'Told you. I'm interested in people connected with Mortimer House.'

Lucy suddenly realised she still wore his homburg. She removed it and placed it on the floor by her feet. Without a hat brim shadowing his features, and with the benefit of a sombre daylight rather than the muted lamps in the club she could see he was younger than she'd imagined. Perhaps early thirties. His hair, sleek with rain, looked jet black and his jaw stubbly and in need of a razor. He glanced at her, laughing soundlessly as his direct gaze made her jerk back immediately into her seat.

'Ask away,' he invited, reading her mind.

'Is Lord Mortimer a friend of yours?'

'We're not friends.'

'So why are you trying to get back his jewels if you're not the police?' A bright idea struck Lucy. 'Do you work for an insurance company?'

'No.'

'So why . . .?'

'For the same reason you work in the Cuckoo Club, Lucy. I'm doing it for the money.'

'His lordship's paying you to get back his jewellery?'

'I hope so, or I'm wasting me time.' His Irish brogue lilted into a little laugh.

'So . . . you're a sort of private detective. Well, I know who took it.'

'So do I – a maid.'

'Audrey Stubbs is her name,' Lucy said helpfully.

'She's a girl with many names.'

Lucy blinked, looking impressed. 'Really? How d'you find that out?'

'Me job to find out these things.'

'Do you know where to find her to get the stuff back?' Lucy was becoming interested in their conversation and turned towards him on her seat so she could read his expression while they talked.

'She's just a foot soldier . . . a good one, I'll give her that.'

'And you're after her boss?'

231

He nodded, pulling over to the kerb. 'You're home.' He jerked his head at the grimy tenement blocks stretching away into the distance.

Lucy had been engrossed and had not realised he'd stopped close to the Bunk's junction with Seven Sisters Road. Oddly, she felt disinclined to get out of the car and it wasn't just because the rain was beating hard against the windscreen. She wished the journey had taken longer so she could have found out more about him. His soft Irish tone was soothing to listen to.

'Thanks for the lift,' she murmured.

'You and Rory Jackson sweethearts, are you?'

'No, we just met up to go out for the evening, that's all.'

'Ah . . . but he saw things differently and expected more.'

'He expected more because he found out where I work. He sees *me* differently now.' Lucy tilted her chin. 'So I put him straight on a few things.'

Sean quirked a smile. 'Yeah, I saw that. Perhaps he should pay a visit to the Cuckoo Club and put his mind at rest. I told you before you're not suited to the work,' he drawled.

'Perhaps you're not suited to *your* work,' Lucy came back sourly, aware of his mockery. 'Taking your time finding the jewellery, aren't you? Some detective! The Mortimer House robbery was ages ago.'

Lucy was about to get out when firm fingers manacled her wrist, holding her in her seat.

'I'll have it, don't worry about that now . . . and more besides.'

Lucy blinked, looked at his fingers. He withdrew them slowly so they stroked her skin.

232

'Stopped raining.' He glanced at the dribbling windscreen. 'Good night, Lucy.' He reached across her, pushed open the car door then swooped on his hat and shoved it to the back of his head.

As Lucy stepped onto a glistening wet pavement she was sure she heard a low laugh and slammed shut the car door with some force.

Jennifer knew her mother's routine on Wednesdays: She would drop Tom at Pooles Park, then go on to her cleaning job in Crouch End. Despite the fact Winifred was regularly away from home during the day, none of the neighbours knew for sure that Mrs Finch worked. She certainly never owned up to it, and Jennifer and Kathy had been warned not to let on to a soul that their mother had a job.

Eddie would have been outraged if a rumour had started that his income was inadequate to keep his family. In fact it was more than sufficient, but he was too tight-fisted to spend much of it, forcing Winnie to supplement the housekeeping with her wages.

Having watched her little brother trudging in through the school gates Jennifer turned her attention back to her mother. Winnie was delving into her shopping bag to check, as she always did, that she had all she needed before setting off towards the bus stop. With a deep inspiriting breath, Jennifer emerged from behind the privet hedge and approached her mother before she went on her way.

'What in God's name d'you want?' Winnie's eyes whizzed to and fro as though to ensure there was no audience to this meeting. She'd accepted Jennifer was gone from her life, and good riddance. The sly probing

233

of neighbours interested in finding out about Jennifer's disappearance was constantly getting on her nerves. She'd had a blazing row with Cissy Dickens when she'd caught the woman trying to wheedle out of Tom what had happened to 'that sister who'd not been seen around in a while'. So far, Winnie had fobbed off all the nosy parkers with curt instructions to mind their own business and leave her to see to hers.

'If you're thinking of begging me to let you back in you can think again,' Winnie hissed. 'Yer father won't hear of it and that's that.' She pursed her lips. 'Tired of you already, is he? Hah! No surprises there, miss! Could've told you you was just one of many where Bill Black was concerned. Well, you've made your bed so you lie on it.' Winnie's voice sounded choked but she determinedly marched past.

Jennifer slouched along behind, lost in thought. She'd been loitering nervously for her mother to appear that morning, dreading that Winnie would fly at her for having stolen from Eddie. But not a word had been mentioned about that, so obviously the theft hadn't yet been discovered. The first person he would have accused would have been his wife because she was the one who usually unearthed his savings. Jennifer remembered her mother had found her father's nest egg one Christmas, years ago when she and Kathy were about nine and Tom just a babe in arms. An almighty bust-up had occurred when Eddie realised Winnie had gone behind his back and splashed out on a turkey and all the trimmings, and lavish presents for the family. Her mother had never done it again after spending Christmas with a black eye.

'Go on, clear off.' Winnie snapped over a shoulder at Jennifer, startling her to attention.

'Not turned up to ask about coming home, honest,' Jenny mumbled forlornly. 'If you'll just stop a moment, Mum, I want to talk to you about something.'

'Off to work, no time fer chatting.' Winnie's impatience couldn't wholly suppress a wobble in her voice.

'Mum . . . please . . .'

'Don't you call me that!' Winnie swung about, pointing a finger close to her daughter's chin. 'You're no daughter of mine, way you've been carrying on.' Her mouth worked but no sound issued for a moment. 'Disgusting . . . that's what you are.' Winnie blinked rapidly against the sting in her eyes. 'Should have known how you'd turn out when you was still at school and acting up chasing after all the boys. Few more good hidings, that's what you needed to learn you a lesson.'

'Brought you this,' Jennifer blurted, interrupting her mother's tirade. She grabbed at the box stuffed in her handbag and showed her mother just enough of it to wet her curiosity. Jenny glanced about for somewhere more private where she could hand over the jewellery. Once, she'd thought it the most marvellous, beautiful possession any girl could wish for. Now, she'd be glad to be rid of it. Bill had changed towards her since he'd found out she'd brought the emeralds with her when she ran away. She was hoping that once she'd offloaded the jewellery on Winnie things would be back to normal between her and Bill.

He was waiting for her in a side street close by to take her back to Lambeth. Jenny wanted to get rid of the box and get going. Dejectedly she realised her mother hadn't softened at all towards her, and secretly she'd hoped she would because she was no longer certain that Lambeth, or Bill for that matter, held the attraction it once had. But what choice did she have now but to go back there with him? She glanced at her mother's pinched features; Winnie's eyes looked as hard as pebbles and there wasn't a hint of forgiveness about her compressed lips.

'What you got there?' Winnie jerked a nod at the edge of tortoiseshell poking from her daughter's bag.

'Come over here and I'll show you.' Jenny started towards an alley that led to a ramshackle mews building, beckoning her mother to follow.

Winnie stubbornly cocked her head but after a moment she joined Jennifer in the shelter of two parallel high brick walls.

'It's for you to take home.' Jennifer closed the lid and held out the box.

As if in a trance, Winnie obediently took it and inched up the lid as though what lay within might leap out and bite. Having taken a glimpse and reassured herself it wasn't a vision, she snapped it shut again. 'You've stolen this, have you?' she whispered.

Jenny shook her head. 'Bill gave it to me to give to you. He owes it to Dad as payment for something. Course, neither of us could meet Dad . . . not the way he is over things. But Bill says he don't welch on deals and wants it handed over. So there it is.' Jenny watched the stupefaction on her mother's face slowly transforming to a more calculating expression. Winnie's nimble brain was already weighing things up, just as Jennifer had guessed it would.

'Right . . .' Winnie croaked. She jammed the box of priceless jewellery into her battered shopping bag. 'I'll see to it then . . .'

'Mum . . .?' Jenny started in a pleading, tearful voice.

Winnie vigorously shook her head and averted her face from her daughter. 'Get going,' she ordered roughly. When Jennifer came towards her, arms outstretched to hug her, Winifred scooted backwards into the brick wall. A moment later she'd scurried down the alley and out of sight.

'Weren't so hard, were it?'

Jenny shook her head and gave Bill a wavering smile.

'Got a bit emotional, did yer, seeing yer old mum?'

Jenny nodded and sniffed.

'Well, only to be expected.' Bill turned the ignition. 'Bit better than facing yer old man, weren't it?'

Jenny grunted a mirthless chuckle. 'Don't want to see him ever again.'

'Don't have to, do you, now I'm taking care of you.'

'Are you . . . taking care of me?' Jenny turned doe eyes on him.

She'd been staying with him at a flat in Lambeth and sleeping on his sofa. She'd imagined he might expect her to join him in his bed but he hadn't and she'd felt a bit miffed about that, and that he hadn't done the gentlemanly thing and offered her the bed and slept on the couch himself. In fact he'd hardly touched her even to kiss her . . . just brief pecks on the lips. She'd begun to think perhaps he had tired of her but when she clung to him he always said about not wanting to get carried away and being respectful. Jenny had wondered whether Bill was scared of her father's revenge. She reckoned that Eddie would go mad about his money going missing but he'd not give a damn if Bill broke her in or got her pregnant. As far as her parents were concerned she was dead to them. Her mother had proved that to her a short while ago.

'Now we've got that out of the way, I've got a couple of friends I want you to meet.' Bill gave her an encouraging smile. 'Nice young ladies, they are, and they're looking fer a gel to help 'em out with a bit of business. I know you'll fit in 'cos you're smart and savvy just like them, and you'd like to earn some decent wages, wouldn't yer, now?'

'Are we getting engaged soon?' Jenny asked, gazing at him with huge entreating eyes.

Bill continued staring ahead for a long moment before grinning at her. 'When the time's right. Getting you a good job, that's what's important, ain't it?'

Jenny nodded, dimpling at him although she felt dejected by his answer. Her mind flitted back to her meeting with her mother, and what Winnie had said about her being one of many where Bill was concerned. Without having any real proof she knew her mother was right. Bill regularly went off in the evening and left her alone in his mouldy bedsit. She'd guessed he'd gone to meet a woman because he'd come back sometimes smelling of perfume as well as booze. But what really surprised Jenny was his home. He'd told her he was doing well so she'd felt sure he'd be living in a swish place.

Jenny's mind turned again to her family. Winnie would do all right now she had the jewellery. She'd sell it then get going, taking Tom with her, and Kathy too if she wanted to escape their father. If she didn't Jenny was sure her mum would see Kathy all right with enough money to rent a room of her own. An idea soothed Jenny's uneasiness. If Kathy had her own home she'd go and live with her if it didn't work out with Bill. She peeped at his rugged profile. But it would. She'd prove to him she was really keen and useful then he'd give up his other girls and concentrate on her. Feeling affectionate she slid towards him, rubbing her cheek against his sleeve. 'Can't wait to get started in a good job.' She glanced up at his set mouth. 'It *is* a good job you've found me, ain't it, Bill?'

'The best,' he growled, then started to laugh.

CHAPTER TWENTY

'Cor, me dogs ain't 'alf barking.' Connie eased off one of her shoes and gingerly peeled her sticky stocking away from her heel where a blister had burst.

'Ooh . . . that looks nasty.' Having dumped down an armful of dirty plates in the Cuckoo Club's boiling kitchen Lucy had emerged to find Connie hopping about in the corridor. 'Do you want a hanky to clean up?' She pulled a scrap of linen from her pocket, leaning back against the cool wall for a breather.

Gratefully, Connie took it and, wincing, dabbed at bloodied skin. 'Should never have let me sister talk me into having these poxy things off her for seven 'n' six. Knew they was too small but Sarah said they'd stretch.' She pulled at the black leather strap. 'Ain't no bigger at all.' She cast the shoe to the floor. 'Charging about like a blue-arsed fly tonight's made me feet swell up like balloons. I've got a ladder in me stocking 'n' all.' She sighed, smoothing into place the black seam running up her calf.

It was a Thursday night and the club was heaving

with customers. Following requests from several diners the entertainment had started early and a woman's husky soulful voice could be heard accompanying the jazz band. Thursday evening tended to be ladies' night. Some of the regular gentlemen had got into the habit of bringing female companions with them when Rita Rawlings was on stage, and the dance floor soon became crowded with smooching couples. Lucy enjoyed the cosier atmosphere created by a more even mix of the sexes, and while Connie dried her wound she began swaying dreamily in time to the music. A moment later she'd nearly jumped out of her skin.

'What you two doing here! Lazy!' Having bellowed at them, Boris angrily smacked an open palm with the back of his hand.

He'd been hurtling along in the opposite direction but on spying his most reliable waitresses standing idle he'd done an about-turn and stormed over. 'Come . . . come . . . lots people waiting for tables. Where's Vera? I said no having breaks till quieten down later on.' He peered at the rota pinned to the wall by Lucy's head, theatrically slapping his olive brow on digesting it was Vera's dinnertime and she was probably disobeying him.

'Just coming, ain't I . . .' Connie huffed. 'Look, me foot's bleeding.' She twisted her leg for Boris to examine the damage.

He waved it away, wrinkling his nose at the cheesy odour wafting his way. 'Get new shoes out of tips.' Grabbing Lucy by an arm he propelled her towards the entrance to the restaurant. 'See . . . Mr Black over there waiting with his friend.' He jerked a nod at the double doors where Bill and a small blonde were stationed at the head of a queue of people. Even at a distance, Lucy could hear his raised voice. 'He all the time impatient. See, Greg Randall nearly finished. Greg like you, Lucy.' Boris gave her a sly wink. 'You go tell him we need table. Quick, off you go.' Lucy received a shove in the small of the back to speed her on her way, then Boris nipped out of sight in the corridor.

Lucy began weaving between tables, smiling and murmuring to customers who tried to waylay her for service. Time and again she reassured people their waitress was just coming. Boris always got in a fluster when they were too busy. Rather than be of practical help he made himself scarce and got the staff to take the brunt of the customers' abuse. On quiet evenings he would swagger about, inviting compliments, or hold court with his boyfriend and their acquaintances. But he was shrewd about profit, and punters got precedence over pals every time. Lucy had seen him shoo away his little gang if an unscheduled party arrived at the top of the stairs wanting to be fed.

Lucy was close enough now to see Greg Randall nodding his grey head in time with the melody. She hated having to hurry customers away before they were ready to leave. She liked Mr Randall and knew he rounded off every dinner with a leisurely brandy.

Another rumble of discontent over by the doorway drew her eyes and through the smoky atmosphere she glimpsed that Bill Black's suit looked almost as loud as he sounded. She was relieved that at least he hadn't brought fifteen-year-old Jennifer Finch out with him. She suffocated a nervous giggle. Dealing with that situation certainly *would* have been awkward!

As far as Lucy knew, Bill's blonde friend had only accompanied him to the club on one other occasion.

She recalled Connie had said her name was Mavis and she was unfriendly. From the way the couple were acting she detected that he wanted to leave and she didn't. Lucy hoped they'd lose patience and go before she reached Greg's side and had to eject him from his seat. But they didn't disappear so with an apologetic smile she came to a halt by the elderly gentleman.

'Would you mind taking your brandy at the bar, Mr Randall? Tables are in short supply this evening.'

Greg Randall put down his glass and slipped a nifty finger along the underside of his clipped moustache. 'If it were anybody else asking . . .' He gave a martyred sigh. 'Very well, I can see you're extremely busy.'

'Oh, thank you, sir, much obliged.' Lucy immediately began clearing the table in case he changed his mind.

'You're too good for a place like this, you know, poppet.' Greg laid a mottled hand over Lucy's flying fingers, momentarily stilling them. 'Boris makes you work too hard,' he crooned. 'If you feel like improving your lot you only have to let me know, my dear. I'm very generous as well as obliging to gels I like.'

Lucy shot him a startled look, feeling disappointed because having served him for many months she'd considered him above the run-of-the-mill lechers who propositioned the waitresses. Besides, he looked old enough to be her grandfather. 'Oh, I don't mind it here on the whole,' Lucy gabbled, freeing her fingers from his hot clasp. In case her rebuff had left him less obliging she whipped up his brandy balloon. 'I'll carry this for you, Mr Randall, and find you a nice comfortable stool not too close to the band.'

Once Greg was perched at the bar, Lucy set off towards the waiting queue of customers. Although the couple had their backs to her she could see Bill checking his watch and hear his coarse complaints.

'About bleeding time!' His fleshy lips curled as Lucy politely addressed him. 'Few more minutes and I'd've been on me way. I know plenty of places appreciate me custom even if Boris don't. Where is the Greek git?'

'Sorry about the wait, sir, we're dreadfully busy tonight.'

Bill's lady friend was drawn from lounging behind him by the curious sound of a familiar voice. Her platinum head was cocked and her eyes narrowed in disbelief as they settled on the welcoming hostess. Lucy's strained smile encompassed her, then froze on her lips before collapsing.

Ada Stone gave Lucy's saucy uniform a scornful once-over but her glee was short-lived. At any other time she'd have revelled in having Lucy Keiver, done up like a tart, waiting on her. But she suddenly remembered the peril in the situation. She blinked in alarm, colour draining from her sharp features at the realisation that Keiver knew things that could bring about her and Bill's downfall. Starting to her senses, she dug Bill in the ribs with an elbow. 'Let's go. Ain't staying here,' she muttered, turning on her heel.

Lucy gathered her wits and was in spontaneous pursuit of her old enemy. A surge of righteous anger formed her mouth into a determined knot, and she put on a spurt as Ada disappeared down the stairs.

Having reached the pavement and the protection of the dusk, Ada darted into a shop doorway and fumbled for a cigarette with shaking fingers. She knew she'd wait no more than a few seconds for Bill to join her before she made herself scarce. Keiver – drat the bitch – had recognised her despite her new look.

244

And she'd recognised Lucy even though she'd cut her hair short and done herself up like a trollop. Ada gave a malicious chuckle then took a deep drag on her cigarette.

'I know what you did at Mortimer House, you thieving so-and-so.'

Ada had hunched her shoulders and ducked down her face in an attempt to conceal herself but Lucy had spotted her white hair and grabbed her arm, pulling her out from her shadowy hidy-hole.

'What've you done with the jewellery you stole? Eh? You give it back to his lordship or I'm getting the police on you. D'you realise what trouble you caused to Mrs Boyd and all the others, you wicked—'

Lucy barely glimpsed Ada's open palm before it struck her face. But she certainly knew about the intense stinging pain in her nose and the rake of fingernails against her forehead. She tottered back, arms outstretched to try to save herself, but there was nothing to grab on to.

'What the fuck you playin' at, Ada? Bill had raced out just in time to see Lucy crash to the pavement.

'Come on, let's get out of here.'

Ada's tense bloodless features made Bill swallow his next outburst. Uneasiness washed over him. 'Woss up? Who is she?' He speared a look at Lucy.

'Bitch recognised me from Mortimer House. Talking about getting the police.' Ada began walking briskly towards the corner where Bill had parked his car.

Bill backed off a step, giving Lucy a venomous stare. She was crouching on the ground, tugging down her skirt over exposed stocking tops while her other fingers knuckled blood from her nose. With a curse he turned and loped after Ada.

*   *   *

245

Sean tipped his hat over his eyes and sank lower in the seat expecting the couple to drive off. He wasn't kept waiting long. After a few seconds the car whizzed past and Sean got a glimpse of Black, his features angrily contorted and turned towards the wildly rabbiting woman beside him.

Before the saloon had reached the junction, Sean had pushed open the car door and jumped out to sprint across the road towards Lucy. A little crowd had gathered to offer her assistance. Sean saw that Boris and Lucy's waitress friend had burst out of the club's doorway and elbowed a path to the invalid.

Sean hung back. He wanted a private talk with Lucy and had been biding his time, hoping to catch her when she finished work. He felt guilty now. If he'd reckoned Ada might floor her he'd have gone into the club to back Lucy up. But he'd got what he wanted: confirmation that Ada Stone was Audrey Stubbs, the maid who'd stolen the emeralds. And Bill Black was pulling her strings.

He noticed that Lucy's friend seemed concerned to help her up off the ground whereas her fat boss was doing the continental shouting and shrugging thing. A minute later Boris had flung his bulk back through the doors of the club and the few remaining spectators began dispersing. Sean strolled closer.

'In the wars, are you now, Miss Keiver?'

Lucy twisted her head then shut her weary eyes with a mutter beneath her breath. If there were one person she'd sooner hadn't happened by it was Sean Napier. She'd thought a lot about him since he'd dropped her off home the evening after she and Rory had argued in the street. She'd hoped in the intervening weeks Sean might visit the club to see her because what he'd told her about his interest in the Mortimers' jewels had intrigued her, but she'd not seen hide nor hair of him . . . till now. And that seemed an odd coincidence . . .

'Some mouthy bitch smacked her in the face,' Connie helpfully said when Lucy seemed tongue-tied by the handsome Irishman's presence. 'Wish I'd got down here a bit sooner; I'd've laid the maggot out.' Connie dipped her head to examine Lucy's scratched face. 'Why'd you go running after her like that, Luce? You never spoke to Mavis last time she came in. Can't have no old scores to settle 'cos she don't know yer, do she? Did Bill try to touch you up? You've only got to say she started it upstairs and I'll go and have it out with Boris and get you yer job back.'

Lucy's eyes slipped towards Sean, noticing a cautionary glimmer in his steady gaze. She gave Connie a non-committal grimace. It seemed her friend had also been deceived by low light and inattention into assuming the small blonde was the woman who'd previously accompanied Bill to the club.

'Just want to get off home, Con. Got a splitting head-ache . . .' As the older woman started again to question her Lucy warned, 'You'd better get yourself back to work or he'll sack you too.'

'He don't mean it! Boris'll have yer back tomorrow when he's calmed down,' Connie soothed. 'Bleedin' hell! I've seen Molly and Vera scratchin' each other's eyes out right in front of the customers and they're still working up there.' She patted Lucy's shoulder before stepping away. Connie realised she *should* get going or she'd miss out on tips from people she'd served all night. It was late and many of them would soon be settling their shots and making tracks. 'Be all right, will you?'

'Course,' Lucy reassured.

Connie hurried inside and Lucy felt Sean's eyes wandering over her dishevelled figure, settling on a grazed knee protruding from a stocking. Unconsciously she tugged at the hem of her skirt. 'Boris can't stop me going back in to get me wages and clothes.' She marched towards the door.

When Lucy reappeared she was in her own skirt and blouse and carrying her handbag and a linen napkin knotted at the top to form a small sack.

'I'll run you home.' Sean dropped the cigarette smouldering in his fingers, pushing off the wall he'd propped himself against while waiting for her.

It didn't occur to Lucy to refuse. She'd known he would be loitering. He was going to question her. In her turn she wanted some answers from him. She allowed him to take her arm and escort her across the road to where his Humber saloon was parked.

'What's in that?' He jerked a nod at the cloth she'd put on the floor in front of her.

'Nothing . . . just something to eat.' Tears prickled the backs of her eyes. She wasn't ashamed of admitting to filching food from the club; she was furious she'd not got a proper dinner to take home to her mother. As far as Lucy was concerned, the six lousy bread rolls that she'd quickly tested for freshness then swiped on her way out were far less than she deserved for running herself ragged for five and a half hours. Boris had angrily waved away her demands for her wages and she'd felt unable to stand and argue with him with her nose throbbing like mad.

'Did you get your pay?'

Lucy was surprised he'd read her mind. 'Boris wouldn't

give it to me. He won't get away with it. I'm going back another time and I won't leave till I get it. I worked bloody hard all evening till . . .'

'. . . Till Bill Black turned up with Ada Stone and you recognised one another,' Sean finished for her. He turned the ignition and set the car smoothly in motion.

For a few minutes they drove through neon-lit streets in unbroken quiet. When the muzzy feeling in her head began to clear Lucy started picking things over in her mind, knowing Sean would be doing the same.

'Have you been waiting for that to happen between me and Audrey . . . Ada?' she asked.

'Didn't want to see you get hurt, if that's what you mean,' Sean eventually said in a tone that held a hint of apology.

'But you knew Bill might bring her here one night and there'd be ructions once we came face to face.'

They stopped at traffic lights and Sean cupped a hand about a struck match, dipping his head to light the cigarette he'd stuck between his lips. 'You seem to me the sort of girl who can take care of herself,' he said, blowing smoke.

'You're right, I can!' Lucy returned pithily. Her spirits were recovering as her headache eased off. 'She just took me by surprise 'cos I didn't recognise her straight off. She's bleached her hair and looks just like the other girl that Bill turned up with. Mavis is her name. I couldn't tell them apart from the back; neither could Connie. But up close Mavis is prettier.' Lucy picked at her nails, her insides writhing angrily as it sunk in that tonight she'd lost face and job in one fell swoop. And it wasn't the first time Ada Stone had deprived her of her livelihood. 'I'll have Ada back for what she did. Don't need Connie to sort *her* out for me.'

249

'Connie's your friend from the club?'

Lucy nodded. 'Connie Whitton's her name.' She levelled on him an old-fashioned look. 'Surprised you don't already know that, considering you're pals with her boyfriend, Ralph Franks.'

'We're not pals; he's . . . a useful acquaintance. That's all there is to it,' Sean drawled softly.

'Same as me,' Lucy muttered sourly.

'You're going to charge me then, are you, Miss Keiver?' Sean looked away, steering around a corner.

'What's that supposed to mean?' Lucy rounded on him.

'Jayzus, you can be touchy,' he protested. 'Just a joke, darlin'.'

'You just make sure you don't touch.' Lucy blushed beneath the sultry mockery in his eyes. 'And don't call me "darling" either.'

'You're a wee bit too young for me, Lucy Keiver. I've no hankering for little girls, even those who dress up to catch a feller's attention.'

'I do not!' Lucy's outrage was spontaneous but within a second she was feeling foolish. She'd been wearing a skirt that barely covered her suspenders less than an hour ago. And she hoped Sean hadn't seen her sprawled on the pavement with her knickers on display. She turned her head and glared out of the car window.

'I'm not like that Rory, thinking you're easy 'cos you work at that place, if that's bothering you now.' Sean's usual wry tone sounded quiet and serious. 'You're a good kid is what I'm thinking.'

'I'm not a kid!' Lucy bit out with repressed fury. 'I stopped being a kid when I turned fourteen and got sent to Southend to work me fingers to the bone dawn to dusk as a scullery maid.' She whipped her face away. '*And* I did all right and worked me way upstairs to lady's maid. So don't patronise me just 'cos you're almost middle-aged.'

Sean barked a laugh behind the cigarette clamped in his teeth. 'And there was me thinking I was still in me prime.'

Lucy hadn't wanted to amuse him. And she could tell he'd found her comment genuinely funny. She tilted up her chin and turned to glower through the side window again.

CHAPTER TWENTY-ONE

If she didn't voice her thoughts soon, Lucy felt her head might explode with tension.

After snapping at Sean, she'd withdrawn, her eyes gliding sightlessly over deserted pavements, and he had made no attempt to talk to her. He was driving effortlessly with one hand, an elbow resting on the ledge where the window had been lowered so he could hiss cigarette smoke into the dusk.

Lucy regretted overreacting to his provocation. It made her appear unworldly . . . which she was, but she'd rather not have brought it so obviously to his attention. She hoped he didn't think she was sulking because he'd carelessly shrugged off her rebuff. Whatever he said about her being too young for him, Lucy reckoned she knew when a man was flirting with her.

Sean Napier didn't seem the sort to waste time charming women he fancied. Lucy reckoned he'd want to get straight down to business. He'd laughed off her taunt about being middle-aged because he knew young women gave him the eye. On the few occasions he'd been into the club it hadn't just been the waitresses doing it. A few of the diners – Bill's girlfriend Mavis included – had stared shamelessly at him. But he'd always left alone. So Lucy was wondering if he had someone at home waiting for him.

She sent a discreet glance at his profile. He had the build and the looks women liked and men envied. And his casual manner and soft accent were appealing. But she'd thought Rory was an attractive fellow until he'd suddenly turned nasty on her. She couldn't accuse Sean of being two-faced; from the start, he'd had an unsettling tendency to look at her or speak to her in a way that made her hackles rise. Yet she found him frustratingly intriguing . . .

As the car accelerated through quiet backstreets, Lucy realised she'd be home soon and it would be too late to find out anything else about him. She'd need to back down and break the silence if she were to empty her mind of all the annoying questions crammed there.

'So . . . you're paying Ralph Franks for information then?' She blurted, sounding churlish.

'Ah, talking to me now, are you?'

Lucy's teeth set on edge but she muttered in a conciliatory tone, 'I've heard Ralph's a copper who's as bent as a nine-bob note.'

'He's not alone in that.'

'Was he worth the money? Did he tell you anything about all this?' Lucy turned fractionally towards Sean.

'He did. There was a similar robbery in town. Before the Mortimers got hit some rings went missing from a rich old feller's mistress in Notting Hill. Franks had heard the maid was the culprit on that occasion.'

'You think it was Ada!' Lucy had fully faced him, interest animating her face.

'I do. But it was all hushed up, like the Mortimer theft. Franks dug out a bit about it for me after I'd dug something out of me wallet for him.' Sean smiled at the sweet scratched face turned to his. Rather than marring her looks the war paint and tangled bobbed hair made her resemble an urchin in a play, in his opinion.

'The girlfriend reported the theft but her sugar daddy wanted the case dropped to save him answering awkward questions,' Sean continued. 'The crooked maid called herself Annie Smith.' Sean chuckled in disbelief. 'Ada lets herself down, doesn't she now. Vanity, to be sure, to stick to her initials on jobs.'

Lucy digested the information. 'The police have had dealings with Ada Stone and Bill Black then?'

'According to me new friend Franks, their names have cropped up for shoplifting on a grand scale. But they've been clever and stayed out of big trouble so far.'

Lucy frowned in consideration, mouth pursed. Suddenly her stomach grumbled loudly, making her start in embarrassment.

'Hungry,' she mumbled, and delved into the little napkin sack to get a dry roll. She was halfway through it when she remembered her manners and offered him one.

'I've had me dinner. Sorry, I should have asked if you'd had yours. Would you like to go and have a bite to eat?'

'Most places will have closed.' Lucy brushed crumbs from her lap. 'It must be almost two o'clock by now.'

'I've got a bit of steak in me pantry, if that's to your liking . . .'

Lucy glanced at him, then quickly away. 'This is enough, thanks anyway. Couldn't eat much; it's too late. Also me mum's expecting me home. She never goes off to sleep till she knows I'm back—'

'I've got the message, Lucy,' Sean interrupted mildly. 'You're not wanting to come home with me. That's fine.'

Lucy frowned out of the window, feeling unworldly again, and a bit cowardly, even though she wasn't sure why. 'Where d'you live, over here?' she asked.

'I'm renting a house in Brookville Road, Fulham.'

'On your own?'

'Uh-huh.'

'But you're going back to Ireland when you're done with this case, aren't you?'

'Yep.'

'So where d'you live over there?'

'I've a place in Waterford.'

'D'you live there alone?'

'Are you after wanting to know if I'm married, Miss Keiver?' Sean asked, his expression unfathomable.

'Well, are you?' Lucy blurted.

'Nope.'

'You look more'n old enough to be wed with kids.'

'So you've told me,' he said, straight-faced, but his voice was warm with humour. 'I'll need some beauty sleep 'cos I'm only thirty . . . all right, might as well admit it . . . close to thirty-one,' he answered her unspoken question. 'How about you? I'm guessing eighteen.'

'Nineteen . . . had a birthday earlier in the month.'

'Well, I'll remember that and buy you a belated present. How about a nice steak dinner as a big thank you for helping me with me enquiries?'

'I reckon you *do* owe me 'n' all!' Lucy compressed a

responsive smile, twitching her lips. 'But you can keep your steak. As Boris wouldn't hand over me wages, you can give them to me out of your reward . . . if you ever get it.' Lucy wasn't wholly joking. She knew it would be difficult getting another job if Boris refused to have her back. She frowned in concentration. 'Why've you told me all this? I could ruin things for you if I blab to the wrong people about what you're up to.'

'Don't take you for a girl who blabs. Her ladyship described you as a loyal and trustworthy employee. But I make up me own mind on things.' He cocked his head to leisurely assess her from top to toe. 'The first time I saw you in the Cuckoo Club, I took a shine to you, if that's reason enough.'

'Don't think it is,' Lucy said succinctly. 'I reckon you're shrewder than that. Before our paths crossed, you'd already found out I'd been working at Mortimer House and got pushed out of me job by a colleague. You knew I could identify the person who scarpered with the jewels, so don't go giving me any old flannel.'

'Is that you angling for me to say there's more to it?'

'No . . . it's not! I'm not angling . . .' Lucy sounded flustered. She squirmed in her seat on noticing a corner of his mouth move upwards. He was deliberately riling her but she'd no intention of snapping at the bait again. 'So how did you know where to find me? Nobody at Mortimer House knew about me working at the club. Rory only found out recently.'

'By lucky chance,' Sean said. 'And you can't have too many of those beauties in this job.'

'What sort of lucky chance?'

'Before Ada snatched the stuff she'd told the house-keeper she had a boyfriend called Bill. Stupid girl, so she was, to do that 'cos it gave me a start. I had me work cut out for a while going looking for Bills with bad reputations and bad girlfriends. None of the women Black hung around with fitted the description I'd been given of a plain-faced maid with mousy hair. I guessed she might have changed her look, so one night, I followed Bill and his lady friend into the Cuckoo Club and stumbled across Miss Lucy Keiver working there as a waitress. Fate was on me side. But I thought I'd picked the wrong Bill to go after when you and Mavis didn't seem acquainted.'

'I'd never seen her before,' Lucy confirmed. 'So why did you carry on following Bill after that?'

Sean tapped the side of his nose. 'Had a feeling about the feller.'

Lucy considered all he'd said.

'But tonight I was after seeing you, not following him. Hadn't even parked me car when lo and behold you were doing me proud by chasing that thieving cu—' Sean swallowed the obscenity before it was fully uttered. 'Sorry . . . nearly forgot, lady present . . .'

'So why did you come over to see me tonight?' Lucy interrogated him.

'Thought it was time I put me cards on the table. You'd've thought me a weird sort of feller, wouldn't you now, if you kept bumping into me round every corner? I thought I'd take a chance and let you in on things.' He turned to grin at her. 'I was going to ask if you'd come to a few places with me and see if you could spot Ada. There . . .that's the truth, and I didn't have to tell you now, did I?'

'You saw me and Ada having a scrap.'

'I did.'

Lucy felt heat flood her cheeks. He *had* seen her

257

displaying her knickers, in that case. 'Thanks for telling me the ins and outs,' she mumbled.

'Not at all. Have you told your friend Connie about the theft at Mortimer House?'

'I promised Rory I wouldn't repeat what he'd told me to a soul. I've stuck to me word on that. Didn't even tell Mum.' Lucy paused, wondering how much Sean knew about the tragedy set in motion by Ada's wickedness. 'I suppose you've been filled in on the scandal?'

'If I say I haven't, will you tell me?'

'I said I've not told a soul and I won't.'

'Good for you, Lucy Keiver. Loyal and trustworthy, as described.'

His lilting praise caused Lucy to frown. If he thought she was being a prissy cow he could come right out and say so.

'Me mother told me all the mucky details about what went on.'

Lucy gawped at him. 'Your *mother*? And how did *she* find out?'

'Her sister told her when she got in touch wanting me to help out tracking down the family heirlooms.'

Lucy's jaw dropped further. 'You said you weren't friends with the Mortimers.'

'No friends of mine.' He grunted a sour laugh. 'But me mother likes her sister well enough, even though she married that pompous eejit.'

'You're *related* to Lord and Lady Mortimer?'

'Don't go holding it against me, will you now,' he said sardonically. 'Poor relations, that's what we are. I'm just after earning me wages, same as you. You're home.'

Lucy had been so engrossed in their conversation she hadn't noticed he'd dropped her right outside her door.

Feeling frustrated because there was so much more she wanted to know, she swivelled towards him on her seat and blurted that out.

'You saying you want to see me again now, Miss Keiver?'

'Well, the least you owe me, *Mr Napier*, is a bit more of an explanation and an apology!' Colour bled into Lucy's damaged complexion and she pointed at her face. 'Look! Bone's probably broken. It wouldn't have happened if you'd come to tell me sooner you had suspicions about Bill Black. I'd've been on me guard.'

Sean skimmed a barely touching finger over the bridge of her nose and down to a blood-encrusted nostril. 'You can't blame me for that now. You and Ada would have come to blows next time you met.' His long fingers firmly gripped her chin, turning her head so he could view her profile. 'It's not broken. You'll probably have two shiners, though.' He pulled a handkerchief from his pocket. Turning her face towards him he rubbed the scarlet lipstick from her mouth.

'Won't want your ma to see that now, will you?' He stared past her at the grimy tenements lining the street. 'I'm thinking you've had a few fights in your time living here.' As he sensed her tense in indignation he leaned in close before she could pull away.

Lucy's eyelids dropped as he briefly brushed his mouth on her clean stinging lips.

'Thought I was too young for you,' Lucy mocked.

'Ah, but you're not eighteen, are you now?' Sean said, feigning seriousness. 'Nineteen . . . well, that's different.'

She laughed despite herself. 'Think I'll have to watch you, Mr Napier.'

'Sure, and I'll let you do that. Meet you Saturday by the caff at the Angel . . . where you met that feller Rory.'

Fleetingly, Lucy considered being contrary. But his authoritative tone didn't sound bullying, unlike Rory's. She nodded without questioning him.

'Seen him since, have you?' Sean relaxed back in his seat.

Lucy shook her head. 'Don't want to either,' she muttered.

'That's good. I've got enough on me plate, so I have, chasing after Bill Black and bad girls without seeing off chauffeurs into the bargain.'

Lucy found herself smiling at that. 'Thanks for the lift,' she murmured, getting out. She didn't look back but knew he would watch her till she disappeared inside the rotten doorway. She hesitated by the banisters until the sound of an engine turned her around. The shadowy vehicle glided off towards Seven Sisters Road. As she climbed the rickety stairs, Lucy felt oddly elated, despite the throb at her temples starting up again.

Lucy crept in quietly, as she always did so as not to disturb her mother even though Matilda was sure to be awake and listening for her to return home. She was used to feeling her way in blackness from door to table to wall on her way to bed. But something seemed different about the stuffy atmosphere, making Lucy hesitate rather than tiptoe straight through to the back room. She remained still and alert in darkness just inside the closed door. Then she heard it: rumbling breathing coming from two people . . . one of them softly snoring.

A rueful smile tugged at a corner of Lucy's mouth. There was no light to see by, but if there had been she'd have ducked down her head to check if Reg Donovan's boots were under her mother's bed.

CHAPTER TWENTY-TWO

Winnie wouldn't have known it but, when the emeralds had been in her daughter's keeping, Jennifer's reaction to their enchanting splendour had been identical to her own. But a sandpaper-dry mouth was the least of Winnie's worries, since her gut had begun cramping in anxiety.

She was beginning to regret ever having accepted the tortoiseshell box, and that was hugely depressing because she'd already started scheming towards a future without Eddie, funded by her ill-gotten gains, miles away where he wouldn't find her. The country may be on the brink of bankruptcy, but Winnie envisaged a vast improvement in her own financial situation.

She knew that such gems must legally belong to rich and powerful people, not working-class housewives with ragged fingernails, but she'd been confident such fabulous quality would tempt a crook to overlook the obvious and offer her a few hundred pounds, no questions asked. She wasn't stupid and she understood the set was worth a vast amount more. But a few hundred pounds was enough for her to get set up in a place of her own with no need ever again to share the same roof as the mean spiteful bastard she'd married.

In her new life, Winnie calculated on getting employment as a full-time shop assistant to bring in housekeeping so she could squirrel away as a pension fund the money raised from the gems. Tom was old enough to get himself to and from his new school and perhaps even do a few errands to earn a little bit. Winnie knew that Kathy was already home and dry. She was ready to be independent and would always do all right wherever she was, whoever she was with, because she had her head screwed on. Nevertheless, it was Winnie's intention to leave Kathy some cash as a parting gift.

But all those plans would wither if Winnie couldn't quickly offload the jewellery and so far she'd had no luck at all in that direction. The longer she kept it hidden the more certain she became that she'd get found out, if not by Eddie then by the authorities. Winnie was starting to feel scared . . .

Last week she hadn't dared approach any local jewellers with the box in case she was recognised. Instead, she'd walked up and down Hatton Garden seeking out the seediest-looking establishments, suspecting such places were more likely to deal in dodgy merchandise.

The first goldsmith had looked at her with weary contempt as she timidly entered his shop. But his attitude had changed pretty quickly. He'd glanced in the box, then started to attention, pointing at the exit without uttering a word. An hour later, having walked around aimlessly trying to pluck up courage, Winnie had returned to the same street for another go. She'd loitered outside a different shop, watching a foreign-looking individual lounging against the counter, picking his nose. From his boredom she guessed he wasn't the proprietor. But it was getting late so eventually she'd forced herself to go in just before closing time. The assistant had taken a longer stare at the emeralds and Winnie's hopes had started to soar . . . until he started blinking and mopping his perspiring brow as though his sense was overriding his greed. Seconds later he'd grabbed her by the elbow and shooed her out of the door.

It had not been a promising start. Winnie had hurried home with thumping heart, looking over her shoulder. She'd stuffed the jewellery box, wrapped in brown paper, deep down in the coal scuttle. Now it was summer the scuttle was out of use. Eddie was too tight-fisted to allow a fire out of season, even on chilly days, so she'd been confident it wouldn't be discovered.

But as much as Winnie despised her husband, she grudgingly gave him credit for the way he ran his business. She was convinced Eddie would have known exactly how much to ask for the gems and who to approach to shift them quickly.

The only associate of Eddie's Winnie knew was Bill, and since the gems had come from him because he wanted – hard as Winnie found it to believe – to hold up his end of a bargain, there was no likelihood he'd buy them back off her. Something else was disturbing Winnie. Her husband was an impatient character; if Eddie were waiting to be squared up on a deal he'd be in a foul mood until it was done and dusted. Yesterday, Winnie had heard him humming as though all was right with his world as he brought in boxes of tablecloths from his van and stacked them in a corner. Eddie wouldn't risk a scrap with Bill for taking up with Jennifer, but Winnie would have put odds on him going down fighting over money due. She pushed the confusion from her mind.

It was getting late and she'd been dawdling in Moorgate for some time. She needed to act quickly or not at all. It would soon be time to get home and get tea on the go, or Eddie would be suspicious as to her whereabouts.

Winnie adjusted her knotted headscarf under her chin. Despite it being a humid day in August she'd donned the plain square of brown georgette in an attempt to hide her voluminous hair because it became remarkably frizzy in such weather. To add to her disguise she'd taken Eddie's reading glasses out of the table drawer and put them in her bag before she'd left home. They were too big for her and although she'd only just put them on they'd slipped down her nose. She shoved them up again and blinked through blurry lenses. She was worried enough now about being in possession of the emeralds to want to hide her identity, even when a good distance from home.

For the umpteenth time she drove a hand into her shopping bag to check that the tortoiseshell box was safely inside. A moment later she'd taken a deep inspiriting breath and, peering over the top of the spectacles, began trotting across the road towards the pawnshop.

Eddie hadn't needed to touch his nest egg since he'd hidden it away many months ago. He'd waited till his wife and kids were out of the way – as he always did – before preparing to dismantle the radiogram. He wanted a hundred pounds because he'd got a new supplier who was demanding cash upfront on a deal. The leather handbags that had dropped from the back of a lorry en route to Bond Street were very nice indeed. As soon as he'd seen a sample of one, Eddie had known there was money to be made. So he hadn't told the old Italian what he could do with his bolshie demands, even though he'd felt tempted to do so.

Eddie found himself inwardly cursing his daughter Jennifer. She'd stirred up family and financial trouble for him. Establishing new contacts hadn't been easy once Bill was out of the equation. If the little tart hadn't made a play for his best business associate he'd still be doing sweet deals. But he'd learned his lesson about putting all his eggs in one basket and now bitterly regretted having come to rely so heavily on Black to supply him over the years. If he were to keep in business he'd need to foster trustworthy people who would extend a bit of credit on quality stuff. Dealing in cheap clobber and household tat didn't bring in the sort of profit he'd got used to when Bill was moseying over with upmarket clothes and gemstone rings. Eddie was still ruminating on his change in fortune as he wielded the screwdriver and deftly set about prising free the front speaker.

He tossed aside the tool, gave the grille a pull and gawped in disbelief. He snatched up some tenners while his other fingers scrabbled to and fro in the cavity to find the rest. Falling to his knees for a better look, he leaned forward to peer into dark crevices, even though he knew he was wasting his time. The envelope stuffed with his cash had gone. Eddie sank back on his haunches, his features rigid in shock.

'Winnie . . . you fucking bitch!' he exploded from between his grinding teeth.

Eddie had a quick wit and soon it was racing away from his wife as the culprit and searching elsewhere.

Slowly he hefted himself to his feet and began pacing to and fro, his expression vengeful. He kicked out savagely at the grille as he trod on it and continued prowling and thinking.

Winnie hadn't stolen from him; Winnie was still around and she'd be long gone unless she'd done the deed that very morning, then fled. But Eddie knew she hadn't because he'd been passing in the van when his wife was walking Tom to school. She'd been carrying a shopping bag, not a suitcase. There had been no hint of anything different about her. As their eyes had clashed there'd been a normal flicker of mutual despising. They'd both carried on their way without any other acknowledgement, as they usually did.

One thing Eddie knew for sure about his wife: if she'd found his savings he wouldn't have found her. He turned to the sideboard and with a shaking hand poured himself a whisky, tossing it back in one swallow.

He stared at the gaping wound in the radiogram. Kathy had asked again yesterday if she could listen to the wireless and Eddie had told her it wasn't yet fixed. Winnie had added her two penn'orth about his selfishness and she wouldn't have done that if she'd not wanted him fiddling with the damn thing. Tom . . . no . . . his young son wasn't a suspect, so that only left Jennifer . . .

Eddie tightened his fist on the scrunched-up banknotes. Whoever had taken the money had felt concerned enough to leave a little something behind. Winnie would have taken off and left him nothing other than two triumphant words scrawled on an empty envelope.

Eddie's mind circled back to his estranged daughter. Incredible as it seemed that the lazy little trollop had outwitted him, it appeared she had. But how had

Jennifer discovered where he kept his money when he was always so careful?

Eddie heard the door slam but made no attempt to conceal the damage to his hidy-hole.

Winnie came in and glanced at the radiogram. 'Fixing it at last, are yer?' She went through to the kitchen. A moment later the noise of cupboards opening and closing could be heard, then the squeak of the brass tap turning.

Eddie followed his wife and stood staring at her back as she filled a pot with water. She turned round to glare at him.

'I've been robbed.'

Winnie's sullen face drained of colour and she swallowed noisily, plonking down the saucepan in a splash.

The guilt flitting across his wife's withered features hadn't escaped Eddie any more than her nervousness. His surprise transformed into viciousness and he took a threatening step closer.

'Know anything about it do you, Win?'

Winnie dropped the peeler she'd been about to attack potatoes with. 'Robbed?' she croaked.

'That's what I said, gel,' Eddie snarled. 'And I was thinking . . . perhaps Jennifer's the thief . . . but now I'm thinking perhaps it was you all along. Was it?'

Winnie had been caught unawares and she felt stupid for not having a ready retort prepared for when her husband challenged her over his missing box of emeralds. If Eddie and his old mate Bill had run into one another, Eddie wouldn't have bothered asking after his daughter but he'd have demanded to be paid up. And Bill would have said he'd already delivered the jewellery via Jennifer, who'd handed it to her mother. . .

For the last few days, Winnie's mind had been

preoccupied with her disastrous visit to the pawnbroker. Once the old Jew had seen her goods, he'd come stumbling around the counter demanding to know her name and trying to wrestle the box from her. Fortunately, Winnie had youth on her side and had outrun him to the door. On the bus home she'd realised that the jewels must be still red hot and giving the shysters the jitters. She'd trembled and wept as her fantasy of a life without Eddie disintegrated, to be replaced by fearful thoughts of arrest and a prison cell. But what had really upset her was that her saviour had turned into a curse.

With an effort, Winnie calmed herself down. She could either brazen it out with Eddie or come clean. Getting rid of the blasted box – even to Eddie – might prove to be a blessing after the frightening incident in the pawnbroker's.

'Not thinking Bill's stitched you up, are you, Ed?' Winnie wiped her damp hands on her pinafore, then swivelled away to handle the potatoes, hiding her tense expression. ''Cos if you are, I can tell you he ain't diddled yer. He's sent the stuff over with Jennifer and she give it to me 'cos she was scared of facing you.' Winnie whizzed a glance over a shoulder, her mouth working silently. 'Ain't said nuthin' 'cos I knew you'd go spare about me being in touch with Jen,' she blurted. 'Been waiting for the right time . . . when you was in a better mood.'

Winnie again peeped backwards and noticed that Eddie was looking dangerously gormless. She'd seen that slack-mouthed, vacant-eyed expression before on him; usually it preceded a violent rage. Before he managed to collect his senses she rushed past to the coal scuttle on the slate hearth. 'See . . . kept it all safe for you right here,' she burbled.

'What?' Eddie had spun about to gawp at her. He was

stunned but still alert enough to keep quiet and give Winnie enough rope to hang herself with.

Winnie overturned the scuttle and scrabbled in soot to swoop on something. 'Here . . .' She thrust out the dirty parcel. 'Jennifer ambushed me. I didn't want to see her, honest, but I admit I stopped and spoke 'cos she's still flesh 'n' blood . . .'

Eddie looked at the filthy offering, then at his wife. Awful enlightenment was making his eyes bulge and twisting his mouth into a strange shape, but he made no move to take the package.

Winnie tore off the wrapping paper with a shrill giggle. 'S'all right, see . . . good as new underneath . . .'

Frowning deeply, Eddie reluctantly accepted the box his wife was vibrating in front of his chest, so keen was she to be rid of it.

'Ain't yer going to open it, Ed?' Winnie watched him warily.

'No point, I know what's in there.'

He tilted his head, gazing at her with such cold loathing that Winnie shuffled away.

'Tried to sell, 'em, ain't yer, you stupid bitch? Turned you down, didn't they? Could've told you that 'n' saved you the trip. Where you been? All of 'em now, every bleedin' one you've been to . . .' Eddie sounded weary, dogging her footsteps as she dodged from fireplace to wall to evade him.

'Been?' Winnie echoed the word as though it were a foreign language, sidling away from where he'd backed her against the table.

'You know what I mean!' Eddie suddenly roared, making his wife shriek in fright. 'You've tried to sell it behind me back, don't deny it.' He shook the box in her

269

face. 'I'm in the game. I get to know about stuff from all me contacts, like jewellers and pawnbrokers. I heard some daft old bag had the Mortimer heirlooms and was out trying to shift 'em.' Eddie suddenly hurled the box into a corner of the room, breaking it open and scattering its sparkling contents on the floor. 'Never guessed for one minute it was *my* daft old bag doing it. Thought Bill had got desperate and sent one of his scrubbers to take the risk of getting shot of 'em.' Eddie swiped Winnie hard across the face with the back of a hand, sending her to her knees. 'I heard on the grapevine that a Jew boy nearly snatched 'em off her so he could get his hands on the reward. He reckoned it was worth the risk.' Eddie barked a laugh. 'Didn't know that, did yer now? Could've got a reward if you'd turned 'em in, and got us all murdered into the bargain.'

Winnie glanced up, blubbering and smearing snot from her top lip. 'What . . .?' she whimpered.

'D'you know what you've done?'

Winnie shook her head, clutching at her aching cheek.

'You've brought the law down on our heads, if we're lucky . . . the IRA if we ain't.'

Winnie blinked up at him through blurry vision. 'IRA?' she mouthed in incomprehension, wondering if Eddie had gone nuts.

'Them jewels got stolen from a lord living in Mayfair. He wants 'em back 'cos, as you can see, they're worth a few bob. So he asked some Irish gangster to fetch 'em back for him and he'd give him a nice fat reward to buy guns with.' He ground his teeth. 'Whichever way you play it you've got to lose. Give 'em back to his lordship, the Irish bloke don't get his cut, so he's after yer. Don't give 'em back, the Irish bloke's after yer.'

Winnie hauled herself upwards with the help of a chair. She swung a look between her husband and the broken box. For minutes she alternately wiped her hands and smoothed her pinafore.

'See the worst of it, Win?' Eddie asked, ferociously jolly. 'Them emeralds are worth a fuckin' lot in an Irish thug's hands, but in yours or mine they're not worth the paper you had 'em wrapped in.'

'Well, we can just hand it all back, can't we, 'n' say we don't want nuthin'?' Winnie began retrieving the jewellery. She laid it reverentially on the table, fingers fluttering over it to make sure nothing was damaged by Eddie's savage treatment. The box seemed beyond repair but she determinedly wedged the lid against its broken hinge. 'I'll get a bit of string . . .'

With a bellow of frustration Eddie smashed a fist into the side of Winnie's face, sending her again flying. 'You really don't get it, do you, you fucking idiot!'

Ignoring his howling wife, he tried to finish what she'd started, jamming the lid impatiently onto the box. 'Ain't just about his lordship getting back his stuff now, is it? It's about revenge. And an Irishman shopping fer guns.' He pulled out a chair and sank into it, looking shattered while his gasping wife cowered in the corner with the back of her hand pressed against her bleeding mouth.

'Bill tried to get me to take them emeralds months ago and I turned him down,' he explained quite gently, as one might to a child. 'So you know what he's gone and done? He's got Jennifer to steal all my cash out of the radiogram where I had it hid. Then off she's scarpered to live with him. Then when he's got my savings in his pocket he's sent the little cow back with the box of jewels so he can keep the slate clean between us and point any mad Paddies in my direction.'

Winnie pulled herself to her feet with the help of the door knob. She stood trembling, fussing with her pinafore. Not all of what Eddie had said had sunk in. But enough had, and she knew she'd endangered them all. She felt stupid and ashamed. She blinked at the hole in the radiogram. 'How much?' she whispered.

'Nine hundred.' Eddie's teeth pulled back against his lips in a snarling smile. 'But good enough to leave me five tenners behind, she was, our little gel.'

'What you gonna do, Eddie? What about Tom and Kathy? What you gonna do, Eddie?' Winnie frantically rattled off.

'Do? Fer starters I'm getting shot of you. After that I'm goin' after that bastard Black, that's what I'm gonna do.'

CHAPTER TWENTY-THREE

Jennifer was rather enjoying herself. She might not be working in Kensington in a way she'd dreamed about, but she was in Derry and Toms, surrounded by luxury goods and wonderful fragrance.

At present, powdery scent was luring her towards the beauty counter to test samples as she'd seen other ladies do.

A bottle of Jicky caught her eye as she dipped her head to sniff her wrist. Jennifer would have liked to slip that out of sight into a pocket. She had read in magazines about glamorous people favouring Jicky and decided she had similar taste. But unfortunately, stealing expensive perfume wasn't on today's agenda. Reluctantly, she replaced the fancy bottle on the counter and walked on.

In the short while that she'd been part of Bill's team of shoplifters, she'd come to learn that the other girls considered it beneath them to wear hoisted togs. They preferred to dispose of the stolen goods, then on days off swan about in the West End making expensive purchases with their wages.

Jennifer would have enjoyed such a shopping trip, but so far she'd not been invited along. Besides, Bill had given her very little cash of her own, despite the fact that she was sure she was bringing home her fair share of the bacon. He'd argued that she was still an apprentice, but Jenny reckoned he simply wanted an excuse to keep her close to him. Although she'd sulked for a bit, in a way she liked him being worried the older girls might lead her astray. He'd promised to look after her and she imagined that it was his way of doing so.

Today they had summer dresses in their sights, but Jennifer knew Bill would be pleased to have any other finery that stuck to their nimble fingers. In addition, he wanted some sturdy leather luggage because he had a client lined up ready and waiting to go on his holidays. Jennifer caught sight of her reflection in a mirror as she sashayed past. It startled her momentarily before a pleased smirk twitched her ruby-red lips. She barely recognised herself.

Although there were sometimes up to five of them working together in the gang, Daphne and Ivy were married with kids and only turned up when a major onslaught on the West End was planned. Ada Stone and Mavis Pooley seemed to be the girls Bill relied on most.

Jennifer knew Ada didn't like her much. Mavis was friendlier and had shown her how to use cosmetics to make herself look older. So she wouldn't stick out like a sore thumb when mingling with fashionable people in the shops, Bill had got her some sophisticated outfits. Her lightweight ensemble of dark blue linen dress and matching gloves and shoes gave her the appearance of a well-to-do young lady in her late teens. She might have been the pampered daughter of a rich banker, bred in a grand Mayfair townhouse instead of the offspring of a petty criminal reared in a poky Islington cottage.

Jennifer sensed Ada's eyes on her as she walked abreast of her in a parallel aisle looking sourer than usual. Jennifer could guess why. Her colleague had on a smart cotton coat but the roomy inside pockets already bulged with merchandise from the gentlemen's department on the first floor, making her appear pregnant. Jennifer wouldn't have taken kindly either to being loaded down on such a close afternoon. As they arrived at a spot where aisles intersected, Jennifer discreetly nodded, letting Ada know she was primed to go into action.

A young gentleman was approaching, giving Jennifer appreciative looks, and he slowed down as she boldly stared back. She'd already decided he could be of use. When he was closer Jennifer adopted an air of embarrassment while fingering some silk lingerie. The elderly woman assistant glared over the counter at the hovering fellow till he cleared his throat and strode away from the array of ladies' unmentionables. Jennifer whispered her size requirements while dangling a pink silk brassiere from her fingers. A few moments later she replaced the scrap of silk with a sigh and regretful smile. Jennifer calculated that while she'd had her head together with the sales assistant her partner in crime had had enough time to whip some négligés inside her coat.

Without a glance passing between them, the two young women proceeded in opposite directions. Jennifer knew she was on her own now; Ada had grown to a suspicious size and was heading towards the exit. Jennifer felt her heart thudding in a mixture of trepidation and excitement. In a few moments she must for the first time attempt to make off, bold as brass, with large items openly on display.

She knew exactly where the suitcases were stacked. Had she not, a pleasant tang of leather would have drawn her in the right direction. She had eyed up the luggage previously then calmly walked past. Bill had ordered her to get two good-sized trunks and Jennifer knew there was no time to fiddle about trying to fit one inside the other so she must carry one in each hand. She strolled on, discreetly eyeing up customers and potential situations that might suit her purpose.

A woman with an infant was browsing in the vicinity. Jennifer noticed that the brake was off the pram so she came to a stop close by. The baby patted his hands on the coverlet and gave her a gummy smile. While his mother flexed her fingers inside a kid glove, Jennifer extended her foot to the wheel and pushed so the pram silently rolled on. The sudden motion made the boy's fingers flutter and his bottom lip quiver.

'Who on earth is minding the little chap?' Jennifer's loud concern made people swivel about just as the baby let out a wail. 'He doesn't seem to be with anybody.'

The woman dropped the gloves she'd been trying on and rushed towards her whimpering son. The two assistants faced one another to tut their disapproval. Other customers congregated and moved closer for a gossip, allowing Jennifer to merge into the background. She picked up the trunks she'd selected earlier and walked swiftly away.

Outside the shop, Jennifer began walking as fast as she could, the luggage painfully bumping her legs. She turned a corner and, thankfully, saw that Charlie North was in position. As she hurried towards him, he gave her a grin but they didn't speak. Jenny noticed that the back seat of his car was already loaded with the lingerie and gentlemen's trousers that Ada had offloaded previously. Charlie snapped up a lid and deftly positioned one case inside the other. He opened the boot, slid the trunk in and within seconds was in the car and driving away. Jennifer planted her hands on her hips and gave a long whooshing sigh, still high on excitement but glad she could now head off home.

In Ada's opinion, the new recruit was a natural, and too damned good for her liking. Jennifer Finch had been with them only a short while yet she'd proved to be an excellent decoy. Mavis Pooley, on the other hand, had never cottoned on to the fact that creating a drama was unnecessary and could do more harm than good.

Ada sent a spiteful glance at her rival over the rim of her glass. Being in competition with a kid of fifteen was infuriating. She knew Jennifer might topple her and be top dog in Bill's books before long. He tended to turn on the smarm with new girls to keep them keen but the little cow already seemed to have wormed her way into his affections. Ada suspected Bill fancied Jennifer, despite him insisting she was living innocently at his place because she was homeless.

When Ada got paid up on the cursed Mortimer job, she had watched Bill count out her cash from an old envelope bearing Eddie Finch's name and address. Bill had told her the tale about Jennifer's brutal father, and that the girl had proved her worth as a new recruit by exchanging the emeralds for Eddie's savings. Ada had grudgingly admitted Jennifer was clever for pulling that one off. But Ada wasn't convinced that they were home and dry. Eddie Finch would be in a rage and gunning for them all – his thieving daughter included. And at the back of Ada's mind was Lucy Keiver. She was sure her old colleague wouldn't have taken kindly to being knocked to the ground. If she knew Lucy she'd be out for revenge and ready for round two . . .

'What're you sitting over there on yer own for, Ada?' Bill called. 'Got a face like you been sucking lemons, gel.'

Bill and his trio of regular hoisters were in the back room of the pub, mulling over the day's events. Mavis and Jennifer were seated with him but on arrival twenty minutes ago Ada had flounced to her own table.

By the side of Bill's chair were the two expensive leather suitcases. He gave the largest a pat. 'Good gel, you are, Jen, to bring them out. Nice size . . .'

Jennifer beamed and sipped from her port and lemon. Bill had said she wasn't allowed the gin and tonic the other girls drank and insisted she had wine. He and the landlord knew she was underage but it didn't seem to bother either of them that she was drinking alcohol. Jim Trent had simply muttered at Bill to keep his crew in the back room. Jennifer had never been allowed to drink at home. A few years ago when at her late granny's house for Christmas dinner, she and Kathy had been given a glass of Sauternes each as a special treat. Jenny had taken a sip, pulled a face, and let Kathy have the rest.

Most adults she knew enjoyed a tipple, so Jennifer had finished every port and lemon Bill bought her because she considered herself grown up. She'd come to rather like the taste, and the fuzzy feeling that made her giggle and sway when she stood up.

Jennifer sneaked a look as Ada scraped back her chair, intending to join them. She was secretly pleased that the older woman was sulking because she was jealous. Mavis had said that Ada had cold-shouldered her too when she'd been Bill's favourite.

Having fished a cigarette out, Mavis pushed her pack across the table to Bill. He withdrew one and Mavis flicked the box towards Jenny.

'Go on then . . .' Bill sighed as Jenny glanced at him for approval.

Once Bill had lit the cigarette for her, Jennifer sucked energetically, then coughed as hot smoke abraded her throat.

'First one? Soon get used to it,' Mavis chuckled as Jennifer knuckled her watering eyes. She turned her attention to Bill. 'Is Charlie coming over this afternoon?'

'Yeah, don't worry, gel, you'll see him.' Bill hadn't been offended when Mavis started cosying up to his underling Northie. In a way it was a relief because she'd not proved to be much use and he'd already replaced her with Jennifer in his business, if not yet in his bed.

Ada plonked herself down in a spare seat, looking bored. She brightened up when Bill flung a welcoming arm about her bony shoulders. Gamely he gave her a smile as she shoved her empty glass across the table, silently demanding a refill. He deliberately held her gaze with low-lidded eyes until she understood and leaned back, satisfied he'd be in her bed later. Bill got to his feet, collecting all the empties in his large hands. 'Same again,' he bawled out to Jim Trent – lost to sight in the saloon bar – as he sauntered off.

To escape Ada's scowl, Jenny got up and went unsteadily to join Bill.

'You're getting all grown up.' Bill's voice was throaty as he looked her up and down.

Done up to the nines in classy clothes and makeup, with a boozy flush on her cheekbones, Jennifer looked dollishly pretty. He'd thought previously he'd leave her alone till she turned sixteen. If her father came looking for him – and Bill reckoned Eddie would be over any day now – he could honestly tell Finchie he'd not touched his daughter . . . and he wouldn't, so long as the old git kept his mouth shut and accepted the emeralds deal as done and dusted. The news had got all over the place that an Irish nutter was on the trail of the stolen jewellery, and Bill had heard enough about the maniacs across the water to be glad he was out of it.

Bill didn't hold out much hope that Eddie would take it all lying down. Even Jennifer's likely abuse wouldn't turn Eddie's mind from getting his cash to saving his little girl. So Bill reckoned some day soon he'd take her to bed because he'd started feeling horny around her. Useful girls always turned Bill on, even those like Ada with little on offer in the looks department.

Over Jennifer's crown of fair hair, Bill noticed Ada's chin was up and she was squinting, letting him know she was watching them. Following the run-in with Lucy Keiver outside the Cuckoo Club earlier in the week, Ada had the next day dyed her hair black in a renewed attempt to disguise herself. Bill understood her motives but reckoned it had done her no favours. The harsh tint seemed to sharpen her narrow features and drain what little colour she had in her pale complexion. But she was still his number one hoister and far too talented to upset so he gave her an exaggerated wink.

*   *   *

'Get yer job back, did you?'

In response to her mother's urgent demand, Lucy closed her eyes, sighed, then flopped down into a chair opposite Matilda at the table.

'Oh, no, Luce! Didn't he give you yer wages wot he owed you?' Matilda groaned in dismay at the sight of her daughter's dejected expression. 'Have you brought in a *Gazette* to find a new job? Not that there's much advertised these days.'

'Thought you'd be pleased, Mum.' Lucy gave a despondent huff. 'You didn't want me working there in any case, did you?'

'No, I didn't like the bleedin' idea of it, but it helped pay the rent!' Matilda stated defensively.

'And it put dinner on the table,' Lucy chipped in, her eyes still pressed shut. 'And those shifts I got good tips we managed to put a bit by in the Christmas jar, didn't we?'

'Good dinners too, they were,' Matilda recalled wistfully.

'Too fatty at times, though, remember . . .'

At last, Matilda was attuned to a tinge of playfulness in her daughter's voice. She levelled on Lucy a beady-eyed look.

Sensing her mother's stare, Lucy opened one big blue eye.

Matilda jumped to her feet. 'You having me on, miss?'

Lucy grinned, pulling some cash from a pocket. 'Got paid up and Boris took me back straightaway, same shifts as before. He said Connie had persuaded him it wasn't my fault that horrible cow started trouble. I told him we'd worked together and she had it in for me from ages ago.'

'Shame I weren't there that night. I'd've showed *her* trouble.' Matilda shook the kettle, gauging from a sploshing sound whether it needed filling. 'We'll have a cuppa, then, to celebrate.'

Lucy had thought it best not to go and ask for her job back while still looking bashed up so had waited a couple of days for the marks on her face to fade before she'd returned to the Cuckoo Club. She'd arrived before the club opened, knowing Boris would be alone then, poring over his accounts books. She'd approached him with a ready apology, prepared to beg, if necessary, to keep herself in work. After giving her a token telling-off, Boris had crushed her to his fat bosom declaring all was forgiven and Bill Black and his friends were banned from the club. Privately, Lucy had thought that Bill and Ada would choose to steer well clear of the place now they'd been rumbled as the Mortimer House jewel thieves.

Lucy hadn't told her mother *all* of what had gone on the night she'd had a scrap with Ada Stone. Any mention of crime and intrigue would beg more questions; in particular, why Lucy hadn't offered up the whole juicy tale in the first place. But Matilda was aware that the maid who'd done the dirty on Lucy had visited the club as a customer, and a confrontation had taken place between them with Lucy coming off worst.

As for Sean Napier . . . just a thought of him made a feverish chill curl through Lucy's veins. She hadn't mentioned a word about him to her mother. She didn't know what to say because she still wasn't sure whether seeing him again was sensible. He had told her things that could endanger his life – hers too perhaps, if Bill Black and Ada Stone turned vicious and came looking for her. They were obviously professional criminals and she had no idea how far they'd go to protect themselves from arrest.

She couldn't lay all the blame for that at Sean's door. From the moment Rory had told her about the theft and scandal, Lucy would have challenged Ada over her wickedness had they bumped into one another.

But there was something about Sean that was unsettling Lucy and she guessed her niggling uneasiness stemmed from suspecting he had lied or withheld important facts about himself. Sean was handsome and charismatic, and she was attracted to him, she knew that. But excitement was one thing, trust was quite another.

They'd spoken on only a few occasions but she'd known straight away he fancied her and that he was guarding his tongue. It wasn't so much that she thought him a married man out for a good time; he seemed too classy for cheap thrills. Yet confusingly, and despite his charm and eloquence, she found it easier to imagine him being a Bill Black type of character than the nephew of an aristocrat. With sudden clarity Lucy realised she feared he might be more dangerous than the villains he was after.

Suddenly conscious of her mother's thoughtful glances, Lucy asked brightly, 'Where's Reg got to? Are you meeting up with him in the Duke dinner time, Mum?'

Matilda vigorously swirled the teapot to mix the brew, then plonked it on the table. 'He's got to find himself work. Or get himself down the dole office,' she replied flatly. 'Told him straight, we ain't landing ourselves with a parasite. Times are tough and it's trouble enough feeding two mouths, let alone three.'

Lucy knew her mother and Reg yearned to be properly reunited but the awkward idea of the three of them living together was prompting Matilda to send him off most nights to a dosshouse further along Campbell Road.

The morning after Lucy had returned home to hear Reg snoring in her mother's bed, Matilda's mumbled explanation that they'd had a bit too much to drink and fallen asleep had made Lucy suppress a smile. She was glad her mother had someone to love. She was also relieved Matilda had the comfort of regular company because she knew she couldn't stay with her for ever.

She was feeling restless, as she had when longing to leave Southend, without understanding this time what was causing it. She needed decent regular employment, but the idea of going into service again, and being at someone's beck and call day and night, no longer appealed. She envied her mother and her sisters having their own homes – no matter how rundown they might be. She envied them too for having partners with whom to share happiness and sorrows. Reg had hurt her mum by abandoning her but Lucy was fair minded; her mother wasn't the easiest person to live with. Reg had been man enough to return and admit his mistakes and make his apologies. Lucy liked Reg and she knew her sisters would also be pleased he was back to stay.

In the past her mother's fiancé had been a tinker, stallholder and journeyman. Lucy remembered him as hardworking, never one to shy away from regular employment if it was available. But every day brought new and worrying news that jobs were getting scarcer and people being laid off. It was little consolation to know that other people around the world were suffering similar hardship.

'The Great Depression', as the politicians termed the lack of work and money, was a horrible phrase but it seemed suitable. Lucy sensed a dreadful melancholy *was* beginning to spread around and about. She'd heard that a new ruling was to limit Government help to only the poorest people out of work. Lucy knew too her Mum wasn't keen on any of them accepting charity or interference of any sort.

'What about this Means Test? Will Reg have to do it?'

'Can test Reg all they like; all they'll find is he ain't got a pot ter piss in.' Matilda barked a laugh. 'That's the thing when you've never had nothing, Luce: you've less to lose when things turn rough. Good times have been bad for people like us so don't make a lot of difference, do it? Me 'n' Reg, and me 'n' yer dad before him, we've just scraped by all our lives.'

'Done it, though, Mum, haven't you?' Lucy enclosed Matilda in a proud hug. 'Got over your dreadful injuries too, so you're a tough old bird.'

'Whatever don't kill you makes yer stronger.' Matilda's stout philosophy was accompanied by a wink as she poured out their tea.

CHAPTER TWENTY-FOUR

'Where you off out to then, miss?'

Lucy spun around, dropping her comb on the mantel. She'd been teasing her shiny chestnut fringe into place in front of the spotted mirror.

'Didn't hear you come in,' she breathlessly told her mother.

'Not surprised,' Matilda returned drily. 'You was humming so loud I thought we'd got a swarm of bees flown in the winder.'

Lucy self-consciously tucked a curl behind an ear.

'Who is he, then?' Matilda asked, dumping shopping on the table, and proving Lucy right in thinking her mother had guessed she was getting ready for a date.

'Thought you were meeting Reg at the caff for tea.' Lucy changed the subject.

'I was; but he's heard there's a hand barrer going cheap round Fonthill Road so he rushed off to see if he can get it before someone else does. He's had no luck turning up a job so we decided he should give totting a go.'

'That's a good idea.' Lucy sounded enthusiastic.

'I reckon so 'n' all.' Matilda frowned. 'So, miss, you gonna tell me where you're off to all dolled up?'

Lucy's get-up of crisp pale blue blouse and a cotton skirt of darker blue received a maternal assessment. Bred in a rundown tenement maybe, ran Matilda's thoughts, but her youngest daughter could saunter along Oxford Street mingling with classy ladies and not look out of place. She knew the outfit had come second-hand from Chapel Street market – as did most of Lucy's clothes – but it had obviously been bought originally from a top store. Matilda felt a surge of pride, and relief. She wanted Lucy to meet a decent man and settle down. Before too long she hoped to see her with kids around her ankles, driving her mad. It was the natural way of things, and at nineteen her pretty daughter was plenty old enough to be setting up her own home with her husband.

Lucy knew she might as well own up. In the near future she might be introducing Sean to her mother. A warm hopefulness was convincing her this wouldn't be the only outing she had with him . . . unless his mission was complete and he was ready to catch the boat home. She found the idea of saying a final farewell in a few hours' time depressing.

'He's Irish and his name's Sean,' she began with a bashful smile.

Matilda raised her eyebrows. 'A Paddy, eh? 'S'pect Reg'll take to him, then.'

Lucy relaxed. She knew it was her mother's way of letting her know so far she'd heard nothing to make her want to raise objections.

'And what work does he do?' Matilda interrogated, ever mindful of the importance of regular employment.

'He's . . . sort of working in jewellery at the moment.'

'Ooh . . .' Matilda looked impressed, then her expression darkened. 'Suppose you met him at that club, did you?'

'Sort of . . .' Lucy said briskly, keen to get going before her mother's questions became trickier.

'Respectful, is he? Is he a lot older than you?' Matilda demanded, eyes narrowed and mouth pursed.

Lucy nodded, aware her mother suspected she might be getting involved with a lecher looking to be her sugar daddy. 'I think he's very nice,' she blurted, wistfully hoping he'd prove her faith in him justified. 'And he's handsome and can get any girl he likes.'

'Well, seems he likes you. And can't blame him fer that. Not many gels are lucky enough to have your looks.' Matilda gave a proud nod.

Having wrong-footed her mother, Lucy decided it was time to bow out. Besides, it was almost six thirty and she didn't want to be late getting to the Angel.

'Make sure you're in at a decent hour, miss.' Matilda started unpacking a few groceries from her bag. Despite her stern warning a smile moved her mouth as her daughter collected her cardigan and slipped out of the door.

'Thought you might stand me up.'

'Why's that?'

Sean shrugged and came towards her, flicking to the floor the cigarette he'd been smoking while lounging against the wall waiting for her. 'Never know with you, Lucy Keiver, whether to expect sun or storm.'

Lucy cocked her head, a mischievous smile tipping her lips. 'Is that right? Well, don't reckon it'll hurt to keep you guessing a bit longer what sort of mood I'm in.'

Sean smiled slowly. 'The clouds are passing over, I'm thinking.' He came closer, took her chin in a cool grasp and tilted her head to and fro. 'All healed up, aren't you, now?'

Lucy raised her lashes and sensed a tumbling in her guts as his deep blue eyes gazed into hers.

Sean let her go with a stroke of long fingers. 'Now where d'you fancy going?' he asked, opening the passenger door of his car, parked at the kerb. When he'd settled beside her in the Humber he turned to her for an answer.

'It's too warm to go to the flicks, and not easy to talk over the racket anyway. How about we just take a drive and you can let me know how you've been getting on. Have you got the emeralds back?'

Sean pulled out from the kerb. 'Not yet . . . but I'm almost there . . .'

Lucy quietly digested that information till he looked at her for a response. 'That's good. Where are they?'

'Can't tell you all me secrets now, can I?'

Lucy sent him a look of pained indignation.

'All right, Miss Keiver, I'll tell you a little bit. A woman's been trying to sell the jewellery around town. It's grand news 'cos for a while I was worried they might have been broken up. But it's all fine and dandy in its box. I think it's got about that I'd be annoyed to find it otherwise.' He smiled behind the cigarette in his lips.

Lucy digested that. 'D'you think Ada was trying to sell them? How did you find out all this?' Lucy's tone and expression betrayed exhilarated interest.

'It was an older woman . . . middle-aged and nervous.

And I know 'cos people tend to talk to me when I ask them questions.'

'I wonder who it is.' Lucy turned a frown on Sean. 'Perhaps they have an older woman in their gang of shoplifters.'

'Black moved the stuff on to a fence a long while ago and the feller is trying to get rid of it. His missus wanted a few hundred pounds for jewellery worth thousands so they're desperate people.'

Lucy's jaw dropped. 'Thousands? As much as that?'

Sean turned his head and gave a dry laugh. 'Many thousands,' he gently mocked. 'Henry the eighth once presented those emeralds to his mistress, so they're almost fit for a queen . . . but not quite.'

Lucy blinked, wondering how he could sound so casual about something so serious.

'So . . . are you hungry?'

'I am a bit.' Lucy declared.

'Still got that bit of steak in me pantry.'

Lucy darted a glance at him, regretting having given an unconsidered answer. 'You're trying to poison me! It'll be right off by now.' She hoped to sound blasé.

'Matured to perfection,' he said with a long steady look. 'Got a bottle of wine too. Fancy it?'

'Cup of tea and a bun in the caff is fine by me,' Lucy responded lightly.

Sean pulled up and switched off the engine.

'You've had a couple of days to think, and you've come to meet me this evening, Lucy . . .'

Lucy glanced at him with a frown. 'What're you saying?' Even before he told her she'd guessed the answer.

'I think you know I'm saying I'm after you spending

the night with me.' Sean tipped the hat back on his head and tilted his face to watch her expression. 'I can't hang this job out much longer. His lordship wants his emeralds and I want me money off him. But I want you too.'

'You could get them back straight away, you mean, if you wanted to?' Lucy asked hoarsely.

'If I wanted to,' he softly corroborated. 'It's been that way for a while. I just wanted to know for sure Black and Stone were in cahoots over the robbery.' He quirked a smile. 'I know you told me I wasn't much good on the job. But I am. I'll show you.'

Lucy sensed they weren't just talking about him chasing jewel thieves. 'And you've been hanging it out because of me? So I'll spend the night with you.'

'I have.'

Lucy was speechless with shock for a moment. Then a simmering anger began to churn her insides. He expected her to go back to his house and sleep with him so he'd be satisfied he'd done all he wanted to do in London and was free to collect his reward money and return to Ireland.

And forget her.

'Well, you've got a fine cheek, I'll give you that,' she burst out. '*And* you're a hypocrite. You said you didn't think me easy just 'cos I worked at the Cuckoo Club. You said you weren't like Rory. No, you're not like him. You're worse!' she scoffed. 'At least he was honest and told me right from the start he thought me a tart for working there.'

She heard an exhalation of breath, saw exasperation flit over his chiselled features. It was the sort of frustrated boredom a difficult child might arouse in a parent. A similar expression to one she'd seen on Lord Mortimer's face when one of his daughters had refused to attend her piano lesson.

Sean turned on the engine, jammed the car in gear and pulled away from the kerb. Lucy's wrath increased on noting he appeared quite casual; she on the other hand could feel her ribs shuddering over her drumming heart. He couldn't be bothered to talk to her now and was treating her as though she was unworthy of further attention. When he pulled up minutes later at the bottom end of Campbell Road, she felt so humiliated that he'd returned her home that she wanted to lash out.

'Go home, Lucy,' he said softly, and sat tapping the steering wheel as though impatient to be rid of her.

'You're a bastard, d'you know that?' she stormed, her voice wobbling with suppressed tears. 'You might not like Lord Mortimer but you damn well act like you're his equal, don't you? You're not! You're just another one of the staff!' She flung open the door and jumped out. Before she'd moved a yard he'd driven off into Seven Sisters Road.

Matilda had been about to head towards the bus stop with Reg when she spotted her daughter leaping from a black saloon car, which had immediately driven off. She needed no telling what had gone on. She had feared, even if Lucy had not, what a man who was a lot older and worked in jewellery might want with a pretty young woman. What saddened Matilda was that her Lucy – who was particular about fellows – had really liked this one. Her maternal instinct had persuaded her that Lucy's shy smile and careful preparations might be for a man worthy of her. But it seemed she'd been right to have misgivings about the swine.

From the way Lucy was walking, with her face lowered and a hanky in her hand, Matilda guessed she had been crying. To preserve her daughter's dignity she tugged Reg back into the shelter of the hallway so Lucy had a chance to compose herself before bumping into them.

Reg understood his fiancée's expressive facial gyrations well enough: he was being warned to keep his thoughts to himself and his lip buttoned.

'You're back early,' Matilda busily greeted her daughter as Lucy entered the dismal hallway of their house. 'Me 'n' Reg are just off over to Wood Green to see Alice. We're hoping Josh might be a diamond and lend Reg a bit of petty cash so he can get going on the totting tomorrow.'

Lucy quickly stuffed the hanky up her cardigan sleeve and gave the couple a smile. 'So, you got the barrow?' she asked brightly.

'I did, Lucy,' Reg answered. 'Can't wait to get going on me rounds now.'

Lucy smiled although his Irish accent – not as smooth as the one that had enraged her moments ago – made her wish Reg and her mother would set off before more tears embarrassed her.

'See you later then.' Matilda had noticed the suspicious glitter behind her daughter's batting lashes and tugged on Reg's arm. 'Bleedin' Irish git,' she muttered under her breath, making Reg give her a pained look. 'No, ain't you this time,' Matilda rumbled. 'Tell you later . . .' she added on turning round to see Lucy making her slow way up the rickety stairs.

CHAPTER TWENTY-FIVE

Matilda wasn't one to gloat over others' misfortunes. People who in the past had felt the rough side of her tongue – or fist – still had her pity when things went badly wrong.

If kids were part of the problem Matilda's sympathy strengthened. Over many years she'd been knocked sideways with worry over her daughters. She'd known too the humiliation of being abandoned by a man you thought could be relied on because he loved you. Not that she'd have thought Eddie Finch was much of a loss. But people had probably said the same about Reg Donovan when he'd scarpered and left her struggling on her own.

Lucy had told her a while ago that Jennifer Finch had run off to live with a rotter a lot older than herself. More recently, Beattie had rattled off more amazing gossip about the Finches: Eddie had upped sticks, leaving his wife and remaining kids to fend for themselves. Beattie had chortled he must have found himself a bit on the side; Matilda recalled choking out commiserations for whoever the poor cow might be.

As they slowly drew closer, sliding glances at each other while browsing market stalls, Winifred hoped that Matilda might pass on by without speaking. She knew it had spread like wildfire around the neighbourhood that Eddie had abandoned her.

At first Winnie had been too astonished to react when he'd loaded up his van with his stuff. The mean miserable bastard had even taken the radiogram, still in pieces, with him. But he'd left behind the tortoiseshell box. She'd thrown it at his head as he slammed the front door, then swiftly picked up the jewellery in case Kathy or Tom saw it and asked awkward questions.

Considering that Winnie had been planning a life without *him* she'd felt incensed that Eddie had got in first. Neither Kathy nor Tom had seemed overly upset once they'd got over the shock of their father leaving. In fact, Winnie reckoned, like her, they were glad he'd gone. But he'd left problems behind, not least of which was how Winnie was going to make ends meet without his wages. Kathy had promised extra housekeeping and had been good to her word in helping out as much as she could. Winnie had looked for full-time work with no success so had taken on another charring job that paid a pittance.

They were on a collision course, and through the throng Matilda noticed that Winnie was looking more defensive now only a yard or two separated them. It made her more determined to stop and say her piece even though they hadn't exchanged a word since their bust-up over the sweet shop job.

'Sorry to hear you've had a few problems of late, Winnie.' Matilda's voice was gruff with sincerity.

Winnie sunk her chin in the collar of her blouse before

swinging a defiant glance at Matilda's face. 'Yeah . . . well, glad to see the back of him, if truth be told.'

'Know what it feels like to have a man run out,' Matilda replied quietly. 'Know what it feels like 'n' all to be worried sick over one of the kids.'

Winnie's lips tightened. It seemed Matilda had also caught wind of Jennifer's disgraceful carrying on. The neighbours in her terrace were still poking around for clues as to whether Jennifer had run away or got kicked out. Not that Winnie allowed them a second of her time when they tried to trick out of her which version it was. But she knew they'd been chinwagging. 'Glad to see the back of Jennifer, 'n' all,' she rattled off. 'Little cow turned out nothing but trouble.'

'Perhaps she'll see sense in time and—'

'Too late for that!' Winnie snorted, agitated fingers renewing the knot in the headscarf containing her buoyant hair. 'Don't want no more to do with her in me life.'

Winnie hoped nobody had come to hear about Jennifer stealing Eddie's money or handling stolen gems. She reckoned Matilda just thought one of her daughters was a little trollop, although Winnie had to admit the woman had been good enough not to rub it in.

'Give it a few years, you might feel differently.' Matilda gently patted her shoulder. 'When they're little they make yer arms ache, when they're big they make yer heart ache.' Matilda nodded sagely. 'You ain't alone in knowing that, Win. So you keep yer chin up, gel. Know you probably don't think so now but yer luck'll change, you'll see.'

'Bleedin' hope so . . .' Winnie mumbled, her eyes watery.

'You take care of yourself now.' Matilda made to walk on but Winnie stopped her.

'Wanted to say . . . about that time with the Dobsons . . .' Winnie felt guilty for causing a commotion over the sweet shop job. She'd been a fool to make a spectacle of herself on Jenny's behalf.

'Already forgot all about that.' Matilda flicked a hand.

'Heard Reg Donovan's back from Ireland.'

'He is, but ain't gonna make life easy for him. He's not managed to find work so's doing a bit of totting round the streets to pay his way. If you've got anything of Eddie's you want shot of, Win, he'll take a look, if you like. Old clothes or bits 'n' pieces yer old man's left behind could make you a few bob. And every penny counts these days, don't it?'

Again, Matilda touched Winnie's shoulder in farewell. She'd barely moved ten yards when Winnie came trotting up behind her.

'Might have something fer Reg, actually,' Winnie mumbled breathlessly. She cleared her throat and licked her dry lips. She didn't feel guilty at what she was about to do. At times like this it was everyone for themselves and she reckoned if Matilda Keiver was in her shoes she'd do the same to keep her kids safe. The jewellery was no use to her and she just wanted to be rid of the damned stuff. If Reg Donovan would buy it for a few pounds, she'd be happy . . . She spurred herself on with the thought that in any case he was Irish so the thug chasing after the emeralds was bound to be a bit more lenient if he caught up with a fellow countryman.

'Much obliged, Win. Send Reg round to have a gander at it then, shall I?' Having received a nod Matilda gave the woman a smile then she was off again, weaving through the Chapel Street market.

When Winnie got home she found Kathy pacing to and fro, looking agitated. 'What's going on, Mum?'

Winnie frowned until she saw the direction of her daughter's gaze and her jaw sagged. On the parlour table was the broken tortoiseshell box.

'Where d'you get that?' Winnie snatched it up.

'Out of the airing cupboard. Tom's got diarrhoea and messed himself. I pulled out some rags from the back of the shelf to clean him up and found that wrapped in a torn pillowcase.' Kathy knew from her mother's wariness that she'd put it there, not Eddie.

'Dad would never have left that behind by accident, would he? In any case, last time I saw that box, Jennifer had it.' Kathy didn't feel guilty about letting out that secret. Things were very different now from the day she'd promised her sister she'd keep quiet. It seemed very odd that the box was now broken and in her mother's keeping. Kathy had suspected all along that the jewellery really belonged to her father and Jenny had somehow got her sticky fingers on it. Her twin had always been a storyteller and Kathy had found it hard to swallow that Bill Black would give such a valuable present to a girl he hardly knew. Kathy felt renewed bewilderment at how badly her twin had been behaving.

'Did Jennifer hand it over to Dad? Has he left it behind for you to sell as you're not getting housekeeping off him?'

Winnie shouted a laugh. 'She give it to me, not him. And yer father ain't left us that!' She clicked two skinny fingers under her daughter's nose. 'This bleedin' stuff. . .'

she rattled the gems by Kathy's cheek, '. . . ain't worth the box it's in. And that's in bits.'

'They're glass, aren't they?' Kathy ruefully shook her head. It all became clear. Bill *had* given the jewellery to Jenny but it was worthless tat. 'Jenny believed that smarmy sod had given her real emeralds.'

'So you knew all about it from the start, did you, miss?' Winnie glared at Kathy. 'Been acting as deceitful as her, haven't you? Well, let me catch you getting any more like your tart of a sister and you'll be out of that door with my boot up yer backside, and that's a promise!'

Kathy's cheeks grew warm beneath her mother's angry stare. But still she felt dreadfully sorry for her. The day her father had run out on them Kathy had seen Winnie's cut and swollen face. She knew her parents regularly heaped misery on one another but she'd felt disgusted that her father had given her mother a hiding as a leaving present. 'Did Dad go away because the jewels were fakes? Is that what set him off?'

'Jennifer found out where he kept his stash of money and took it with her. All she left him was a few tenners. *That's* what set him off.' Winnie's lips stretched into a thin line. 'Selfish little cow didn't let me in on it, more's the pity. I'd've made sure I was miles away before he found out he'd been stitched up by his own daughter.'

'Jenny took all his savings?' Kathy gasped out.

'And this was what he got in return.' Winnie jerked up the box.

Kathy gawped at her mother's pinched expression. She'd never have believed Jennifer capable of anything so devious.

'You just make sure you keep quiet about it all!' Winnie's finger quivered under Kathy's nose. 'I'm selling them soon. Whatever they are, they're still pretty enough for someone to want 'em.'

Kathy frowned. Pretty they might be but she didn't know of any woman round here who'd spend good money on bits of coloured glass to string about herself. Most people were more concerned with spending what little they had on putting food in empty bellies. Lately she'd seen local families queuing at the soup kitchen in Holloway Road. 'Don't reckon you'll get much,' Kathy said dispiritedly.

'I saw Matilda Keiver earlier and she said Reg Donovan's setting up in rag 'n' boning. He's keen to get stuff to start him off and I know he'll buy 'em. So there's no need for us to say we ever had 'em 'cos soon they'll be gone . . . right?'

'Mum . . .'

Winnie spun about, tugging her cardigan edge over the box to hide it.

'Got bellyache,' Tom whimpered, standing in the doorway of the parlour with his hands pressed to his abdomen.

'Been scrumpin' apples out of the Vicarage, 'fore they're ripe, ain't yer?' Winnie stomped over and clipped his ear. 'Nosy cow next door saw you climbing the fence, and made a point of telling me, so don't go denying it! Told you time 'n' again not to. And if I find out you've been with that Davy Wright and those other tykes from the Bunk you'll get another one of those.' Winnie threatened him with a raised hand.

Kathy heard her little brother's sob, and the gurgling in his belly that terminated in a squish and a bad smell. Before her mother could set about him again she rushed to intercept. 'Come on, I'll take you out back to the privy and get you cleaned up again,' she said on a sigh.

'Don't you ask fer no tea later!' Winnie's bellow followed Tom as his sister led him out of the back door.

Eddie Finch had known if he waited long enough the bastard would sail by before closing time. He'd been parked round the corner to the pub for over an hour, the van's windscreen wipers squeaking to and fro, smearing drizzle and giving him a clearer view through the dusk. For August it was a foul evening but, come rain or shine, Bill Black was always out on the razzle Friday night.

Eddie's fingers tightened about the gun in his pocket. He was sure it didn't work, and even if he'd had some bullets to try it out, he wouldn't have dared use it. The weapon had been brought back from the Somme by an army pal of his who'd said it was a German Luger. Eddie didn't know one pistol from another but he reckoned it looked good enough to put the frighteners on Bill Black. Eddie wanted some of his cash returned and if Bill demanded his jewellery back he could get Jennifer to go and fetch it off her mother.

A scrawny black-haired woman had alighted from Bill's car and Eddie saw his daughter get out after her. Eddie barely hesitated before jumping from his van. The sight of Jennifer hadn't put him off his mission. He'd got a few things to say to that little cow, as it happened.

'All right, Bill?' Eddie had quickly and quietly come up behind the trio while Bill was busy locking his car.

Bill whipped a glance between Eddie and his small harem. He licked his lips. 'Now, I hope you ain't come over to make no trouble, Ed.' Bill's smile was threatening,

301

his eyes shifting side to side. 'No point in going back over spilled milk, mate, is there?'

'Yeah, there is.' Eddie ignored his daughter, who'd turned as white as the summer blouse she had on. He also had no interest in the hard-faced maggot glaring at him. 'And I'll tell you why I'm going back on it, Bill,' he said softly. 'I don't take kindly to getting robbed of me life savings, and I don't take kindly neither to being landed with merchandise I can't sell 'cos a fuckin' Irish thug might slit me throat if I do.'

Ada turned a snarl on Bill. She'd known this bust-up was fast approaching. Bill's praising of Jennifer for thieving her father's cash and getting rid of the emeralds had grated on her nerves from the start. Ada had warned him even a cowardly weasel like Eddie Finch wouldn't take something that serious lying down. Well, she wasn't handing back her share of the cash! She'd done the collar on the poxy job and had waited ages to get rewarded for it.

'I'm off inside fer a drink,' she snapped. 'You can bleedin' sort it out with him.' When Jennifer tried to escape her father's wrath by scuttling after Ada the older woman shoved her away. 'You stay with yer old man. I reckon he wants a word with you. Time you went home, little girl, anyhow.'

Eddie's eyes flitted unemotionally over Jennifer. 'Go round the corner, Bill, where it's a bit quieter, shall we?' He suggested with sinister softness, jerking his head to the shadowy place where his van was parked.

'No point, Eddie. Nothing to say.' Bill's lips flattened against his teeth. He swayed to and fro on legs planted wide apart, flexing his fingers into fists. 'Now you know I can take you easy as anything, even with one hand tied behind me back, so why don't yer fuck off 'fore you end up hurt. Go home to yer missus, mate, and leave it alone.' He leered at Jennifer. 'Like I've left her alone . . .' He paused, letting that sink in. 'I respect you, see, Ed. Ain't taken advantage of yer daughter, even though I could. You wouldn't like that to change now, would yer, 'cos you've pissed me off?'

Eddie snorted his contempt. 'Even if I believed you, it don't make no difference. I'm here for me money, as you well know. You can have her.'

Grabbing Jenny by an elbow, Bill pushed her, stumbling, in front of him towards the pub's entrance. 'All right, Ed, I will have her. And if any of me mates want to join in I'll let 'em so she gets a right good seeing to . . .' He suddenly froze as he felt metal dig into his spine. 'Now what you got there, Ed? That's silly, ain't it?' Bill squirmed, attempting to peer over a shoulder, but Eddie stopped him with two painful prods with the gun barrel.

'Round the corner by me van,' Eddie muttered close to his ear.

Bill squinted loathing but did as he was told, dragging Jennifer with him. If the old bastard had a loaded gun Bill was going to make sure Jennifer was between him and the bullets.

Eddie felt his guts turning to water. He was light-headed with fear but knew there was no going back. If he were to drop to his knees and grovel an apology it'd make no difference now. Bill would kill him just for showing him up in front of his women. Eddie tightened his quivering grip on the revolver, holding it two handed to keep it still. But he wasn't here to grovel or apologise, he reminded himself. He was here for everything in Bill's wallet and he wasn't leaving without it.

Without any ammunition he realised he'd have to clump Bill quick and hard with the gun, rifle his pockets then make a getaway. In a brawl Eddie knew he'd got no chance. Once Bill realised he wasn't going to get shot he'd spring into action and pulverise him.

Eddie was praying that on this particular evening Bill was carrying a thick wad. He knew from past experience that the flash prick liked to wave an impressive amount about even if he spent very little of it. He was always on the ear'ole for drinks. Eddie wasn't expecting to get *all* his money back. But he reckoned Eddie might be carrying as much as a ton if he was intending to go on to a club, or meet up with some pals for a bit of showing off.

Eddie knew he'd only get one crack at this. And there'd be no more living in Islington. But then there wasn't much to take him back . . . although he'd miss Tom . . . His small son had a place in his heart and he reckoned he'd stay there; unlike Winnie, or his twin daughters. To Eddie's mind, women were a pain in the arse and only any use in the kitchen or bedroom. Winnie's cooking wasn't up to much, and when lying on her back with her legs in the air she couldn't keep her nagging gob shut long enough for him to finish what he'd started. It was a crying shame he hadn't wilted sixteen years ago on the night he got Winnie pregnant with the twins, then he'd never have had to marry the cow . . .

Dwelling on his family was his undoing. Eddie missed the moment that Bill pivoted about and thumped him hard in the guts. The blow sent him tottering so far away that Bill had to come after him, intending to give him some more. Those few seconds were exactly what Eddie needed. He gasped in air, finding the energy to whip up the Luger and smash it into Bill's cheek. He followed that up by a dig with a bony knee aimed at his opponent's groin. It was a panicky tactic but worked well enough to fold Bill over. While the bigger man struggled to focus and keep on his feet, Eddie kicked him in the side of the head sending him sprawling on the ground. He was desperate to knock him out so he could dive in his pockets, so drew back one foot then the other, striking out indiscriminately at his head and torso in a maniacal dance. When Bill's head finally flopped to one side Eddie let out the pent-up air behind his teeth in a long sobbing sigh.

He glanced over at Jennifer to see that she was clinging to the brick wall silently wailing. Her face was chalky and she suddenly retched onto the pavement.

Eddie stooped, blindly driving his hands into Bill's pockets till he found a bulging wallet and yanked it out. Stuffing the Luger in his waistband, he snatched at the banknotes then dropped the empty leather down on Bill's chest.

He strode to Jennifer and raised a fist. 'You're lucky you don't get some of that 'n' all,' he spat. 'You filthy little slut. You deserve all you get.' Bill's groaning made him jerk nervously around and sprint over to him. Deliberately he raised a foot to stamp hard on Bill's crotch. 'There. Don't say I didn't do nothing for yer,' he hooted at Jennifer, who was trying to wipe vomit from her chin. 'He ain't gonna be botherin' any woman for a while . . .'

Ada strutted moodily out of the pub to see what was keeping Bill just as Eddie was firing the throttle on the van. Seconds later he was screeching away in first gear.

CHAPTER TWENTY-SIX

Lucy realised she had nobody to blame but herself. From the start, she'd known Sean Napier was only in London for a short while, and had judged him a man who'd not bother wooing women he fancied. Yet when she'd been proved right she'd felt cheated and hurt . . . and stupid because she'd allowed herself to fall for him.

She placed Greg Randall's dinner in front of him with a smile. The old fellow winked, flicking her a sixpence. Politely she pocketed it. She could see he'd like to chat but she moved away, feeling too downhearted to conjure up a jolly façade.

'What's up, Luce? You look like you've lost a florin and found a thrupenny bit.' Connie slid a tray full of empties onto the bar while Lucy waited for her drinks order.

Lucy shrugged, glancing at her frowning friend. 'You don't look that bright yourself, Con,' she replied.

'Not sure how much longer I'll have a job.' Connie let out a heavy sigh. '*And* I'm two months behind on me rent.'

'Not thinking of quitting, are you?' Lucy sounded astonished.

'No, but reckon I'll be shown the door before too long.'

'Why? What have you done?' Lucy guessed Connie had got herself in hot water with Boris.

'I overheard the boss on the telephone to one of his cronies. He didn't spot me earwigging 'cos I kept meself out of sight.' As the barman approached Connie leaned closer to Lucy. 'He was moaning that takings are down 'cos bookings are slow and he needs to put off a wait-ress,' she whispered. 'I know it'll be me. I'm the oldest and gents want youngsters to look at.'

The barman had been making trips to and fro to replenish Lucy's tray; suddenly her friend began rear-ranging the glasses for her.

'Look sharp! Boris is watching!' A moment later, Connie had hurried away to busy herself clearing tables. And there were plenty of them, and very few new arrivals necessitating them being re-laid.

Lucy set off with her load of cocktails and spirits. She knew she should be anxious, having heard Connie's news, but strangely she wasn't.

Even the well-to-do were feeling the pinch. Some of the surrounding nightspots and supper clubs in Piccadilly had already closed their doors as people tightened their belts and stayed at home. It was inevitable the Cuckoo Club might suffer the same fate.

She'd only ever considered the job a stopgap till she found something better. Not that anything better had turned up, so she had no idea where she'd go or what she'd do. But she was now resigned to moving on, if only because the Cuckoo Club would always remind her of Sean Napier and she wanted to forget him. Besides, her mother deserved to have her house back to herself. Reg and Matilda wanted to live again as man and wife and she was the stumbling block. She'd said she'd no objection to sharing their living space with Reg but Matilda's reply had hinted that the right time for that would be when she moved out.

Lucy distributed glasses, flinching away from a male hand that had found the back of one of her knees. Resisting the urge to swing her empty tray against the offender's bald head she sweetly accepted the coins he offered and headed towards the kitchens. Connie was trudging ahead of her, looking glum. The older woman was usually the one to cheer everybody up, and genuinely enjoyed her job whereas Lucy often found it hard to bear.

Lucy decided at the end of her shift she'd tell Boris she was soon leaving London, so there'd be no need to sack anybody.

Ada was perched on the bonnet of Bill's Austin, taking lazy drags from her cigarette, when she spotted him limping through the open hospital gates. She straightened up and stepped on her dog-end. He rarely allowed her to drive his car unless it was for his benefit.

She'd visited him as a patient several times and had been amazed at how quickly he'd started to mend. She guessed his determination to get even with Eddie Finch was spurring on his recovery.

As soon as Bill had been able to get out of bed unaided he'd told the doctor he was going home. The doctor had impressed on him that he was lucky no limbs had been broken and he needed more bed rest. Ada had argued that he'd be a fool to ignore the doctor's advice. But yesterday, following his nagging, she'd turned up at the hospital with a set of clean clothes and agreed to pick him up in the car the next day.

Bill gave her a listless wave and kept going in the same uneven gait till he halted by her side with a wince. His bruises had faded but his body still ached.

'You don't look so bad.' Ada gave him a top-to-toe inspection. He was leaner in face and physique, and his swarthy complexion, beneath unshaven stubble, had a greyish tinge. His nose had been broken during Eddie's beating and now flared at an odd angle. A crusty scab sat on one of his cheekbones where the Luger had dug into his flesh. But all things considered he'd made a remarkable recovery since Ada had first seen him sprawled on the ground, unconscious, with blood pooling under his head.

On that evening, when she had frantically hared back inside the pub to call for an ambulance, Ada had feared the next time she saw Bill Black, he'd be laid out in his coffin. But he obviously didn't plan to push up daisies just yet.

'Want to drive?'

'Nah, be me chauffeur, will you, gel?' He gingerly settled himself in the passenger seat.

'Jennifer still around, is she?' Bill asked as they set off.

'Oh, yeah,' Ada said. 'Can't shift the bleedin' pest.'

'Right . . .' Bill said, a hint of vicious satisfaction in the single word.

During his stay in hospital, Bill had rarely mentioned Eddie Finch or business matters. Ada knew he hadn't forgotten either; but when she'd visited he'd spend an hour either moaning about his treatment or disappearing beneath the sheets to take nips from the flask of whisky she'd sneaked in for him.

But he was out now and she knew he was brooding on revenge before they'd reached the end of the street. Ada could understand his bitterness. Still she felt possessive enough to want Bill to concentrate on her, not Eddie's snivelling daughter. She slipped a sly look at his groin but he had his hands folded on his lap and she couldn't tell if he was already horny. She guessed he must have women on his mind after more than a week without sex. She was just hoping the kicking he'd taken hadn't done any serious damage down there . . .

Jennifer's confession that she feared she'd be in for it when Bill got out of hospital had been followed by her giggling that she'd do whatever he said if he'd let her stay at his place. Ada had then locked Jennifer out of Bill's flat, but reluctantly had taken pity on the girl when she heard her sob story. Ada had never got on with her own mother and had a similar tale of woe in her background. She'd piped down because she'd believed that Winnie Finch would sooner see her daughter go on the game than have her back.

In any case, Jennifer was worth her weight in gold when they were out on a job. Without Bill around nabbing the lion's share of the proceeds, Ada had done a few crafty deals of her own using Jim Trent as a fence. Jennifer had gladly taken her whack but Ada had warned her young accomplice to keep her gob shut about it because if Bill found out they'd cut him out he'd go for the lot of them, the landlord included.

Having sneaked a look at Bill's pursed-lip profile, Ada guessed he might be brooding about what business she'd done recently, so decided to give him some answers before he asked questions.

'Jennifer was a diamond when Mavis got caught in Selfridges with a silver teapot stuffed in her drawers.' Ada chuckled. The story was true. 'She fainted, and made it look real 'n' all. I managed to get away with a nice load of clobber. But Mavis weren't so lucky. You'll like the silver cruets and the men's scarves. Quality silk, they are.'

'Mavis got caught? What's happened to her?' Bill demanded. Even when in hospital feeling like death warmed up his mind had been on work . . . when it wasn't on revenge. But he was keeping his ideas close to his chest.

He'd relied on Ada keeping things ticking over for him so was glad to hear there was a nice lot of merchandise waiting to be looked over. He wasn't so happy knowing Mavis had let him down.

'Silly cow's in custody and up before the beak next week,' Ada said succinctly. 'I've let Jenny stick around 'cos we need her. I reckon Mavis is going down. She got fined last time after getting caught in Gamages, so if it's the same magistrate . . .' She shrugged.

Bill muttered under his breath while worrying at the scab prickling on his cheek. He was a vain man, brooding on his looks being ruined. He was a frustrated man too. After a barren spell in hospital he was ready for a woman but he knew Ada was too much for him to handle. She'd suck the life out of him and he wasn't sure what damage that bastard Eddie had done to his knackers. At first he'd been in agony, pissing blood.

Bill knew Jenny was a virgin. She wouldn't laugh, however badly he performed, not if she didn't know

311

any different . . . and not if she knew what was good for her . . .

The door slammed and Jenny jumped up with a start. She shifted from foot to foot, eyes pinned to Bill's face. She knew she was in trouble when he flung his keys on the table without giving her a glance.

'You look well . . . better, that is.' Jenny licked her lips. She dropped back to the settee and buried her nose in a journal. She'd decided it was best not to draw attention to herself until he seemed happier.

Bill poured himself and Ada whiskies, ignoring Jennifer darting glances at him from under her lashes. Ada smirked, as she swung a glance between the two of them. She was satisfied that Bill was hers for the night.

Having downed another tot in swift succession Bill turned hard eyes on Jennifer. 'Get in here,' he muttered, striding to the bedroom door and pushing it open.

Reflexively, Jenny shot to her feet, then sank down again. She'd never before seen such an ugly frightening expression on Bill's face and she knew he'd nothing but punishment on his mind.

'Want me to come and get you, is that it?' Bill leered. 'No use acting dumb, Jen; you know you gotta make it up to me fer what yer dad's done. He said I could have yer and I reckon I will. Things need putting right, and I'm gonna teach yer how you can do it.' He rumbled a dirty laugh, stepping menacingly towards her. Jennifer's look of startled innocence had put a bulge behind his fly and his confidence was soaring that his wedding tackle was in full working order.

The game Bill was playing was arousing Ada. She

liked the way he was stalking Jennifer and backing her into a corner. He never did that with her; usually she ended up making all the moves and doing all the work.

The excitement firing Ada's eyes and the way her tongue was poking at her lips hadn't gone unnoticed by Bill. He growled a laugh, penning Jenny against the wall with his body. 'I know what you're after, Ada. Suppose I owe you a favour, don't I, fer sorting stuff out while I've been laid up? Anyhow, if I ain't up to the job, you can lend a hand.' He tugged Jennifer by the arm towards the bedroom, lobbing over a shoulder at Ada, 'Come on then, dirty gel, let's have some fun . . .'

'Get anything good off Winnie, did yer, Reg?'

Matilda had been pegging out a damp sheet in the back yard, hoping the last rays of the sun might dry it by nightfall, when she spotted her fiancé in the hallway and called out to him. Hurriedly she entered through the back door that led to the washhouse and privy and met him by the banisters, washing basket beneath an arm. She cocked her head, guessing that whatever Winnie had offered to sell him had been no use. Yet his furrowed brow spoke of bafflement rather than disappointment.

'Hear what I said?' Matilda gave his arm a good-natured prod. 'Was it a waste of time going round Winnie's?'

'Well, I don't know about you, Til, but I'd say these are pretty.'

Matilda frowned. Not only did her fiancé look odd, he sounded odd. Reg fished out a box from his pocket and lifted the lid carefully because the hinge was broken.

The wicker basket escaped from under Matilda's

slackening arm. As a low sunbeam entered the hall and hit several emeralds, she gasped at the sudden explosion of colour. Seconds later she'd jerked to her senses, snatched the box and stuffed it in her pinafore pocket. Swiftly she swooped on the washing basket and was soon setting off up the stairs with Reg following behind her.

'They must be nicked. Eddie Finch was one fer dodgy deals.'

'Agreed. But why would he leave them behind?'

'Perhaps he didn't know he had. Perhaps he had everything packed up ready when Winnie managed to have a crafty rummage. Can't say I blame her fer that.'

'What I'm thinking is she could get more than two guineas for them, Til, even if they are fakes.'

'Desperate times, you snatch at anything to feed yer kids.'

'It seems to me there's a bad smell. I wasn't sure whether to have them. Shall I be taking them back now?'

'No! You shan't!'

'How much d'you think they're worth?'

'More than two guineas. You'd need to be a blind man to miss that.'

'Winnie doesn't seem a stupid woman to me. She could have pawned them for more. It's what I'd do. So why didn't she, now?'

'In case Eddie found out, perhaps . . . Oh, I don't know!'

Hissed conversation had batted back and forth between the seated couple until Matilda had erupted in exasperation. But still their eyes remained fixed on the open box midway between them on the pitted table. The diamonds encircling the emeralds were throwing rainbow light to dance on cracked plaster.

Reg was feeling suspicious and uneasy. Winnie Finch had told him the gems were glass and she'd take a few pounds for them. But she'd avoided his eyes and been keen to do the deal to get rid of him. She'd nothing else to sell; it seemed her husband hadn't left behind an old shirt but had forgotten to take the tortoiseshell box with him.

From the outset Reg suspected she was lying. But spontaneous greed had overcome him. It was only as he'd sped back towards the Bunk, pushing his barrow, that niggling doubts had set in. He feared he might have got himself into bad trouble and lost his two guineas into the bargain.

Matilda's thoughts were similar to Reg's: Winnie might have pulled a stroke and landed her and Reg with something too hot to handle. The last thing Matilda Keiver wanted was the police round banging on the door. She brooded on what to do next. Her nephew Rob Wild was a businessman known to have a few useful contacts. He was getting back on his feet after the fire at his warehouse a few years ago so perhaps she might pay him a visit and take the jewellery with her . . .

Matilda's hand flew to the box as she heard her daughter's key strike the lock. A second later it had been slipped out of sight into her pinafore pocket. A finger was whipped to her lips and she gave Reg a meaningful stare.

'Cup of tea's what I'm wanting.' Reg pushed to his feet and found the empty kettle. He understood Matilda's caution and agreed wholeheartedly with it. He'd no intention of letting anybody know just yet about his good fortune, because he wasn't sure if the deal he'd done with Winnie was about to turn sour on him.

CHAPTER TWENTY-SEVEN

Kathy had just finished her shift at Barratts and had emerged from the factory gates to find her twin loitering outside.

It was a sunny August afternoon and, at first, she hadn't recognised Jennifer huddled into a coat with the collar turned up. But her sister had called out, making Kathy halt and peer towards a low-branched tree nearby.

'What on earth's happened to you?' Kathy whispered, hurrying under a canopy of branches.

Jennifer started quietly sobbing, burying her face deeper into her lapels to try to hide her yellow complexion.

Kathy took her twin's arm, propelling her further into the shadows behind the trunk. She'd noticed a couple of her colleagues staring and she didn't want anybody coming over to be inquisitive.

A huge ache swelled in Kathy's chest as she gazed into her sister's bloodshot eyes and gently touched the fading bruise on a cheekbone. But Jennifer's dead-eyed expression spoke of more harm done than a beating.

'Has Bill hurt you?'

Jennifer gave a single nod. 'Have you got yer own place yet?' she blurted, sniffing to clear her watery nose.

'Own place?' Kathy frowned. 'How would I get me own place on what I earn?'

'Didn't Mum hand over some money when she sold the stuff I gave her? She must have got rid of it by now.'

Enlightenment shaped Kathy's features. 'Do you mean the jewellery?'

'I reckoned she'd sell it straight away and leave Dad,' Jenny mumbled. 'S'pose he found out and put a stop to that, did he?' She used her coat sleeve to dry her eyes. 'I expected her to take Tom with her and give you something to set you up on yer own. That's what I hoped . . .' Jenny sounded forlorn.

Kathy had forgotten her sister knew nothing about their father running out, or the tortoiseshell box holding worthless baubles that had been sold to a rag 'n' bone man. She could have laughed. She was hardly likely to get her own place following the deal her mother had done with Reg Donovan.

'Dad's gone.' Kathy's blunt information brought Jennifer's head jerking up.

'*Gone?* What, left you all?' Jennifer's voice was hoarse with astonishment.

Kathy nodded. 'He beat Mum up badly when he found out about you taking his savings and giving her that box of tat in its place.'

'Weren't tat!' Jennifer exclaimed. 'Was worth a lot of money. It was a fair exchange,' she added defiantly. 'But if I'd known Mum would only get a hiding out of it . . .'

Kathy put a comforting hand on her sister's quivering shoulder. 'It's rubbish. Mum's sold it to Reg Donovan for a few pounds 'cos he's totting.' She twisted a wry smile. 'Bill Black's done the dirty on you all round. Bet you wish you'd never gone off with him now, don't you, Jen?'

Jennifer nodded miserably, but suddenly brought up her chin. 'He's horrible but I ain't lying about the box of jewellery. I've overheard them talking and know it's real. Bill got a woman he knows called Ada to get a job as a maid so she could steal it from a big posh house in Bloomsbury. He's got a few girls work for him doing dodgy stuff . . .' Jennifer bit her lip. She was too ashamed to admit to Kathy she was one of them and regularly went shoplifting. 'But his lordship who owns the jewels wants it all back 'cos it's valuable and been in his family for ages so he's sent an Irish bloke to find it for him. Dad called him an Irish thug so he must know a lot about it.'

An hysterical giggle was Kathy's reaction to that far-fetched tale but something in her twin's expression soon withered away her laughter. 'You're kidding?' she murmured.

'No, I ain't,' Jennifer stated grimly. 'When I found out I really hoped Mum had quickly sold it in case the Irishman came round and set about you all.'

Kathy turned white. She had a quick intelligent brain and dreadful facts were slotting into place and making sense. 'D'you think Bill passed it on to you 'cos he found out he was in danger?'

Jenny nodded. 'I reckon so. He's a coward!' she sneered. 'Look what he's done to me 'cos he hates Dad. Dumb, ain't I, to think he'd give me emeralds out of the goodness of his heart? *He* tricked me into stealing Dad's savings.' Her mouth drooped in self-mockery. 'Bill went crackers when he found out I'd brought the cash *and* the jewels with me when I left home. So, I met Mum and handed them over. But I wouldn't have done if I'd know then that a thug was after them. I'd've chucked the lot in the dustbin.' Jenny wrinkled her nose in regret. 'Thought I was doing Mum a favour . . . thought too that if you had yer own place I could come 'n' live with you.' Jenny raised pleading eyes to her sister's face.

'I'd let you, swear I would. But I can't afford a room of me own.' Kathy enclosed Jenny in a hug. 'D'you want me to ask Mum if you can come home?'

Jenny's shoulders shook as she again started to cry. 'No use. She won't let me,' she wailed. 'I'll have to go back to Lambeth . . .'

Kathy knew her sister was right; Winnie wouldn't allow Jennifer over the threshold. When her sister quietened Kathy asked, 'Bill's got what he wanted so why's he taken it out on you?'

'Dad ambushed Bill outside a pub so he could get back his savings. He had a gun, Kathy!' Jennifer hissed, bloodshot eyes popping. 'He managed to get the better of Bill and whacked him in the face with it, then grabbed all the cash in Bill's wallet.' Jenny grimaced revulsion at the memory. 'It was disgusting!' she gurgled. 'Dad kept kicking Bill on the ground and there was blood everywhere and I was sick and . . .' She tailed off into racking coughs.

Kathy's mind had become overloaded with awful images; she gawped at Jennifer as though she'd garbled in double Dutch. A low brick wall edging a garden lawn was behind her and she backed away to sink down on it. Jennifer followed at a dragging pace and kneeled on grass beside her.

'I want to get away from Bill. But I can't. I'm in such

a mess and it's all me own fault. I don't know what to do . . .'

'Is Bill going after Dad for what he's done?' Kathy urgently whispered.

'S'pect he will when he's well enough. He's not long out of hospital and is still limping. He don't tell me nuthin' about what he's up to. Anyhow, don't care if Bill does beat Dad up.' Jennifer's expression hardened. 'He deserves it. It's all his fault! Dad's always been up to no good and that's how I come to meet Bill. I hate them both!' She fell silent for a moment. 'After he got out of hospital . . .' Jennifer swallowed repeatedly then turned her face away in shame at the memory of the disgusting things she'd been forced to do to make up for her father's crimes. Once, she'd yearned to have Bill kiss and touch her, now Jennifer flinched if he came close. During that first assault, when Ada had joined in, he'd not kissed her once, nor touched her gently. Ada had been the one she'd turned to to escape his brutality . . .

'You won't get pregnant, will you?' Kathy had guessed from her sister's mournfulness what Jennifer was unable to say.

'If I do I'll get rid of it. Don't want a kid of his.' Jenny forced her mind away from such a dreadful possibility. 'When I get back I'll tell Bill Dad's run off, then he'll not bother coming over yours looking for him.' Jennifer started picking at her fingernails and for some seconds the twins remained quiet, burdened by inner troubles. 'Those emeralds are cursed, I reckon,' Jennifer muttered. 'Wherever they go it's trouble.' She pushed herself to her feet. 'Walk back with me to the bus stop, Kath?'

Kathy stood up and dug in her bag. 'I've got a few shillings if you're short.'

Jenny pulled a couple of half-crowns from a pocket. 'Got money.' She gave her sister a wistful smile. 'But never got enough to set up on me own, Bill makes sure of that.' She made an effort to cheer up. 'I'm gonna start saving every penny I can. I know I can get stuff to sell—' She broke off, hoping Kathy didn't ask where it would come from. Jenny was confident she could hoist without assistance from a decoy. She had the knack when it came to thieving, so Ada had told her, and her colleague rarely praised anyone. 'All I need is a fence who'll promise not to let on to Bill what I'm up to,' Jenny continued outlining her plans. 'Then I'll be doing all right for meself, Kath, and I won't be back bothering you for anything . . . honest.'

Kathy gave her sister a weak smile but didn't voice what was on her mind: Jennifer might despise their father and his work but it seemed she was keen to follow in his footsteps.

'You knew, didn't you!'

'What you on about?' Winnie continued plunging clothes up and down in the kitchen sink while slanting Kathy an irritated glance.

'You knew the jewellery was real and that whoever's got it could be in danger.'

'Who you been speaking to?' Winnie yanked at the plug, then turned the tap to rinse the washing of soap.

'Jennifer. She said the box was stolen and an Irish thug's out looking for it to return it to the rightful owner.'

Winnie dropped the wet garments onto the wooden draining board, lips writhing, but she didn't answer her daughter or meet Kathy's eye. Having grabbed a tin bowl she jammed the washing into it, pushed past Kathy and jerked open the back door.

'Haven't you got anything to say?' Kathy squeaked in astonishment, sprinting after her mother as she marched towards the mangle in the brick shed.

Winnie suddenly dropped the bowl with a clatter and a few of Tom's socks flew onto concrete. She rounded on her daughter. 'I'll say this: you'd best keep away from yer sister if you know what's good for you. That one's no good.'

'I bet you didn't tell Reg Donovan he risked bad trouble if he bought the jewellery off you.'

'Should've kept it then, should I, and got all of us murdered instead?' Winnie gritted out between her teeth. She glanced at the boundary fence, hoping no neighbours were outside to eavesdrop.

'Should've chucked it out soon as you found out about it,' Kathy cried. She calmed herself down. 'There's no need for anybody to get murdered.' Her agitated fingers combed through her fair hair. 'You can take it to the police station and they'll give it back to the rightful owner. If you just give Reg Donovan his money back and explain to him—'

'Ain't giving him back nuthin' or explaining nuthin'.'

Winnie picked up the socks and started feeding them through the mangle, whizzing away at the handle. Kathy noticed her mother's hands were shaking so much she nearly caught her fingers in the rollers.

'Can't believe you'd be so wicked as to put people in danger like that.'

'Ain't wicked. It's looking out for us, not them,' Winnie snapped. 'Rent's overdue and me new lady has put me off already. Her husband's lost his job. So if you want to go round and give Reg Donovan his two guineas back, you do it. If you want to take the stuff down the police station, you can do that, 'n' all. First, I'll tell you what yer father told me while he was punching me in the face: if the Irish bloke don't get his reward for returning those jewels he's gonna be real upset. And he won't get a penny once the police are involved. So you think about that. Now if you don't like living here you know where the door is.' Winnie dried her raw hands on her pinafore. 'I'm getting Tom in for his tea and I'd better not find him round in the Bunk playing football.'

Kathy heard her mother's voice quavering and knew she was close to tears. She bit her lip. There was no point in saying any more. In a way she understood Winnie's logic of looking out for number one. But now Kathy knew about the perils surrounding the jewellery her conscience wouldn't allow her to do nothing. The Keivers might be a rough-and-ready family but they had a streak of kindness that put the Finches to shame.

She hadn't forgotten that Lucy had stuck up for Tom against the playground bullies and got a load of abuse from Winnie for her pains. If she had two guineas she'd take it round to the Bunk and offer it to Reg Donovan. She knew he might not believe her story. He'd probably think she was trying to pull a fast one to get back the stuff because her mother had sold it too cheaply. But at least she'd have done her best to keep innocent people safe.

Lucy was browsing the *Gazette* for jobs when the knock came at the door. She pushed back her chair from the table and went to open it.

'Oh, hello.' Being naturally hospitable, Lucy gave her unexpected visitor a smile. 'Nice surprise to see you. Coming in for a mo? I'll stick the kettle on.'

323

Kathy craned her neck to see past Lucy. 'Just come round to see Reg . . . is he in?' she rattled off.

'He and Mum have gone over to Wood Green to see Alice. But they've been gone a while; they should be back soon.' Lucy chuckled. 'I expect they're after another loan off Josh to oil the wheels of Reg's barrow. I think he's doing all right in his new job and seems to be enjoying it.' Lucy set two cups, frowning as she looked about for a bottle of milk.

Kathy's spirits wilted on hearing the people she really wanted to see were out. It had taken all her courage to come round to the Bunk. During the short walk she had picked over in her mind different versions to offer the couple of why her mother might callously jeopardise neighbours.

'Oh . . . have you got something to sell?' Lucy asked. She'd suddenly realised why Kathy might have turned up out of the blue. She'd overheard her mother and Reg talking about Winnie having some bits she wanted to get rid of.

'No . . . it's not that . . . well, it is in a way about something to sell . . . that's been sold . . .' Kathy bumbled, then sighed miserably. 'Don't know how to start,' she told Lucy truthfully.

'Sit down.' Lucy kindly pulled out a chair. She could see that Kathy was close to tears. She'd heard that Eddie Finch had done a runner. No doubt the family were now strapped for cash but embarrassed about needing to sell off stuff.

'Bad times for everyone,' Lucy said sympathetically. 'I'm just looking for another job.' She tapped the paper on the table, hoping her little problem might help Kathy open up about what was bothering her. When the younger girl sat at the table with her fair head slightly bowed, Lucy prompted her again. 'It's about something you want to sell, is it?'

'Mum sold something to Reg,' Kathy blurted. 'I . . . I've come to tell him to get rid of it quick as he can. Take it to the police, or better still just throw it away.' Kathy remembered her mother had said police involvement wasn't wise. 'I know Reg paid Mum two guineas for it and I'll give him back the money soon as I can 'cos it's not his fault she wasn't completely honest. I'm sorry she never said . . .' Kathy suddenly looked up, eyes glistening. 'But can you tell him to get rid of the jewellery 'cos it's dangerous to keep it. An Irishman might come looking for him to get it back. I know it sounds ridiculous but it's true.'

Kathy abruptly shot upright and made for the door but Lucy darted to intercept her before she'd fully pulled it open. So far Reg had brought in old shoes and coats and smelly clothing to sort out, but nothing else.

'What jewellery?' Lucy whispered. Trepidation was making blood pound in her ears. Danger and jewellery and Irishmen had been linked in her mind too often recently. When Kathy answered her it felt as though her heart had become wedged in her throat.

'Emeralds,' Kathy murmured. 'In a box. It's my dad's fault. He used to do business with someone who . . .' She felt ashamed to admit outright that her father dealt with criminals . . . *was* a criminal. 'It's a complicated story but when Dad ran out on us he left a box of jewellery behind.' She made a hopeless gesture. 'Mum just wanted to sell them to get some money 'cos she heard an Irish thug was looking for them . . .' Her voice tailed away as she became conscious of Lucy's increasing pallor. 'Sorry, Lucy. I know she shouldn't have done it.'

'Was Bill Black involved somewhere along the line?' Lucy asked, dreading though expecting to learn he had been.

Kathy nodded glumly.

'How long ago did Winnie sell it to Reg?' Lucy's eyes were unblinking, fixed on Kathy's face.

'Sell what to Reg?'

From Matilda's merry tone as she entered, it appeared the couple had stopped off at the pub on the way home from Wood Green.

'Has your ma something else to sell now?' Reg asked brightly, following his fiancée through the open door. 'I'll take a look at more stuff any time.'

Tears again welled in Kathy's eyes and she appeared scared witless.

'I'll tell them,' Lucy murmured as Kathy gazed beseechingly at her. 'Go home, go on . . .' she urged gently.

Kathy nodded gratefully and squeezed past the couple to hurry out.

'What's that all about?' Matilda frowned at the closed door. She was tipsy but not so far under the influence that her nose for trouble was affected.

'What have you done with the jewellery Winnie sold to you?' Lucy felt angry that her mother had kept the deal a secret.

Matilda suddenly noticed that her daughter's lovely face was white with strain. But she'd not liked Lucy's tone of voice and told her so, then followed her scolding with, 'Kathy Finch had no right interfering. What's she think she's doing coming round here stirring up trouble?'

'She came to try and prevent trouble,' Lucy said

quietly, pacing to and fro. 'Have you still got the emeralds?'

Matilda and Reg exchanged a glance. They were rapidly sobering up as they sensed Lucy's agitation and her questions stemmed from a serious problem.

'Emeralds, are they?' Matilda grunted a laugh. 'Oh, I see. Winnie's found out they're worth more and wants 'em back, 'cos she's sold 'em too cheap. Well, that's her lookout.'

'No . . . it's yours . . .' Lucy laughed bleakly. 'You have to give them to me so I can give them back.'

'She ain't having them back!' Matilda argued. 'A deal's a deal . . .'

'No! Not give them back to Winnie!' Lucy cried in exasperation. 'She doesn't want them, that's why she's shifted them over to you. They're stolen, Mum!' Lucy raked ten fingers into her soft wavy hair. 'Lord Mortimer wants them back and he's sent somebody to find them. He's paying the man a big reward.'

'Lord Mortimer . . .? What, the Mortimer you used to work for?' Matilda garbled.

Lucy nodded.

Matilda's jaw dropped open. 'Bit of a coincidence, ain't it?'

Lucy gave an impatient shrug. 'Just let me have them so I can return them.'

She'd suspected Sean Napier was concealing something and might be dangerous. But there was no satisfaction for her in being proved right; she felt desolate.

'Why don't we wait till the fellow shows up, then he can give us a little something for our trouble?' Reg suggested, elevating his eyebrows. 'That way it won't leave us out o' pocket, will it now?'

'The something he gives you won't be to your liking if he *is* an Irish thug.'

'*Irish* thug?' Reg had started to attention. Men in his homeland did wicked things to collect for the cause. 'Big reward he's getting from Lord Mortimer, is it?'

Lucy nodded. 'Oh, yes . . .'

'What's this fellow called, now? I know lots of people over there.'

'Sean Napier.' There had been barely a pause before Lucy offered up the information. She was eager to find somebody who did know Sean so she might get an honest opinion about him.

'Napier . . . Napier . . .' Reg tested the name. 'It rings a bell, so it does. 'IRA, I'm thinking . . .'

Matilda had been listening in disbelief. Suddenly her mouth formed a tight knot. 'Irishman works in jewellery, eh?' she sarcastically enquired. 'Handsome and can have any girl he wants, ain't that right? Well, no wonder he was sniffing round you! He was tracking down stolen emeralds that was just round the corner. Now we're landed with 'em and could get a knock on the door from the police or the bleedin' IRA! You've got some explaining to do, miss!'

Reg caught hold of Matilda by the arms as she lunged to box Lucy's ear. 'Can't be sure it is IRA, Tilly,' he soothed. 'Might be a decent enough feller, so he might.'

Matilda struggled free. '*And* I was going to give 'em to yer uncle Rob to sell through one of his outlets. As if he hasn't had more'n enough on his plate lately. Just getting back on his feet, he is, and it would've been me pulled the rug out on him!' she roared.

'Give them to me, Mum,' Lucy said, swallowing the lump in her throat. 'I know what to do . . .'

CHAPTER TWENTY-EIGHT

'Where've you been then this afternoon?'

'To see me sister.'

Jenny gave Bill a wary look. She never knew what to expect from him any more: it might be a cuff if he'd been staring at his wonky nose in the mirror and picking at his scab. Or he might shove her on the bed. She knew the only time he was in a good mood was when she and Ada brought him back nice stuff following a shoplifting spree. Earlier in the week Bill had given her a lovely kiss as a reward for some nice golf clubs, carried out of Gamages beneath both armpits so she looked like a martinet. He'd been pleased as punch with those, and Jenny had wistfully glimpsed how it used to be . . . before her father had turned Bill against her.

Jenny liked it best when Bill and Ada carried on drinking in the pub after a major haul and she slipped off home. He then came back to the flat drunk, smelling of Ada's perfume, and fell straight to sleep on the couch. Those were wonderful evenings when she was safe for hours. Sometimes he stayed at Ada's for several days and Jennifer lived blissfully alone. At other times they both came back. She had come to prefer Ada's softer touch to Bill's rough pawing but she'd gladly never clap eyes on either of them again.

'See your old man over Islington way, did you?' Bill asked.

'He's gone.' Jenny was glad to have an opportunity to bring that up about her father. She wanted Bill to know there was no point in him tormenting her family because they didn't know where Eddie was any more than she did. If she had the foggiest clue she'd grass him up like a shot.

Bill came over and sat next to her. His hand travelled up under her skirt and he squeezed her thigh while his other fingers fumbled open his fly then shoved one of Jenny's hands inside. He spread his legs and leaned back, hands clasped behind his head and his eyes closed. 'Slow 'n' easy, gel, and keep going till I tell yer to stop,' he muttered when Jenny's hand fluttered away after a couple of clumsy pulls. 'So where's Eddie gone, then?'

'Nobody knows. He ran out on them and give me mum a clump before he went.'

Bill grunted a laugh. 'The lot of yous are better off without him.' He squirmed his buttocks further into the seat, settling in for some enjoyment.

'Know that, don't we!' Jenny muttered acidly. 'He never liked me and Kath anyhow, and him and Mum were always fighting. He only had time for Tom. Bought him stuff . . . footballs and toys.' Jenny pouted sulkily.

'Is that right?' Bill panted, gripping Jenny's labouring hand in one of his and pumping it up and down. He jerked and shuddered but kept their slimy fingers clasped together for a few seconds more till he'd relaxed. With a sniff he drew a handkerchief out of a pocket and wiped himself, then threw it on Jenny's lap so she could clean up. 'So yer dad likes little Tom, does he?' Bill got up and turned his face to and fro in front of the mantel mirror, inspecting the damage from different angles. 'That's nice to know.'

Whistling, he strolled off towards the kitchen to get himself an ale.

'You're too late now. I cooked that steak a while ago; wine went down a treat too.'

Sean opened the door wider, tilting his dark head to one side to assess Lucy with narrowed blue eyes.

Her heart had done a silly flip at the sight of him and her reaction was greatly annoying considering how they'd last parted. 'Don't want your steak, your wine or anything else from you. I'm here to give you something,' Lucy announced crisply.

'Are you now,' Sean drawled. 'That's nice. Come in.' He stood aside, one hand jammed in a pocket, mouth slanting in amusement.

If only she could trust him enough to sail past into his hallway and demand some answers! Lucy felt as though her body were coiled tight as a spring, securing her to the spot. Throughout the journey to Fulham she'd been praying that he would still be at this address. She'd been determined to hang on to the jewellery until she'd got a full explanation. But nervousness was chipping away at her confidence.

She glanced at the house next door, considering just thrusting the box of emeralds at him and turning on her heel. But that would be cowardly. It wouldn't get Reg his two guineas back, neither would it satisfy her

331

hungry need to know that he was just a man, who happened to be Irish, working for his wages.

'Are you wanting to go and sit in me car for a talk like we usually do?' Sean kept a straight face as he nodded at the saloon parked at the kerb. The dusty black vehicle had identified the house for Lucy. She'd stood staring at it for some minutes while readying herself to march up the path and knock on the door.

She gave him a pained smile and stepped over the threshold with admirable aplomb. It was a fine house, semi-detached and set on a leafy street. She guessed the rent was expensive. 'Which way?' she enquired, glancing at the three large doors that opened off the wide hallway.

'Well, now . . . that depends on what you've got for me.'

Lucy spun round to find him leaning back against the closed door, arms folded. She'd never seen him dressed so casually, with shirt buttons open at his throat and sleeves rolled back on muscled forearms. The white linen made his skin look uncommonly dark, or perhaps it was the dimness of the corridor making it appear so.

'Let's get one thing straight.' Lucy tilted up her chin, cleared her throat. 'If you think I've come here to spend the night, you're wrong . . . so you can take your eyes off the stairs. I won't be heading up 'em.' She backed away as he came towards her, then stopped and flattened herself against a cool wall.

'What have you got to give me, Lucy?'

He stood in front of her, too close, looking down at the top of her bowed head.

'Why haven't you gone home to Ireland?' She glanced up at him. 'Have you lost track of the emeralds?'

'Maybe . . .'

She tipped her head back, meeting his eyes squarely. 'Careless.'

'Had me mind on other things.'

Lucy guessed he was hinting he'd been thinking about her. Despite everything she hoped he had because she couldn't put him from her mind. But she wouldn't ask. It would sound teasing, and she was unwilling to start something she'd shy away from allowing him to finish.

She might have fallen for him – properly fallen for him, rather than feeling infatuated as she had with Rory – but she was still her mother's daughter: a good girl, decent to the core because she'd had drummed into her the consequences of straying. It was no idle warning; Jennifer Finch was just the youngest of several teenagers Lucy knew who had allowed men to wreck their lives. Neither was it only in slums like the Bunk that randy fellows came and went as they pleased, leaving women to pick up the pieces and rear the bastards they left behind. Lucy had heard of similar sad cases when working in Southend, and she imagined Ireland had its fair share of bitter, abandoned Colleens.

'Shall we go in there?' Lucy indicated the closest door.

'Help yourself.' He turned the handle and pushed the door ajar.

Lucy walked into a room that appeared to be a gentleman's study and immediately sat down in a chair by a large desk.

'Would you like a drink?'

'Tea?'

'If you want.'

'No, it's all right . . . don't really fancy anything, thanks.' Lucy had recognised his amusement.

'You're being very polite, Lucy.'

333

'Usually I'm not?' she stiffly enquired.

'Usually you come right out and say what's on your mind, no holds barred. This evening I'm thinking you're too scared to do that.'

'Well, you're thinking wrong.' Lucy jumped to her feet. She dragged from her bag the tortoiseshell box and placed it on the desk.

'You after me reward now?' Sean took out a cigarette pack.

Lucy blinked in confusion. She'd expected him to snatch it up or at least look taken aback. But he'd barely given the box a glance. 'And what would you do if I said I was going to Lord Mortimer with that to claim the reward?' She flicked a finger at the jewellery.

'Suppose I'd have to protect me professional credibility and fight you for it.'

'Ah, well, fighting is something *you'd* know all about, isn't it?' Lucy pounced on the opening to launch an accusation. 'Because you're a thug. An *Irish* thug.' Her heart pounded while she waited desperately hoping he would deny everything.

Sean eased up the lid of the box to see the gems, then let it fall. 'Does Reg Donovan know you've got these?'

That took the wind out of Lucy's sails. She remained silent for several seconds. 'How d'you know about Reg?' she breathed.

'It's me job to know. We talked about that before.'

Lucy licked her lips. He'd told her he knew a middle-aged woman had been unsuccessfully trying to sell the jewellery. 'You knew Mrs Finch had them?'

'I told you I did.'

'You didn't say her name,' Lucy cried.

'OK, I didn't say her name.'

334

'Winnie Finch told you she sold them to Reg?'

He stuck a cigarette in his mouth and struck a match. 'She didn't need to tell me anything. I've got eyes in me head. A feller turns up with a handcart with old clothes on it; he's after buying stuff nobody else wants. That box of jewellery fits the bill.'

'He's my mum's fiancé.'

'I know.'

Lucy gazed at him, aware he was watching her right back through a haze of tobacco smoke. 'You've been round our way spying on what goes on . . . spying on us all.'

'Like I said, it's me job.'

'Nobody's seen you . . . I've not seen you.'

'Wouldn't be much good at it if you had, would I now?' He grunted a laugh, flicked ash into the empty fire grate.

Lucy flopped down again onto the seat. An extraordinary idea popped into her mind. 'You guessed I might bring them here?'

'Yes.'

She hooted scornfully. 'You bloody fool! You could have knocked on Winnie's door and given her two guineas. She'd have sold them to you days ago and you could have got the boat back to Ireland with Lord Mortimer's reward in your pocket.' Lucy felt her laughter choke her as it turned tearful. She sniffed loudly, her mouth covered by her hand. When composed she stood slowly and stuck out a palm. 'Give me two guineas. That's all I want and I'll be on me way. Reg borrowed the money off my brother-in-law to pay for those and now he's out of pocket. If you don't give me two guineas you won't get them.' She snatched up the box and held it to her chest.

'Still working at the Cuckoo Club, are you now?'

'Only till the end of the week.'

'You'll be needing more than two guineas to take home then.'

He held her gaze with his, and Lucy could tell he wasn't mocking her any more. The atmosphere between them was heavy with tension.

'Are you an Irish thug, a terrorist?'

'Would you have come here if you truly believed that?'

'Yes . . .'

'Ah, still you brought the emeralds for me. That's sweet of you, now.'

Lucy swung a hand at his face, cracking an open palm against a lean cheek.

'I'll make you tea.' He turned to go.

'I don't want bloody tea!' Lucy stormed, leaping in his direction.

He swung back, colliding with her and lowering his face as she looked up so their mouths merged quite naturally in a perfect blend of size and shape. Lucy's small hands had balled spontaneously against his chest to push him away but her fingers unfurled as quickly as they'd formed fists. The tension between them had exploded, leaving her feeling drained of fight.

She'd thought him a man who'd not bother with seduction, yet it was the sweetest kiss she'd ever received. Far nicer than the brutal assault Rory had inflicted on her. As Sean gently coaxed her lips apart to taste her tongue with his, Lucy sensed warmth firing her veins, melting her bones. She remained submissive when Sean's fingers traced her breasts through her blouse. No man had ever touched her so intimately. She wouldn't have allowed it because she'd never met one she liked enough, yet she found her back arching so she might have more of his caress. When he lifted her against him his mouth was still fused to hers. He took two steps, seating her on the desk and wedging his body between her parted thighs. Lucy tightened her hands on his nape, sliding her fingers to span the breath of his shoulders, then anchoring them there as Sean lowered her, torso to torso, until her back was on leather. His mouth relinquished her lips to nestle against the base of her throat and tantalise the madly bobbing pulse in a delicate hollow.

Lucy moaned, squirming in pleasure as his thumbs circled her tight nipples beneath cotton.

'Ah . . . Lucy . . . Lucy . . .' Sean murmured in a voice of anguished amusement. 'You've got me thinking I shouldn't be doing this, with me heading home.' Gently he touched his mouth to her swollen, reddened lips. 'Should I . . .?'

Lucy curved her fingers around his nape, bringing his head back to hers. She'd heard his gentle taunt and despite intoxicating desire knew she should sit up and act with some modesty. But she craved just a little bit more of the exquisite bliss shivering through her . . .

She felt the warm stroke of his lips, sensed his hesitation before he withdrew. She blinked up at him, reading raw longing in his eyes. A moment later he'd jerked her to a seated position, then put her back onto her feet.

'So . . . leaving the Cuckoo Club, are you? Why's that, now?'

Lucy hid her furious blush by picking up her bag and rummaging needlessly in it. She felt like a brazen hussy and imagined Sean must think her one too. But he was giving her a chance to compose herself by making

337

conversation. That small kindness made her heartache even more poignant.

'The club's not as busy as it was,' she blurted huskily. 'Boris is laying off. Connie reckons he'll pick on her as she's oldest.'

'So you decided to take the bullet instead, did you now?' He slanted a smile at her.

'It's no great sacrifice.' Lucy felt still too bashful to look at him for long. 'I never intended staying there. It just happened that I did.'

'What d'you want to do?'

Their eyes clung and Lucy knew he was asking her more than what work she was after. He was letting her choose to go upstairs with him. He was a decent man, she realised. He could have taken her up there a few minutes ago when she'd lost her wits and she'd have offered no resistance. No thug would have done that.

'Time to go . . . it must be getting late.' Her eyes strayed to the window to gauge the fading light. She knew without mentioning it again that Reg would get his two guineas back. What she feared was that Sean might offer her more. She wouldn't take it. Neither would she plead with him to come back from Ireland soon to see her, even though the words were on the tip of her tongue.

CHAPTER TWENTY-NINE

Tom glanced behind to make sure his mother wasn't watching him. He knew that sometimes she came out into the street to stare at him and check he was playing on his own with his football. She didn't like him being friends with the other kids any more. Last time she'd seen him setting up goals in the road with some pals she'd dragged him indoors.

Since Jenny and his dad had gone away, his mum thought everybody was talking about them and trying to find out things. But the boys Tom had hung about with hadn't asked much at all. They'd only wanted to have a kickabout with his football.

Nervously Tom bounced the ball up and down watching his front door. He knew if his mum caught him before he could disappear he'd get a belt in front of anybody who happened to be outside. She didn't care about showing him up. But Tom reckoned Winnie was too busy to spy on him because he'd heard her shouting at Kathy that she'd got enough on her plate. At the time she'd been doing the ironing and Tom had seen a big load of washing soaking in the sink when he'd gone to rinse his hands before tea.

Confident that his mum would still be doing laundry, and might even be pegging out in the back garden, Tom made a sudden dash for the end of the road. He was fed up of playing on his own, and if he couldn't lark about with the boys round here he'd go and find Davy Wright in the Bunk. His mother would never know . . .

He was heading towards Campbell Road along Paddington Street, kicking and chasing the ball, when it bounced off the pavement and he hared into the road after it.

A car swerved to a halt and Tom jumped to safety on the pavement. The driver got out and Tom knew he was in for a telling off. And he deserved it. He shouldn't have run into the road.

'Now what you doing, son, nearly getting yourself run over like that?'

'Sorry,' Tom mumbled. He reddened on seeing it was somebody he knew because he realised it might get back to his mother that he'd been misbehaving.

'I seen your dad not long ago. He'd've ripped me off a strip if he knew I'd nearly knocked you down. Wasn't my fault, though, was it? Silly boy, y'are.' Hairy knuckles grazed gently on Tom's jaw, swaying his small head aside. 'Yer dad was asking after you. You remember me and your dad are pals, do you?'

Tom nodded, clutching his football. He knew this man was Bill Black although he looked a bit different today, with an odd shape to his nose and a bright pink mark on a cheek. He hadn't seen him in a while but once, out of his bedroom window, he'd watched Bill and his dad laughing together and shaking hands before loading up his dad's van. So he knew they were pals.

'Shame you don't see so much of Eddie now. Bet you miss him, don't you?'

Tom nodded. He lowered his eyes. He did miss him. He hadn't thought he liked his dad much, but now his mum had turned really grumpy he wished his dad had taken him with him when he went away. His dad used to belt him now and again, but so did his mum. And at least his father had been out at work a lot and hadn't followed him around, treating him like a baby in front of his friends. And he'd bought him presents. He'd promised him a bike just before he'd left . . .

'Eddie told me he'd like to see you, y'know.' Bill took out a Woodbine and lit it, leaning back casually on the bonnet of his Austin and blowing smoke skywards. 'But he don't want to come round and see you 'case it make things bad for you with yer mum.'

'Where is he?' Tom piped up, squinting at Bill's face.

'Where is he?' Bill echoed with a faraway smile. 'Ah, well, that's a bit of a secret and he told me not to say. As I said, he don't want a lot of shouting with yer mum, see, and he reckons if she comes round after him there will be.'

Tom could understand that. Winnie never stopped yelling. He nodded with a sad grimace and started to trudge on towards Campbell Road.

'Yer dad got you a present,' Bill called. 'I know he wants to give it yer.'

Bill had kept himself slumped down in his car observing Tom for fifteen minutes before the boy made exactly the right move and hared away from outside his front door. He'd followed him slowly, trying to decide how to casually intercept Tom and get him talking. The lad had done him a big favour by running in front of his car. He knew Tom was feeling obliged to chat politely.

'Present? Is it a bike?' Tom trotted back to gaze up expectantly at Bill.

Bill chuckled. 'You can't make me say, y'know. Said to yer old man I could keep a secret, didn't I?'

Tom pulled a face and turned up his collar against the first spots of rain. He was wondering whether to go back home when Bill made him prick up his ears.

'Shall I take you to see him? Not far . . . can be there and back quick as yer like . . .' Bill trod on his dog-end, keeping his face lowered to his swivelling toe.

'Mum'll go mad . . .'

'Ah, she won't know, son. If you don't tell her, I won't. Be our secret, won't it?' Bill took an encompassing look around, pleased to see Paddington Street remained quiet. There were a couple of people in the distance but nobody close enough to be taking much notice.

'Seen Tom, have you?'

Kathy had taken over from her mother doing the ironing while Winnie finished the washing. Usually, Winnie complained that she ironed more creases in than out, but today her mother had been glad of her help. She'd found a new lady to clean for, but the woman wanted Winnie to take home her laundry as well so they were always run off their feet catching up with things at home.

'Thought he was playing out.' Kathy pushed the iron to and fro and blew a wisp of hair off her damp brow.

'He's not in the street.' Winnie started to undo her pinafore her expression grim. 'Bet yer life he's gone round the Bunk to see Davy Wright. I'll have his hide.'

'Any sign of my Tom?' Winnie was just about to march onto Campbell Road from Seven Sisters when she bumped into Beattie Evans turning the corner, fiddling with an umbrella.

Beattie frowned. 'Not seen him, Win.'

Winnie peered into the distance. The street looked quite empty, probably because a light drizzle was turning to rain. She certainly couldn't see any boys playing football close to where Davy Wright lived.

Margaret Lovat walked up behind Beattie, pulling her scarf over her hair to keep it dry.

'Seen anything of Winnie's Tom up there, Margaret?' Beattie asked helpfully. As the rain got heavier she shared her umbrella with her companions.

'There was a lad in Paddington Street talking to a bloke. Might have been your Tom but, with my eyesight, it was too far away to be sure. Looked about the right size to be him . . . had fair hair.' Margaret frowned. 'There was a saloon car parked up close by.'

'Your old man, was it, Win?' Beattie asked sympathetically. She'd heard, as had most people round these parts, that Winnie Finch's husband had done the dirty on her. 'Perhaps Eddie stopped to speak to Tom if he saw him out playing.'

'My husband don't have a car. He's got a van.' Winnie was feeling the first niggles of fear. 'Must've been someone else's kid.'

'Yeah . . . that's it,' Beattie agreed rather unconvincingly.

'Gotta dash or I'll miss the bus.' Margaret hurried on, hunched into her coat.

Beattie loitered. She liked a drama and she had a feeling one was in the offing. Besides, she had nowhere in particular to go. She'd been on her way to see her sister in Hackney but could never be sure what sort of welcome she'd get there. 'I'll help you look for him if you like, Win.'

Winnie started off up the road, giving Beattie a grateful smile.

'You've gone too bleedin' far this time.' Ada was staring at the boy's eyes, wide with fright, peering over the top of the gag Bill had put on him. 'What the fuck have you brought him here for? I don't want nuthin' to do with any of this!'

'Can't take him back to my place, can I, not with you know who being there?' Bill thought Ada must have forgotten the boy's sister was holed up at his place.

When he'd bundled Tom Finch into her flat, the lad had been sobbing. But he'd calmed down and sprinted to the window to shout for help while banging on the glass. Bill had dragged him back, a hand over his mouth. He'd then stuffed a tea towel between Tom's lips and knotted it behind his small head.

'He won't pipe down, will he?' Bill muttered, tying Tom's hands behind his back so he couldn't pull out his gag. 'Won't be here long, anyhow,' he snapped at Ada. 'As soon as Eddie pays up, the kid'll be gone.' Bill knew he was after more than money from Eddie. He wanted the satisfaction of giving the weasel a pasting he'd never forget.

It had got round the manor – as he'd feared it might – that his stay in hospital had come about because he had been beaten by a bloke almost half his size and twice his age. He'd seen the laughing glances. But folk all made sure to keep their thoughts to themselves when

344

he was in earshot. Behind his back they were having a field day, and because of it simmering rage was constantly making Bill's guts writhe. He knew his reputation as a hard man would be in tatters until he put this right.

'And how you gonna let Eddie know you've got his son when you don't even know where he is?' Ada spat sarcastically. 'Even if you do find him, what if he don't pay up?'

Bill carried on pacing to and fro, shooting threatening glances at Tom. The boy's glassy gaze was tracking his every movement from his position on the sofa. He was perched on the very edge as though at any moment he might again spring up and try to escape.

'The police might turn up looking for him. Then you're for it, and you ain't dragging me down with you. Hoisting stuff's one thing, kidnapping people is another!' Ada lit a cigarette with shaking fingers.

Bill snatched the packet of Weights before she put it away and helped himself. 'Wasn't nobody about to see, so nothing to worry about.' He took a ferocious drag and filled his lungs with nicotine.

For a moment they both stood smoking and spearing glances Tom's way.

'Gotta get a message to Eddie. How we gonna do that?' Ada squashed her dog-end in an ashtray.

'Soon as his missus finds out the boy's gone missing she'll do that for us.'

'He'll get the police straight on to us!'

'He won't grass; I know enough about him to put him away. He won't risk going inside. He'll try and do this nice and easy at first.' Bill knew he wouldn't allow Eddie a second time at it. As soon as he turned up to collect his son and pay up he'd have him. But Bill didn't intend to harm Tom. He'd drop the boy off close to home while his father went to hospital.

'What if Eddie's wife don't know where he is now he's done a runner?'

'Reckon she does. Anyhow, he knows where she is, and bet yer life he's keeping a crafty eye on things. Jenny reckons the old man's keen on his little boy. Eddie'll make sure he keeps tabs on him.'

Tom had started at the sound of his sister's name and he swivelled on the sofa to gaze about at doors leading off the sitting room, longing for a glimpse of a familiar face. He was sure Jennifer wouldn't let him down and if she were in one of the other rooms she'd rescue him.

'She ain't here, son, and she don't know where y'are.' Bill had interpreted Tom's frantic glances. In a way he felt sorry for what he'd done. He'd got nothing against the boy, but his need to get even with Eddie burned like acid in his gut. He went to the mirror to stare at his deformed nose and reinforce his determination to see things through.

CHAPTER THIRTY

'What's up, Mum?'

Before Sean had pulled up outside her home, Lucy had been frowning at the sight of a gaggle of neighbours by the railings. The rain had stopped and a late sun was glistening off wet pavements as she jumped out of the car to call to Matilda. The moment she'd spotted the mother's meeting, she'd rattled off to Sean, it looked as though something bad must have happened.

'Winnie can't find Tom,' Matilda announced, approaching her daughter. Her eyes slew to the man getting out of the car. She cocked her head and pursed her mouth, giving him a top-to-toe summary. She knew this was the fellow Lucy had fallen for. She recognised his car from the time he'd brought her home very upset. She accepted her daughter's description of him had been a fair one. Tall, dark and with eyes as blue as the sky above . . . but in Matilda's mind, handsome is as handsome does, and she'd gladly share her theory with him. If she ever again saw her daughter crying, big shot or not, she'd have his guts for garters.

Sean rounded the car in swift strides. 'Who is it now who's gone missing?'

From her mother's sour expression, Lucy guessed she was expecting the courtesy of a proper introduction, followed by some answers. 'Oh, this is Mr Napier,' she blurted. Before Matilda could demand information about the emeralds and all the rest of the tangled mess that surrounded them, she said, 'Is Tom with his dad? Perhaps Eddie's taken him home with him.' She could tell that Sean – usually so effortlessly relaxed – was keen to find out more, and a pang of uneasiness curdled her stomach.

'Is it Tom Finch you're looking for?' Sean demanded.

'Been looking all over for the little lad,' Beattie pushed forward to announce. She waved an arm to indicate the surrounding area then leaned closer, having spotted Winnie trotting down the street looking frantic with worry. 'Between you 'n' me 'n' the gate post, I reckon Eddie Finch *has* got him. Margaret saw a small boy with fair hair talking to a fellow with a car. It was too far in the distance for her to properly recognise them. Winnie says her old man don't have a car, but perhaps he treated hisself to one now he don't have a family to keep.' Beattie nodded, widening her eyes to emphasise her point.

'I'll take a drive around and look for him. Fair hair, hasn't he now . . .?' Sean was back at the Humber before he'd finished speaking.

His immediate offer of help brought Lucy's eyes veering to him. Over the roof of his vehicle their eyes met and his steady stare let her know he wanted to talk to her in private.

'I'll come with you,' Lucy blurted. 'I know Tom and can point him out.' Her apprehension had increased.

Beneath Sean's calm exterior she sensed that he was also anxious about the boy's safety.

'What is it?' She turned to him as soon as they set off.

'Bill Black's got him, I'll stake me life on it.'

'But . . . why would he?' Lead settled in Lucy's stomach.

'Bill came off worse in a fight with Eddie and I'm thinking he's not liking being made to look a fool. It's not only his dented pride. There'll be a scrap over money for sure, and perhaps Eddie is worried about his daughter Jennifer living with such a man. I'm guessing a whole lot of hatred has come out of the emerald deal going down and the tactics are getting mighty dirty.'

'You seem to know all about it,' Lucy said, hanging on to the dashboard as Sean steered around a corner, barely touching the brake. As he glanced at her she gave a wry smile. 'Yeah, I know, it's your job.'

Lucy whipped her head to and fro, scouring the streets with narrowed eyes as they motored on. 'If you don't slow down a bit we might miss him.'

'If me theory's correct and Bill's got young Tom we won't be finding him this side of the water. I'm heading towards Lambeth.'

'There's nobody in but Jennifer Finch.' Sean got into the driver's seat and drove a hand in a pocket to find a pack of cigarettes.

He had just startled Jennifer when he'd knocked at Bill Black's door. She'd opened up, dressed in her night-dress, wafting her painted nails to dry them. Following some Irish blarney, and a tale about about an urgent deal with Bill, she'd offered up his whereabouts. He

349

knew the poor kid had been suspicious but hadn't wanted to risk her boss's wrath by doubting one of his associates. And he'd not wanted to tell her about her brother going missing in case she went into hysterics. Sean had had a feeling Bill wouldn't use his own flat to hold the boy. Jennifer was there; she might be under his thumb but was nevertheless likely to create merry hell on finding out her brother had been kidnapped.

'Did Jennifer tell you where to find him?'

Sean nodded. 'He's with Ada, she thinks. And I think so too.'

The idea of sweet little Tom being at the mercy of *two* bullies was enraging Lucy. The poor little lad hadn't been able to stand up to kids his own age and size in the school playground. 'If Ada has hurt him I'll swing for her,' she vowed grimly. 'Did Jenny tell you where Ada lives?'

'She did, but I already knew where that one is to be found.' Sean gave Lucy a look, slid a finger down her warm cheek. 'Are you ready for this, Lucy Keiver?'

Lucy nodded, nibbling her lower lip. 'Perhaps we should get the police . . . do you think so?'

'No police. They're not my favourite people. Ask questions, don't they now . . .'

Lucy twisted a smile. 'You sound like my mum.'

'A fine woman, to be sure,' Sean said in his lilting way. 'I can tell she doesn't trust me one inch.'

Lucy's smile faded and she gazed earnestly at him. 'Are you a bad man, Sean?'

'When I need to be . . .' He turned the cigarette in his fingers to stare at its glowing tip.

Lucy watched his profile, saw his long lashes lower to almost touch his cheekbone as he brooded on whether to tell her more.

'When you were just a little girl about nine years old, I was fighting in the Irish civil war. It's not over for all of us. So me uncle's money will come in handy when I get home. Soldiers need equipment . . .'

Lucy started to question him but he brushed a silencing thumb over her lips. 'Not now, darlin'. When we get there, you listen to me and do what I say, and we'll be taking Tom home in a very short while.' He half smiled. 'Are you scared?'

Lucy gave a single nod.

'I'll take care of you now, don't worry.'

'You might as well let me in Audrey . . . Ada, or whatever your name is. I know you're in there.' Lucy recommenced banging her fist on the closed door, keeping her eyes on a strip of light on the threshold. If it disappeared Lucy knew Ada would think she'd not seen it and pretend to be out.

Ada and Bill had been sitting on the sofa stewing on how to blackmail Eddie when Lucy had first hammered and called out. Startled by the commotion, they'd scrambled to their feet, to stand goggling at one another in astonishment. Lucy Keiver hadn't even been on the list of people they'd thought would be bothering them this evening.

'Come on, open up. You must've known I was coming after you, Ada. You gave me a black eye and I reckon you're due one in return.'

'Open the door to the bitch,' Bill mouthed quietly, having come to his senses. 'She'll have a crowd down on us the racket she's making.'

Still Ada hesitated. Questions were whizzing around in her mind and she started airing them in a whisper.

'How's she know where I live or me real name? I never told her anything about meself.'

'Never mind any o' that!' Bill hissed, baring his teeth in annoyance. 'Just open the fucking door so I can shut her up.'

'*I* can handle her. Did so before, didn't I?' Ada's expression had turned malicious. She was going to enjoy laying Keiver out for the second time.

Bill opened the door of the bedroom and pushed Tom inside. He put a threatening finger to his lips miming he expected the boy to keep quiet. 'You don't want me to make you shut up, do you?' he whispered in his ear as intimidating knuckles pressed into the boy's soft cheek. 'No kicking at the door or I'll be kicking you, right?'

Tom's small head vibrated agreement and he backed away till his legs banged against the bed and he abruptly sat down.

Bill closed the door, then nipped into the kitchen, out of sight.

Ada jerked open the door, pouting. 'You're gonna regret you was born, Keiver, promise you that.'

Lucy gave her a defiant smile, noticing she'd changed her hair colour again. Black didn't suit her any more than had the platinum shade; Ada was a mousy kind of a girl, Lucy realised contemptuosly. She suddenly barged past, knocking her foe aside, allowing Sean – who'd been flat against the wall some yards away – seconds and space to follow her into the flat.

'Well now, where's wee Tom? We'll be taking the lad off your hands and be on our way.' Sean darted glances around the room to locate the boy.

A weird smile was contorting Bill's features as he swaggered out of the kitchen and came to a halt, licking his lips. He swayed from side to side on the balls of his feet. 'So, the smooth Paddy from the Cuckoo Club. Didn't have it down to be you causing all the trouble with the emeralds. Didn't reckon it'd be you here after the kid either. My mistake.'

'We all make 'em,' Sean drawled sympathetically. He closed the door behind him with a backward kick.

Bill whipped his eyes between the room's occupants. He'd never been sure about this man and regretted now taking him at face value: too rich and sophisticated, he'd thought, to bother messing with spud-bashing terrorists. The last time he'd seen Napier had been months ago when the fellow had been chatting up Lucy Keiver outside the club. When the girl walked off alone he'd dismissed Napier as just another mug punter, down on his luck. Bill had been with Mavis that night. Then he went back another time with Ada. He rued the day he'd done that. Of all the things that might have ruined him over the years it seemed too ludicrous that a stupid scuffle between Ada and Lucy could bring about his downfall.

'Tom!' Lucy rushed to a door and shoved it open. She glimpsed a cracked toilet cistern and turned to another door. It was then she heard the muffled sob. She whipped a look at Sean to see if he'd heard it too.

Ada moved to block her path into her bedroom. 'What d'you think you're doing, nosy bitch?'

Lucy elbowed her aside and Ada retaliated by swinging a fist. Lucy had anticipated that and ducked. She didn't relish a fight and hadn't had one since she'd punched Winnie on the chin for pulling her hair. But she had no such qualms on this occasion about thumping another woman. She punched Ada as she had Tom's mum, short and sharp, sending the older woman staggering back against the door handle she'd been guarding.

Sean smirked on seeing Lucy could look after herself without his help. 'Suppose it'd be rude not to join in,' he said, taking a swift stride to land Bill a low body blow.

Bill had been anticipating a move from Sean but had guessed he'd go for his healing face and that's where his guard had flown to when his reflexes kicked in. As he folded over, his foxy eyes darted to find a weapon. He craftily staggered a step closer to Ada's sideboard and swiped a brass candlestick, swinging out immediately with it. It caught Sean's side, making him grunt out air.

Bill struggled upright and began tossing the candlestick from palm to palm. 'Come on then, you thick Mick, let's see what yer made of.'

Sean circled him, darting concerned glances at Lucy. He could see that Ada had hold of her hair but Lucy was fighting back and he couldn't prevent a growl of approval as Lucy stamped hard on her opponent's foot. As Ada howled Lucy got enough space to free a hand and slap her face.

Sean concentrated on Bill. He knew the candlestick might have cracked a rib. He managed to swing a right hook to connect with Bill's odd pink cheek, splitting it open, but although his opponent tottered, Bill stayed on his feet, slicing the air with his brass weapon.

Nobody heard the bedroom door creak. At first Tom just gazed at the scene of mayhem with huge glistening eyes. He'd heard somebody fall against the door and had tiptoed towards it on seeing a sliver of light flicker on the wall. Through a crack he saw Bill Black bleeding and swinging a weapon at a man who was bobbing to and fro and hitting out with his fists. He could see Lucy Keiver, too, wrestling with the woman who was Bill's friend.

Tom wriggled his hands in their binding but he couldn't free them so he used a foot on the edge of the door and pulled it inwards. Bill had said he'd kick him if he didn't do as he said. Well, Tom had heard that off the bullies at school and once when he'd kicked first the boy had left him alone afterwards. He crept up behind Bill and struck out at his ankles with a small foot, with all his might.

Bill turned with a snarl to see Tom's face close to his waist. He lashed backwards with a fist, catching Tom's shoulder and sending him flying.

Sean got a clean shot at his face, then another. He kept going, raining down fast wounding punches till Bill collapsed back on the sofa like a rag doll, the candlestick falling from a limp hand.

Sean put Tom on his feet and ruffled his hair as he passed on his way to the fighting women. He dragged Ada out from where Lucy had her pinned under an armpit. 'You're enjoying yourself, Lucy, aren't you, now? Come on, leave off, it's time to go.' He gazed with a mixture of love and admiration at her flushed sweaty face. She was panting, holding her sides, unable to answer him. But her expression told him everything she'd like to say in retaliation to his teasing.

Ada swivelled in Sean's grip, attempting to knee his groin but he'd anticipated that and propelled her away from him with one hand so she bounced onto the sofa beside her unconscious boyfriend.

Sean picked Tom up because he seemed frozen in shock and, steering Lucy by an arm, hurried them out of the flat, a single foul curse from Ada following them.

*   *   *

Lucy had settled in the back of the car with Tom so she could cuddle him and calm him down. She'd rubbed at his bruised shoulder, then quickly untied his hands and wiped his tears with her hanky. But they'd only been motoring for a few minutes when Sean pulled over. She met his eyes in the rearview mirror.

'Why've we stopped?'

He indicated a telephone box. 'Now we call the police.' His next words emerged in a voice that wouldn't have sounded out of place in the Bunk. 'Concerned people, ain't we? Walking past, mindin' our own business when we heard a racket like someone gettin' murdered.'

Lucy smiled as Sean got out. She relaxed back into the car seat. Her face was stinging from the grazes Ada had given her and she rubbed at her features, thinking she must look a fright. Beside her she felt Tom take in a shuddering breath. 'Soon have you home again,' she whispered against his brow, and tightened her arm about his small shivering form.

Bill Black had been right about one thing: Eddie Finch might have dropped out of sight but he was keeping a close eye on his old stamping ground. Eddie still had business contacts in that area and crept quietly back to see them. He'd known Bill would be out after him so usually came at night, slipping away again as soon as possible.

He'd settled in a quiet backstreet in Edmonton and always made sure to park his van some streets away from his door, so if by chance Bill or one of his cronies drove this way searching for him they'd knock up the wrong house. As soon as he could afford to he was going to change the vehicle for something different. He had already made small alterations to his appearance; his hair was shorn short and he'd grown a small moustache. He always wore an oversized flat cap that could be pulled low over his eyes.

Sometimes he managed to convince himself that Bill had accepted his beating as rough justice: the man knew he owed him a lot more than the eighty quid he'd taken from Bill's wallet. Bill had stitched him up good and proper with those emeralds and he'd deserved his come-uppance.

But there was more than business luring Eddie back to Islington. He wanted to see his son. He'd not realised he'd miss Tom so much so he had loitered, hidden from view, outside the school gates on a couple of occasions hoping to speak to him. Winnie had been with him one morning and Eddie had drawn back into shadows. He had nothing to say to her! He was still bitter about her going behind his back trying to sell the jewellery to all and sundry, starting off dangerous rumours in the trade into the bargain. He'd come back the same afternoon to catch Tom when lessons finished, but Kathy had been waiting to walk her brother home. Once the playground had emptied Eddie had slipped away. He was wary of being seen. Gossip got round like wildfire . . .

'How you doing, Ed?' A fellow clapped a hand on Eddie's shoulder, startling him from his reverie. He sat down at the pub table, uninvited.

Mr Dobson had come over to a council meeting in Edmonton. He and his colleagues had got together with their counterparts in neighbouring north London boroughs to discuss finding ways to make economies now the Depression was becoming entrenched and Joe Public was struggling to meet even basic costs. Soup kitchens were springing up everywhere and public assistance wasn't available unless people had next to nothing. Mr Dobson had seen houses virtually cleared of furniture, to be carted off and sold, before the authorities would grant benefit money.

He sat back in his chair with a smile for his fidgeting companion. He held no grudge against Eddie Finch; it was that cow of a wife of his he couldn't stand. He hadn't forgiven Winnie for causing such a commotion in his sweet shop even though it had been months ago. He waved to some colleagues at the bar, letting them know he'd be talking to a mate for a while.

Eddie shifted uncomfortably on his chair then took a swig from his tankard. He wished Dobson would get lost.

'Ah, don't worry, won't say anything to your missus about seeing you.' Mr Dobson had latched on to Eddie's mood. He tapped his nose and winked. 'I'll keep shtoom.'

'How's thing's over there?' Eddie asked gruffly. It was too good an opportunity to miss quizzing the fellow. Nevertheless, tomorrow he'd be moving out of the area to somewhere new, just in case Dobson's lips became unsealed and word got around that he'd been spotted drinking at the Angel, Edmonton.

'More or less the same,' Mr Dobson said. 'Nothing much changes . . . trade's slackening. We had to let the new assistant go after a few months, so just as well your Jennifer found herself something else.'

Eddie gave a faint smile and sipped beer.

'There was a bit of a commotion going on when I was driving past Campbell Road this evening to come here. A woman stopped my car and asked me if I'd seen a boy who'd gone missing. That lot in the Bunk!' He shook his head. 'Can't look after themselves, let alone their kids . . .'

Eddie turned pale. 'A boy?'

'Mmm . . . said he had fair hair and was about seven. Don't know too much about it. I was late for my meeting so I shooed her away.' He grimaced. 'High time that slum was pulled down, in my opinion. I might make mention of it, actually, but with the way things are . . . no funds available . . .'

Eddie scraped back his chair.

'You off already, Ed?' Mr Dobson nodded at his half-empty glass. 'Not going to finish that?'

Eddie shook his head and made for the door. Mr Dobson upended what was left of Eddie's ale into his own glass, then went to join his colleagues at the bar.

CHAPTER THIRTY-ONE

Kathy bolted into the passage as she heard the key in the lock, praying it would be her mother returning with Tom. Her chin sagged in astonishment.

'Yer mum in, is she?' Eddie wearily trudged over the threshold, closing the door behind him. He could tell from Kathy's swollen bloodshot eyes that he was about to have confirmed something he was dreading to hear.

'Tom's gone missing. Mum's out looking for him with neighbours and people from the Bunk 'cos they think Tom was going round there to see some pals when he disappeared. He was outside playing football when we last saw him.' Kathy's voice broke and she snuffled through her tears, 'Mum told me to stay here in case he comes back, but I want to go and help. Will you stay here so I can help search for him?'

Eddie put a clumsy hand on his daughter's shoulder to try to comfort her. 'I'm back . . . I'll find him.'

'Did you hear he'd gone?' Kathy gurgled.

Eddie nodded. 'Come straight over.'

'People think you took him.' Kathy fished a sodden

handkerchief from up her sleeve and wiped her eyes. She was desolate; she'd clung to a hope that Tom was safe with their father and now that had been whipped away.

Winnie had been harbouring the same hope. Much as she hated her husband she'd sooner know Tom was with him than with a stranger. Eddie loved Tom, in his own way.

She let herself in with her key. She'd come back to find out if Kathy had had any news. Now it was dark outside, helpers were drifting home, urging her to call the police. She yelled that information to Kathy before she'd properly closed the street door, then took dragging steps down the quiet hallway. She'd been hoping against hope she'd enter the house to the sound of Tom being ticked off by his big sister for worrying them all to death.

Winnie gazed at her husband with defeated eyes. She gulped a deep breath, trying to dredge up the energy to tell him what she thought of him, but instead the air filtered out of her lips in hiccuping sobs and a long silent wail.

Eddie tentatively put a hand on his wife's arm, expecting to be elbowed away, but Winnie had no will either to welcome or reject his comfort.

'No need for the police, Win.' Eddie's voice sounded thick with emotion. 'I know where he is. Bill Black's got him, I'll put me eyes on it. I'll give the bastard me life if he wants it. But I'll get Tom back whatever it takes. Come and sit down. Kathy's gonna make us some tea . . .'

'You're home, sleepy head.' Lucy gave Tom's cheek a gentle tickle to wake him.

Sean got out and opened the car door, helping Lucy to set the stretching boy onto his unsteady feet.

'Will you take him in?' Sean glanced at the house. A light was on in the front room.

Lucy shook her head. 'Too many questions and I don't have the answers. They do.' She jerked a nod at Eddie and Winnie's house. Dipping her face, she kissed Tom on the cheek.

The lad rubbed his eyes, then swung a look between her and Sean.

Lucy knew that even at his tender age he was trying to focus so he could thank them. She could tell too that he was nervous of crossing to his house on his own in the dark.

'I'm gonna wait right here till you're inside, promise.' She gave him a gentle tap. 'Off you go, and tell your mum the truth now. She won't be cross. She knows Bill Black and so does your dad. I reckon they'll understand.'

Lucy hoped they both felt thoroughly ashamed of themselves. They were to blame. If they hadn't got involved with Bill Black in the first place . . .

Tom trotted off and banged on the door.

A moment later, Kathy opened up and swooped on her brother, hugging him to her chest and rocking them both to and fro.

Lucy saw the young woman look over at the car but Sean was already reversing away down the road.

'If I smoked I'd take a cigarette off you.'

'In need of calming down, are you, darlin'?' Sean sounded amused.

Lucy tilted her head back against the car seat. 'Aren't you? What a night . . .'

362

'We make a good team, you and me.' Sean blew smoke into night air. He turned to look at her. 'What are your plans?'

'Plans?' Lucy echoed.

He'd parked close to the junction with Seven Sisters Road so they could talk before he dropped her outside her door.

'You're out of work next week.'

'And you're back in Ireland next week.'

'Tomorrow. I'm catching the boat back in the morning.'

That blunt information stabbed at Lucy's heart. 'With your reward?' she murmured.

'Certainly hope so. I'm off to see Mortimer tonight.'

Lucy turned large luminous eyes on him. She wasn't ready to lose him. 'You want to get going?'

'Nope . . . not yet.'

'It's very late, past midnight, I guess.'

'Well, he'll have to get himself out of bed for me, won't he, now?'

Lucy's lips twitched but the band of sorrow gripping her chest tightened. It was pointless drawing out the agony. She might just as well say goodbye and go. The longer she stayed . . .

'Come with me.'

Her head whipped around. 'What?'

'Come with me to Ireland. I want you to. I want you, you know that. I'll say I love you if you want to hear it. It's the truth, but I don't expect you to believe me after such a little while.'

'I can't . . . my mum . . . I've got no money . . . nothing . . .' She scoured his features, wondering if he meant what he'd said. She knew she'd fallen for him, but love . . .

'While I've got money, you've got money: eight thousand pounds, perhaps more if I can prise a bit of a bonus out of me dear uncle for a job well done. No bodies to bury, are there, now? He seemed worried there might be.'

'*I can't* . . .' Lucy sounded despairing, yet her heart was hammering.

'You can. You're a brave girl, a girl after me own heart, wanting an adventure.'

Lucy gazed up at the stars and sliver of moon, and a dark blue sky that stretched away into infinity.

'Not so far, is it now?' Sean said softly, reading her wistful expression. 'And if you're homesick, or sick of me, I'll bring you back. Swear I will.'

Lucy shook her head and grabbed at the handle and turned it.

Sean caught her wrist, pulled her back, kissed her with cruel demanding passion.

'If you change your mind I'll be at the Angel at five o'clock in the morning.' Another punishing kiss and he let her go, sitting back in his seat.

Lucy walked with tears blocking her throat, too shocked still to let them fall. She'd heard the car drive off straight away. There was no going back, no way to negotiate terms, or demand he say again that he loved her while she carefully watched his eyes.

His way or nothing at all.

Dawn was striping a light on the ceiling when Lucy woke from an hour of fitful sleep. She sat on the edge of the bed with her face in her palms. She knew she shouldn't even consider going with Sean but still the longing wouldn't go away.

Her mouth felt dirty so she tiptoed through into the front room to get a cup of water, trying not to make a noise and disturb her mother and Reg.

He'd stayed again. He was becoming a more frequent overnight visitor, despite her mother insisting he couldn't move in permanently yet . . . because she lived with her daughter. And if she didn't, she'd be happier, Lucy knew that.

She looked at the sleeping figures on the bed wrapped in each other's arms. They'd been like that when she'd got home in the early hours and she'd had no opportunity to talk to them. She knew she could wake them, tell them the thoughts tormenting her. Her mother would try and make her see sense . . . there would be a row. She wouldn't want to leave under a cloud so she'd stay. She'd bucked against her sister Sophy's advice when in Southend and had come to London seeking pleasure and excitement. And she'd found it in amongst the dangers and disappointments. She hadn't regretted relinquishing security to test the unknown. But the restlessness squirming in the pit of her stomach now was sharper, almost a physical pain.

Lucy put down her cup of water and walked to gaze down at her mother's profile, blurred by straggling hair and faint light. Close to the mattress the air smelled faintly of stale sweat and stale whisky. Lucy glanced at the clock on the wall and went back into her room.

She opened the battered chest of drawers that held most of her clothes, drew out a pencil and piece of paper and started to write.

She left the note propped up on the mantel, under the spotted old mirror that reflected back at her a face a little bit pale and battered. But her eyes were glowing and she gave herself a smile. She quietly placed her key by the letter. She took a long look around as one might when understanding it might be for the final time.

With a blown kiss and a silent prayer she went out and closed the door.

EPILOGUE

'Ain't that yer mum comin' down the road?'

Tom booted the ball to Davey Wright then looked over a shoulder to see his mother marching in his direction.

'You gotta go in then?' Davey asked glumly. He knew the football would disappear at the same time Tom did.

The other boys playing with them started shuffling. One started kicking at cabbage stalks in the gutter, looking fed up.

'Ain't going in,' Tom said. 'Whack it back.'

His three friends exchanged glances. Tom Finch wasn't allowed to play with them. Winnie Finch had bawled that out many a time when dragging Tom off down Campbell Road with his football tucked under her arm.

Winnie stopped some yards away and beckoned Tom. When he ignored her, she called, 'Come on, love, teatime.'

'Be home later.' Tom didn't turn around to answer his mother.

'Yer dad's fetching in some fish 'n' chips,' Winnie wheedled.

It was tempting but still Tom held his ground. Things at home had changed since Bill Black had taken him off. Although he didn't know all the ins and outs, Tom realised that what he'd suffered was somehow his mum and dad's fault. And now they were both being nice to him because they were feeling guilty and wanted to make it up to him. His dad had promised to get him a bike for Christmas.

'I'll get me own chips,' Tom said, having a brainwave and making his mates' ears prick up. He strolled to Winnie with a palm outstretched. 'Only want tuppence,' he mumbled but his small features held an amount of defiance.

Winnie hesitated, frowning, then delved a hand into her pinafore pocket for two coins. 'Just this once,' she said, ruffling his hair before he could duck his head aside.

Tom was off immediately, smiling with pride. He knew he'd impressed his friends. They'd want to share his chips. And he'd let them. 'Kick us the ball, then,' he demanded of Davey, who immediately obliged with a clumsy toe punt.

'Be back before it gets dark. Or yer dad'll be out after you,' Winnie warned, then turned and trudged back down the road towards Paddington Street.

'Alright, Win,' Matilda called. She'd been girding her loins for the clamber up the stairs to her room. On spotting Winifred, she emerged from the dingy hallway of the tenement to speak to her.

'Yeah . . . so . . . so . . .' Winnie answered, looking bashful.

Matilda knew that the woman was feeling awkward following the drama of Tom's kidnapping. 'All's well that end's well.' She patted kindly at Winnie's arm. The woman had thanked her more than once for Lucy's help in bringing Tom home. She started to do so again, but Matilda wafted a hand, turning the subject to one of Winnie's daughters instead. 'Been in touch with your Jenny since all the carrying on?'

Winnie shook her frizzy head. 'Eddie's dead against it.'

'Perhaps he'll come round . . . now he's back home.'

'How's your Lucy . . . not seen her about . . .?'

'Well . . . I'd best get in, Reg'll want somethin' fer his tea.' Matilda briskly stepped away, a farewell drifting over a shoulder.

"Ere, Til, hold up.'

Beattie, shopping bag bashing against her leg, hurried across the road to catch Matilda before she disappeared up the stairs.

'This right wot Reg told me?' Beattie gasped, plonking a supporting hand on the banisters while she sucked in air. 'Your Lucy gone off to Ireland with that tall handsome bloke who helped her rescue little Tom?'

'Reg told you, did he?' Matilda's mouth pursed. She'd have something to say to him when he got back from work about how Keivers kept their lips buttoned on family matters.

Beattie nodded, eyes gleaming with curiosity. 'Wondered why I'd not seen Lucy.'

'Well, now yer know,' Matilda retorted.

Beattie grinned. 'Can't say I blame her burnin' bridges fer such a good-looker.' She nudged Matilda in the ribs. 'I'd've gone off with him like a shot 'n' all.'

'Yeah . . . and if you was thirty years younger, coupla stone lighter and as pretty as my Lucy, he just might have asked yer.' Matilda crossed her arms over her chest, giving Beattie an old-fashioned look. 'And she ain't burned no bridges. She's welcome back home any time.'

Beattie wasn't offended by any of it; she cackled a dirty laugh. 'I just saw Connie up the road. She's got a bit o' the green eye over it. Told me straight out, she did, she had a *pash* for Sean Napier first time he turned up at her supper club.'

'Anybody else you been gossiping to about me daughter's business?' Matilda demanded drily.

'Oh . . . don't be like that, Til.' Beattie sounded plaintive but her expression was lively as she dwelled on recent, exciting events. 'You know, half the neighbourhood's nattering about what went on. Your Lucy and that Sean fellow are sort of heroes after what they done.'

'Yeah . . . well . . .' Matilda's expression softened slightly. She couldn't argue with Beattie over that. News had got round and she and Reg had been bought drinks galore in the Duke by people wanting to praise Lucy's efforts in saving Tom Finch from danger. Of course, those folk also hoped to winkle out of her some more details about the scandalous goings on. Matilda didn't know any more because she'd not had an opportunity to question Lucy, but she always kept that small detail to herself while toying with her empty glass.

Matilda had wailed like a banshee on finding Lucy gone the morning after Tom's disappearance. But after the shock had worn off, she'd felt a glimmer of admiration subduing her anger. She'd always known her youngest wasn't like her other daughters; regular work and a humdrum life weren't for Lucy. But she was nobody's fool and wouldn't have gone off with Sean if she didn't trust him to look after her. Matilda felt proud, and a little bit envious, when dwelling on Lucy's brave, adventurous spirit. Of course, she'd tear her off a strip as soon as she got the chance . . .

'So . . . that'll be all your gels married soon then?' Beattie enquired slyly.

Matilda gave Beattie a smug smile. That morning she'd received a small packet from Ireland. In it were two guineas and a photograph of Lucy and Sean arm in arm. There'd been nothing much on the back of the snap in the way of a message, other than Lucy telling her not to worry because she was happy. But Lucy had been holding out her left hand to the camera. 'Asked her to get wed, ain't he, and he's already bought her a lovely ring.'

Beattie's jaw dropped. 'Ring, eh?' She nodded to show she was impressed. 'Big 'un, is it? Diamonds?'

Matilda chuckled privately, starting up the stairs. 'Probably . . . couldn't tell, but I do know it won't be bleedin' emeralds . . .'

Read on for the next compelling novel
to feature the residents of Campbell Road.

Coming from

Kay Brellend

in Autumn 2013.

CHAPTER ONE

February 1936

'Have you killed her?'

'Don't care if I have,' the big man growled. 'The slag deserves to be six feet under for what she's done.'

'What could she have done to deserve this?' The young woman bellowed.

Kathy Finch weighed seven and a half stone and stood five foot and three inches in her shoes but she was trying to wrestle the brute away from the prone, bloodied body of his young wife. He swatted her away as easily as he would an irritating moth.

Kathy regained her breath and balance then launched herself at the stevedore again. This time when she grabbed his hairy forearm he allowed her to pull him away, having delivered a final lazy stamp to the figure on the floor.

Ruby Potter had curled into a foetal position in a vain attempt to protect herself and her unborn baby from her husband's boots. But, whereas moments ago she had been gamely fighting back – punching and slapping at his thick shins – she was now motionless, her face fallen away to the wall.

Satisfied with the punishment he'd inflicted, Charlie Potter sauntered off to get his donkey jacket from a filthy armchair. The child sitting on it barely flinched as the coat was whipped from under her posterior.

'I think you know right enough what she's done Miss,' Charlie finally answered Kathy. 'Don't come the innocent with me. Ruby talks to you about all sorts of stuff, I've heard her.'

'She talks to me 'cos I'm her midwife!' Kathy yelled. She'd dropped down beside Ruby and was feeling her limp wrist for a pulse. She swivelled on her knees, aware that at any time the vicious bastard could again let loose his temper and she might be on the receiving end. She felt ire well up inside. She'd go down fighting, like Ruby had.

She'd no idea what had led up to this beating, having arrived after it had started. The blood-curdling commotion had made her race down the passageway and burst into the room but by then her patient was already on her knees. The punch she'd seen Charlie deliver had looked savage enough to fell a horse. It had certainly put Ruby out like a light.

Kathy's eyes slew to the chalk-faced child sucking her thumb and watching everything with unblinking intensity. Kathy's concern was how to protect the other females present. She knew she was relatively safe but a maniac such as Potter, who believed his family were his chattels to do with as he would, wouldn't think twice about chastising his small daughter if he thought she was being insolent.

'You'd better get out of here! I'm warning you . . . I'm calling for an ambulance and then I'm calling for the police.' Kathy's fear was subdued by fury.

Charlie Potter swooped on Kathy pinching her chin between his calloused fingers. Her neck strained as he hauled her up using just those remorseless digits until she was on her feet and gritting her teeth in agony. When standing in front of him she tried to jerk back from his leery gaze but the pain increased so she settled for despising him with china-blue eyes.

'If she's a goner I've got friends who'll say I was with them. I've got other friends who'll turn things bad fer you.' He patted her cap and gave her a tobacco-stained grin, making her recoil from his stinking breath. 'Just 'cos you're friendly with the coppers don't mean nuthin'. My friends have got mates in the constabulary 'n' all, if you get my drift. So you think on, Miss . . . you've been about long enough now to know how we do things round here.' His crafty eyes slipped over her slender figure beneath her Gabardine mac. 'We don't need you comin' round, interfering. I've told you that before. Ruby's got all the help she needs with friends 'n' family . . .'

'Leave her be!' The weak command came from behind and Kathy spun around so quickly and violently that Charlie's fingernails scored into her skin.

'Are you alright?' Kathy crouched, her hand instinctively moving towards Ruby Potter's distended belly. A tiny undulation beneath her fingertips made her whisper a relieved prayer. She turned to glare at the thug behind. There was no flicker of remorse or thankfulness at this sign that his beating hadn't proved fatal. He simply scowled, pointed a menacing finger at his battered wife that promised more was to come. A moment later he swaggered out of the room.

'Help me up, will you Miss Finch?' Ruby asked wearily once she'd heard the front door crash shut.

'You stay there. I'm just going out to call an ambulance for you, Mrs Potter . . .' Kathy blurted.

'No! Don't do that, it'll just make things worse if busybodies get to hear what's gone on.'

'But . . . your face needs stitching,' Kathy said gently, not wanting to upset the woman. The gashes on her face were sure to leave nasty scars if left unattended. Ruby looked a dreadful state and the shame of it was that she'd probably been quite a pretty woman in her time. Kathy glanced at her patient's tangled dark brown hair and sallow complexion. From Ruby Potter's medical notes Kathy had gleaned that the woman was only six years older than herself. Had she not read her age as twenty six she'd have guessed her to be in her mid thirties.

The child jumped down from her seat now she knew the coast was clear. As Kathy gripped her arms under Ruby's and strained to lift her, little Pansy shoved her mother on the posterior trying to do her bit to help.

There was an iron bed set against one wall and having settled Ruby on the edge of a grimy mattress Kathy gently lifted up her chin to get a better look at the damage Charlie had inflicted. 'You should get yourself seen to at the hospital . . .' she urged.

'Can't you do it Miss?' Ruby pleaded.

'I can't stitch you up . . .' Kathy had guessed that might come. She was a nurse, not a doctor and had not been trained to close wounds.

Kathy did her rounds in this East End quarter of London where slum conditions and rough people made the job unpredictable. But Kathy was determined to continue in her vocation no matter how unpleasant it was at times. For every vile brute like Charlie Potter there were twice as many salts of the earth who were terribly grateful for the work she did.

'Don't care how it looks. Just don't want no germs getting in. I'd be grateful if you'd do what you can.' Ruby attempted a smile but it simply made blood leak again from the corner of her mouth. 'Don't want to get you into no trouble, of course, Miss Finch,' she mumbled, lifting a corner of her pinafore to dab her face.

Kathy shook her head to herself and delved into her nurse's bag to find something to clean her up. 'I don't carry any equipment for stitches . . . sorry . . .' Kathy knew if she did she'd probably flout regulations and risk her job for Ruby Potter's sake. As she looked at the pathetic spectacle sitting with hunched shoulders on the bed, she felt tempted to run after Charlie Potter and let fly with her fists even though she knew it would make her no better than him.

'Make Miss Finch a cup of tea Pansy,' Ruby's fat lips made the words sound slurred, as did the muffling edge of the pinafore she was again pressing to her face to staunch the bleeding.

The little girl shook the dented kettle and satisfied it had water in it set it on the hob grate then squatted down in front of the fire to wait for it to boil.

'Probably got no bloody milk. Suppose that selfish git's used it all in his tea . . .' Ruby muttered. 'Christ me head aches . . .' She clutched at her forehead and closed her eyes.

Pansy jumped up and found a milk bottle. She swung it to and fro to let her mother see there was a little bit sploshing about at the bottom.

Kathy wetted some lint under the tap and dabbed it on Ruby's face, rinsing and repeating the process. She drew from her bag some antiseptic and a clean piece of wadding.

'Suppose you're wondering what set him off this time,' Ruby mumbled.

'Your husband seems to think I know all about it. He thinks you confide in me.' Kathy's clear blue eyes drifted from the split cheek she was tending to Ruby's brown eyes.

'He's jealous.'

'Even so he has no right to beat you unconscious . . .'

'He's got a right to be jealous, though,' Ruby interrupted, sounding sheepish.

'I know he has,' Kathy sighed. She knew gossip was going around these tenements that Ruby Potter was a shameless baggage. In Kathy's opinion the woman was a fool not to have run off with the other fellow rather than stick with a brute like Charlie. But young and single as Kathy was, she realised life wasn't that simple for these slum dwellers: Ruby's boyfriend was quite likely to be married too with a brood of children and no money and no job. Charlie Potter was considered one of the lucky ones to be working at the docks and Kathy had heard him loudly impressing that on Ruby on previous occasions when she'd visited.

Kathy couldn't condemn Ruby for wanting a man – any man – to show her some love and tenderness.

'All the men round here would've done the same,' Ruby volunteered, in her queer voice, breaking into Kathy's introspection. 'Sal Turpin got a fractured skull off her old man when he caught her with a fancy man.'

'There's no excuse for any of them to act like savages.

Kathy replied. 'What are you waiting for, the pair of you? Pine boxes to leave in?'

'Where shall I go with no money and three kids?' Ruby grunted an astonished laugh. 'Got one under me feet, one at school and one in me belly.' She shook her head. 'Ain't that easy, Miss Finch, fer the likes of us. You take it from me, 'cos you'll never know, will you. Nice clever gel like you'll be set up fine and dandy. Doctor or someone posh like that'll walk you up the aisle.'

Kathy felt a flush warm her cheeks. Ruby was being either sarcastic or diplomatic. She liked the woman so gave her the benefit of the doubt and decided Ruby probably didn't want to accuse her of being a copper's nark to her face, as some folk did. It had soon got around these Whitechapel tenements that Nurse Finch was walking out with a local police constable. And nobody liked him: it was David Goldstein's job rather than his character or his Jewish roots they took exception to. East End slum dwellers' roundly despised coppers.

'Go on just do it . . . start on me cheek if you like.' Ruby suggested gamely.

Kathy continued working as gently as she could on Ruby's face, wiping blood and pressing together edges of skin. She knew the woman was doing her utmost not to flinch. She knew too that Pansy had come closer to watch her tending to her mother. When Kathy allowed her eyes to dart quickly to the child she noticed Pansy's eyes were bright with curiosity rather than fright.

'Got that tea made, Pansy?' her mother asked, eyes squeezed shut against the pain in her face. 'Can hear the kettle steaming.'

The girl trotted off and splashed hot water onto tea leaves. She put milk into chipped cups a drop at a time so as not to waste any, just the way she'd been told.

'Don't forget to give it a good stir, Pansy. And don't spill none in the saucer fer the nurse.' The curt warning made the child turn large eyes on the adults.

'She's always very quiet.' Kathy remarked without looking away from her delicate work of patching up Ruby.

'She natters sometimes,' Ruby said flinching at the antiseptic stinging her lip.

Kathy had done what she could and started packing away her things.

'She keeps schtumm when strangers are around.' Ruby gingerly touched her face feeling for the damage. 'Then when Petie gets in from school he never stops, so poor Pansy don't get a word in edgeways even if she wants to.'

'When is she going to school?'

'No rush . . .' Ruby said with a hint of defiance.

Kathy guessed that Pansy was already of an age to attend school. She was small and slight from under nourishment – as were most of the local children – but Kathy suspected she was over five years old. She bent to smile into Pansy's face. 'Is that my tea?' Kathy tipped her cap at a chipped cup and saucer with an unappetising weak brew in it.

Pansy nodded.

'Thank you.'

The little girl's response to unwanted personal attention was to shuffle towards her mother and press against her.

'If you lie down Mrs Potter I'll listen to the baby's heart before I go and make sure there's nothing amiss.'

'Ain't no need, Miss Finch; I can tell you the little

blighter's strong as an ox. Lays into me almost as hard as its father does . . .' her words faded away.

Ruby knew for sure, even if Nurse Finch did not, that Charlie Potter wasn't this baby's father. Charlie knew of course and that was what was making him nastier than usual. He could count months as well as she could and knew he'd been away courtesy of Her Majesty when the baby was conceived. Anyhow, her husband would know for certain when the kid was born; Ruby feared the child would look foreign being as the man who'd knocked her up was Chinese.

'You promise me you won't say nuthin' about this commotion?' Ruby pleaded, eyes widening.

Kathy could see she was close to crying. The woman had taken a beating off her husband without shedding a tear yet might weep now but for having her vow of silence. Around here the disgrace of interference from the hated authorities was always greater than being married to a brute. Kathy nodded, sighing agreement. 'Now I'm here I'll just take a look at you and make sure everything's alright with the baby,' she insisted.

'Never had none of this fuss and bother with me other two,' Ruby muttered easing herself back gingerly on the bed. 'Me mum's friend Ivy from across the street took care o' me before when I was due with Peter and Pansy.'

'Things have changed Mrs Potter and people like Ivy Tiller mustn't deliver babies unless they want to get into trouble.'

Kathy inwardly sighed. She was used to coming up against resistance from women – and their husbands – who had been used to calling in local handywomen to care for them during labour. Rather than risk arrest most of the unofficial midwives adhered to the ruling, if rather grudgingly. Kathy sympathised with those women: their livelihood had been bound up in their unofficial profession. Times were hard for everybody and jobs not easy to find.

Kathy listened to the strong heartbeat feeling amazed at how resilient these working-class wives were. Her own father had been a bully, yet absurd as she knew it to be, Kathy considered him better than Charlie Potter because his brutality had been controlled. Potter didn't give a damn about the consequences of beating his wife. He believed his criminal acquaintances protected him from trouble. Eddie Finch had not risked drawing attention to himself, or his career fencing stolen goods in Islington, with a charge of wife battering.

He'd floored Winifred with his punches but had refrained from following them up with a kicking while she sprawled defenceless. Like Ruby Potter, her mother had no intention of allowing outsiders to know her business. Winifred Finch's greatest terror had been giving the neighbours a reason to gossip about her, so she'd hide indoors till bruises had healed rather than go out and face knowing looks.

Dwelling on her family prompted Kathy to take out her watch and have a quick glance at the time. She'd told her sister Jennifer she might call in and see her while she was in the area but time was short and she had a postnatal visit to make to a woman who was still confined to her bed. Besides, after the disturbance with the Potters, Kathy didn't think she could face going into Jennifer's fetid dump and bumping into the unsavoury characters she kept company with.

'Baby seems fine . . . surprisingly enough . . .' Kathy

said having concentrated for some time on the rhythmic thud in her ear. 'There's a nice strong heart beat.'

'Hear that, Pansy?' Ruby turned to her daughter standing by the side of the bed. Your little sister is doing right as rain.'

Pansy nodded her small head.

'You want a girl do you?' Kathy asked, picking up her bag in readiness to leave.

'Don't want no more men about the place, that's fer sure.' Ruby said. 'Peter's already getting his father's swagger about him at times . . . he's only eight 'n' all.'

Kathy could see her patient was grimacing in pain and touching her swollen mouth. 'I think you ought to get checked out at hospital, Mrs Potter.'

Ruby shook her head as violently as her injuries would allow. 'I'm alright now . . .'

'Will you come to the antenatal clinic next time for a check up at the surgery? It's on Wednesday afternoons at two o'clock.'

'If I can,' Ruby said, as she always did.

Kathy knew that she wouldn't turn up. If the pregnant women in these tenements would just attend the local clinic for a quick check up it would save her the job of home visits.

Kathy gave little Pansy a wave as she went towards the door. Throwing a last glance over a shoulder she saw that Ruby was, head in hands, sipping the weak cup of tea Kathy had left untouched on the table. She felt a surge of hatred for Charlie Potter and all his like. It was wasted passion. The women would never leave. As Ruby had pointed out, they had no choice but to stay with the brutes and take a bit of fun where they could with other men.

CHAPTER TWO

'What have you done to your hair?'

Blanche Raven turned her head, inspecting her new hairstyle in the hallway mirror. She was pleased with the permanent wave she'd had put in, even if her mother wasn't, and she guessed Gladys didn't like it from the tone of her voice. But then her mother could find fault with anything and sound sour when discussing the weather on a fine day.

'Is Dad in?' Blanche asked, ignoring her mother's question. She was after a sub off her father having just spent all her wages at the hairdressers. She knew asking her mother for a few bob would be a dead loss, even though Gladys was flush having just got paid from her job as a machinist.

'Your father's gone out. I think he's meeting Nick 'cos he heard he might have a job for him, but 'course I don't get anything.'

The mention of her estranged husband made Blanche excitedly prick up her ears. She'd only been in minutes from the hairdresser's but in a flash she'd buttoned her coat ready to again leave the house.

Gladys Scott eyed her daughter grimly. 'Thinking of going chasing after Nick again, are you? Won't do you no good, my girl. He still won't take you back, and you know it.'

'Oh, shut up, Mum,' Blanche muttered, crashing the front door shut behind her. She hunched her shoulders against a sense of dejection and the bitter February wind. She feared her mother was right. Nick had given her the brush off earlier in the week when she'd turned up at his place with seduction on her mind. She'd felt humiliated when he'd practically bundled her out of the door and told her to go home. He hadn't even offered her a lift in his car and she'd had to catch the bus.

Hearing a bus wheezing to a stop at the corner, Blanche trotted towards it and managed to jump on at the last minute before it pulled off. She settled down on a seat next to a fat woman with a basket on her lap. The woman gave her a glare even though she was taking up most of the seat with her porky backside.

When the bus reached her stop, Blanche got off and walked briskly in the direction of Grave Maurice pub. She was hoping that Nick would be in his local as he usually was at dinnertime and that her dad would be with him; Nick was more tolerant of her company when her father was around because the two men liked one another. If only she'd listened to her father's advice rather than her mother's she'd never have let Nick Raven slip through her fingers . . .

Blanche dawdled outside peering through the pub windows. She was itching to creep inside and see if Nick and her father were propping up the bar but she had been brought up right – as her mother would term it – and knew it wasn't nice for a young woman to enter such a rough house on her own. Besides Nick didn't like pushy women – he'd never got on with her mother – and wouldn't appreciate her marching in on him if he was with pals rather than her father. But Blanche didn't fancy loitering outside freezing to death so she had to make a decision.

'Who you after then?' A burly fellow had just emerged from the pub and seen her on tiptoe trying to peer into the saloon bar over the frosted glass pane. He gave Blanche an appreciative top-to-toe look. She was a pretty brunette with an ample bust and curvy figure undisguised by the heavy winter coat she wore.

'Me dad and me husband, Nick Raven,' Blanche answered. She was always proud to let people know who she'd married. 'I think they might be having a drink inside.' Despite the fact he looked like a scruffy navvy Blanche preened beneath the fellow's leer, unconsciously patting her crisp dark waves.

'Yeah . . . they're in there,' Charlie Potter said giving her a grin. 'And depending on which old man you're after, could be you turned up just in time, Luv. Nick's got an admirer moving in on him.'

'Oh, has he?' Blanche snapped and, chin high, stormed past, bristling as she heard laughter following her.

She pushed open the pub door and once her eyes adjusted to the smoky atmosphere, managed to spy the men she was after. Her husband was leaning on the bar just yards away. It was a crowded pub but his height and fair hair made him easily recognisable. Her short, balding father wasn't quite so easily located at his side. Blanche heard his gravelly laugh before spotting him perched on a stool. She was relieved to see that there didn't appear to be any women with them. Not that she'd have been surprised to see Nick with somebody else. He made no secret of the fact that he'd had affairs since they'd split up.

Blanche pursed her lips indignantly. Perhaps the navvy had thought he was being funny by riling her. She reckoned he'd known her identity even before she told him she was Nick's wife, although she hadn't a clue who he was. Blanche was glad people knew of her association with Nick despite the fact they'd been separated now for over three years.

Her father had turned and spotted her. He gave her a frown but raised a hand in greeting. The movement drew Nick's attention. She noticed he didn't seem so pleased to see her, nevertheless she weaved through the crowd to join them.

'What'll you have, Blanche?' Nick asked mildly.

Blanche had to give it to her husband: even though she'd done the dirty on him he'd always remained generous and polite to her. In fact she knew if she had an opportunity to ask him for money before they parted he'd probably hand over a note to her.

'Gin 'n' orange, thanks.' Blanche gave him a coy smile.

'What you doin' here?' her father demanded in a whisper when Nick turned away to get her drink.

'Mum said you was with Nick . . . getting a job . . . so I thought I'd come and see you both,' Blanche muttered defiantly.

'Well, I'm more likely to get me job if you ain't around,' Tony Scott retorted, but not too unkindly. He knew his daughter had a renewed hankering for Nick, and he knew why that was. Much as he feared his daughter was wasting her time, he nevertheless wished the couple would get back together. That way at least he'd have a bit of a peaceful home life.

Nick Raven was doing alright for himself now. He might not have been when he did the decent thing and married Blanche having got her pregnant. At the time Nick had been driving a lorry for a pittance and his lack of cash and prospects had been the problem where his Tony's wife and daughter were concerned. Blanche had acted as though she was doing Nick a favour by agreeing to marry him rather than the other way around.

Blanche was too much like her mother; always wanting to be envied and decked out in expensive stuff. In Tony's opinion it was a crying shame that Gladys and Blanche hadn't managed to curb their impatience for a year or two because by now they both would have got their wish. Nick was on his way up and Blanche would have been going places with him but for her greed and her mother's influence.

Tony knew that it had been with his wife's encouragement that their daughter had started an affair with Wes Silver. Wes was an important fellow around this manor, with property and gambling clubs and a reputation for putting people out of business or in hospital if they crossed him. Wes also had a wife and a couple of kids and when push had come to shove he'd chosen to stay put rather than set up home with Blanche. May Silver was too useful to him to be dumped for a younger woman, no matter how keen Blanche had been to make that happen. A lot of people, Tony included, believed May ran the show where Wes's business was concerned and he merely provided a bit of muscle and credibility.

Irony of ironies, Nick Raven was now coming up fast on the inside and likely to take Wes's crown. He didn't seem so keen to take Wes's wife and really rub it in. Tony knew it was sticking in Blanche's craw that her husband's lack of emotion made it seem Wes Silver had actually done him a favour by sleeping with his wife and breaking up his marriage.

'There you go . . .' Nick slid glass of gin and orange towards Blanche.

She pouted him a thank you kiss.

'Done something different to your hair, ain't you?' Tony asked to break the silence that had settled on them since his daughter's arrival. He could tell Nick was pissed off by Blanche's presence. And he knew why. A young blonde seated at a window table had been quite obviously giving his son-in-law the eye, and Nick had been encouraging her with subtle glances. Tony knew her name was Diane Groves because she worked in the café up the road. For a moment Tony had thought trouble might start. Then he'd realised that the fellow sitting with Diane was her older brother rather than a boyfriend. He recognised Kenny Groves from way back when he'd been in the same class at school with Blanche.

'What job you getting then, Dad?' Blanche asked, her tongue loosened by a few quick gulps of gin.

'Ain't really spoke about that just yet,' her father answered, glaring from beneath his brows. 'Ain't long been in here so not had a chance.'

'Well¯. . . I've gotta be off in a minute,' Nick said, looking at his fancy wristwatch. 'Got to see some bloke in Shoreditch.'

'No . . . stay and have another. My round . . .' Tony Scott said quickly. If Nick went off without offering him a job he'd tear Blanche off a strip for sticking her oar in and ruining his chances.

'Can you start on a house in Commercial Street in the morning?' Nick asked. 'It needs decorating from top to bottom, interior and exterior. I know the weather's a bit against us for outside work but . . .'

'Course I can,' Tony snapped at the offer of employment. He was a painter and decorator by trade but had been picking up any sort of work he could find lately just to keep some wages rolling in. Although Gladys did piecework, sewing coats for a Jew boy she never let him forget it was her regular money keeping them all afloat. 'Be glad to start this afternoon on the preparing, if yer like,' Tony burbled, keen to get his foot in the door.

'Thanks . . . appreciate you getting going straight away as I've got tenants lined up ready and waiting to move in.' Nick took out a notebook from an inside pocket and ripped out a page. Having written down the site address he handed it over, upending his glass and draining it in a one gulp. 'Gonna get off now . . .' He started towards the door.

He'd only managed a yard or two when Blanche rushed up to hang on his arm.

Nick kept on walking trying not to look too impatient when his wife wouldn't take the hint and leave him alone.

Outside the pub he turned up his coat collar then removed Blanche's hand from his arm. 'What do'you want?'

'Thought you might like to go to the flicks tonight?'

'No, I don't want to go to the flicks with you tonight or any other night,' he said mildly. 'We've been through this. We ain't married now, Blanche . . . well, we are,' he corrected himself. 'But it's over between us and has been for a long time.'